Tony Macaulay comes from a family of novelists but is best known as a songwriter. His thirty-eight top twenty hits have sold more than fifty-two million records world-wide. He has won the British Academy (BASCA) Award eight times, and has twice been named British 'Songwriter of the Year'. His first West End musical, *Windy City*, won both the British Academy and *Evening Standard* Drama Awards and is currently in production in the USA. In 1985 he was commissioned to write a musical work to celebrate Her Majesty the Queen's sixtieth birthday, which was performed by 6,000 children inside Buckingham Palace.

Tony has three children and lives in Sussex. His first novel, *Enemy of the State*, is also available from Headline Feature.

D1614754

Also by Tony Macaulay

Enemy of the State

Brutal
Truth

Tony Macaulay

First published in 1996
by HEADLINE BOOK PUBLISHING

First published in paperback in 1997
by HEADLINE BOOK PUBLISHING

A HEADLINE FEATURE paperback

10 9 8 7 6 5 4 3 2 1

ISBN 0 7472 5025 1

Typeset by Palimpsest Book Production Limited,
Polmont, Stirlingshire
Printed and bound in Great Britain by
Cox & Wyman Ltd, Reading, Berkshire

HEADLINE BOOK PUBLISHING
A division of Hodder Headline PLC
338 Euston Road
London NW1 3BH

To
Daniel, Laura, Matthew,
Marika and Aris
with love.

ACKNOWLEDGEMENTS

My sincere thanks to Stewart Mitchell, Maggie Phillips, Ed Victor, Sophie Hicks and Marion Donaldson for their continued help and support on this project. My gratitude to Brian Thomas, Dr Frank O'Connor, John Wheeler and Professor James Sang for their invaluable technical expertise.

T. M.

PROLOGUE

Joel McKinnon ducked low and ran along the flat roof of the cell block. The discordant rattle of the fire alarm receded into the distance.

Below, the sound of running feet told him prison officers were answering the alert, sweeping through the wing as he'd seen them do on the drills.

A shaft of hard white light sliced through the darkness. McKinnon flattened himself into a shadowy space behind a ventilation duct as a searchlight began to pan across the roof. His throat burned. His breath vaporized into mist in the chill air.

In around ninety seconds they'll reach my cell, he told himself. Then they'll find out they have a helluva sight more on their hands than a phoney fire alert.

The pool of light began to move away from him, across the roof. For a few precious seconds it would shine directly into the lens of the surveillance camera, blinding it. Then he would make his move.

McKinnon turned and peered at the chasm of blackness ahead of him – the wide gap between his block and the next. He steadied his breathing.

I could piss a jump like this when I was a kid, he told himself. What real difference does it make that it's six storeys up?

One helluva lot.

1

Trip, lose you nerve, and you'll end up spiked through the gut on the railings beneath. A bad way to die . . .

'Only a madman would make that leap, would hole up right under their noses,' Devereux had said. 'But then only a madman or a genius will ever break out of this place. And you ain't a genius, McKinnon. If you were, you wouldn't be in here.'

McKinnon checked the progress of the searchlight again.

Now! It has to be now . . .

He broke cover and ran. The guttering gave a little beneath his feet as he took off into the void.

The roof of the administration block came up to meet him. But he'd jumped short. Not much, but enough. His ribcage smacked against a low coping-stone, crushing the breath out of him. He began to slide down. His left hand shot forward and locked around some pipework. For several seconds he hung motionless in the darkness, seventy feet above the railings.

His foot began to search the wall for a toehold. His shabby trainer struck what he guessed was the spout of an overflow pipe. He tested it for strength, and then, with infinite care, began to lever himself upwards until his right hand, too, could lock around the pipe. A moment later, he was standing on the roof of the admin. block, steadying himself against a strong south-westerly wind.

There is a God. And tonight, he's all mine.

McKinnon stumbled forward, heading for the fire escape he knew would lie to his right. He fell as much as climbed down it, and sank into the shadows of a vehicle servicing shed.

The distant fire bell was now drowned out by the hammering clang of the main security alarm. Almost immediately, the door to his left was slammed back, and armed prison guards began to spill out on to the compound, spreading out in all directions.

As soon as it was safe, he moved deeper into the shed, and began to burrow his way into the mountain of truck tyres that lined the back wall. Satisfied he was thoroughly hidden, he settled down to wait. Through the skylight, barely visible through the forest of rubber above him, he could see the first glimmer of daylight.

The muscles in his left leg were beginning to cramp. He massaged them, pressing his fingers deep into the hard tissue.

How, in the name of God, did I ever get myself into this? he asked himself for the hundredth time. By doing what I do best, what I've done all my life: making a damn nuisance of myself. Just picked the wrong outfit to screw around with this time, that's all. Folk smart enough to mount an operation on that scale cover their backs. You got sloppy, McKinnon. Slow and sloppy. And this is the price you paid.

If I ever get a second bite of the apple, Sweet Jesus, that won't happen again! I know what I'm dealing with now. Something vast, highly organized. Absolutely lethal.

So much depends on Hannah. Please God she comes through . . .

CHAPTER ONE

There was a dull scraping sound, like something heavy being dragged across stone flags – the rattle of a steel bolt. Slowly, the kitchen door of the house at the corner of Fielding Street and Ponce De Leon opened.

Special Agent Holden, thirty yards away in the woods that overlooked the backyard, tightened the focus on his binoculars, and muttered into the mouthpiece of his short-wave radio. The two dozen M16 rifles, spanned out along a wall of sandbags that stretched as far as the adjacent property, trained on the dark space between the door and the architrave. Holden sucked air in through his teeth. Maybe now . . .

Black garbage bags were tossed from inside the house on to a pile of trash in the centre of the yard, sending a fat rat scurrying for cover amongst some bushes. Holden watched as the agent in front of him swung the barrel of his weapon, following its movement across the yard. For a fraction of a second he thought the man was going to take a shot at it.

Jesus! One mistake now . . .

An FBI agent ran through lines of men and vehicles, drawn up on the east side of Ponce De Leon, crossed the street sealed off by two troop transporters, and ducked into the woods. He moved up to Holden's side, and handed him a single sheet of typescript. 'The latest fax from Kerensky, sir. Just came in.'

Holden studied the text for a moment. The ache in his lower jaw was beginning to ease up a little now. Once you had a tooth filled, the pain was meant to stop, wasn't it? That was the whole idea. He swallowed another painkiller and began to walk back to the command vehicle.

For three days and nights, Holden, 270 agents from the FBI and the Alcohol, Tobacco and Firearms Bureau, and a SWAT team had surrounded the building, allowing in only food supplies. For three days and nights, Holden had tried to succeed where the police had failed, to evict Daniel Kerensky, self-proclaimed reincarnation of Christ, and about ninety of his followers.

De Leon House had been a private clinic for more than seventy years. In the early nineties its ownership had become the subject of a bitter legal dispute, and it had been unoccupied for some time when the squatters broke into it fifteen months ago.

The mayor had been under pressure to get Kerensky out from the beginning. A report, put together by the local residents' association, on the activities of Kerensky's cult since it'd taken over the place, spoke of bizarre ceremonies running into the early hours of the morning, of loud music and chanting that terrified the children of neighbouring families. When Holden had first driven up to the house, set on the eastern corner of one of the wealthiest enclaves in Atlanta, he'd seen the battered cars cramming the narrow driveway, the Arabic symbols daubed in garish colours around the doors and windows, and was in little doubt that the locals were as much concerned over the falling tone of the neighbourhood as they were for their children's mental welfare.

The authorities had found out soon enough that there was no easy way to evict ninety people. Court orders were routinely ignored, bailiffs repulsed. Daniel Kerensky had played this hand before, and he knew so long as his followers kept their children close to them, little more would be done to get them out in the short term. There would be no salvos of teargas canisters, no police heroics. Only a waiting game to be played out.

But now the local elections were only months away. Politicians – the mayor amongst them – who relied on local captains of industry to underwrite their campaigns were beginning to sweat. A number of notables who'd been generous in the past had homes on Ponce De Leon, and had made it clear that the Kerensky problem would have to be taken care of before they'd consider opening their cheque books again.

Fate seemed to take a hand, however, when, after months of surveillance, a concealed cameraman was able to get shots of assault rifles and other weaponry outlawed in the Clinton gun law reform bill being carried into the old clinic building. The mayor sensed a breakthrough.

A study of Kerensky's published writings and the transcripts of recent speeches he'd made to his followers, gained through audio surveillance, convinced the Georgia state governor that he was faced with a situation that, left unchecked, could mainfest itself in a bloodfest that could eclipse even the Waco disaster of 1993. Anxious to distance himself from an operation that showed every sign of turning into a PR fiasco, he had wasted no time in passing the case over to the FBI.

At first light, three mornings before, AT & T engineers had set up a wire-tap on Kerensky's phone, and the first he had known of the massive firepower now marshalled against him had been in a phone call from a trained negotiator that had roused him from sleep. Furious at being classified as one who might be susceptible to talk-'em-down-gently psycho-babble, he'd terminated all live contact, opting instead to communicate via his fax machine.

Holden climbed the steps of the command trailer. His operations and risk management team were studying Kerensky's latest communiqué. Holden didn't need them to tell him how the odds were stacking up. This wasn't a rational mind they were pitted against. Kerensky was a psychotic, capable of anything. Experience gained from similar events had shown that there was a strong likelihood he would follow through on every one of his threats.

Two hundred miles away, Pieter Kleig studied a copy of the same fax: 'Unless all troops and police are withdrawn immediately, I will instruct my followers to torch the building. We will die together in the flames. Our deaths will be on your hands.'

Kleig hurried out across the wide lawn that ran down from a rambling ranch-style home, and made for the gazebo at the west end of the property.

J. Richmond Fiske sat at breakfast. His small fingers selected mint from a bowl and placed it in a Moroccan tea-glass. He lifted a tiny silver teapot, its top shaped like a minaret, and poured in boiling water, drawing the vessel away from the glass as the steaming liquid flowed.

Kleig stepped into the gazebo and Fiske motioned for him to sit. The South African took the chair opposite his employer and passed him the single sheet. 'We intercepted this five minutes ago. It's Kerensky's latest communiqué to Agent Holden.'

Fiske read it quickly, folded it and laid it on the linen tablecloth. Then he gazed down at the valleys way beneath him, deep in thought.

From this secluded eyrie, high in the mountains of

North Carolina, J. Richmond Fiske had plotted the rise of the sect he had founded, with almost unerring judgement, since its earliest beginnings more than twenty years before. He'd seen the Apostles of Christ grow to become the largest and most powerful Christian sect, outside the mainstream, in America. Now, it seemed, the movement was to face its gravest threat.

Fiske had long regretted that Daniel Kerensky had ever come into his life. He had travelled to Machin County, Georgia, one spring day in 1989, on the advice of one of his scouts to see the young man speak. The venue was a piece of waste-ground on an industrial estate, the crowd that had come to listen had been small but, ten minutes into his oration, Fiske knew that he had found a great new evangelist.

Over the next months, he took care to vet every aspect of Kerensky's character and beliefs before inducting him into his movement at the highest level.

But, as his young protégé began to relax into his role as heir apparent, it became clear to Fiske that he had a hidden agenda of his own, one that no amount of vigilance could have anticipated. The more Kerensky began to reveal his true nature, the more it seemed to the cult's creator that the man he had chosen to take the Apostles into the next century was a dangerous extremist whose ravings could destroy a lifetime's work.

Kerensky was stripped of his authority and expelled from the sect, and a damage control operation mounted to erase the effects of his teachings. Although it was largely successful, a hard core of fanatics had left with the man they called the Messiah to form a breakaway group.

Kleig broke the silence. 'If this ends in a bloodbath, the knock-on effect to us could be very damaging.'

Fiske's small brown eyes met Kleig's. 'Why else do

you think Kerensky would threaten to pull a stunt like this? It's his last chance to strike a blow at me. Don't you see that? He wants to draw us down into the mire with him. He wants the media coverage, wants eyes in Washington turned our way.'

Fiske began to examine the problem. 'If this plays out the way he intends it to, we have to find a way to lessen the impact on us . . . To change the media emphasis. We have to rewrite Kerensky's script a little . . .'

He gazed down at the white dogwood blossom, scattering into the wind beneath him, and began to weigh up his options. Kerensky's spin-off cult, with its bizarre magic rituals, polygamy, even paedophilia, so it was claimed, had captured vast media attention. Each TV feature and newspaper article made much of the sect's beginnings, dragging the Apostles of Christ further into the spotlight. The Apostles' own teachings, their recruitment and intitiation methods, had often been condemned, compared to the more extreme sects, but, thus far, negative publicity had done little real damage.

'We need to change the world's perception of this whole event,' Fiske mused. 'If we can intercept Kerensky's faxes, surely we can send them too, send them as though they were from him?'

Kleig poured himself mint tea. 'Sure we can. So long as no one finds the "grabber" we have wired in their direct line. We'll need to get a match on the printer Kerensky's using, of course. Then we can use one of these fax sheets with his letterhead as a master, and simply change the text.'

'Yes, but find another copy of Kerensky's signature. We must have a dozen samples of it on file . . . Is the field operative standing by?'

Kleig nodded. 'Ready to go whenever you say.'

Fiske looked down. The early morning mist had cleared. Five hundred feet beneath him, the entrance to a labyrinth of caves where the last of a generation of Cherokee had taken refuge during the Indian Wars was clearly visible now. Here they had fought and died to the last man rather than be taken to the government reservation in South Georgia.

'Then I think Special Agent Holden is going to receive one last communiqué from Mr Kerensky,' Fiske said softly.

He began to walk back to his study, already drafting the letter in his head.

Few decisions that had the smallest influence on the billion dollar, multinational conglomerate that the Apostles had become escaped its founder's attention. Fiske was, at sixty-seven, the man he'd always been, a hard-nosed entrepreneur with a finger on the public pulse. These days, others were left to shape the religious rhetoric. Fiske shaped the corporate leviathan that underpinned it all. The letter he would write now would, he hoped, ensure that all that he had worked for would stay in place.

The old clinic was drenched in floodlight now. Special Agent Holden moved out on to the steps of the command trailer, shielding his eyes from the glare. The press pack closed around in a tight knot.

'We have just informed Kerensky that unless he and his followers vacate the building by nine pm this evening, appropriate action will be taken to remove them.'

NBS correspondent Joel McKinnon elbowed his way forward. 'But isn't there a real chance that Kerensky and his followers will do precisely what they're threatening – torch the building and kill everyone inside it?'

'There are always risks involved with this kind of

operation,' Holden said. 'But we're confident that lessons learnt in the past will pay off here, and that events will never move in that direction.'

'What about the children in there?' the CNN correspondent asked.

'Provisions have been made for them, but I'm afraid I'm not at liberty to tell you what they are.'

'Do you have an accurate assessment of the kind of fire-power Kerensky can deploy?' a local correspondent enquired.

'We know he has a number of assault rifles and handguns. Perhaps some grenades.'

An anorexic-looking woman from ABC seemed determined to get her question in. 'Will you be using what's come to be called the "Weingreen Technique", that's to say, pump teargas into one wing of the building, to bottle the squatters up in the rest?'

'I'm sorry, I can't elaborate in that regard.'

The crowd broke up and McKinnon and his cameraman began to head back to their truck.

As McKinnon held the line for his news editor, he watched police begin to herd the press pack, which had grown rapidly over the last three days, back to barriers that had been set up a safe distance from the target area down the street. Amongst them was a tall woman about thirty, with long copper hair. McKinnon had seen her here a couple of times before, and had assumed that she was with one of the local papers or radio stations. She behaved like she was. But when police had run a security check, the previous evening, she'd had no press pass and, much to her fury, she'd been moved back, to stand with the general public behind the main cordon. Now here she was again. She seemed to be caught up in a heated toe-to-toe with a police sergeant. Why are you

12

so anxious to get your head blown off, lady? McKinnon wondered. You don't look like one of the ghouls and weirdos that hang out at these things. You look smart and kind of classy, as a matter of fact. If I get five minutes to myself, I might try and get a few answers.

The house opposite the clinic was typical of those in the area – an old colonial-style home, one of the tens of thousands of 'Tara' replicas to be found across the South. The flat-roofed wing to the right had a foreshortened view of the target building, but provided an ideal vantage point for grenade-launchers.

An ATF agent, with a pock-marked bull neck, stationed at the eastern end of the position, strained to hear the message on his radio, then shouted to the man sitting on the Coke crate further along the roof.

'Okay, hotshot, you're on dinner break. Bring me a coffee, will yer?' The man grunted something and moved gingerly through the line of grenade-launchers and headed for the stairs.

A minute later, the French doors of the master bedroom that led out on to the flat roof swung open and an ATF special agent moved into view. Bull Neck hastily spat out his gum, and got to his feet. He tried to place the man. You ain't with my unit, he thought. And how do you get away with wearing your hair that long?

The senior man turned away from him for a moment and looked down the line of launchers. When he turned back, he had a Glock 9 mm in his right hand. The first shot – muffled to a percussive smack by a silencer – opened up a small hole above the other man's left eye. Surprise never had a chance to register on his face. He dropped to his knees and began to tip forward. The special agent caught his shoulder and put two more shots into the top

13

of his forehead. He took a small box, the size of a Lucky Strike packet, from inside his jacket, and laid it by the man's left temple. Then he checked his watch.

Two streets away, in the command trailer, the fax machine chattered into life. A single sheet pumped out, and the machine switched off. It would be fully three minutes before anyone would have a chance to read it.

The killer on the roof top, a hundred yards away, spun around and deftly fired the grenade-launcher behind him. Immediately, high in the night sky, there was a whistling sound. Now he hurried for the first time, moving down the line of launchers, firing each one. By the time the task was over, the sky was alive around him. A series of explosions, seconds apart, rent the silence. The killer threw himself to the ground, his ears ringing, as chunks of roof tile, glass and brick showered down around them.

For some seconds afterwards, the only sound was the crackle of fire. Flame and smoke billowed from the roof of De Leon House. Then, from a second storey below, came the rattle of an automatic rifle, answered, almost instantly, by the sibilant crack of the M16s from the ranks of the FBI.

Holden had been thrown to the floor of the command vehicle by the impact of the explosions. He pulled himself to his feet and staggered to the door. There was so much smoke, it was almost impossible to evaluate the situation. Back inside, the radio officer clapped his headset tight to his ears. The noise of gunfire was making it hard to hear what the men in the target area were trying to tell him. As the echo of the grenade bombardment began to die away, one of Holden's team moved up to his side. 'I think you'd better look at this, sir.'

Holden's jaw slackened as he read the single short paragraph on the fax: 'For the sake of the children

14

amongst us, it has been agreed that we will vacate the building by the stipulated time, on the condition that we are all allowed to leave the city unhindered.' It was signed, 'Daniel Kerensky'.

Holden clasped a hand to the top of his head. What the hell is happening! This is all craziness!

'When did this come?' he shouted.

The man could barely make himself heard above the barrage of gunfire. 'A couple of minutes ago, just before . . .' He gestured around, utterly confused, '. . . all this.'

While those in command tried to bring the situation under control, Holden typed furiously, begging Kerensky to hold fire while the two of them worked out the details of what was now clearly a resolvable situation. As his fingers rattled over the keys of the computer, he knew men outside were dying.

'It's no good, sir.' The telephone engineer, drafted in three days before, shook his head. There was a gash in his forehead and splinters of wood in his hair. 'It's just not going through. I think the fax machine is okay. The line must be down . . .'

By the time ATF agents reached the garden of the property from where the grenade barrage had come, the roof-top killer was deep into the woods beyond. He pulled a remote detonator from his pocket, swung around, and pressed the plastic button on the side of it. Seventy yards away, a small bomb blew Bull Neck's bloody head to pieces.

Let the ballistics boys put that lot back together, he thought, as he crossed Gardener street. Those Glock slugs should have been scattered anywhere within a fifty-yard radius.

He headed for the dark blue Audi parked amongst the trees.

Five minutes later, he crossed the county line and moved on to the freeway. He reached for his mobile phone and dialled Kleig's number in South Carolina.

Nothing in Holden's experience had prepared him for the chaos growing around him. It had taken longer than he dared think about to bring the men under his command back under control. But the volume of gunfire pouring from De Leon House seemed to dispel any hope that a peaceful outcome might still be achieved, and his men were now returning fire again. The order was simple enough: 'Neutralize the gunmen as a matter of the highest priority.'

The agent in charge of the squad sent to inspect the site where the grenade-launchers had been set up – acknowledged by witnesses to be the flashpoint of the trouble – radioed in to Holden.

'It's hard to be sure what happened up here, sir.' The noise around him was deafening again. 'It looks like the agent manning the position took it into his head to fire off a barrage at the place . . . And then got hit in the returning fire.'

Holden watched as the first salvo of teargas canisters was lobbed at the barricaded windows of the first floor of the house. Returning gunfire tore into the sandbags piled in front of him. He put on his gas mask and thought, Dear God, the sick sonofabitch has killed them all.

By sunrise, the mansion was a burnt-out shell. Huge screens of yellow plastic sheeting had been rigged around the site, while fire-damage experts picked through debris.

Several streets away, Joel McKinnon sat in the back

of the Toyota truck that served as a mobile editing and dubbing suite, and toyed with the wording of the voice-over he was about to record. The cameraman, with whom he'd worked for more than a year, ran the final cut of the video report that would be sent down the line with it. There was obvious camera shake on one section – .44 calibre shells had peppered the side of the truck they were hiding under – but McKinnon had learnt long ago that such flaws only added to the sense of drama. The key thing was that they had footage of the hottest part of the action, taken yards from the front line. Police had moved in to force pressmen further back within seconds of the grenade bombardment, but McKinnon and his cameramen had broken away and taken cover under a transporter, parked within view of the whole shooting match. They were in little doubt that the stuff they'd file would become the definitive record of the bloodiest confrontation the state had seen in a century.

McKinnon cleared his throat, still raw from the smoke he'd inhaled. 'Okay, let's take a shot at it.'

The cameraman spooled the tape back to the top and set the audio to record. As the report played through on the monitor, McKinnon spoke in a clear, steady voice: 'Daniel Kerensky, self-styled messiah, and some ninety of his followers, including seventeen children, are dead. Their bodies lie only yards away from those of eleven federal law enforcement officials who perished in an attempt to bring the carnage to an end. Why they died will be the subject of debate for many months to come. This much, however, is certain: minutes before grenades blew the roof off the building where the cult members were holed up, Kerensky contacted the official in charge here, and told him he and his people would leave peacefully. Quite why FBI Special Agent Holden chose to answer that offer with such a deadly assault is unclear. A provisional statement claims it was the result of "unauthorised action", in other words, an accident, one it seems that has claimed the lives of children, cult members and law enforcement officers alike . . .'

CHAPTER TWO

Joel McKinnon ordered himself another whiskey, and strained to hear if the mishmash of sounds, breaking through the noise in the airport bar, was his flight being called.

He'd stayed on a further week in Atlanta, conducting what his news editor described as a mopping-up operation. He'd filed interviews with local government figures on the AFT's handling of the Kerensky affair, reports on the progress of the injured, and the effects the tragedy had had on the local community.

The day after the shootout, McKinnon had pleaded with his news editor to let him develop the Apostles of Christ angle. 'Kerensky wasn't the cause, Bruce, he was the effect. He did what he did because of the indoctrination he underwent inside the cult . . .'

But his boss was adamant that McKinnon stay on in Atlanta, and cover the human interest end.

'We're gonna go with the report on cult terrorism we have in the can,' he was told. 'Update it, add some new footage.'

McKinnon sipped his whiskey. Bruce Van Stratton was finally losing his touch. What had that psychiatrist the network had shipped in said on air a couple of days back? Something to the effect that the current view was that for every killer out there who was a product of his environment, there was another who was just born bad – bad blood, bad genes, whatever – who was destined to take himself and a good many of those around him straight to hell, one way or another. And Kerensky was simply a prime example of the second category.

Good, straightforward thinking; bad TV. Van Stratton and the shrink had missed all the key indicators. McKinnon had been around crackpot renegade régimes – weren't Kerensky's lot, and the Apostles, little more than that? – and knew the territory better than most. There were parallels here. And a much bigger story.

As a foreign correspondent for NBS, McKinnon had stomped through minefields, sat out artillery barrages, endured week-long bombardments, marauding looters, virulent epidemics, and everything that the armies of a dozen military juntas could throw at him, for the better part of five years. He had watched Tutsi villagers in Rwanda desperately trying to sell off the last of their belongings to him – not to buy their release from their Hutu captors, as he'd first thought, but to simply buy a quick, clean death by firing squad – and realized that even if he was to give them all he had, it could not save them and their children from being slowly hacked to death with machetes. He had watched Bosnian Serbs perform strange ritualistic little dances on the gagged and trussed bodies of their Moslem captives, as they put out their eyes with bayonets. Seen the victims' feet drum the ground in agony, almost in time to the singing. A thousand nights he'd woken from deep sleep, soaked in sweat, and asked himself, 'Why, in the name of God, do I make myself a witness to such barbarity?'

But the answer was simple enough: in the end, for someone like McKinnon, there was no other place he could be. When you'd lived in a world where human resilience is stretched to the limit every waking hour, the trivialities of normal civilized existence became impossible to relate to. A hundred times McKinnon had sat through dinner parties in New York, consciously retreating deeper and deeper into himself. The rising price of pork bellies, how the Yankees were measuring up, Jack and Jeannie's new holiday home in Hawaii; what did it really matter, any of it? And then there had been Macedonia. Seventy-two hours that changed McKinnon's life for ever . . .

For a while he'd thought of getting out of the business altogether. But then NBS had offered him the job as South-eastern States stringer and he'd thought, well, what the hell?

If the noise, the smoke, the tensions of the last few days had made him feel like he was back in the front line again, the reassuring buzz of his native tongue, the glare of ads for familiar products around him, told him he was unquestionably at home.

He took another slug and tried to unwind. He craned his neck to get a view of the flight monitor that hung across from him, then paid for the drinks, and began to make for Gate Seventeen.

The stewardess's smile revealed several grands' worth of dentistry. McKinnon waved away the copy of the *Georgia Constitution*, and put on the headset of his cassette machine.

His recent researches had turned up a tape Kerensky had made only weeks before his expulsion from the Apostles of Christ movement. McKinnon put the cassette into the portable recorder he always carried, and played it through. Almost involuntarily, his ear began to dissect every inflection, to log every nuance of Kerensky's delivery.

21

His interest in psycholinguistics had begun almost accidentally. He'd learnt long ago that, to succeed as a war correspondent, one needed two qualities above all others: patience and tenacity – the capacity to sweat away mind-numbing chunks of one's life in dusty bars, shabby hotel lobbies, on blistering street corners, to survive seemingly endless treks over roads that were little more than dirt tracks, in jeeps and trucks that in any organized society would have been consigned to a breaker's yard decades ago, still with the determination to come through with that key report the network was demanding. Often local radio was the only source of information. McKinnon would spend hours switching from station to station, searching for accurate updates, trying to separate news from propaganda. He had a natural ear for languages, and, in the absence of an interpreter, could quickly assimilate essential vocabulary and key phrases. Nevertheless, much of what he monitored, delivered in countless dialects and accents, would remain an impenetrable babble. So other faculties were forced into play. To the untutored ear, the rantings of one foreign demagogue can sound much the same as the next. But McKinnon soon found that, whilst the exact sense of what was being said might elude him, the way in which it was delivered could tell him much about the speaker.

When he returned to the States, he found he involuntarily applied these skills to those who spoke his native language. Only now he was able to add to his assessment of them an analysis of their character, personal philosophy and a dozen other elements of their make-up.

McKinnon began to make notes on the recording he was listening to. It had obviously been made at some mass rally where Kerensky had given the address. It was soon clear that the man who would later proclaim himself

22

to be the living reincarnation of Christ was an extremely accomplished speaker.

All the oratorical tricks were here: the commanding rhythmic delivery, punctuated by sudden rises in vocal inflection, the vivid 'them and us' comparisons, the triple repetition of key phrases. Kerensky was expert, McKinnon noted, in setting up a 'claptrap' – not a term for gobbledegook, as he'd discovered when he'd first checked it out, but that for a device designed to catch applause. He would create 'rapid fire claptraps', waiting about seven seconds each time, until the applause began to diminish in intensity, and then 'bite into' it. By talking over the clapping, he knew that the audience would be prevented from giving full vent to its feelings, and their response would then became 'bottled up'. One effect of this was that Kerensky could create the impression that he had not invited their applause, and by talking in competition with it, paint the picture of a modest sincere man, more concerned with the development of his argument then the plaudits of the crowd.

When McKinnon fast-forwarded the tape, and listened again, the further benefits of the technique became apparent. The audience approval here was loud and sustained – Kerensky had finally allowed them full voice – and by repeatedly breaking off in mid-sentence, he could create the impression that, such was their enthusiasm, he was losing the fight to be heard.

Kerensky, McKinnon concluded, had been a consumate professional, entirely in control of himself and his audience. This recording had been made only weeks before the evangelist's expulsion from the Apostles of Christ movement. So where was the radical, the raving subversive that insiders had said the heir to J. Richmond Fiske's mantle had become? If you didn't know who this guy was, you'd take him to be another Oral Roberts or Jim Bakker. Flashy theatrical sermonizing, the usual preposterous claims made in the name of the Almighty; it was all here. But is this the word of some kind of anti-Christ? Hardly.

McKinnon lifted the tin foil that covered the white plastic dish on the tray in front of him, and stared at the contents. Times that tough, huh?

In the tapes McKinnon had heard of the radio broadcast Kerensky had made days before his death his speech patterns had been entirely different. The even delivery was gone. The throat sounded constricted, the voice reedy, devoid of the bass tones that had characterized it in the earlier tapes. He sounded high, like he was on something, speaking in fast bursts as though he needed to breathe in between. You could almost sense the cortisol and adrenaline flooding his metabolism, as the 'fight or flight dichotomy' took hold of him, starving the brain of blood as the muscle tissue was prepared for action. His rhetoric, in this recording, had been full of threats, apocalyptic references. Here was a desperate man, wildly out of control, lost entirely in a world of his own imagining.

McKinnon balanced a quantity of the damp confetti-like substance he guessed the airline billed as some kind of casserole on the tiny fork, and steered it towards his mouth.

The tape backed up everything he'd told his news editor a week ago. The central focus of this story from Day Two should have been: what happened to this man in barely eleven months to turn him from a relatively sane individual, into someone who believed he was the reincarnated Son of God, capable of immolating himself and all his followers?

24

McKinnon knew the hack behind the network's forth-coming feature on cult terrorism from way back, knew that it would be little more than a make-over, a set of graphic montages, high on impact, low on insights.

There'll be no attempt to examine the real issues, McKinnon told himself. He put the cassette machine back in his attaché case. Written on the yellow legal pad beneath it, were the lines he'd used to sell his boss on his angle for the story: *'Kerensky was not the cause, but the effect.* The effect of something far more sinister and all-pervading that is still flourishing unchecked'.

He tore the sheet off, scrunched it into a ball, and sighed.

Damn shame. Lost opportunity.

McKinnon lowered two heaped spoonfuls of sugar into the mug of strong black coffee that stood in front of him, then thickly buttered the white toast that lay on a plate beside it.

One morning, a year ago, when he'd first quit the foreign correspondent job, he'd dumped fifteen dollars' worth of perfectly good groceries into the trash: two jars of decaffeinated coffee, the sweeteners he always took around with him, several loaves of wholewheat bread, and the low fat spread that he'd covered it with since he'd first come to America.

So my blood pressure and cholesterol levels go up, my waist and my arteries thicken, and my teeth rot. Big fucking deal. For five years, I watched people, brimming with health, being tortured, shot at, and blown to pieces. In the final analysis, what's a little caffeine and a few calories, for Christ's sake?

As he breakfasted, he looked around him. The kitchen was in reasonable shape – well, it would be when he put a few things away and cleaned the floor. Oh, and pasted back those ceiling tiles. But the living room was a tip. Unopened packing cases stood stacked shoulder-high where the removal men had left them a year ago. The normally habitable area in the south-facing corner – Mission Control – a cable-strewn complex of electronics that included a TV set, a video, telephones, fax and PC, was currently ankle deep in newspapers, unopened mail, carry-out food packaging and beer bottles.

It's dump day, McKinnon resolved. He loved to throw stuff out. It was more than just a cleansing process. For him, a trashfest could border on the spiritual. He began to plan his campaign. He would deploy the garbage bags along the Eastern Front – the hallway – and blitz the capitalist debris with ancient vengeance until noon.

His eye caught the blinking light on his answering machine. It had been close to three am when he'd let himself in to the apartment he'd rented on New York's Upper West Side since his marriage had broken up. He'd seen the light blinking then, but he knew that few, if any, of the calls waiting for him would be anything other than work-related – these days he counted only two people as true friends, a photographer, who was currently working in Italy, and a journalist, who worked for a rival network, and was still, for reasons which McKinnon had yet to establish, harbouring some grudge against him. The previous night, he'd regarded the flickering light balefully, and thought, I've been on the road for this shoddy outfit for close to five days. They don't want any more on the Kerensky story, well, not the wider aspects of it that interest me, so fuck 'em! If Saddam Hussein just took Washington, it ain't my watch. Anything else can wait till morning.

Now, he picked his way through the packing cases, took a notepad from under a half-finished can of Labatts, and began to play the tape through. There was the usual crap from the NBS newsroom. Most of the later calls superseded earlier ones. He listened, bemused, as queries on stories he was no longer involved with were satisfactorily cleared up, while he had remained blissfully ignorant of them ever having arisen.

There were two personal calls from that tall woman with the bad posture. Why don't I just tell these women the truth? he wondered. I don't fancy you, and I won't be seeing you again, okay? Because I know what it feels like to be slung in the dumper, that's why . . . And not calling back was the easiest way out.

The last voice on the tape was one that McKinnon had not heard in close to six years.

'Joel, it's Caitlin. Call me when you can, will you?' She'd left a whole list of numbers where she could be reached, so it had to be important.

McKinnon checked his watch, worked out the time in London and began to work through the numbers. He found her at her office.

'Caitlin. Christ, it's an age since we've spoken. How the hell are you?'

'Okay. I was concerned about you.'

'Why, how should I be?'

'Oh, so you haven't heard.'

'Heard what?'

'There's been a lot happening here, Joel.' It was obvious she was unsure as to how to proceed. 'Well, for a start, some guy who's just been sent away for life for a whole bunch of murders and armed robberies has confessed to the Marchmont killing.'

The Marchmont killing. McKinnon had last heard those

27

words in what seemed to him now to have been a different lifetime.

'According to *News at Ten* last night, he's admitted to setting up your father and his partner. Joel, are you still there?'

McKinnon reached for a chair and sat down. Slowly the implications of what was being said began to register.

'There was an interview with the partner, Sudley, that's his name isn't it? He was pretty shaken up, as you can imagine. He's been released from jail. There's talk of him getting a full pardon, but that hardly . . .'

'What about my father?'

'Well, that's when I heard. I hate to be the one to tell you this, Joel, but . . . I'm afraid he's dead. He died nearly four months ago. A heart attack, so the Home Office is saying. I knew you hadn't been in touch with him for a long time, and it occurred to me you might not know about all this. I tried calling you in Atlanta but they said you'd just left.'

But McKinnon was no longer listening. He was conscious of a knife-like pain turning in his gut.

'You're right, I didn't know any of this.' He struggled to frame the next question. 'Why didn't they let me know about this when it happened?'

'Does the Home Office have your address in the States?'

'No . . . Now I think about it, they don't.'

'Well, there you are. Now your mother has gone, who else would they tell?' Silence. 'You're gonna have to take it up with the Prison Service or whoever. All I can think is that they sent something to your mother's old address and, when they heard nothing from anyone in the given time scale, made funeral arrangements of their own. Look, I've got a bunch of press cuttings for you here. They'll tell you

28

a lot more than I can over the phone. Let me fax them to you. I'll be here all night. Please call me any time you feel you want to. It doesn't matter what time. I'm so sorry, Joel. Sorry to open all this up again . . .'

McKinnon hung up and made for the closet in the living room that doubled as a bar. He poured himself a stiff Scotch and watched numbly as paper began to snake out of the fax machine that stood on a packing case in a corner of the room.

Now they were both gone. His English mother had married his American father – she'd met him at a dance at the US Airforce base in Bushy Park in the south of England – when she was barely twenty. After the army, Frank McKinnon had never really settled into civilian life. Over the next decade he moved from one job to another. Joel had begun working for a newspaper in Sussex when his father started the painting and decorating business, the only enterprise that was ever to bring him in a regular wage. For three years, life for the McKinnons took on some sense of normality. In due course, Joel graduated from newspapers to local TV and was soon a regular face on current affairs programmes.

Then, one warm spring night in the late eighties, a CID officer and two uniformed policemen arrived at the family's terraced home in north London.

Joel felt the same gnawing ache in his gut now that he had felt when his father had emerged, ashen-faced, from the kitchen and taken his son in his arms. 'There's been a terrible mistake . . . I don't know what's happened here . . . I'm gonna go down to the police station to get it all sorted out. You stay here and take care of you mother.'

He soon learnt that a seventy-year-old spinster, who lived in the apartment above the one Frank McKinnon and his partner had been decorating, had been found raped and battered to death. The place had been ransacked and her jewellery stolen. Police claimed to have found one of her earrings in a toolbag belonging to the men that had been left at the site overnight, and had brought the decorators in for questioning.

While Frank's solicitor argued that his client was the target of an obvious set-up, police, acting on an anonymous tip-off, began to dig up the garden of 17, Hillside Avenue. Joel had stood with his mother at the French doors and watched in horror as a muddy cardboard box containing more of the woman's jewellery was lifted from a hiding place in the rockery. Cries that Frank had been framed were lost in the furore that engulfed the family when, after hours of questioning, Sudley confessed to the killing, implicating his partner in every dreadful deed.

The next months became a nightmare from which Joel had never fully recovered. Certain that Sudley had been forced into the confession, he stuck loyally by his father through the trial, and was stunned into shock and grief when he was found guilty of murder and sentenced to life imprisonment.

Joel had always known his father was a flawed character, but had loved him nonetheless. But his mother, who had been miserable in the marriage for years, now began to discover that her husband had been involved in a number of shady dealings along the way, and, to her son's dismay, began to turn against him. Soon, her visits to Marston Moor Prison in Yorkshire ceased altogether.

Joel became increasingly haunted by the fear that people would connect him with his killer father. Soon after being passed over for a job as a correspondent with a major network, a position he'd been confident of getting, he changed his name by deed poll, taking that of his mother's family – Mackenzie. Two years later, his fortunes no better improved, he resolved to leave England for America. By now many of his mother's doubts regarding his father's innocence had became his own.

Three weeks after his twenty-fifth birthday, depressed and traumatized, Joel moved to New York to stay with relatives. As he began to make a new life for himself there, his contact with his father petered out altogether.

In recent years, to think of his father had been to relive the agonies of those years, to know again the shame and uncertainty that had consumed him. His last word from his father had been in a Christmas card seven months before.

Although Joel had long ago reverted to using his real name he, not surprisingly, still went to some lengths to keep the fact that he was the son of a convicted murderer from those who came into his life. But Caitlin, who had been his girlfriend at the time of the trial, knew the whole story. Knew too that Joel had had no personal contact with his father for years. Now, as he read through the press coverage of the new development on the case, he was glad that she, at least, had been aware of the truth. But for Caitlin I might never have known any of this, he told himself.

As he read the statement made by the Marchmont woman's real killer, and that of his father's partner, a man whose life he'd ruined, the old gut pain twisted inside him. Only this he knew was not fear. It was guilt.

I should have stood by him. He swore to me a thousand times he was innocent, that he had nothing to do with that woman's death. I stopped believing. And so he died alone. Forgotten, unloved.

* * *

It took all McKinnon's journalistic skills to extract the name of the department head responsible for information regarding his father's death from the Home Office in London. Having been passed through a succession of 'Estuary English' Tracys and mumbling 'Mockney' Sharons, McKinnon was put on hold for the prison director's office. After a long wait, he was connected to a spokesman who announced himself, in ringing county tones, as one Aubrey Stamford-Smith.

Stamford-Smith fielded McKinnon's questions with unctuous efficiency. Yes, the case was of course known to him . . . A complex and disturbing matter that was receiving a full investigation. He would in the meantime write to McKinnon laying out the details surrounding his father's death.

A week later, Mckinnon received a letter marked 'On Her Majesty's Service'. It told him little more than the press cuttings had.

Four months ago, his father had had a minor heart attack in his cell at Marston Moor Prison, where he was serving his sentence. He'd been transferred to the prison hospital, but had died from a massive coronary only hours later.

As Caitlin had suggested, the Home Office had then written to him at the only address they had on file: the house in Acton, London, where his mother had lived until her death two years before. The present owners had been unable to provide a forwarding address when a police officer called some days later.

After some unproductive detective work, the details of which were unspecified, it seemed that the authorities had given orders for Frank McKinnon's body to be released from the mortuary of York District Hospital, and handed over to funeral directors in the city. After a short service, presided over by the assistant governor of the Prison, the body had been cremated.

Good of the assistant governor to make the time, McKinnon thought.

An urn of Frank McKinnon's ashes was available for collection, the letter went on to inform him. As regards the consequences resulting from the confession made by the real killer of the Marchmont woman, Stamford-Smith would say only that matters were being further investigated by the Home Secretary, and a report could be expected soon.

McKinnon scratched his head. Okay, so the Home Office didn't know where to reach me. But the prisoner's brother-in-law, my Uncle Stan, is still kicking around south London. Why didn't they notify him? And if they did, why didn't he call me?

McKinnon checked his watch. It was late lunchtime in England. A good time to catch Uncle Stanley. He flicked through his address book and reached for the phone. Let's just see how thorough these Whitehall jerk-offs have been.

Uncle Stanley was clearly in the middle of the midday meal he always insisted on calling his 'dinner'. All he seemed to know about his brother-in-law's death and the other recent revelations was what he'd read in the paper.

'But some fella did call up a couple of days ago. He wasn't from the Home Office though. Said he'd been your father's cellmate for a while, wanted to get in touch with you, as a matter of fact. I couldn't put my hands on your number at the time. I was going to call him back. But now you might as well call him yourself.'

It was late evening, Eastern Standard Time, when

McKinnon reached the man who'd contacted his uncle. Arthur Jessop sounded like a sick man.

'Where did you say you were calling from . . . New York?' The voice was hoarse, roughened from years of smoking, the breathing laboured. 'I can't talk about this over the phone . . .'

'You knew my father?'

'Shared a cell with him for three years, twenty-three hours a day. I liked him. Every con I ever met told me he was innocent. Your father was the only one I ever believed was.' There was a pause, filled with a racking cough. 'The Home Office are selling you a crock of shit, Mr McKinnon. That's all I'll say over the phone.'

'In what way?'

Silence. 'Do you have any plans to come here in the near future?'

'I honestly don't know. My whole life has been turned upside down in the last few days. It's possible, I suppose.'

'Well if you do, give me a call. We'll meet up.' More coughing. 'You won't be wasting your time . . .'

McKinnon slept little that night. The growing compulsion to meet with this man who claimed to be his father's friend was, he knew, fuelled by his own guilt. Hadn't his father died simply for lack of a reason to live? If I'd stood by him, supported him, given him some hope, McKinnon told himself for the twentieth time, perhaps things might have turned out very differently. If the cellmate has more to tell, has information that can exorcise that dread . . .

McKinnon twisted in the bed sheets, damp with his sweat.

I need to hear it.

Aubrey Stamford-Smith's bar – a walnut cabinet that

stood in the corner of his office in London's Queen Anne's Gate – was seldom put to use until, as his father put it, the 'sun was over the yard arm'. This translated, regardless as to the time of the year, as five pm.

Stamford-Smith checked his watch. Three forty-five. He put his hand to his stomach and swallowed hard. The dry white wine he'd taken with his fish at lunchtime had never given him acid indigestion before. He got up and walked to the cabinet.

Ah, the hell with it.

He poured himself three fingers of Scotch, and filled the cut glass to the top with ice. He took a sip, crossed to his private line and dialled.

This time the called was answered. A male voice said simply, 'Yes?'

'It's Stamford-Smith. I've been trying to reach you for two days.'

'What's the problem?'

'The McKinnon case . . . The son's been in touch . . .'

CHAPTER THREE

Laser light sliced through the darkness. Fingers of red-gold spread out in a semicircle like rays of the sun, and the vast half-dome that dominated the stage began to open.

Now a pulsing rock rhythm filled the night air. Seven thousand Byelorussians sat in mute amazement as blue mist spilled from the dome. Crashing power chords, from a brace of guitars, announced the arrival of a band. They rose slowly through the mist on a hydraulic platform, as though being forced from a giant metallic womb. A black rap singer began to gyrate to the pulse of the music and, as the wall of sound widened, a massive choir and orchestra were revealed, silhouetted against the night sky.

To those in the West, where entertainment wizardry is an accepted part of life, the open air show would have been impressive enough. But to the families of peasant farmers, struggling for survival in the empty plains of the Russian steppes, the spectacle they were presented with was nothing less than astounding.

The lyrics of the songs, belted out on the stage in front of them, spoke of the search for love, much in the way pop music always has, but it was soon clear that the 'lerve' in question here was not that of man for woman, but of Jesus for all mankind. But the few in the audience who might have felt duped by the con were already too caught up in the gathering excitement to care.

Vast movie screens, each half a city block in length, enclosing the audience, now came to life. They swivelled in their seats to follow the images of dancing people, watched enthralled as the scene gradually gave way to a depiction of the Sermon on the Mount.

A man at a lectern began to address them now in their own language. Here was a new way to speak to God, he told them – as new and fresh as the free lives they now led. Here was a new way to listen to God's answers . . . The audience began to settle down to their first taste of evangelism – US style.

A chill wind, blowing off the Urals, was making it hard for those at the back to catch everything the speaker was saying. Svetlana Volochek, in the fortieth row back, strained to hear. At seventeen, she was typical of many of the young people gathered there.

At first, when the churches in her neighbourhood had reopened their doors after seventy years of Communist suppression, the Gregorian chant, the icons and the incense had held a certain fascination. But the teachings of the most fundamentalist sect in the Christian mainstream, she soon knew, had little to say to her. When a black-robed priest had turned up at her home one night to berate her parents for letting her spend the weekend at her boyfriend's house, Svetlana had shut her mind to the Russian Orthodox Church, and all that went with it.

But these people, these Apostles of Christ, seemed to be a different lot altogether, she thought as she swayed to the music. They seemed to understand how it felt to be a teenager in a struggling new republic in the middle of nowhere.

In the row behind her, Hannah Rostov looked nervously around as she tapped notes into a word processor no larger than a pocket book. As the stadium lights brightened, she could see men patrolling the aisles. She lowered her face, and pulled the fringe of the mousy wig she was wearing down a little lower on her forehead.

These men she knew were sentinels, the cult's own security police. They'd been on to her for three months now. It had only been her talent for losing herself in a crowd that had prevented them from ejecting her from the rally she'd attended in Riga. She'd resolved that she would see this new show too, to get a measure of the kind of impact it was having on the people it was designed for, and no pack of redneck thugs was going to stop her.

A heavy-set man in a fawn suit – standard dress for sentinels at these events – was moving up the aisle towards her right. He appeared to be checking the exits, but Hannah was getting a bad feeling about him.

She'd spent almost two years investigating every aspect of the Apostles of Christ. She'd gone to great lengths to ensure that her researches were known to very few. But someone, no doubt one of the disaffected converts she'd interviewed, had clearly turned informer and dished the dirt on her. Now a force high in the movement, possibly even its founder, J. Richmond Fiske himself, wanted her silenced. How far they would go to achieve that end, she was as yet uncertain. But she'd seen the other faces of this organization in all their ugliness. She knew the lengths Fiske's people could go to keep their followers in line, to keep their public image unsullied. The mess in Atlanta had been the latest evidence of that. The media could lay the Kerensky massacre on the FBI and the ATF all it wanted but Fiske had had a hand in the carnage down there, Hannah was certain. There seemed little doubt, too, that the journalist whose body had been fished out of the Potomac a couple of months back, with a ten-inch-length of baseball bat rammed down his throat, had also been working on an exposé of the cult, as he'd interviewed some of the sources Hannah had.

Another sentinel was closing with the man near to Hannah, from the back of the stadium now, and radioing in for instructions as he went. Neither of the men shot even so much as a glance in her direction, but every instinct told her that they were there for her.

How have they got on to me so quickly? she wondered. Well, if they really intend to shut me down and lose me, Hannah thought, where better than here in the middle of nowhere?

The first part of the sermon was over. The lights dimmed to black again, and Hannah took the one chance she knew she had. To much angry muttering, and cries of pain as feet were trodden on, she fought her way along the line to the far aisle and hurried down towards the stage. A hand reached out for her in the darkness, almost caught her coat, but she twisted away. By the time the lights had come up again, she'd reached the area to the right of the stage. Keeping low, she hurried to the wall of the stadium. There was no exit here, but she had seen them putting these amphitheatres up before. The inner walls were just black cloth, hung on a framework, built around the seating.

As the choir began to pump out another song, sentinels moved in to cut off Hannah's retreat. She dropped to her knees, lifted the cloth and was through and off into the labyrinth of vehicles behind it in seconds. Soon, she could hear voices, twenty or thirty yards off.

Run backstage, her mind screamed. *It's the one place they'll never think to look.*

She headed off to the right, threading her way between trucks, trailers and pounding generators. In front of her was an open space. Stagehands stood in groups around what Hannah guessed to be the stage entrance. She moved around the area cautiously, then ducked under a truck.

How were the sentinels able to track her so accurately? she wondered. Had they planted a bug on her somewhere? As she searched her clothes, she became aware of voices. Angry voices. A few feet from her.

'You don't think I could, do you? You don't think I've got the guts to just walk away. You've all made damn sure there's nothing for me to go to, that's why. My family wouldn't have me back now, not after what you made me do to them.' The speaker's voice cracked.

Hannah could just see his face from where she was hidden. A young black guy . . . The lead singer of the rock band.

'The friends I had gave up on me years ago. But I'm not like the other God-fodder here. I've got more respect for myself than that . . .'

Hannah could only see the back of the other man. His body seemed to vibrate with anger, but his voice was only a whisper. 'I don't need to give you answers, Christian. I have all the answers I need . . . Right here.' His hand went to his hip pocket. He produced what looked like a black leather wallet, and held it aloft. But Hannah knew it was a bible. All sentinels carried them.

The black guy put his hands on his hips. 'Don't hand me that standard operational bullshit. It doesn't work anymore. I'm out of here, pal. I don't know how I'm gonna get home, or even if I'm going home. But you'd better find yourself a new singer.'

The other man checked his watch. 'You're due on that stage in three minutes, fella.'

The singer turned to walk away. 'I'd like to see you try and make me.'

The sentinel began to radio in for assistance. The black

kid closed the distance between them and put his whole weight into the right hook. The sentinel's head threw off a spray of sweat as it resonated with the punch. Hannah was surprised to see him stand his ground. He shook his head like he was trying to unscramble his brain, and swung back at the black kid. The boy ducked away, goaded him to come for him.

But, instead, the sentinel turned around and began to walk towards the stage entrance. He nodded slowly to himself.

'I think it's time we worked out a little re-education programme for you.'

The black kid sat down on the step of a trailer and let out a howl – anger, fear and frustration all wrung together into one anguished cry.

Hannah listened for a moment. The only sounds now came from the stadium. She moved slowly out into a space between the vehicles. The black singer turned to face her.

They stood staring at each other for a moment, then Hannah said, 'I heard what happened.'

The eyes narrowed a little. 'So?'

'So . . . If you're looking for a way to get out of the Apostles, I may be able to help.'

The rented BMW inched forward in the rush-hour traffic. McKinnon stared out at the ugly terraced houses flanking the dual carriageway that cut a swathe through a dozen Hammersmith streets and wondered again at his decision to use valuable vacation time to pursue what might easily turn out to be a dead-end mission. At least Caitlin's offer of a bed for a few nights would keep costs to a minimum.

He collected her house keys from her neighbour, as

42

arranged, and let himself into her elegant Kensington home. The last time he had seen her had been at his mother's funeral. She had been living in a studio flat in Earl's Court then. McKinnon examined the oil-on-canvas landscape above the marble fireplace in the living room, the sculpture that stood on a plinth by the French doors. Caitlin, it had to be said, had done very well for herself. He'd never been able to equate the high-spirited young woman he remembered from that last year he'd lived in London with the sedate world of merchant banking. Clearly there was another side to the woman.

There was a note for him, propped against the flower vase on the kitchen table. 'I'm free for lunch. Call me if you want to meet up.'

McKinnon dialled Arthur Jessop's number and waited. The ex-con showed little surprise that his friend's son had turned up in London so soon.

'I could see you tomorrow around three,' the cracked voice informed him. 'I'll meet you at the newsstand outside St Pancras Station.'

McKinnon crossed the floor of the Italian restaurant and searched the faces of the diners. His eyes locked on to the smiling woman in the corner.

Caitlin rose and he kissed her on both cheeks. 'How are you feeling? Jetlagged to hell?'

'No, I had a couple of hours' sleep at your place. I feel okay.'

Caitlin had changed little in the last two years. Her dark hair was cut very short at the sides and back now, but it seemed to highlight her high cheekbones and violet eyes.

'So, you look very elegant,' he said.

'To hell with elegant. What happened to sexy?'

'You look sexy too.'

'I should think so.' She took a step back and looked him up and down.

'Don't tell me how I look. I don't want to hear.'

'Not bad. Too thin. You need feeding up.'

They sat down. 'Thanks.'

'It's okay.'

He tried to catch a waiter's eye. 'So how's the world of futures and derivatives?'

'Well, I haven't done a Nick Leeson and broken the bank yet. But I'm working on it.'

'Excellent.' A waiter came over and McKinnon ordered a whisky and water. They studied the menus. 'And your love life?

'I spend most weekends with a painter who's got a place in Dorset. He's mean and moody and . . . magnificent in an insanitary kind of a way.'

'Still going for the same type then?'

'No. You were just mean and insanitary,' she said.

'Ah yes . . . That's right.'

'So . . . I take it you're here because of your father.'

He told her about Jessop, and how he felt about the whole business of his father's death. As he talked, she studied the man who had once been such an important part of her life.

No one knew better than her the impact his father's conviction had had on him. Caitlin and Joel had been lovers for almost two years when his father was arrested for murder. For a while, the stress had thrown them together. Then, as Joel McKinnon began to change his view, began to believe that perhaps his father was guilty as charged, their relationship had started to disintegrate. She knew he felt deeply sullied by the whole experience. She had watched helplessly as the man she loved slowly withdrew into himself, pushed away all those who cared for him, turned with fear and suspicion on those who sought his friendship. And tortured himself with the question, am I my father's son? Am I capable of such terrible deeds?

By the time he announced that he was emigrating to the US, Caitlin and he were all but strangers. An occasional postcard from Bosnia, Rwanda, or Macedonia, told her the kind of life he'd lived since, told her something of the way he felt about himself.

That gaunt look she remembered from a few years ago was gone now. So was the slightly hunched bearing. His manner was bright and animated enough. But, to her, it was as though every bloody assignment, every shattering salvo of gunfire, had knocked a little more out of the man she knew she still cared a great deal for.

'Are you Joel McKinnon?'

McKinnon turned around to face a bent figure in a threadbare overcoat. His thinning hair was scraped off his lined forehead and tied in a ponytail at the back. The flesh of the face was streaked with broken veins.

'Yes, I am.'

Jessop offered his hand. The fingers were stained with nicotine. 'Okay.'

They moved off in silence at a good pace, leaving the forecourt of St Pancras Station behind. Soon McKinnon found himself under the arches of the old Victorian station. Curled up in sleeping bags, under soiled blankets, were dozens of derelicts. Others sat in the shadows in sullen groups drinking cider from plastic flagons.

'Welcome to Cardboard City,' Jessop said.

'Do you live down here?'

'Used to.'

'Then why are we here?'

Somewhere in the hacking cough that followed was the remnants of laugh. 'It's the one place you can be certain there'll be no government snoopers hanging around.'

Whatever the truth of that statement, Jessop clearly felt secure talking down here, and that was all that mattered right now. The old con stopped and began to roll himself a cigarette.

'Like I said, I shared a cell with your father for close to three years. We were both transferred to Marston Moor when it was first completed. You need a friend to survive in that place, believe me. And your father was the best one I ever had. I knew he had nothing to do with that killing, long before all this recent stuff came out. I've been around cons half my life, you get to know when a guy's on the level.'

'What kinda frame of mind was he in?'

Jessop shrugged. 'Resigned to the situation most of the time – a damn sight more so than I'd have been in his shoes.'

McKinnon had to steal himself to ask the next question. 'Did he ever . . . talk about me?'

'Sure he did. He was proud of you. Thought you were a winner. He felt guilty about you, I think, thought he'd let you down.'

'Let *me* down!' McKinnon turned and looked down the row of blackened arches that supported the old station. 'I was the one that didn't come through, for Christ's sake.'

'He understood about your taking off to the States. He felt you only went because of the hell he'd put you through.'

'How was he towards the end?'

Some of the tobacco had dropped out of the half-made

46

cigarette on to the ground. Jessop seemed not to notice. He rolled up the meagre remains, and reached for a light. 'Can't tell you. We were separated a year ago, and I didn't find out what happened to him till recently.' Jessop took a long drag. 'Your dad didn't die four months ago, Mr McKinnon.' His face was half hidden in a wreath of smoke. 'I saw him alive . . . Four weeks ago.'

McKinnon turned to look at him. 'What did you say?'

'I saw your father alive in the prison hospital about a month back.'

'Are you certain?'

'Absolutely. Well, I say alive. His face was wasted to the bone, his flesh covered with sores. But it was him all right. I recognized him from that scar on his neck. I was in the hospital wing, waiting at a lift with a prison guard to go to X-ray. Your father was brought out on a trolley. He tried to speak to me, but he couldn't get anything out.'

'Wasted flesh . . . sores. Those aren't the symptoms of a heart disease.'

'The Home Office is feeding you cattle wham, Mr McKinnon.'

'What did you think he was suffering from?'

'I really don't know. As I say, he couldn't speak. But his eyes . . .' The ex-con looked at McKinnon steadily for the first time. 'I guess that look in his eyes is why I'm here.'

Till this moment McKinnon had taken Jessop's claim as no more than the ramblings of a man, broken by years of institutionalization. But now he sensed that perhaps the man was telling the truth. He studied him and wondered what he could possibly hope to gain for himself from fabricating such a story. A handout? Hardly. How would this disclosure increase the likelihood of that?

47

'If you put this to the Home Office, they'll tell you there was no one in Marston Moor called Jessop.' He was caught in a coughing fit for a minute. 'And they'll be right. See, Jessop ain't my real name . . . It's just one I need to use right now.' He studied the vagrants across the street, drifting aimlessly around under the arches. 'It's hard to explain to someone who's not been inside Marston Moor what it's like . . . It's one of the new privatized joints. It's clean, efficient, sure, but it's also the most soulless hole on the globe. I've been in some of the toughest slammers in this country, but that place, it's a state-of-art gulag, a santized Devil's Island . . . Only a handful get paroled out of there in a year. I was one of the lucky ones. Getting out of that place was the greatest achievement of my life. One wrong move and I'm back in. I told you what I told you because I owed it to your dad. But this is as far as it goes. Where you take it from here is entirely your business.' The dull blue eyes held McKinnon's. 'The phone you called me on was a mobile – I'm sure you realized that. It's not mine, and it's not traceable to me. See, I know from your father, you're a real hotshot in the news game. So before you get any ideas about trying to rope me into this . . .'

McKinnon sighed. 'Okay. I get the picture. It was good of you to do what you've done.'

How the hell do I take this thing further without this guy's cooperation? he wondered.

The group of deadbeats squatting, drinking under the arches across the road, was starting to break up. The wine and cider were gone now, and there was nothing more to keep them there. One elderly vagrant turned back to the one remaining drinker, who took a tattered overcoat from around his shoulders and passed it back to its owner. The vagrant stood in a bemused stupor, for a moment, watching his newfound friend – any fella who turns up out of the blue, toting three bottles of booze, has to be considered a friend – as he brushed fluff and fragments of the newspaper that had lined the coat off his pristine suit. Then the bum turned around and headed off after his friends, all thought of stealing the fancy little camera the guy had been using lost in a chemical haze.

CHAPTER FOUR

'Move out into the light with your hands up . . . Or I'll send in the dog!'

Silence. The security guard peered cautiously around the door frame, into the empty corridor ahead. The Rottweiler bitch strained on the choke-chain, its breath coming in panting snorts.

Where the hell were Pastorelli and the others? The guard radioed in again.

'Keep your teeth in, Shydner. We're at the main door of Lab Seven,' came the reply. 'We'll be there any second.'

Suddenly there was the sound of running feet. The guard broke cover in time to see the edge of the white lab coat flap around the corner. The man he'd seen photographing classified files, only seconds before in D Section, was going to make a break for it. Shydner snapped off the dog's lead. The animal moved off so fast its feet skidded on the tiled floor. It made the turn on the corner and was gone. A second later, two gun shots echoed through the building. There was one short, desperate howl and then silence.

The man in the white coat lurched onwards. His heart hammered so hard in his chest it seemed to blank out all other sound. He swung through a set of double doors, out on to a staircase, and began to make for the ground floor. He was halfway to the exit at the west end of the laboratory block, when he heard barking. He threw back the doors with a clatter and he raced across the forecourt of the Falk Pharmaceutical Research Center towards the parking lot. His throat burned as he fought to catch his breath.

Two more Rottweilers burst through the exit doors like hounds from hell. They skidded to a halt and sniffed the warm night air, then tore off after their quarry.

The man in the lab coat stumbled, skinning his knees. The tiny camera he'd used to photograph the files clattered on to the Tarmac. He scrambled on to his haunches, and groped for it in the darkness, then froze, listening.

Dogs.

The security guards arrived from two directions and joined the hunt. 'All exits now sealed,' one radioed through. 'He can't leave the complex.'

The fleeing man put his own short-wave radio to his ear as he ran. It was tuned to the same frequency. He'd caught enough. He veered to the right. This route would take him closer to the dogs, but it was his only chance now. The section of the perimeter fence that he'd half cut through the day before lay no more than a hundred yards ahead.

A wall of razor wire loomed into view. Close behind, the dogs streaked through the shadows towards the hard white light that enveloped it. The man spun around. One hand searched desperately for the wire-cutters, the other locked on to the butt of the Mauser automatic.

'Zero! Boston!' Thirty yards back, Shydner was yelling for the dogs to come to heel. They'll need this guy alive, he told himself. Why don't the dogs respond? What's gotten into them tonight, for Christ's sakes? Then he knew. *They can smell the blood of one of their own on him . . .*

The fleeing man scanned the section of fence that stretched up into the darkness in front him, searching frantically for the marks of wire-cutters. He reached through the wire. Stiletto-edged fingers of steel sliced into him. He cursed, shaking the blood from his gashed hand, spun around, and tried to get his bearings again. A glistening black shape hurtled through the air towards him, level with his neck. He threw himself to the left and fired twice. The Rottweiler smacked into the perimeter fence with a rattling crash. In the same instant, the second dog hit him like a Scud Missile, driving him back against the wire. Its fangs ripped into his throat, cutting short his scream as they severed his vocal chords. *Let me die now . . . Let me die now*, his mind screamed, as teeth slashed and tore at his flesh.

Dark faces turned to watch, squinting into the sunlight, as the squad of soldiers picked its way down the stony path that ran between the tents and cattle pens. Two men in the front broke rank and ran forward to help an old woman move a cart, laden with earthenware water jugs, out of the way so that the rest could pass. Gradually the word spread. The vast noisy crowd began to close behind the soldiers as they moved on, straining to get a glimpse of the prisoner in their midst.

The squad took a turning to the right and began to trudge down a slope, and out into a vast open pit that had been hacked out of the earth. The crowd began to line the edge. Soldiers behind the prisoner, a tall cadaverous man dressed only in a loincloth, pushed him out into the centre of the pit and withdrew. Without a word, the multitude stooped down. For a moment it seemed as though they were about to pray. But it was suddenly clear that this was anything but an act of devotion, as each man and woman gathered rocks from around them and stood up ready to hurl them.

A man mounted on the wide arm of a camera dolly, reaching out over the crowd yelled, 'Cut! Okay, thanks everybody. Twenty-minute break.'

J. Richmond Fiske, seated with a dozen others on the roof of a building to the left, sprayed himself again with mosquito repellent and watched the vast cast and production team of *The Lost Gospel* move off towards the refreshment tents.

Only God knows what the establishment churches will make of this, he thought. But if you're going to tell the story of the killing of Christ, tell it like it was. Like it must have been. It's been a long journey to this moment.

'Mint tea, sir?' The voice of his aide all but broke through his reverie.

'*Mint tea, Jeffrey?*' In a distant part of his mind, he heard another voice. His mother's. He closed his eyes. Suddenly around him was their old home on Gardener Street.

He was the bastard child of a St Louis hooker. He'd spent his pre-school days with his grandmother, playing in the shabby living room that adjoined the kitchen of the café she ran on West Franklin street. At supper time he went home to his mother. Home was a rented clapboard house, three streets away. There was a bedroom into which he was never allowed to go. He was nine before he asked his mother why.

His mother always picked him up and hugged him when she came for him. She always smelt of carbolic soap. Sometimes, it seemed to him that he must be the heaviest thing in the world when she tried to lift him. Occasionally, she would stop by the café during the day, to see him too. Then she would smell like the

54

perfume stuff grandma used to spray around the café when vagrants had been in. He'd know then that this was not really his time. Just by the smell. In the strangest of ways, it was a cloistered existence.

Nothing could have prepared him for the odium, the naked aggression he was to encounter when he first went to school. None of the children who persecuted him could have had any real idea as to why Jeffrey Fiske was to be regarded as such a pariah. Their parents' reaction whenever his mother turned up at the school gates to collect him was all they needed to see, to know that the hate campaign had to be maintained.

Fiske changed school several times. But it was a small community and word travelled. What sustained him through this, the worst period of his life, was his Christian faith. Until he was around seven, he always regarded the Sunday mass his mother took him to as a chore, to be endured for the sake of peace in the household. But as his schooldays wore on and he became further and further isolated from his peers, Jesus took on a new significance in his life. Sometimes, when the jibes became unbearable, he would take his sandwiches to the church, across the road from the schoolyard, and sit alone in the nave to eat his lunch.

In the years that followed, few men would more thoroughly re-invent themselves than Jeffrey Richmond Fiske. At fourteen, he was a slightly built, sandy-headed youth, barely five foot seven in height. To withstand the bullying, he'd joined a local gym – one of the few in the area at the time to have a comprehensive range of body-building apparatus – and embarked on a work-out routine that was maintained to the present day. Later, he acquired coloured contact lenses which changed his eyes from almost-colourless blue to dark umber, and allowed him to ditch the glasses that, to him, consigned him to everlasting dorkdom. In strong sunlight, he found the sandy hair he so loathed faded to the colour of straw, the skin – normally freckled and pink, like a sow's belly – turned to smooth brown.

Fiske walked to the parapet of the roof, and called down to the second assistant director for a copy of the latest script revisions. His voice was thin and reedy and, at first, failed to get the man's attention.

Over the years Fiske's confidence in his abilities had begun to build. But he'd accepted, from an early point, that he would never be a natural leader of men. Nature had simply not dealt him the cards. This conclusion would, in later years, cause him to rely on the skills of front men, like Daniel Kerensky, to sell his message.

Now Fiske watched as the movie's director took the actor cast as Christ through the next scene they were to shoot. Fiske knew every detail of the script – he'd structured it himself. But it had been a long hard journey that had brought him to the point where he felt adequately equipped, for such a task. That journey had begun on the day of his mother's death.

One afternoon, when he was in eighth grade, he'd come home to find her lying crumpled up on the living room floor in a pool of blood. His grandmother, who had been trying to get an ambulance for half an hour, told him she had been attacked by a burglar. But Fiske knew better.

When it was clear that no ambulance would be there inside an hour, he called the only person he knew might help them. Father Doyle had an old station wagon they could lift his mother in to, and take her in to the St Francis Hospital, downtown.

There'd been a drunken slur in Doyle's speech when he picked up the phone. It was mid-evening when he finally staggered up to the open door of the Fiske house. The boy lay sobbing in his grandmother's arms in the corner of the kitchen. His mother's body still lay where it had fallen in the living room, covered in flies. She had died without receiving the last rites, more than an hour before.

His sense of loss, both personal and spiritual, was to mark the rest of his life. It did not find full voice until he was nearly twenty when some findings, based on research carried out by Cambridge postgraduates, using the first linguistics analysis computer program ever developed, were published in a learned journal he took.

The program had taken to an exact science a concept long accepted by linguistic experts: that no matter how intelligent or educated a writer may be, he will consistently repeat his vocabulary and syntax over a given volume of work, often no more than a few dozen pages. The identification of this inherent 'literary fingerprint' had often proved invaluable in authenticating writers' work in the past. But, with the development of the computer program, the process had taken on much greater significance. For the first time, manuscripts of doubtful provenance could be scanned and analysed with considerable accuracy.

One of the most sensational findings came from an examination of the original Aramaic manuscripts of *The Gospel According to St Mark*. According to the program, the document was the work of no less than eleven writers, four of whom had made their contributions as late as the Fourth Century, AD.

Many readers of the article had been outraged by what they considered to be blatant blasphemy, but Fiske wrote that this verdict, on one of Christianity's most treasured texts, had had an almost liberating effect on him. He had waited impatiently for analyses of the other three gospels

57

to be published. None appeared, but the gradual erosion of his faith, a process which had begun with the Father Doyle incident, seemed all but complete. Fiske became certain in his own mind that the whole Christian faith – perhaps even religion itself – was one giant lie. There was no God. The evidence to support the existence of a Christian Messiah was minimal. If Christ had ever lived at all, Fiske told himself during these years, he was, at best, a charismatic faith healer who'd rattled the collaborators amongst the Jewish establishment of his day enough to drive them into shopping him to the Roman forces of occupation. A cursory study of the contemporary laws of the region showed that heretics and subversives were invariably stoned to death – along with pimps, prostitutes and adulterers – so that even the account of Christ's death on the cross was almost certainly apocryphal.

As Fiske's depression began to lift, he was forced to ask himself the inevitable question: so why had Christ's story, the teachings themselves, endured as long as they had? Firstly, because they were undeniably a force for good. If Christ hadn't existed, he concluded, someone would have had to invent something very like him. So, somewhere under the mountain of rhetoric, somewhere in the doctrinal labyrinth that reflected centuries of man's ambition, greed and obsessive need to control his fellows more than any real desire to spiritually enrich them there was a truth. If somehow, one could get back to that . . .

For much of the next decade, Fiske devoted himself to his chosen career, writing for television. Trashy scripts for soaps, often churned out in a day, gave way to science-fiction classics like *Star Voyager*, a series that ran for nine seasons.

It wasn't until the mid-seventies that Fiske, and a consortium he put together, was able to initiate the analysis of the other three gospels. This showed that all four were the work of some thirty-seven different writers in total, with many contributions having been made as late as 450 AD.

When Fiske had the work of the most spurious contributors extracted, there was just enough material left to construct one complete telling of Christ's life. This slim tome was then checked against every available historical, archaeological and geographical source then available.

Fiske's income from television, in a time when TV merchandising was just coming into its own, was considerable. But all this work put a strain on his finances, nevertheless. Quite what it was all leading up to, even he himself was unsure of at the time. He knew only that he had embarked on a personal odyssey, one that might perform some kind of exorcism within himself. In rediscovering the story of Christ, he was in some way rediscovering, in a sense rewriting, his own past.

But the final draft of *The Lost Gospel* was a supreme disappointment to J. Richmond Fiske. Accurate it might be, but the greater truth he'd worked so hard to rediscover, to purify, had, if anything been diluted. The new work was, in short, dull. In taking Christianity back to the drawing board and purging the spurious elements, he had turned an inspirational account of the Messiah's life into routine biography, peppered with platitudes regarding the human condition. Fiske called it, 'Fortune cookie philosophy – without specificity, with little or nothing to say for today.'

Christ had brought a lofty ideal down from the temples to the streets, coloured it with imagery designed to capture the imagination of the ordinary man. But if his message had held a more timeless, more universal truth than the one that has come down to us, Fiske resolved, it must have been bound up inextricably in the messenger himself. Hundreds of hours of movie footage were testimony to the fact that that had been so with one of history's greatest Antichrists – Adolf Hitler. Perhaps, in some sense, it had been true, too, for the Messiah? The tale had been in the telling.

Meanwhile, Fiske's career in television was flourishing. The enormous success of *Star Voyager* – at this point in its sixth season on NBC – had inevitably led to the commissioning of a big screen feature, and the show's creator now set to work on the script. The storyline, which, like the TV show itself, called for its characters to intellectualize endlessly about the meaning of life, and man's place in the universe, would prove an interesting platform for a man still smarting from the failure of a serious exercise aimed at answering many of the same questions.

Here, Fiske felt free to extemporise and elaborate, to give the credos, required in the fictional work, all the bite and gusto he felt the final draft of *the Lost Gospel* had lacked.

The movie proved to be a box office sensation, the merchandising spin-offs grossing as much as the picture itself. A catch-phrase – 'Feel the strength in Him, feel the strength in you!' – went straight into the language.

One night, the picture's director, drunk on success, called Fiske at home. 'Jesus, Jeffrey, this thing is bigger than either of us now! Everywhere you look, you see that fucking slogan! We've created a new fucking religion, man!'

Of course, they hadn't, and interest in the *Star Voyager* cult waned as all fashions spawned by movies do. But it had sparked something in Fiske. He went back to *The Lost Gospel*.

Working at night and at weekends, he began to reshape it. The text began to change, to become more cosmic, more surreal. Above all, more modern. Later, Fiske would say there were times when he wrote as though directed by an unseen hand. But, in fact, by the time the work was complete, every last vestige of the little spirituality he'd retained was gone. It had been replaced by something he felt even more devoutly, something that, for him, was now very real, very practical, and would over the next twenty years make him a multi-millionaire.

The Lost Gospel was published in 1974. The mainstream churches were outraged by it. Here was a Christ with human failings, sexual desires, searching questions about the relationship between God and mankind. Most importantly, one with contentious views on issues that could not possibly have come within the experience of a man living two thousand years ago.

To many, he became more real, but the book's sternest critics claimed that it should have been called *The Gospel According to St Fiske*. The *Georgia Constitution* called the work, 'The most blasphemous creation ever published in the English language.' Several fundamentalist groups urged that Fiske be burned as a heretic.

But, prophet or pariah, by the early eighties, *The Lost Gospel* had found its way into three million households. And it had, by then, become the theological handbook of the fastest-growing cult in America.

The Apostles now boasted more than 1,750,000 members worldwide, more than a million of them in the US. There was an Apostles' place of worship in almost every town in America, usually an anonymous building in a back street – people often lived in the same neighbourhood for years without ever knowing what the building was.

New converts would say, 'Fiske's creed uplifts, empowers, and enriches as God's word always has. But it speaks to us of now, not of twenty centuries ago. The lessons it teaches relate to concerns, issues, situations that Christ and his followers, even those who rewrote the gospels generations later, could have no knowledge of.'

Other initiates summed up their conclusions more prosaically, 'It takes away that knot in the stomach you get from fear and uncertainty, that, before, only booze or dope could ease.'

These days, Fiske himself was presented to his flock as a distant mythical figure, a world-weary recluse, living out his final days in spiritual meditation on some tiny island in the Pacific. The fact that he oversaw every aspect of the corporate leviathan the Apostles had become with a ceaseless, fanatical energy was known to very few.

Now the cult's creator was to bring the work that had started it all to the screen for the first time, as part of a vast promotion campaign, aimed at taking the movement into an era of influence that would eclipse all that had gone before.

'It is our right to feel that those who seek to hold sway over us, to control and rule our lives, do so with the guidance of God's new word – a word that was lost to us, but is now refound,' Fiske stated in the preface of the most recent edition of the book. 'It is our bounden duty to bring that word to all those who would have their voices heard.'

Although he publicly supported the Christian Coalition, he would often tell close associates that 'it may influence governments, even create them. But it's an artificial union of utterly disparate forces that can't survive in the long term. What is needed is one force that can rise above the others, that can create the theocracy that should have been adopted as the system of government in this country from the beginning: church and state as one body, capturing the hearts and the minds of the people.'

My church . . . my state . . . my body . . .

Fiske watched impassively as film extras, playing the mob, began to hurl fibreglass 'stones' down upon the stuntman, standing in for the actor who was playing Christ.

Real change is never bloodless, he thought.

Both sides will suffer losses before it's done. And it will be done. Quietly in hidden places. With noise and flurry in public places, unrecognized for what it is.

My will be done.

'Mr Fiske? I'm sorry to bother you, sir . . .'

Fiske looked up to see the anxious face of his assistant. 'Mr Kleig said it was urgent.'

Fiske shook away his thoughts, took the satellite phone, and pressed his hand over his free ear to cut out the clamour of the crowd below.

'I'm sorry to bother you while you're on location, sir, but this really can't wait.'

For close to three minutes, Fiske listened to his security chief's report on the killing at the Falk Pharmaceutical research facility, a corporation in which the Apostles of Christ had had a controlling interest for many years.

'What do the authorities know?' Fiske asked at last.

'Nothing yet. I've screwed the lid right down on the whole thing. I wanted to get your input on the situation before I did anything more.'

'Do we have any idea what files this Corrigan got access to, or for whom he was working?'

'Not as yet, no, sir.

'What was the nature of the data found on him?

'A thirty-five mm film negative. Copies of files on

research done into REGENS development. Mostly old stuff. Fairly inconclusive by itself, I'm told.'

'Yes, but we don't know what he already has.'

'He was only on the payroll for six weeks.'

'If he knew where to look, that was long enough. What's his background?'

There was a pause, while Kleig found the relevant file. '"Stephen R. Corrigan. Qualified as research chemist at UCLA, 1993. Three years with Western Pharmaceuticals . . ."'

'Yeah, followed by a crash course at the Food and Drug Administration's Investigations Unit, no doubt.'

'Or maybe he never really left Western,' Kleig said.

'This isn't Western's style. Whoever's behind this wants it to look like industrial espionage all right. But my gut tells me this is Caulfield.'

Kleig sighed. 'I thought we'd taken the steam out of that.'

'You don't take the steam out of that sonofabitch. The President plans to shut down the movement any way he can. He obviously knows about our connection to Falk, and enough about what's going on down there to sense that it could be the weak link in our defences. If this was some kind of covert federal operation . . .'

There was complete silence for a moment. Then Fiske said, 'I want to know everything about this guy, Kleig. Who he really was, and who he was working for.' He seemed to be examining his options for a moment. 'How well can you tidy this up?'

'I've had sentinels speak to the security men involved. They get the picture, believe me. Mercifully the incident happened at night, so there are no other witnesses. I can have the whole situation thoroughly sanitized within twelve hours.'

'Okay. If the authorities do come nosing around, Falk's line with them should stay as close to the truth as possible. They should say that they turned up evidence of industrial espionage at the facility, but by the time they identified the spy himself, he'd taken off.'

'I have people going through the apartment he was leasing right now,' Kleig said. 'We'll need to make it look like he packed a bag or two.'

'That's right. The line of communication between Corrigan and his paymasters has been silent for close to ten hours already. If they can be made to believe he's still operational somewhere, just not calling in, they'll start getting fidgety. Maybe take the view we got on to him, and got him talking to us. Give it a week or two and someone from their end will come sniffing around his apartment or the bar he drinks in. It's just a matter of time.'

Fiske sat alone that night in his hotel suite, the food on the plate in front of him untouched. The more he thought about the incident at the Falk research facility, the more he became convinced that it was a part of the Presidential initiative aimed at shutting down the movement he'd devoted a life's work to creating.

It had been six years since the nation's eighty-three million church-goers had first flexed their electoral muscles and, in a move calculated to show they would no longer tolerate draft-dodging, pot-smoking womanizers in the Oval Office, had swept devout Presbyterian Preston Caulfield to power. Taking advantage of a strong mandate in both Houses, Caulfield had set to work on a flurry of legislative reforms. Gays were immediately discharged from the armed services. Abortion, for anything other than *bona fide* medical reasons, was made illegal in all but three states. Controls on violent or sexually explicit material in the media, the internet, even video games, proliferated at a rate that would have been considered nothing less than apocalyptic a decade before. Loopholes in the law that allowed those on Death Row to string out their appeals almost indefinitely were closed with a slam that resonated through penitentiaries across that land.

Terrorist outrages committed by the Aum Supreme Truth sect in Toyko and Branch Davidian sympathisers in Oklahoma, and the recent bombing of an airliner over Paris by the Circle of Light movement, had massively raised public consciousness of extremist religious groups. So now President Caulfield, egged on by the evangelical right, to whom he'd made a whole string of promises during his campaign for a second term, was turning his energies to eradicating cults and sects that, in the mind of the establishment, had presented a security risk for far too long. Word on Capitol Hill had it that the Apostles of Christ had been marked out for special attention.

But now, in the middle of his second term, Caulfield was being forced to work with a weakened mandate. Fiske had mustered all his political resources – a wide-ranging group of senators, congressmen, members of the judiciary, the media, captains of industry – to slow down and subvert the President's initiative. For the last months it had seemed that the promised purge would amount to little more than rhetoric, aimed at pacifying the establishment churches.

But now it was beginning.

Fiske left the table, and began to ready himself for bed. Tonight he would take a sleeping pill.

Did Caulfield have those around him who could make sense of the data on file at Falk? There were only a handful on the planet who fully understood the capabilities of the systems under development there. If he did . . .

In time of war, men were shot for hatching such schemes.

But time for this administration was running out faster than anyone there knew.

My church . . . my state . . . my body . . .

Real change is never bloodless. Few, even those peering down from the highest vantage points, have the foresight to see what is best for us, Fiske told himself again. Casualties were inevitable. The cause was worthy, and those who stood in its way would begin to perish soon.

Pieter Kleig closed the buff-coloured file, and came to a decision. He crossed his office in the administration building at the Apostles of Christ's headquarters in South Carolina, and dialled a number on his private line.

This new matter was of no great import. The old man should not be bothered with it. He had enough on his plate right now. The Caulfield initiative, the Corrigan infiltration, *The Lost Gospel* picture . . .

This Jessop matter was no more than an irritant. He would handle it himself.

CHAPTER FIVE

The master bedroom of the semi-detached house in north London was very dark now. Scrivens sat sullenly on the double bed and drew heavily on a cigarette. 'You got a problem?'

French, a tall wiry man with heavily lidded eyes, shrugged. 'Yeah, you're my problem.'

'What the hell have I done?'

'What does it matter? It's just . . . you, that's all.'

Scrivens thought for a moment. 'If you have a problem with me, I want to know what it is. Call it professional pride, if you like.'

'You make me nervous. It's something about you. You sit there on that bed, sucking on that cigarette. They kill you. Didn't anyone ever tell you that?'

'It's the fucking stink in here, if you must know.' He took another long pull and got up. 'How can anyone live in this filth? Okay, maybe I am kinda jumpy. I just want to get on with it that's all.'

'Shh!'

They fell silent and strained to hear. Footfall.

The man McKinnon knew as Jessop had had a basinful tonight. But at least he'd eaten, so his head was clearer than it was usually by this time. Bennie from the pub had asked him back for a meal. His wife hadn't been any too pleased at having to make their dinner go for three, but

Jessop was hungry and the last of his giro was gone. And, for the first time that day, so was the knot of pain in his stomach. I should never have contacted McKinnon's boy, he told himself again as he struggled with his door key. What is any of it to do with me?

The hallway was cold and smelt of damp, but Jessop had grown used to it long ago. The fire in the tiny living room had burned down to ash. A piece of coal had fallen out on to the rug. He kicked it back into the grate, and rubbed at the black mark left on the rug with the end of his boot.

His alcoholic stupor did little to block out the stench of urine in the downstairs lavatory – the only one that worked now – so he held his breath, leaning on the wall as he pissed. It hurt to piss these days. Was that his kidneys giving out? Probably. He zipped up his pants and made for the stairs. I could have done with another drink, he thought as he pushed open the bedroom door and switched on the light.

His whole body shuddered with shock. A man in a black leather jacket stood facing him, a gun levelled at his chest. Jessop was about to speak. A hand was clamped to his forehead and a piece of cloth stuffed into his mouth. The man behind him moved forward and snapped handcuffs on to his wrists.

'Downstairs. Move!'

Jessop's bloodshot eyes blinked uncomprehendingly. Scrivens put the Mauser to his forehead. 'Move!' Jessop stumbled down the stairs sandwiched between the men. These aren't police, can't be. Police don't behave like this. Christ, I should know! he thought.

They half-dragged him through the kitchen, and through the door that led into the garage. French snapped on the light. Jessop peered into the room, then pulled back violently, his eyes wild with fear. He was sober now, the most sober he'd been in a long time.

Hanging from a wooden beam in the centre of the room was a rope, the end knotted into a noose. Beneath it was one of the dining room chairs. Beside it, a stepladder. Jessop clung to the doorframe as the men tried to inch him forward. 'Don't mark him, for fuck's sake!' French muttered.

'I'll mark him! I'll mark him all right!' French drew on his cigarette, wrenched up Jessop's ponytail and rammed the butt hard in under it. Jessop let out a muffled cry and stumbled forward.

'You damn fool!' Scrivens yelled.

It took a full minute to force Jessop up on to the chair. French climbed the stepladder and pulled the noose tight around the man's neck. 'Do it!'

Scrivens kicked hard at the chair. Jessop lost his balance and swung off. French hurriedly pulled the chair away.

For a minute, the ex-con, his eyes bulging crazily, kicked, jerked and twisted. Then Scrivens reached up, grabbed his legs and pulled down.

Five minutes later, French checked the hanged man's pulse.

'Come on, let's get out of here.'

'Good morning, my name is Garson, Michael Garson,' McKinnon said. 'I wonder if I could make an appointment to see Doctor Alderbrook as soon as possible.'

'I'm afraid he's at a medical conference till the twenty-second,' the secretary said without looking up. 'I could give you an appointment with his partner if you like.'

Two weeks, way too long. 'No, it's Doctor Alderbrook I need to see. I'm only in the country another few

71

days. Thanks anyway.' McKinnon smiled and crossed the
secretary's oak-panelled office and headed for the door.

The smile faded as he hit the street.

Damn it. Back to square one.

McKinnon had begun to have serious doubts about
what his father's one-time cellmate had told him. If the
face Jessop – or whatever his real name was – saw, a
month ago in the hospital wing at Marston Moor Prison,
was as disfigured as he said, how could he be so sure
that it was Frank McKinnon? Because he'd shared a cell
with the guy for three years, McKinnon had reasoned,
and knew his face as well as his own. And he'd seen the
scar. If the man was his father, then he'd died not from
a heart attack four months ago, but from some kind of
cancer or wasting disease within the last few weeks.

According to Jessop, Dad was convinced that he'd
wronged me, McKinnon agonized. That my fleeing
Britain for the US was entirely a result of the publicity
the murder case attracted. But even if that's true, does it
justify my breaking off all contact with him? No.

But how could I know he'd been set up by a hardened
killer? Because he told me so. And if I was any kind of
a son I'd have held faith with him.

Jessop said my father seemed to be reaching out to him
with his eyes, entreating his help. If I'd been around, he
would have had me to turn to. By telling me what he has,
Jessop is giving me the chance to do something now.

Subconsciously McKinnon began to recognize that he
couldn't exorcise his guilt by rationalizing his actions.
But he could perhaps atone for them.

The old con had made it very clear that he now
considered his obligations to his ex-cellmate fulfilled,
and that any allegations the son chose to make against
the Home Office, as a result of what he'd told him, would

72

have to be done without his support. McKinnon was sure that to confront Stamford-Smith with his suspicions, without that evidence, would prove to be a fruitless exercise.

The journalist in him began to kick in. Hammer away at a weaker link in the bureaucratic chain. Get to some of the hospital staff who had treated his father direct. Finesse them, catch them off-guard, before the authorities have a chance to warn them he was sniffing around.

First, he needed names. He began to go through the stuff the Home Office had sent him more thoroughly. The letter from the prison director's office had included copies of his father's death and cremation certificates. The first had been signed by someone called Everett, and showed that Frank McKinnon had died from myocardial infarction – a heart attack – four months before. The cremation certificate bore two signatures: Everett's and one which was virtually unreadable.

Now, in a cafe around the corner from Dr Alderbrook's surgery, McKinnon took out the cremation certificate and examined it again. The second name scribbled at the bottom could have been a dozen things – it almost defied being read.

The previous day, he'd faxed a copy of it to NYPD's chief consultant graphologist, a woman he'd got to know during a blackmail case he'd covered in his first year as a journalist in New York. The fax he'd received back from her colleague – it seemed she was out of town – ventured that the name of the signatory was probably 'Aldenbrook' or 'Alderbrook' and that the initial was an 'L' or 'C'.

The British Medical Directory, in the local library, showed a Michael Everett was in general practice in York. It had only an L. Alderbrook listed, with a practice in Harley Street. He was an oncologist.

An oncologist – a cancer specialist.

What Jessop had said suggested that McKinnon's father was suffering from some kind of cancer . . .

This single link changed McKinnon's whole attitude to the old con's story. If the cellmate was totally wrong, what on earth was the signature of a cancer specialist doing on his father's cremation certificate? And if he was suffering from cancer, what was so fascinating about the case that it should attract the interest of a specialist based two hundred miles away?

McKinnon was sure that, had he not heard Jessop's story, this link would have almost certainly gone unnoticed. But in the light of what he now knew . . .

But Alderbrook, it seemed, was out of the country, and McKinnon was no nearer an answer to any of these questions.

He drained his coffee cup and finished his sandwich. You put that little pastrami in a sandwich in New York, the customers would torch the building, he thought dejectedly.

There was one distant possibility. Alderbrook's secretary had had a modem on her desk by her computer. So that meant she was periodically on-line. An on-line computer could be hacked into. Muddy Harbin had chopped into the Vaphiadis database without too much difficulty, that time when McKinnon was in trouble with that report for the network. If he could take a trawl through the private files of a Macedonian arms dealer, a Harley Street quack shouldn't present too much of a problem.

McKinnon hailed a cab, and gave the driver Caitlin's address.

A block behind him, an overweight woman, trailing a miserable-looking Yorkshire terrier on a lead, muttered into a concealed mike in the lapel of her coat. A minute

later a car pulled out of a turning and moved up to
her. The door swung open. She lifted the terrier, and
she got in.

'Look, McKinnon, people don't use their birthdates or
the name of their pet poodle as entry codes anymore.
Not if they've got half a brain in their heads,' Muddy
said through a mouthful of reheated chicken enchilada.
'Sure, sometimes you can get a toehold with a little
social engineering, finesse a code out of a rat-assed
employee, or some such, but I don't see that as a feasible
option here.'

'Neither do I.' McKinnon clamped the phone between
shoulder and ear.

Muddy chewed for a moment. 'Well, what I'm trying
to get into your head is that this could take some time.
If you're gonna be waiting on me, my advice is get back
on the plane to the US, and get on with your life.'

McKinnon hung up.

Caitlin called through from the kitchen of the Kensington
house, 'Unless you want this pasta to taste like bill-
poster's paste, you'd better get in here and start eating.'

McKinnon hurried through and took his seat at the
heavy wooden table that dominated the room.

'My day off is the only time I ever get to cook,' she
said. 'So you're seriously privileged.'

'When we've eaten, I'll kiss the hem of your gown.'
McKinnon helped himself to food. 'If I remember right,
you used to do a more-than-passable impression of
Madonna.'

'Eh?'

'Talking, not singing.'

'Oh . . . Oh yeah, stuff from that on-tour movie she
did in black and white. Kind of all whiny and spoilt.'

'Can you still do it?'

She looked thrown. 'I guess.'

As they lunched, he brought her up to date on the events of the last two days, and then explained what it was he wanted her to do.

'See, Alderbrook's secretary has already heard my voice.'

She shook her head slowly and laughed. 'You don't change, Joel.'

'Hope not.'

She shrugged. 'Well, I'm not exactly Glenn Close, but I'll give it a whirl.'

Later, Caitlin poured them coffee and McKinnon checked his watch. 'She should be back from lunch by now. And the time in Miami fits, so . . .'

She reached for the phone. 'Give me the number.'

She waited for it to be picked up. 'Doctor Alderbrook's secretary please.' Her voice suddenly took on a kind of mid-Atlantic twang. 'Oh, this is Doctor Kirstner's assistant, calling from Miami. The doctor has asked me to check if Doctor Alderbrook plans to be at the Kessler Foundation Conference here on Tuesday . . . Oh, he is? Well, that is a pity. Doctor Kirstner was looking forward to seeing him again. Well, thanks for your help anyway. Goodbye.'

Caitlin hung up, a broad smile on her face. 'Alderbrook's at an oncology conference in Chicago. How's that?'

'Good girl!' McKinnon got up and punched the air. 'All right!'

'This is fun. Do you need any more calls like that made?'

'Not right now, but thanks. Chicago? I guess I could drop in on him on the way home. I've come this far, so what's another few hundred miles?'

'The BMA should be able to tell you where the convention is being held. The event organizers should page him for you, they do at the things I go to.'

'You look as though you didn't expect me to turn up.'

Wes Tyrell was taller than Hannah remembered. He also looked a good ten pounds lighter than he was when they'd first encountered one another in Byelorussia. He stood in a corridor of her apartment building, looking nervously about him, as though he felt he was being watched.

'Frankly, I didn't. Your Mr Fiske casts a broad net. Not too many fish get away.'

He walked in, and looked hard at her. There was fear in his eyes. 'I'm not away, Hannah. I'm just putting a toe in the water.' He peered around her entrance hall. 'The water the rest of the world swims in.'

'Come in and sit down.' Hannah took him through to her small living room. The walls were stacked with books and files. The dining table doubled as a computer terminal.

'I'd have come sooner, but I had a helluva job slipping by my minders.'

'They're keeping you on a tight rein, huh?'

'Uhuh. They don't know I'm here though. They think I'm out visiting a couple of potential converts – that's the one Outland excursion you can make where they don't breathe down your neck.'

'Sit down, relax,' Hannah said as gently as she could. 'Would you like some coffee?'

Tyrell spun around. 'I'd kill for a beer, if you have one.'

Hannah laughed. 'Two sins in one, huh?'

'You bet your sweet life.'

Tyrell sipped the Budweiser like it was Puligny Montrachet.

Hannah poured herself coffee from a pot on a filing cabinet. 'Have you and your brother had a chance to talk?'

'Some. We have to do a lot more. This would be a massive step for us. If you know anything about the Apostles, then you know that.'

'Of course.'

'Well, in my case it's not some great crisis of conscience that's caused me to consider leaving. I just feel I'm being used. I front the band, write the material, do the arrangements. I'm a crucial part of the Evangelical Army. You saw the show in Byelorussia, you know the kind of impact it makes. We take the message wherever we're told to. We've played nineteen countries this year already. We obviously don't get paid, we're expected to give our best for the good of the church. They have us on the go eighteen hours a day. We're told what to think and when to think it.'

Tyrell obviously had a lot he needed to get off his chest. Hannah had made it clear at their backstage meeting and in subsequent phone calls that she would be there to listen, even help him and his brother get out of the cult, if that was what they ultimately wanted to do. She knew now, as she listened to Tyrell talk, that she had been the first person in his life to make that even a possibility.

'It took me a while to see it for what it was. It's fucking slavery, Hannah. It's the only word that fits. Don't get the wrong impression. All the applause hasn't gone to my head. I don't want money, or any more accolade than I get. I don't even want thanks. I just want to be treated like an adult human being with a life and mind of my own.'

78

'Well, you're in the wrong organization for that.'

'You saw what went down backstage. It's like that every day.' He got up and paced the room. 'That whole experience has made me take a hard look at the Apostles in a way I don't think I would have otherwise done. It's made me question everything I was brought up to believe.'

'You and your brother are second-generation disciples aren't you?'

'Yeah, we were born into the thing.'

'So tell me about your brother. How does he feel about the set-up?'

'He's thoroughly disillusioned too. Like me, he lives in a closed order. He's at the commune in Highlands, North Carolina. Most of the disciples there work at the organization's central database. They have hardly any contact with the outside world at all. He's been a data processor there for four years. He sees a lot of what really goes on at the core of the operation. When he's not working at the database, he's expected to help with the induction of new members, those who have computer skills the organization needs. Like me, he finds it harder and harder to reconcile the teachings with what he knows to be the truth.'

'Well, at least you've had a taste of the real world. That should help you to cope with life outside of the cult to some extent.'

'Oh, if you take the mighty word of Fiske as holy writ, the Outland is a hotbed of iniquity and disease, and the Devil lurks in every corner.'

'That's what I'm getting to. From what you say, your brother has had little or no exposure to life as the rest of us live it. If you do both leave, he'll probably need to undergo some professional exit-counselling. You may

79

need to too. I'm in touch with one of the best in the field. When you're ready, I'll make arrangements for you to meet.'

'Yeah, I know about that stuff. Part of the technique is to expose the cult member to the true face of the organization, the illicit end of it. As I say, Jerry's had five years of that already. He confronts it every day, working at the database. That's why he wants out. It won't be easy for him at first, I know that, but he'll cope. We just need a place to hang out for a while, and enough cash to bridge us till we can get started again.'

Hannah took out a yellow legal pad and began to make notes. 'Well, here's the deal on that, then. I have a small place in the Adirondacks, about two hundred miles north of here. It's nothing special, but it's clean and dry. If you're looking for a wild time, forget it. It's in the middle of nowhere. That's why I got it. That's why I think it's where you should both go. Fiske, the Apostles of Christ, and a division of the National Guard will never find you up there. There's a phone, and I'll lend you a fax machine. That way you can start networking, putting out feelers, building new lives for yourselves. I can let you have a thousand dollars, enough to keep you warm and fed for a while. When that's gone . . .'

'We'll be up and running, don't you worry about it. We'll be halfway to paying you back.'

'Well, we'll talk about that down the line.'

'That would be great . . . wonderful.' Tyrell was lost in thought for a moment. Then he looked at Hannah hard. 'How much do you really know about Fiske?'

'Enough to be certain that he wants me out of the picture already. If he knew I was planning to get involved with you guys . . .'

'Right. The guy's a fucking monster. He thinks he's

80

God. He thinks he's in control. Rattle his cage and he bites. He devours. I'm replaceable. I can't do him any more harm than any of the others who've got out of the organization in one piece. But Jerry . . . He's not the kind of guy Fiske wants walking around shooting his mouth off. He's gonna get madder than hell when he finds he's gone. Why do you want to be on the receiving end of all that? I mean, what do you expect to get out of this?'

Hannah shrugged as though it was the first time she'd thought about it. 'Anything and everything you and Jerry can tell me about how the inner circle of the movement works.'

'I take it that means you want Jerry to get you into their database.'

'It would be helpful, yes.'

Tyrell smiled. 'Ah . . . So that's what this is all about.' He put up his hand 'Not that that's a problem or anything. Hell, you take all the heat, you're entitled to get something back.' He scratched at his scalp. 'Well, as soon as Fiske finds out Jerry's gone, he's gonna have the entry codes changed. So Jerry needs to get out of there, and to wherever you want him to be, before anyone at the Highlands commune notices he's gone.'

'Yes, ideally.'

'That's gonna take some figuring out. Especially as I have to make plans of my own.' He drained his glass and wiped his mouth. The foamy head smeared across his moustache like it was ice cream. 'It's not often I get the chance to have a beer. Christ, I enjoyed that.'

Hannah laughed. 'So, you'd like another one?'

'You bet.'

She got up and walked through to the kitchen. 'Listen, don't let this freedom stuff go to your head.'

'Don't worry about it.' Tyrell sat and thought some

more. Then he said: 'The hardest part for me is gonna be leaving Elaine. She and I have been together a while now. But she still believes in the Apostles. I've tried to make her see, but it's just no good. I guess it's the price I'm gonna have to pay to get Jerry and I out of there.'

He looked up at Hannah. 'See, I love my brother too, and they know that, know I won't leave so long as they still have him. And they feel secure about him, we've made sure of that. So pulling this all together won't be easy. It's gonna take a lot of setting up. We're gonna have to synchronize our plans to the minute.'

Hannah put out her hands. 'Well, I'm here for you, Wes. Both of you. Call me, any time, day or night, and if need be, I'll come to you.'

As soon as Wes had gone, she began to make copious notes. The book on the Apostles of Christ movement, that had occupied her solidly for the last eighteen months, was intended to be more than a definitive exposé. Her intention from the beginning was to strike a blow against the cult that would fatally damage it. She knew from first-hand experience just what a vile and pernicious organization it was, and readily recognized that part of her motive in doing the work was to exorcise personal demons. But the deeper she'd dug into the cult's affairs, the more she felt justified in pursuing her cause.

Careful networking amongst disaffected cult members had led her to the belief that Fiske was set upon a course aimed at putting his movement in the forefront of the country's affairs, into a position of power that no religious body, let alone an extremist cult, had ever occupied before.

Her first book, *Chain of Command*, had exposed to public view aspects of the Bosnian arms scandal that had resulted in the resignation of three senior army officers and a senator. This book, she was determined, would provide President Caulfield, a man committed to the eradication of sects like the Apostles, with the impetus he needed to put an end to Fiske and all he had created.

Hannah knew she would never conclusively prove her theories regarding Fiske's despotic dreams until she got access to classified files she was sure must exist in the cult's vast database.

Frustrating months of failure to open up that end of the research had led her to examine other aspects of the cult's activities, in particular the methods used in their drive to make new converts in Eastern Europe.

Her motives for offering help to Wes Tyrell had, to an extent, been humanitarian – all too aware of the suffering the cult could cause, she'd played that role a number of times before – but were also aimed at adding a further dimension to this new aspect of her book. But the fact that Wes had a brother who might be capable of accessing the very classified material she needed to see had come as an extraordinary and unexpected bonus.

The week before, when Wes had first talked about Jerry, Hannah had written in her diary, 'It's a funny thing; the harder I work, the luckier I get.'

The brother will need to know precisely what I'm interested in extracting from the database, she thought now, as she walked through to the kitchen to make coffee. He may need to finesse entry codes out of colleagues before he leaves. I'm closer now than I've ever been to tearing these bastards down. Please God, don't let these kids chicken out on me.

Muddy turned out to be far more resourceful than McKinnon could have hoped. Within hours of getting his instructions from his client, he'd put together a profile of Dr Alderbrook, using the on-line files of relevant professional bodies, public records offices and TRW bureaus. He soon knew a great deal about his subject, and was sure the doctor would have been a little inventive about choosing a codeword that would access his database.

Alderbrook had called his home in Kent 'Thelworth'. Thelworth turned out to be a village near Cambridge, where it seemed Alderbrook had studied medicine in the seventies. With this in mind, Muddy decided that the doctor was probably one of those professional men who retain an intense nostalgia about their university days, so he set a computer programme to scan all available data on the town and its environs, and had names that might be suitable as codes scheduled into a list. This he then compared with notes he'd made on Alderbrook's life-style.

Muddy knew that he would probably only get three shots at getting into the doctor's files. After that, the system would shut him out. He selected his choices with great care, using instincts built up over years.

He wasn't surprised when the second word proved to be the key. An examination of Alderbrook's credit card statements had shown that wine played an important part in his life. That had inspired the choice. It seemed that the magic word had been 'Godfreys' – apparently the name of a wine bar in the town that was still popular with medical students.

Muddy had said that Alderbrook's secretary had not been on-line long enough in the last few days for him to get a great deal out of the doctor's database. It did seem that there was a medical file on Frank McKinnon, but the hacker was unable to access it. The name appeared on some kind of patients' list, however – about a dozen names on a page in an otherwise unrevealing file.

McKinnon had recognized one of the other names on the list the hacker had sent him as that of a man convicted of a series of murders shortly after his father was sentenced. Caitlin recognized another, a man involved in a kidnapping and killing, who had been sent down for life a few years back.

McKinnon then contacted an old colleague from his days in England as a local radio correspondent. The man now worked at the *Daily Telegraph*, and agreed to get McKinnon access to the newspaper's press-cuttings library.

'I need to find out if the other guys on this list are convicted killers too,' McKinnon told Caitlin that night, as they dined at a restaurant in Islington that had been a favourite, years before. 'And, if they are, why they should be of interest to Doctor Alderbrook.'

'Maybe he's just making a study of them or something,' Caitlin said.

She knew nothing of the hacker. McKinnon simply referred to Muddy as 'my man in New York', like he was some kind of researcher he employed from time to time.

'My man also turned up a letter from Alderbrook to someone called Gerald Rosendorf, outlining some changes he wanted made to a contract he was about to sign – it seems the existing one has only weeks to run.' He took another mouthful of *Boeuf en Croûte*. 'There's no indication from the letter what organization Rosendorf works for, but the new deal guarantees the doctor an annual income of almost £370,000. So what I need to know, Caitlin, is why a Harley Street specialist, who could command that kind of salary from a single source, should be remotely interested in a bunch of deadbeat cons. What's so goddamn fascinating about these guys, that he should want to leave valuable private patients behind in London, and trek the better part of two hundred miles to their bedsides in York?'

When they walked back to McKinnon's rented BMW, shortly after midnight, they found the offside rear quarter window had been smashed. The interior of the car was covered in broken glass. The radio was missing; a tangle of coloured wires protruded from the dashboard.

McKinnon's good humour vanished. 'Great. You can't even go for a meal without having your car vandalized.'

'Has anything else gone?' Caitlin asked.

He opened the unlocked door, and began to pick up the few fragments of glass that had come through to the front seat. 'I don't think there was anything else much to get.'

'Well, you know what they say: these days, BMW stands for Break My Window. I don't know why you rented a car. You could have used mine. I use cabs and tubes most of the time, so it just sits out there, rusting away.'

'Force of habit, I guess.'

'Well, if you're going to hang on to this, you'd better stick it in my garage overnight while you're here,' she said, as they pulled on to the Pentonville Road. 'I rent one in a mews at the back of my place.'

'And what are you gonna use?'

'Old Renaults are beneath thieves in Kensington. It'll be fine on the street for a night or two.'

McKinnon said very little more on the way home. To Caitlin, it was as though he'd retreated back into some kind of private sanctuary. There was a sense of *déjà vu*. For a few precious hours she'd had the old McKinnon – animated, positive, the McKinnon she remembered from the time when they'd first been together. And now here again was the sullen, withdrawn man she knew from the days of the murder trial. It was as though the evening had been a microcosm of their whole relationship.

The rental company's insurance would cover the damage to the car and the loss of the radio. McKinnon knew that, and yet it seemed to Caitlin as though he was taking the incident personally.

CHAPTER SIX

Aubrey Stamford-Smith ordered steak and kidney pie from the diminutive septuagenarian waiter, who had been serving in the dining room of the Marlborough Club for as long as he could remember, and turned to his guest.

'So, we have a troublesome relative.'

Stamford-Smith sipped his drink. 'Not just a troublesome relative. McKinnon's son . . . An NBS correspondent for Christ's sake!'

'Well, there's an upside. At least we had people in there who could get us his address in England. Without that we wouldn't have been able to put a tail on him.'

'He's becoming a serious problem. I did my best to defuse the situation when he first called, sent him the approved material, everything we agreed. If the father's cellmate hadn't got in on the act I think the whole thing might have gone away.'

'It's a great pity we didn't have the report on that end of it earlier.'

Stamford-Smith's eyes met his guest's. 'If it hadn't been for me, you'd have never have had it at all! You've no idea how carefully I had to tread to get what we got. If I'd known in time that the cellmate had seen Frank McKinnon alive, I'd have made damn sure he stayed in Marston Moor. But he'd already been paroled, and was beating a path to McKinnon's son.'

Stamford-Smith's guest sipped his drink. 'Well, as you know, that matter's been addressed.'

'Too damn late! Joel McKinnon has made the Alderbrook connection, has been nosing around his surgery, and God knows where else!'

'Calm down, Aubrey. I've told you, our people are following the situation very . . .'

'Look, I needn't tell you what's at stake here. If this isn't handled properly . . .'

There was silence at the table for a moment as the waiter served lunch.

Stamford-Smith lowered his voice to a whisper. 'If this isn't handled properly it could compromise the whole arrangement. It's been of great benefit to both of us, I'd be the first to admit. But unless I get assurances that . . .'

'Let me take some advice, Aubrey, and come back to you.'

Stamford-Smith crossed Pall Mall and hailed a taxi. It's times like this I wish one of these terrorist groups would do the whole nation a favour, and blow this damn government to kingdom come, he thought. The Home Secretary stands up in the House and promises: 'More punishment, tougher penalties,' and before he's drawn breath, the Chancellor slashes back budgets to finance tax cuts! How can you run an effective prison service faced with that kind of subversion?

The international attitude to crime and punishment was now pretty much uniform. It was accepted that prison was no answer in itself, but as long as persistent offenders were in jail, they were not on the streets committing further crimes. But the policy of incarcerating murderers for terms of at least twenty-five years before considering them for parole had created massive problems in the

British Prison Service. A killer in his twenties, with a long record of violence, or one who'd premeditated his crime – and the maximum security jails were full of them – might now expect to spend fifty years behind bars. Total cost to the government, allowing for inflation, around £3.5 million, per head and climbing. No one was more aware than Stamford-Smith that every time a Crown Court judge shouted 'Life!', another few square feet of precious cell space would disappear off the vacant list for perhaps the better part of half a century. He had remarked many times that, these days, the value of some cell space made real estate in Mayfair look positively worthless.

The prison population – already 65,000 – was now growing at the rate of nine per cent a year. Recent plans to build seven new prisons, despite heavy investment from the public sector, had stalled, and then had been scaled down to provide for only five. Three of the jails would not be ready for occupancy for another two years.

Overcrowding, especially amongst prisoners who by the very nature of their crimes warranted complete isolation, was now so bad there were concerns in some quarters that the whole system was close to meltdown.

Stamford-Smith's private view was that around 30 per cent of the current prison population should never have been incarcerated in the first place. They should have died at the end of a rope, or by some more fashionable means if need be, years ago. But so long as that remained a pipe-dream, the pressing question was: where the hell does one put new high risk prisoners when the 'Category A' prisons are full, and the killers in them can't be freed, and resolutely refuse to die?

Nearly six years had passed since he'd first spoken to his old Cambridge friend, a director of the corporation that held the largest private prison franchise, of the pressures the service was facing. His concerns had been met with the most unexpected of responses. The friend too, it seemed, had problems. These related to another company in which he had an interest, and were linked to the development of new products they were hoping to market.

Stamford-Smith needed to look at the problem laterally, the friend advised. To open his mind to new options, ones he might not yet be aware were available to him. The matter would require the utmost thought and discussion of course, but there might be a way that they could help each other . . .

The special arrangements that had been in place at Marston Moor Prison ever since had certainly not been unuseful, Stamford-Smith thought now, as the taxi pulled into Queen Anne's Gate. Who could have foreseen that the Frank McKinnon case would have brought them such unwelcome attention?

If this begins to get out of hand, I'll need to pull the plug very quickly. What I don't yet know, is how much damage has already been done.

J. Richmond Fiske turned over and watched the girl slip from the bed. He studied the smooth olive skin of her back and buttocks as she crossed to the bathroom.

Lucia had been barely seventeen when she'd first come into his life. She was now just twenty-one. Officially, she didn't exist in his household. She was never ever referred to by his staff. She was simply a fact of his life. To the extent that he thought about it at all, he believed that she saw him as some intricate composite: seven parts father figure, three parts lover. He saw her as someone who he could trust. Someone who actually loved him for him. There had been few enough who loved him for any reason.

Fiske showered and dressed, and walked out on to the balcony where his butler had laid out breakfast. With the mail that morning were several reports from Pieter Kleig.

There was no good news today.

The first document dealt with the much-publicized federal initiative, aimed at eradicating – as the President framed it to Congress – 'the many corrupt and repellent cults that operate in this country, whose doctrines violate the most fundamental of human rights'. If Kleig's information was to be relied upon, there was evidence of a gradual build-up of pressure on a whole range of fronts. Slow but inexorable. The number of initiates defecting to the Outland had risen sharply in recent months. From Kleig's report it seemed many were talking to FBI investigators, shooting their mouths off about matters they'd sworn to keep secret until death.

Let 'em yap, Fiske thought, as he picked through the files of the deserters. What could the testimony of a bunch of miscreants and dropouts really add up to?

Kleig confirmed that district attorneys in at least eleven states, where the movement had multiple interests, were digging through records of every transaction they'd been a party to, in the hopes of turning up evidence of corruption.

Fiske put the document to one side. You don't build an organization with the degree of influence the Apostles now commanded by leaving loose ends lying around. If the authorities got really lucky they might inflict a little peripheral damage, nothing worse.

The infiltration of the Falk Pharmaceutical research

facility, Fiske knew, might turn out to be another matter entirely. He opened the next report – an update on Kleig's investigations into the incident that had resulted in the death of a research chemist there. Kleig had clearly spread a wide net, had dug as deeply as he dared into the cloistered enclaves of Wall Street and Capitol Hill for information, but still there was no word on who had planted the industrial spy caught photographing classified data at the base.

Normally, little disturbed Fiske's slumber. But in recent weeks, there had been more than a few sleepless hours. Within the walls of the research facility there were projects no more than a handful of men had knowledge of. Programmes that, developed to their full potential, could reshape the political map of the western world. The mere chance that Corrigan had accessed them, taken what he'd found to the authorities . . . Not that Fiske was frightened for himself. His concern was for his organization, and the impact such revelations might have on all that he'd built.

He poured himself more coffee, and opened the last report that had come with the post that morning. It was from his legal department. Three sets of parents, who were currently bringing legal proceedings against the movement, aimed at breaking the hold they allegedly had over their offspring, now had hearing dates.

Fiske made careful notes in pen as he ate. 'The timing of these actions could be highly deterimental, given the interest the authorities are currently taking in us. I believe several, if not all, of these actions can be closed down, or severely frustrated, by re-employing the strategy used in the Harrowman case.'

He rang the bell under the heavy oak table to signal to his valet that he had finished breakfast, and made for the elevator in the hallway. He tapped a code into a panel on the wall and a metal door slid back.

For almost a minute, he was winched silently down into the substructure of the building, and then into the body of the granite mountain beneath. He walked out into a small lobby, slid a plastic card into a slot in the door ahead of him, and let himself into a large octagonal library.

In this room, the Apostles of Christ movement had been born. Every edict that had shaped it since had been drafted at the oak desk that stood facing a balcony set into an opening in the rock face. Books of every size and description, many bound in leather, lined the shelves. Set into alcoves between them were display units containing ancient documents.

Fiske unlocked a drawer of a filing cabinet and began to search through it. The document under glass on the wall in front of him was a single page of a letter written by St Ignatius Loyola, the founder of the Jesuit Order. Written in 1541, it was uniquely valuable in that it contained the first known version of a dictum that was to become synonymous with the teachings of the Jesuit doctrine: 'Give me a boy till he's seven, and I will give you the man.'

Fiske had given that old boast much thought over the last thirty years. It had still been, in some measure, a reflection of the relationship that existed between church and state till the dawn of the twentieth century. But two world wars and the liberalism of the sixties had swept away much of that ethos. The same hypothetical seven-year-old, living today, was, when he became a teenager, likely to hold his parents' attitudes and beliefs up to scrutiny, reject or reshape them to his own needs, as few generations had been free to before. It was in these same crucial years that sexual preference was usually decided, Fiske had argued, when the principles of the Apostles movement were first hammered out in the late seventies. So was it not in this time of tumult and change that an individual would be most open to a new philosophy, a new life-style? Turbulent teenagers needed the understanding and approval of a valid peer group. Research had shown that those from over-protected backgrounds were often unable to succeed in the real world, and would reach out to an alternative family just as readily as their less cosseted counterparts. Fiske had determined that the Apostles of Christ would become such family.

He knew, too, that there were potential converts to be made amongst the professionals and high achievers who, by the demanding nature of their jobs, often failed to develop worthwhile relationships, and might have turned to the church for solace had their questioning minds not found the dogma of the establishment bodies so rigid, timeworn, and unconvincing.

Fiske's induction teams still played heavily on the feelings of isolation many potential initiates had felt in their personal lives – in the Outland.

'Outlanders will ostracize and ridicule you for your convictions. Many will simply be jealous. Jealous of the contentment you've found, the esteem you're held in, by your new family. Your friends and relatives in the Outland have had their chance; they failed you. The question you must ask yourself now is: do you believe they are still worthy of you, that they can still bring something of value to your life, something you do not already have in abundance here?'

The doctrine was backed up with daily sessions of 'love-bombing', in which the initiates would be smothered with affection by their new peer group. Then, when they were high on their newfound self-worth, the love would be temporarily snatched away and replaced with hours of humiliation and abuse, inevitably leaving the cult member feeling totally disorientated and craving re-acceptance from those on whom they'd come to depend. Love would be regained at a price: many initiates gladly signed away their life savings, as a tithe to the movement, knowing that, by doing so, they gave their new family a clear measure of their faith.

Over the years, Fiske's legal department had defended dozens of actions brought by distraught parents desperate to rescue their offspring from a cult they believed was destroying them. Few ever got as far as a hearing. Parents were inevitably told by trial attorneys that, under the constitution, American citizens were free to join any movement they wished, on any terms they felt were reasonable, which was precisely why the cult rarely allowed the initiation of minors, over which the law had greater control.

One exception had been the Harrowman case. Harrowman, a wealthy lawyer from Boston, had gone to considerable lengths to extricate his daughter from the clutches of the Apostles of Christ. The daughter had made it very clear to her commune elders that she wished to stay where she was. Anxious to avoid a damaging public wrangle, Fiske had moved in to direct the events that followed.

'How much does this movement mean to you?' he'd asked the Harrowman girl.

'Everything.'

The girl was hypnotized and given a mild hallucinogenic. 'When you were small . . .' Fiske's voice was a whisper. 'Maybe eight years old, perhaps ten . . . When you were a little girl . . . There were times your father came into your bedroom, weren't there? Into the bathroom when you were changing for bed. Then he'd touch you, touch you in places you knew, even then, he should not . . .'

The girl had screamed, vomited. But still Fiske had persisted. 'He told you that, if you loved him, you would kiss him too. Kiss him and suck him . . .

'If you want to stay with our family,' Fiske's voice was urgent in her ear, 'and we want you to stay with us, you must try to remember, for your own good . . .'

When the affidavit containing the daughter's counter-claims reached her father, family friends said he aged overnight. He made no further attempts to extricate his daughter from the Apostles.

Fiske crossed to his desk. Ignatius Loyola had been right for his time. Fiske's own dictum was: Give me a child who has glimpsed the world beyond the schoolyard, the wasteland beyond the city wall, and found it a cold and cheerless place. It is that child I take and have for ever.

Are these new legal proceedings being brought against us one more part of the Caulfield Initiative? Fiske wondered. One more attempt to drag us into the media spotlight?

It's of little import; these issues at least will be dead inside a month. I've not worked a lifetime to build all that I have, to have this bloodless servant of the right tear it down before my eyes.

The fax in the corner of the room chattered into life. As Fiske finished reading the sheets that pumped out of it, the phone on his desk rang. He knew that it would be Kleig.

'I wouldn't have bothered you with this normally, sir. But with things shaping up the way they are, I felt you should be briefed.'

Fiske scanned the sheets. 'Yes, you were right to call.'

98

'Do you remember the Frank McKinnon case?'

'Of course,' Fiske said.

'It looks like the son has really gotten up a head of steam,' Kleig said. 'He's got the makings of a major troublemaker.'

'Because of the NBS connection? We have people in there, don't we?'

'Sure. I'm not concerned at this point about keeping the lid on their end of it. I'm concerned about the resources the son might be able to call on in an investigation of his own. As you see, he's been pretty busy already. I've taken steps to slow him down. But in my view the situation's now bordering on the critical.'

McKinnon's expedition to the press cuttings library at the *Daily Telegraph* proved to be highly productive. It was soon clear that all the names on the list found in Doctor Alderbrook's database were those of men serving life sentences at Marston Moor Prison.

When, through old cuttings, he was able to contact a number of the men's relatives and friends, another common factor emerged: it appeared that all the criminals were effectively forgotten men – no one who'd ever cared for them had been near them for years. Indeed, a number of them had since died in jail, almost unnoticed. Several, like his father, had met their ends in middle age. All but two had died of cancer.

Again, McKinnon was forced to ask himself why this eminent specialist should go out of his way to treat these particular men. Many top consultants did charity work. But why would he choose patients he would have to travel two hundred miles to see?

Was there some kind of medical research involved here? McKinnon wondered, as he walked to where his car was parked. Secret stuff, that you could only get away with performing on forgotten lifers who no one in the outside world gave a damn about? In the fifties, prisoners were used as guinea pigs to test LSD, so it wouldn't be anything new. It would explain why Jessop had seen his father in the state he did. Might even explain the discrepancies on the date and cause of death.

Alderbrook is working on my father when the ballon goes up, McKinnon speculated. Dad is suddenly cleared of the murder charge, and the spotlight is turned on his whole case. Those involved in the research panic, desperately start to try and clean up their act, before the authorities, and relatives like me, start nosing around, asking awkward questions. Dad has guessed what they're doing to him, and so he's killed to shut him up, and his death certificate is backdated. The cause of death is shown as being from heart failure to draw attention away from what has really been going on.

He stopped at the kerb and levelled the small plastic remote control unit at the BMW, parked ahead of him, and pressed. There was a click as the central locking was deactivated.

Am I the first, McKinnon wondered as he climbed in and started the car, or have other families of deceased prisoners, once held at Marston Moor, felt the need to know more? From all they've said, it seems that I am.

It had gone midnight when McKinnon reached Caitlin's place. The mews, behind, was little different from a score of others in the district. The nineteenth-century stabling and staff accommodation had long ago been converted into garages and chic cottages. He drove down the narrow cobbled street to the lock-up Caitlin rented,

100

got out and searched for the keys she'd given him only the morning before.

Movement in his right peripheral vision made him look around. Ten yards up, on the other side of the mews, a man stood in the doorway, sipping a can of beer.

McKinnon's eyes focused on him for no more than a second. He judged him to be in his mid-twenties. He looked fit, alert. McKinnon found the key, moved over to the doors of the garage, and pretended to wrestle with the padlock for a minute. All the time, as casually as he could, he scoured the mews.

The perfect place for a set-up. Narrow, dark. If there's a second man . . .

At first, McKinnon didn't see him. His clothing merged with the stonework, his face was hidden from view. But when he moved, McKinnon could see him at the top of the mews, closing off the the only line of retreat.

In that second, he was certain. They're here for me. They'll steam me. Roll me for my watch, my cash and credit cards . . . If I'm lucky.

He moved closer to the door, so they couldn't see what he was doing, and continued to fumble with the padlock.

Sure enough, within seconds, the man across from him began to move closer – McKinnon couldn't see him, but, in the silence of the night, he sensed the slap of his trainers on the cobbles.

Covering his actions with his body, he lifted the heavy padlock free, and closed his right hand around it. The other guy was moving in too now, coming down the mews fast.

Don't panic. Panic, and you're fucked! These guys look like they know what they're doing. Take one out first, then you stand a chance.

101

Scrivens was ten feet from McKinnon now. He weighed him up as he came. Stringing up the old con had been a piece of piss. But this fella looks like he could give us more trouble, Scrivens told himself. Take it carefully.

His right hand tightened around the handle of the knife in his coat pocket.

'Excuse me. Can I have a word with . . .'

Fuck all that! Let's see what you're really here for.

McKinnon's answer was short and to the point. He swung the garage door back with all the force he could muster, catching Scrivens hard in the side of the head.

The guy was totally surprised by such an act of aggression. For a precious second he lost his balance. The hand holding the knife jerked into view. It was all McKinnon needed to see. He could hear the other man running now.

His fist tightened around the padlock and, using it for weight as a crooked prizefighter would a horseshoe, he threw his whole body behind a deft right hook.

Scrivens went down hard, his head striking the cobbles with a dull smack.

McKinnon turned to meet the other assailant. He too had a knife. He was bigger than the other guy. Looked like he worked with weights. McKinnon dared him to come on, any fear he felt drowned in adrenaline. Behind the garage door, caught in the street lights, he could see some garden tools. He grabbed for one as the man came for him. It was a garden fork. McKinnon wielded it as threateningly as he could, but it made a pretty pathetic weapon.

French's face twisted into a smile. You've got to be fucking kidding. I haven't got time for this. He stepped back, shaking his head.

He stopped, calmly folded the blade of the knife back

into the handle, and put it back in his pants pocket. Then his hand moved upwards, inside his jacket.

Christ, he's carrying!

McKinnon knew that when the hand emerged it would be holding a gun. He swivelled the fork around in his hands, and launched it into the air. The heavy wooden handle caught French full in the chest, knocking him back. Before he could right himself, McKinnon was on him, one hand around his throat, the other around the gun wrist. They both lost their balance now, and staggered backwards down the mews. McKinnon wrenched the gun hand round, smacking it against a garage door further down. French instantly headbutted him. For a second McKinnon thought he was going to black out. Some part of him seized the moment, and his left knee came up into French's crotch like a jackhammer.

The man's head went back, and he let out a grunt of pain, but still he wouldn't let go of the gun. The two grappled and bumped down the row of garage doors for some thirty feet, each struggling to get an advantage.

Blood ran freely into McKinnon's eyes from a gash in his forehead now, but he could see a lantern bracket on the wall ahead of him – an old-world wrought-iron job someone had put up. With the last of his strength he swung French's arm back, slamming his wrist against the iron support. The gun got caught up in the bracket for a second, and McKinnon judged the moment was right. He let go of the arm, locked his fists together, and let the guy have it in the jaw with a great rolling punch. The man sagged, his arm still caught up in the bracket. Then he shook his head wildly, trying to unscramble his brains.

I can't knock this guy out. I don't have what it takes.

McKinnon searched around desperately for a new weapon. Suddenly he was caught in a beam of hard yellow light. He shielded his eyes, heard the juddering whine of a starter motor, then the revving of a car engine.

The other man . . . He's in my car . . .

The BMW roared down the mews, zigzagging across its width as it came. There was no more than three feet clearance on either side. McKinnon turned and ran.

Ahead, there was a bend, then an arch leading out to the street. He'd never make it in time, he knew he was all in. He could see lights in the front rooms of some of the cottages here. He hammered at a knocker, rang a doorbell, then spun around. The car was twenty feet from him. The gunman was upright now, silhouetted in the headlights, and staggering down the mews towards him. McKinnon wiped the blood out of his eyes, and tried to clamber up on to a high pile of trash and junked building materials.

As the car passed the gunman, he made a grab for the passenger-side door handle, but the door was locked. Clinging now to the wing mirror too, he levered himself up and, hanging on precariously, was swept along with the car. It turned into the bend and screeched to a halt in front of McKinnon.

At the same moment, doors in the mews began to open. A large man in a soiled T-shirt, his upper arms green with tattoos, stepped out into the street. Other men appeared from a doorway to McKinnon's right.

Scrivens cursed, and swung the wheel hard left. The BMW lurched forward and raced for the archway. It was low and narrow. If the gunman kept his head down and tucked himself in, it looked like he might just make it. The car made a tight turn to line up with it. The gunman, on the outside of the turn, had to grip on to the door handle with both hands to stay on.

McKinnon lifted the small remote control unit from

his pocket, levelled it at the car and pressed the button on top. He was too far off to hear the central locking system release, but the door the gunman was clinging to, heavy with his weight, immediately jack-knifed open, swatting him against the stone wall to the right of the arch, like a giant horsefly. His broken body folded into a dark heap in the shadows.

CHAPTER SEVEN

'That's what I'm trying to tell you! They *weren't* trying to rob me.' McKinnon leaned back in his chair and ran his fingers over the dressing on his forehead. 'They were trying to kill me. I don't have a doubt about it.'

The police officer closed his notebook. 'I'm not saying you're a liar, sir. I'm sure that's how it seemed to you. But, as you say yourself, you don't know anyone in this country anymore, and, in all the circumstances, it seems unlikely that that was their prime motive. I'm sure we'll find the motive was robbery.'

Caitlin came through from the kitchen carrying a glass of brandy and some painkillers. She looked down at McKinnon's pale face.

'Here, take some more of these.'

'And you didn't find any . . . body or anything?' McKinnon asked.

'No. The witnesses I spoke to told me that one of the assailants was hurt. But it seems by the time we got there he'd taken off.'

'*Taken off*! I saw that guy get swatted! No one could survive that.'

'Perhaps someone came for him, took him away,' Caitlin said.

The officer moved into the hallway. 'And we haven't

had any reports of anyone turning up in casualty who fits the description you gave us.'

McKinnon looked at Caitlin. 'It doesn't make sense. Any of it.'

The policeman turned in the doorway. 'When you're feeling a little better, I'd like you to come down to the station and look through some mug shots, see if we can put names to faces.'

McKinnon sighed. 'You won't have those faces on record.'

'What makes you say that?'

He shrugged. 'It's just a feeling I've got.'

McKinnon slept little that night. The pain of the stitched gash above his hair-line nagged through the codeine. His thoughts pitched and rolled, until he got up and made himself tea.

He rose early and began to pack for his flight home. If I could somehow get Jessop, or whatever his name is, to go on record with his statement, he thought, my case against Alderbrook, if I do get to confront him, would be a thousand times stronger.

Caitlin made them breakfast, while McKinnon tried the ex-con's number again. This time a youngish-sounding woman answered. It took a moment for McKinnon to make her understand who it was he wanted to speak to.

'I'm afraid my father . . . Well, the fact is, he's dead, Mr McKinnon. Three days ago.'

'Good God,' was all McKinnon could say for a minute.

'Were you a friend of his?' the woman asked.

'Son of a friend. I hope you don't mind me asking, but how did he die?'

There was a pause. He guessed the woman was trying to compose herself. 'He ended his own life, Mr McKinnon . . . At least, that's what they tell me.'

Five minutes later, McKinnon walked slowly through to the kitchen, and sat down to breakfast with Caitlin.

'*At least, that's what they tell me.*'

There's doubt in her mind.

'Are you okay?' Caitlin asked. 'I mean apart from the war wound.'

'The man I told you about – Jessop. The one who raised this whole question about my father's death. Well, he was found hanged, three days ago. His daughter doesn't believe he'd ever do that to himself. Pills maybe, but not that.'

'She thinks he was murdered?'

McKinnon looked up. 'Well, it could hardly be a fucking accident, could it?' He saw her flinch at the tone of his voice. He forced a smile, reached across the table and took her hand. 'I'm sorry. I'm wrecked. My head's killing me. And, well . . . This news has really thrown me. I nearly get wasted by two thugs, and in the same week Jessop comes to a bad end. Can that be coincidence?'

'What else could it be?'

'Retaliation. An attempt to tidy up a messy situation.'

'That's kind of a leap in the dark, isn't it.'

'Well, right now, that's about the only place I have to go.'

'No. You have Chicago.'

McKinnon crossed the packed lobby of the Marriott in downtown Chicago, and made for the reception desk. The desk clerk was clearly a member of that vast clan whose motto read, 'Resigned to a life of coping with irksome pricks.' His face was dominated by a lower lip that made him look like disgruntled sturgeon. 'We have nothing for tonight,' he said flatly, in answer to McKinnon's enquiry. 'I suggest you try the Hyatt.'

'I'm with NBS.' McKinnon gave him a business card. 'I'm here to cover the conference. You should have something for me.'

The desk clerk moved his fingers over the keys of his computer as though he'd been asked to check that a week had seven days. 'Nothing. You'll have to speak to the organizers.'

McKinnon was halfway across the lobby when a hand touched his sleeve. He turned to see a woman of around thirty. A card on her lapel identified her as an employee of the pharmaceutical company hosting the seminar.

'Sorry, I couldn't help overhearing what you were saying. I'm Maggie Phillips. I'm with Falk's press office. I'm sorry, I didn't know NBS was covering this. I'm delighted they are, of course.'

'Well, they are if the local office comes up with a cameraman,' McKinnon said.

'Actually, we've just had a cancellation. If you come with me, I'll see to it that you get a room.'

Five minutes later, they walked to the elevator together. 'There's a Doctor L. Alderbrook here some-where,' McKinnon said. 'Do you have any idea where I might find him?.'

She checked her watch. 'The programme's pretty much finished for today. I guess he'll either be in his room or in one of the bars.' She checked through the papers on her clipboard. 'His room number is 3011. If you have any problems, let me know.'

McKinnon let himself into the room he'd been assigned to, showered and changed. He unzipped his bag, took out a neatly folded press cutting, and opened it out. It was a piece from a back issue of the British medical journal, the *Lancet*. The picture in the centre showed a group of doctors. The man to the far left was a short, balding, overweight figure of about fifty. The caption gave him as, 'Dr Laurence Alderbrook'. Well, if it comes down to it, I shouldn't have any difficulty picking that ugly little runt out of a crowd, McKinnon thought as he headed for the elevator.

First he tried Alderbrook's room. The doctor wasn't home. McKinnon took the stairs to the lobby and had him paged. When that, too, produced nothing, he began to trawl the hotel bars.

Just what the fuck am I doing here? he asked himself as he drained his second glass of Budweiser. Even if I do confront the jerk, there isn't one good reason why he should open up to me.

As he turned into the back lobby he encountered the press officer again.

'Did you link up with Doctor Alderbrook all right?' she asked.

'No, as a matter of fact, I didn't. Tell me, are there any others in his party?'

She checked the notes on her clipboard. 'No. He seems to be here on his own. But that woman sitting over there at the bar was trying to find him a while back. She might be able to help you.'

The woman in question sat with her back half-turned to McKinnon, her long russet hair masking her profile. McKinnon thanked the press officer and crossed to the bar. She turned as she saw him approach.

He took her to be about twenty-eight. He studied her as he closed the distance between them. Now I know that face, McKinnon told himself. I've seen you recently. But where?

'Excuse me. I'm trying to find a Laurence Alderbrook.'

The wide green eyes stared at him impassively.

'The press office said you were trying to find him too. I wondered if you . . .'

As soon as he heard her voice, McKinnon was sure that, even if they had met before, they'd never spoken. Her voice was light with a faint Texan twang. 'I think you must have the wrong person,' she said.

'You aren't looking for Doctor Alderbrook?'

The full mouth lifted into a smile. 'I'm afraid not.' She got up, leaving a barely touched drink, and headed for the lobby beyond. He watched her rhythmic passage across the bar, followed her with his eyes till she disappeared into a crowd of conventioneers in the lobby.

Now he remembered where he'd seen her before: in Atlanta, at the Kerensky shootout. She'd been amongst the press corps there. She has to be covering the conference here for someone, McKinnon decided. He ordered himself a whiskey and waited. When it was clear she wasn't coming back, he thought, Now something here doesn't add up. The press woman tells me this woman was looking for Alderbrook, actually points her out – she wasn't the kind of lady you could easily confuse with anyone else – and the lady herself denies it. Then she leaves a nine-dollar cocktail, with no more than a sip out of it, and takes off.

Soon after, he'd downed a final drink and headed for the elevator. It was now eleven forty-five pm. It was worth trying Alderbrook's room just once more.

This time there was a light showing under the door of room 3011. The moving shadows told him someone was in there.

At last.

McKinnon hastily began to ready his opening salvo.

Alderbrook might be the worse for drink: catch him off guard and you might get somewhere.

He knocked on the door, three spirited raps, and waited. Nothing.

Come on, you sonofabitch, I know you're there.

He knocked again, and this time called the doctor's name. No response.

He's on to me. Someone's tipped him off that I'm here . . .

There was hardly any point in calling the room. If Alderbrook wasn't going to answer the door, he certainly wasn't going to take a phone call. Okay, I got you bottled up now, and you ain't going no place.

As a young reporter, when he freelanced for Sunday papers, he'd staked out some of the sleazeballs he'd been sent to investigate for days at a time in the hope of 'door-stepping' them. This matters one helluva sight more than any tabloid piece, so what's one lousy night? he told himself now. You gotta come out sometime, you fucking creep. And when you do, I'll be waiting.

McKinnon ducked into the doorway of a linen room, where he had a clear view of the corridor, and settled in for a long vigil. What if Alderbrook calls security, with some crap about being harassed? Deal with that when it happens.

Before more than ten minutes had passed, there was the creak of a door. McKinnon peered out from his hiding place. The door of 3011 was opening slowly, like someone was being real cautious. McKinnon readied himself to make his move. A head peered out and checked the corridor.

It was the woman from the bar.

Christ! Is she screwing Alderbrook, is that it? McKinnon

113

remembered the picture of the doctor in the back copy of the *Lancet*. Now that would take some believing.

McKinnon stepped out of the doorway.

'Well, hello again.'

The girl was clearly startled. She recovered herself within a second, but her initial reaction told McKinnon all he needed to know – he'd seen that look too many times before to mistake it. She was in Alderbrook's room for no good reason.

'So it seems you and Alderbrook know each other after all,' he added.

The green eyes looked at him coolly now. 'I don't think that's any of your damn business.' She tried to move off but he moved to close off her line of retreat.

He took his mobile phone from his coat pocket. 'Fine. Then let's get security up here. The doctor should be back any time now. If he's okay about your being in his room, then there isn't a problem, is there?'

McKinnon watched her weighing up her options. Thankfully, they didn't seem to include making a run for it.

Is she a thief? Or is she just a journalist with a hard nose for a story? She may have been through his papers, might even have a few of the answers I need . . .

'Look, I'll make this easier for you. I know you're a journalist, I saw you in the press pack at the Kerensky shootout in Atlanta. As a matter of fact I'm here to get some answers myself.'

She seemed to relax a little.

'You want a beer?' Hannah said at last.

'You don't have a cigarette, do you?' Hannah took a sip of her beer. 'I quit smoking a year ago. But right now . . .'

'No, I'm afraid not.' McKinnon scanned the hotel bar for a waiter. 'I could get some for you.'

'Forget it.'

'Look, my name is McKinnon, I'm with NBS, which is how I happen to know you were in Atlanta that time. Don't tell me you and Alderbrook are an item, because I won't buy it. You don't strike me as an inveterate felon. So my guess is you have to be on a story. I have no interest in muscling in on your territory, I swear it. But I am out here to get a few answers of my own. It's a personal matter, to do with my family.'

Hannah shot him a look as if to say, You really expect me to believe that? There was a long pause, and then she said, 'What do you want from me?'

'Well . . . You could tell me your name.'

'Hannah Rostov,' she said sullenly.

McKinnon shrugged. 'Well, talk to me, Hannah.'

She stared at him for a while, wondering how to proceed.

'I write books. I'm an investigative journalist.'

'Anything I'd know?'

'I doubt it. They don't have pop-up pictures.'

McKinnon tipped his head on one side and sighed.

'My last book was called *Chain of Command*,' she said.

McKinnon looked up. 'On the Bosnian arms scandal. I was there in ninety-three. That was damn well researched. You really wrote that?'

She nodded, then took a copy of the conference programme out of her purse and slid it across the table to him. 'Well, I'm out here nosing around on something new.'

The programme was open at a page advertising a lecture: 'REGENS – Remedial Genetics Systems. The Road Ahead.'

'Is this Alderbrook's field?'

'He's here, isn't he? That's the central issue under discussion at this conference, you know. There are aspects of genetic medicine and the development of treatments for diseases currently considered incurable that interest me.'

McKinnon sensed she was treading very carefully.

'I thought Alderbrook might have some of the answers I needed,' she went on. 'I tried a little social engineering the other night, to get him to open up, but he wouldn't play. I knew he was at dinner in Evanston tonight – I even managed to appropriate his key – so . . .' She shrugged. Then the green eyes caught his. 'So, Mr NBS, tell me you've never crossed the line in search of a story.'

He laughed. 'How long have you got! How could you be sure he wouldn't turn up when you were in there? What did you do, "dead-end page" him?'

'Do you know a better way? I had him paged at the restaurant in Evanston, hung up when I heard his voice . . .'

'Certain it would take him thirty to forty minutes to drive back, if he left right then,' McKinnon said.

'Then I went straight to his room. Trouble was, so did you.' Now she laughed for the first time. McKinnon found himself laughing too.

She stood up. 'Okay, NBS, that's all she wrote. If you wanna book me, do it now. Otherwise . . . I'm hitting the sack.'

McKinnon studied her. 'Have breakfast with me?'

She put her head on one side as if to say, Where's this going now?

She turned and walked away. 'Fine, if you wanna be down here for six fifteen. I have a plane to catch.'

McKinnon stopped at the elevator and turned over what

Hannah had told him. Then he decided that confronting Alderbrook should wait. *There's a connection or two I need to make first.* He sat in the lobby for a moment, and checked through the notes he'd taken on the data that Muddy Harbin had extracted from Alderbrook's database.

The convention PR woman looked about all in. She sat forlornly at a trestle table, to the left of the reception desk, nursing a large cocktail. 'Was the lady any help?' she asked, as McKinnon approached.

'Yes, she was. Thank you. Tell me, is there a Mark Rosendorf here?'

She checked. 'Yes. Do you want his room number?'

'No, that's all right. Just remind me, who's he with?'

'With Falk. He's senior vice-president . . . They're the hosts here, Mr McKinnon.'

He headed for his room.

Got it! Rosendorf was the man Alderbrook had written to, regarding changes he wanted made to the new contract he was about to sign. So it was Falk that was planning to pay the good doctor the equivalent of $550,000 per annum for his services. Alderbrook had to be here primarily to see him, to discuss 'the principle issue under debate here'. What was the term Hannah had used? REGENS: Remedial Genetic Systems. From the correspondence it looked like the Falk thing was a done deal. So why would he make the transatlantic trek?

Could there conceivably be a tie-up between Falk, Alderbrook and his work at Marston Moor Prison? McKinnon wondered. *Again, it all points to some kind of research project, one that perhaps involved my father. Was that the reason for the cover-up? Were the ex-cons on the patients' list Muddy had turned up all human guinea pigs?*

* * *

'Kerensky was in over his head from the start,' Hannah said. She sipped her coffee. 'Richmond Fiske – he's the founder of the cult as I'm sure you know – wanted some new blood at the top. The man who had been fronting the set-up from the beginning, McBain – he kinda played Christ to Fiske's God Almighty – was played out, and he wanted to get a new charismatic figurehead trained up before he snuffed it.'

McKinnon buttered his toast. 'Kerensky was certainly a hell of an orator. I got the feeling, listening to some tapes he'd made, he'd just been put through more changes than he could handle.'

'Well, that's right. My view is that Fiske didn't reckon on the kid's idealism – it's a fairly rare commodity in that end of the God game. I think the more the kid found out about the organization, the more he realized what a vile, pernicious bunch they were . . .'

'And the more he wanted out.'

'Or the more he tried to change it. Fiske's people probably got nervous, and went to work on his head – they have stuff that makes *The Manchurian Candidate* look like *Forest Gump* – and he flipped.'

'You're really into this stuff,' McKinnon said.

'Uhuh. You might say I got dragged into it. My partner of four years got sucked into the cult, a few years back. I tried to get him out. Found out a lot about them, about the whole cult industry, along the way.'

'I got packed off to Atlanta to cover the Kerensky thing because of a report I did on fringe Christian churches for the network last year,' McKinnon said.

'Saw it. Covered the Christian Scientists, the Scientologists, the Church of Christ, and a few others.'

'That's right.'

'Well, that's the soft end of the spectrum from my

118

point of view. I'm more interested in the hard end, the extremists – the Brethren of Christ ... You up on them?'

'Yeah, I read a few things . . .'

'Kinda mail-order Manson set-up, with a little Jeffrey Dahmer thrown in for flavouring; the Church of the Redeemer: they're a Southern-based bunch of sweethearts using Jesus as a cover for a whacko Survivalist movement. And then, top of the heap, there's the Apostles of Christ.'

'I wanted to widen the follow-up piece I did on Kerensky to include an in-depth look at them, but I was getting the hurry-up, and, well, there's just so much you can pack into a fifteen-minute slot.'

'Well, they're brand leader, believe me. Estimates vary, but the Evangelical Alliance reckons they may have as many as two million members, worldwide – they've made a lot of new converts in the old Soviet block. They're a multi-billion dollar conglomerate. Data from Cult Watch shows they have a controlling interest in at least a dozen Fortune 500 corporations, and a powerful lobby on Capitol Hill, too well camouflaged to fully assess. Once in, you don't leave. The Apostles have their own secret police to keep the faithful in line. They corrupt, they cripple, they kill.'

'Sounds like you got a book there somewhere.'

She shrugged. 'Maybe.'

McKinnon studied her as she finished breakfast. How about, you bet your ass!

Her eyes met his. 'If I published a fraction of what I know about Fiske, I'd have to live the rest of my days like Salmon Rushdie!'

'Yeah?'

'I've been high on Fiske's burn-in-hell list for a while as it is.'

'How so?'

'I did a piece on the Apostles for the *New York Times*, on how he got female initiates, whose parents were trying to get them out of the cult, to claim that their fathers had sexually abused them – I had the testimony of two disaffected sect members to back the story up.'

'And Fiske sued.'

'No, not in the end, he's too smart for that.' She wiped her mouth with her napkin. 'I think he has something more exotic planned for me down the line though.' She shook her head. 'How intelligent people can actually believe that that animal has the ear of God is beyond me.'

'Perhaps you have to start out with some Christian faith, to see it from their perspective.'

'I had some once. When I was in school. But I was always the kid with the awkward questions they never wanted to answer. Like "if Jesus fed the five thousand, who did the dishes?" As a child, I was one of those brats that always had to get to the root of everything. I'm still like that. If something intrigues me, before I can think, is it safe, is it legal? I'm off.'

'So I noticed.'

She stopped and studied him for a moment. 'You're working well, McKinnon. You know how to listen, I'll give you that. But that's as much as you get this time out.' She made a little jabbing motion with her chin as if to emphasize the point. 'Okay, your turn. Tell me about you.'

He thought for a moment. Then he told her something of his early life in England, skating over his family troubles. An instinct told him to hold back on that until he knew more about her.

'Are you married?' she asked.

'No. I've been divorced a while now. I was a foreign correspondent through most of the marriage, so . . .'

'She went through a lotta lonely nights.'

'The separations weren't easy. But she was pretty clear about what she was getting into when she married me, had her own career, her own friends. She coped pretty well. No, the problem was me. I just lost the capacity to re-adapt to . . . ordinary life.'

As he spoke, she studied him. She judged him to be in his early thirties. The most striking feature was the eyes – blue, ringed with black. There was a sharp intelligence in them, and more than a hint of humour. Was there something Slavic about the set of them, about the cheekbones too? But the thick wiry hair was almost raven black, the skin light: taken with the eyes, his was classic 'Black Irish' colouring. Could his father be a descendant of one of those Spanish sailors washed up on the the Irish coast after the destruction of the Armada?

All in all, a good face. A striking face. He was looking at her steadily now.

'Anyway, eighteen months ago, some terrorist with a rocket launcher did me a favour. I took a piece of shrapnel in the back, and that put me out of that end of the game for good.'

'You seem to be in pretty good shape now.'

'It didn't really mess me up physically, Hannah. It changed me.' He took another sip of his drink. 'Anyway, I took a job as a stringer here. But it was too late for the marriage. She'd had enough of my moods, my introspection. And I don't blame her.' He put up a finger. 'But! I have changed.'

She checked her watch. 'Good. I'm glad to hear it. Okay, I'm outta here. I have a meeting with a source in

New York. Someone with key data I need, if I can ever get to grips with it.'

McKinnon, too, checked his watch. Alderbrook should be stirring any time soon. 'Technical stuff?'

'Very. But that's the least of my problems. I don't know yet, but, down the line, I may need some real computer whizz to get me to where I need to go.'

'I have a couple of tame ones.'

She stood up. 'Well, if I get bogged down, I'll give you a call.'

'And if you don't?'

She tipped her head on one side and smiled. 'I might anyway. Thanks for breakfast. Good hunting.' She turned, and headed off towards the lobby.

He watched her go. Ask for her fucking number, you ditz. McKinnon hurriedly opened the check the waiter had slotted under a plate.

Inside was her business card.

'Doctor Alderbrook!'

The small man at the elevator stopped and turned. 'Yes.'

McKinnon crossed the corridor towards him. 'My name is Joel McKinnon.' He passed Alderbrook his card, hesitating long enough for the doctor to absorb that he was with NBS. 'My father, Frank McKinnon, was one of your patients.'

'He was?'

McKinnon took out Stamford-Smith's letter, folded open at the cremation certificate. 'Well, you signed this.'

Alderbrook gave it a cursory glance. 'Sadly, in my position, I sign all too many of these. But I remember the name from the stuff in the papers. Was that your father? Bad business.'

The elevator came, and McKinnon followed the oncologist into it.

Play him carefully. Draw him in.

'My father had been dead some weeks by the time I was put in the picture. The Home Office sent me this, but it leaves a number of unanswered questions. I heard you were here, so I thought I'd track you down.'

Alderbrook took the letter and looked through it. 'I hope I can help . . . Only fifty-five . . . Bad business.' He looked up. His mouth lifted into what McKinnon took to be a smile. 'I'm always happy to talk to relatives in these circumstances.' They moved out of the elevator into the lobby. 'I'll need to have my secretary fax your father's records to me, of course.'

Alderbrook eyed a group of conventioneers heading in the direction of the ballroom. 'And I'll need to get clearance from the Home Office. But that's just a formality.' The small eyes engaged McKinnon's. 'If you call me tomorrow evening about six, I'll update you on the position, and hopefully we'll be able to meet for a drink and get things squared away.'

'Well, there's a couple of questions I'd like an answer to right now . . .'

Alderbrook's unlovely face set into the steely smile all senior medical consultants learn to effect.

'As I remember, I had only the most peripheral involvement with your father, and it would be wrong for me to say anything until I've had a chance to consult the file.'

Alderbrook hailed some colleagues across the lobby and turned to go. 'Now if you'll forgive me I have a lecture to attend. I'll see you tomorrow night, Mr McKinnon.'

He moved off. McKinnon turned his back, and slammed the heel of his hand into the wall.

'Damn it! Damn it to hell!'

Alderbrook left his colleagues, and moved hastily through the ballroom without even looking for a seat. He emerged through the entrance at the other end, and made straight for a bank of pay phones.

CHAPTER EIGHT

McKinnon reached blindly out of the shower, and grabbed at the bathroom wall phone.

'Joel? It's Laurie? I don't know if you remember me. I'm the one with the eating disorder and the crush on Danny DeVito.'

'How could I forget. I'm in the shower, kiddo. I'll call you in ten.'

Laurie Thomas had run McKinnon's day-to-day life at the network for more than a year. 'I didn't hear from you for a week, I thought you might be dead.'

I damn nearly was! he thought

'Okay, call me back,' she said. 'I have a fax from some freak called Alderbrook. It sounded like it might be . . .'

'It is. Read it to me.' McKinnon trapped the receiver between ear and shoulder, and reached for a towel.

'"The Home Office takes the position that, in view of the fact that your father's case is currently the subject of an enquiry, it would be entirely inappropriate for me to discuss this with you privately. I'm sorry, sincerely, Laurence Alderbrook."'

'Sonofabitch. Thanks, Laurie. I'll see you Monday, kid.' McKinnon hung up and dialled the front desk.

Fifteen seconds later it was clear the man he'd come to Chicago to see had checked out.

*   *   *

Hannah Rostov put down the phone and took a deep breath. The Tyrell brothers were on their way. Wes hadn't gone into any detail, but he'd said that Jerry had with him entry codes that could access Fiske's classified files.

At last, Hannah thought. She walked through to the linen closet, and began to make up the beds in the two guest rooms. The phone rang again. She waited until the answering machine kicked in and listened.

Her heart hammered in her chest. It was Fenton.

They know. Fiske's on to me. He has to be. Why else would Fenton call now?

The first time Hannah had heard of the Apostles of Christ had been from the lips of a girl who roomed next to her, during their sophomore year at college. She extolled their virtues with chilling zeal to anyone she could corner.

The Faculty of Comparative Religions at the college had had a file inches thick on the cult and its doings. Having waded through it, Hannah was far from surprised when the kid became immovably entrenched in the sect, and left college for good.

The movement had raised its head again, crucially, some years later. Fenton Dellaplane was ten years older than Hannah. He'd been running a small but well-respected business consultancy in Boston for five years when she met him. The following spring, certain that she was in love for the first time, she'd left her native Texas, headed north and moved in with him.

She was in the final year of a PhD in English literature when Fenton's business went down in the recession, a few years later. When he couldn't get started again, she'd taken a teaching job to keep them going. He'd played house husband for a while. She'd been too busy, too tired most of the time, to notice how strange and preoccupied he was becoming. Then they started having fights. One night he'd gotten into this whole thing about 'the state of her immortal soul', spread out all this Apostles of Christ literature, and she began to realize then how desperately lost he was.

For weeks Hannah tried every argument she knew in an attempt to break Fenton free, even thought of joining the cult herself at one point, doing whatever she had to do to reach him at his own level. But once the Apostles had her pegged as a negative influence, they began to deploy every weapon in their psychological arsenal to drive a wedge between the couple.

One night Hannah came back to the house to find all Fenton's stuff gone. The last she heard – in a hurried phone call on New Year's Eve two years before – he'd risen to the position of Senior Elder at the cult's commune in Chicago.

And now he'd called again.

Why now? To threaten her, to warn her not to get involved with the Tyrell boys? They were not from his commune. It was hard to imagine he would know already what was in their minds. Unless the cult had specifically deployed him, knowing his previous connection to her.

I have to call him back. I have to know what's behind this, before the Tyrells get here. For all our sakes.

Fenton could be charming and beguiling. He could also be secretive, devious and cajoling. When he came to the phone, Hannah could hear none of those Fentons in his tone.

'I . . . well, the truth is, I just wanted to hear your voice,' he said flatly.

'You're hearing it. What are you expecting it to say?'

There was a pause. 'After all this time . . . not a great deal, I suppose.'

Hannah sighed. 'You made your choice, Fenton. It was the Apostles or me. They won. What's your problem?'

'I'm trying to make changes here. I know you know all about the movement, about the book you're doing and everything – I didn't ring to give you a hard time about that. Go ahead and write it, if that's what you feel you want to do. I'd probably agree with some of it anyway, about the . . . more troubling aspects of the work. But there's a lot of good in the Apostles, Hannah. Good I want the world to know about too . . .'

She listened to him yammer on for a while. He's cracking up, she thought. The strain of justifying his actions is getting too much for him. The important thing is, he's not calling about the Tyrells.

'Why are you telling me all this, Fenton?' she said at last. 'Me of all people?'

Again a pause. 'I dunno . . . We were a good team, you and I. At times like this, I miss your . . . input, that's all.'

She laughed mirthlessly. 'Fenton, you wouldn't want my input on anything you're involved with right now, believe me! I don't mean to be offhand, but I have to be somewhere. I'm sorry you're having a rough ride. You'll come through, you always do. When you speak to your mother, give her my best.' Hannah rang off, and made a mental note to have her phone number changed to an unlisted one.

Two hours later, she peered through the glass peephole in the door. Then she slid off the security chain, and let the Tyrell brothers into the hallway of her apartment. They came in like the dogs of the Devil were snapping at their very heels.

128

She took them through to the kitchen. 'How'd it go?'

Wes Tyrell immediately moved to the window, and scanned the street below. 'We're here. I guess that says it.'

The other boy turned to Hannah. 'Hi, I'm Jerry.'

Hannah took his hand. 'Hi yer. It's good to meet you at last.'

'I wanna thank you for what you're doin' for us,' he said nervously.

'I'm just glad I could help.' Hannah surveyed the two battered-looking backpacks they'd brought with them.

'Is that all you have?'

'We thought it was best to travel light,' Wes said.

'Were you seen?'

Jerry Tyrell shuddered. 'I keep tellin' myself no . . . But with that outfit, you just never know for sure.'

Hannah opened the fridge and took out sandwiches. 'I didn't know what time you'd get here, so . . .'

Wes fell on the food instantly, but Jerry continued to pace. Then he spun around. 'Here, take these.' He handed her an envelope. 'I just wanna get rid of them. Jesus, if Kleig knew I had them, I'd be a dead man.'

Jerry was smaller and of slighter build than his brother. He'd no doubt spent the hours Wes had spent working out slouched in front of a PC.

Hannah knew the envelope contained entry codes and decryption software. 'Well, we'll get to those later.'

'No, we can't,' Jerry said. There was urgency in his voice. 'The minute they figure we've split, they'll change everything. If you wanna get into Fiske's database, you gotta get movin'.'

'Well, get some food inside you, for heaven's sake. The PC, modem and stuff are in the living room. Like I said on the phone, it's not exactly state-of-the-art, but . . .'

Jerry bit disconsolately into a sandwich. 'It's not your hardware that concerns me . . . The weak link in the chain is me.'

'What d'yer mean?'

He stared up at Hannah. He looked about all in. 'Like I told you on the phone, I don't have enough information to access more than a small part of the database. I can find my way around that pretty well, but . . .'

Wes helped himself to another sandwich. 'Jerry is worried because he can't get you into the holy of holies, the mega-classified stuff.'

Jerry started to speak in a gabble. 'Don't get me wrong, I can get you part of the way . . . I mean that's the deal, isn't it? I'm sure you're a very decent person and all that, but it's part of the reason you're helping us, I know that . . . But unless you know a real smart hacker . . .'

McKinnon let himself into his apartment. The emaciated-looking fern in the living room had finally given up the ghost; a few more plastic tiles had detached themselves from the kitchen ceiling; but otherwise the place looked much the same.

He checked his voice mail. There were several relating to meetings set for the following day at the NBS Building. Another from the woman with the bad posture, to say he was a ratfink for not calling her. And there was a message from Hannah.

'I do want to see your cute little face, but the truth is NBS, I'm floundering here. I need one of your computer whizzes. Does whizz have a plural? Probably not. Call me as soon as you can.'

'Do I look like the kind of guy who consorts with hackers?'

130

Hannah threw the rest of her pizza at the grimy-looking pigeon pecking around at the trash under the bench opposite.

'Well, you seem happy enough to consort with me. What was your term? An "inveterate felon". So it didn't seem like a giant leap to assume . . .'

McKinnon watched the traffic snake around Columbus Circle. 'Actually I said I thought you weren't . . . Oh, never mind. I know . . . people. But I'd have to have a very clear idea about what you wanted of them, and the risks involved, before I'd consider putting you in touch with them.'

Yeah, I bet you would, Hannah thought.

'Well, I'll have to check back with my sources on that one. But time is a key factor here. Unless I get something moving on this in the next few hours, the opportunity I have is gonna be lost.' She got up, and brushed bread crumbs off her coat. They began to walk.

Slow down, girl, don't get the guy nervous, she told herself.

She put her arm into his. 'It was good of you to see me so quickly. So tell me, how did Alderbrook pan out?'

'He skipped town, got the Home Office in England to cover his ass. So I'm right back to square one. Look Hannah, I need to know about this REGENS stuff, what's involved in the research stage.'

It was then he told her about the events of the last two weeks. He played down the attack on himself, and edited out Jessop's killing entirely. What he did not tell her was that, in the last twenty-four hours, he'd begun to put together all he could find on Falk – telling the NBS researcher that it was for a future feature could, he'd told himself, turn out to be the truth – and on Hannah herself. He'd resolved that if he was to get any further, any time soon, he would have to take someone, other than Muddy, into his confidence. Hannah had checked out – she seemed to be all that she said she was – and it was starting to look as though there might be some kind of useful trade-off achievable here.

By halfway through the tale, Hannah had that message loud and clear: I get you to a tame hacker; you fill me in on REGENS.

By the end of the tale, she had a great deal more. When he told her about the experiments that he believed were going on at Marston Moor, that he believed involved his father, and the link that he'd established between them, Alderbrook, and Falk Pharmaceutical, a light went on in a recess of Hannah's mind. She now knew why he'd needed to speak to the oncologist so badly, why he needed to know about remedial genetics systems.

'REGENS are medical treatments, designed to arrest and reverse the effects of mass killer diseases – cancer, tumours, melanomas, conditions for which there are still no effective cures,' she began. 'They're the world's next multi-billion dollar industry. Pharmaceutical companies have spent a fortune over the last ten years trying to develop a whole range of them. The treatments involve identifying the faulty gene, and replacing it with a synthetically produced obverse gene, using a patented process. We're talking here about remedies that could give tens of thousands of desperate people – rich and poor alike – a whole new hope of life.'

McKinnon could see that she was weighing up all he'd told her about his father, debating how much she dare give him in exchange.

'About a year ago I got the chance to debrief a disaffected employee,' she went on. 'A woman who worked in the marketing division of a major pharmaceutical company. She told me that, although very few people yet knew it, they had a whole line of REGENS ready to go. But the general public would never get within a mile of them. Until other companies started to produce them, and they became readily available – that, according to her, could be years in the future – they'd be kept back, and used sparingly. As "a priceless power-broking tool" – that was the term she used. The only people that would get miracle cures would be those who were in a position to benefit Falk's directors politically or financially.'

'Have you any evidence to back that up?'

She sighed. 'I was in Chicago to do just that.'

'And?'

She turned to face him. 'I'm not telling you one more thing than I have to, McKinnon. Let's just say I believe her.'

'Can I ask where Alderbrook fits into the picture?'

'He's in the forefront of REGENS development. A lot of the key research had been done in the UK, by the British end of the company who developed the patent. And what you've just told me adds a whole new dimension to the thing. You see, McKinnon, the only human guinea pigs pharmaceutical companies can experiment on legally are terminal volunteers. What you ideally need are healthy patients in a controlled environment, ones where you can know everything about their life-style – diet, stress levels, and so on.'

'Marston Moor,' McKinnon said.

'Exactly. It would be the perfect place to set up research on something like that.'

McKinnon stopped. 'Look, Hannah we can help each other here.'

Here it comes, she thought.

'I'll give you all I get on what's really going on inside

the prison, and I'll do what I can to get you with a computer whizz. I can't make any guarantees; the guy I have in mind is a law unto himself – and that's gonna involve me in a certain amount of risk. In exchange, you help me stand up my theory about my father's death. As I say, if you want my contact, you're gonna have to come clean with me about what's involved.'

Hannah walked on silently.

'It's pretty obvious that the pharmaceutical company in question is Falk,' he said huffily. 'Like I say, I've already established that Alderbrook is tied up with them.'

Jerry Tyrell had been crystal clear, Hannah reminded herself: no hacker, no holy of holies. She came to a decision.

'Okay. I guess your man's going to have to know names, so you might as well. It is Falk. But the key thing is, well . . .' She gave a long sigh. 'Falk is owned by J. Richmond Fiske, by the Apostles of Christ.'

McKinnon turned to look at her. 'You're kidding?'

'Don't ask me to tell you how I know. It took months of networking, finessing, searching through *Share Watch* data to establish. But it is so.'

'So that's why you're so up on the Apostles.'

'And that's why I was in Atlanta. Falk and the Apostles are all one story.'

'And it's Fiske who wants to control the distribution of REGENS for his own advancement. You're doing a book on the whole tie up?'

She smiled. 'I might be. That's why I'm being so cagey. REGENS are a new kind of power, McKinnon. To give that power exclusively to someone like Fiske . . . Can you imagine what kind of tool these cures could be in the hands of his recruitment people? Figure it out. You're a political bigshot; you've been told you have months to live; all the money and influence in the world suddenly becomes meaningless. Then, out of the blue, comes someone like Fiske with a REGENS package. What're you going to do?'

'Bend down and kiss his feet,' McKinnon said.

'New Testament miracles – today and to order. You retranslate that into political terms, and you start to see why the tie-up is so dangerous.'

'Marston Moor . . . Alderbrook . . . Falk . . . Fiske, all joined at the hip.'

'So it would seem,' Hannah said. 'If you're right about what's going on at the prison, it's Fiske who will have instigated those experiments. He wants to make damn sure these cures work as they're supposed to. The buck stops with him.'

'I knew when I started reading up on the Apostles of Christ, during the Kerensky assignment, that that was just the tip of something far more sinister. I never imagined I'd get caught up in it myself.' There was a pause. Then he said, 'If all our assumptions are correct . . . Fiske killed my father.'

'Indirectly, he may well have.'

What she was not yet prepared to tell him was that the day her primary source on the project, the disaffected employee, was due to swear an affidavit, regarding all she'd told Hannah, she'd disappeared, and that Hannah believed that Fiske was behind that too. She felt that as long as McKinnon believed the woman was still around, and that her evidence was pivotal to the investigation, he would be hamstrung from pushing ahead with it on his own.

'And your dad didn't die so that sick people all over the world might live,' Hannah went on. 'He died so that Fiske could turn the most loathsome organization operating

135

in the West into a world force. President Caulfield is passionately committed to wiping the Apostles off the map. He's right up-to-date on remedial genetics too. He's fighting hard to bring in legislation that will control the manufacture of REGENS, and the practices associated with them.'

'I'll bet he is.'

'He wants the whole subject discussed in open forum and guidelines developed. There isn't just money involved here. In the gay community, where the benefits of new cures are obvious, you're talking votes. Fiske and REGENS-producing pharmaceutical corporations are two of Caulfield's main targets right now. If I can show a link between one of the key organizations, Falk, and Fiske, demonstrate the abuses that the cures are gonna be put to – are perhaps being put to right now – I can help him strike a blow against two abominations in one move.'

McKinnon stopped and looked hard at her. 'What exactly do you want my man to do, Hannah?'

'Well, the fact is, I've acquired some entry codes, codes that'll access crucial data I need to stand this thing up. For all I know, there's stuff there that could help you too. But to get where I really need to go . . .'

'You need a hacker.

Her eyes fixed his. 'Yes. And very, very soon.'

'Or the codes might be changed?'

'You got it.'

'Well, I'll have to act as go-between – my man's kinda choosy about who he meets. I'll have to give him assurances. And I'll need to know about the whole scam for that to happen.'

CHAPTER NINE

'Show me a hacker and I'll show you an a compulsive gambler. An obsessive, an insomniac, a recluse. A man for whom the lonely art of codebreaking is an all-consuming passion, for whom sexual entanglement, social intercourse, and physical exercise are just a plain waste of good calories.'

McKinnon's special report for NBS on computer hackers, which had aired three years before, could have been written with Muddy Harbin in mind, although they had yet to meet. All except the sexual part, Muddy had said, when he finally saw a tape of the piece.

He lived in an elegant apartment on Central Park West. The office and master bedroom were always in what Muddy referred to as an organized clutter. Trade papers, journals and magazines of every description were stacked four feet high in some places. Somewhere in each of them was a scrap of information, a minor business fact or personal detail, that he knew might come in useful at some future date, and therefore needed to be 'filed'.

The kitchen of the apartment was the only room that was seldom less than immaculate – his other great passion in life was cooking. Muddy bought his virgin olive oil – reputedly the finest manufactured – from a tiny wholesaler in Little Italy, and dispensed it as though every spoonful had been personally blessed by the Pope. He bought delicacies like foie gras and truffles from Polanski's, the Polish deli on 56th, and spent hours working them into exotic concoctions, often of his own devising. And then he'd sit down to eat them – alone. Occasionally the call-girls who graced his bed were elevated to a higher status: that of dinner guest. Muddy would think nothing of paying the madam who ran the service extra, so that a lady of his choosing could stay on and sample a new recipe he had developed.

Muddy was a respected member of the hacker élite and spent hours conversing with various far-flung members of the fraternity by various means. But, like McKinnon, he had few real friends. He considered the tall English journalist one of them, however.

In a sense, McKinnon was the man Muddy would have liked to have been. Outgoing, tenacious in the field, he was the only newsman he knew of to regularly use the services of a hacker, a fact that, to Muddy, said a great deal for the man's character.

Few of Muddy's clients ever entered his domain. Most deals were done, and information passed, by fax and mobile phone. McKinnon was one of the trusted few who was allowed to know where and how the hacker worked. Muddy hated meeting new people anyway, and had insisted that if Jerry Tyrell and Hannah were to come to his place – and if anything was really to be achieved it seemed they would have to – McKinnon himself would have to be present.

He peered nervously through his pebble glasses as the three crossed his threshold at seven forty-five am – he'd made clear that, given the events surrounding the boys' defection, to wait later in the day was to risk finding the entry codes changed. He poured them coffee in his kitchen, and they made small talk for a while. But soon

Hannah's hunch that there was a natural bond between computer buffs paid off, and Tyrell and Muddy were deep into technospeak.

Apparently satisfied that the two newcomers could be trusted, he took them through to his work room. Jerry walked over to a monitor on his left and studied the text of an e-mail letter on the screen, fascinated.

'What language is that?' he asked.

Muddy laughed. 'As a matter of fact it's Klingon.'

'Klingon?' McKinnon came over to study it.

'Uhuh. Show me a hacker and I'll show you a Trekky. If hackers want to communicate they often do it in the tongue of Captain Kirk's great enemy. There are five places in this city that teach it already. There's even a bible in Klingon now.' Muddy went over and pointed to a word on the screen. 'Each correspondent has his own name. Mine is *Iwlijijachjaj*. That's means: May Your Blood Scream.'

McKinnon smiled. 'Figures.'

Muddy sat down at his work station. 'Okay, let's get started.'

Two hours later, Jerry Tyrell, having given Muddy all the worthwhile input he could, lay curled up asleep on the sofa in the hacker's living room. A beer and a sandwich lay on the coffee table in front of him, untouched.

Muddy sat at his work station in the next room, trawling the Apostles' database for files that might equate with the ones Hannah had listed as being of prime interest to her. He checked his watch, and turned to Hannah and McKinnon.

'Well, I've been downloading stuff to disc for ninety minutes now. I'll stay in for another thirty, then that's it. Even if the entry codes aren't immediately changed, going back in again for anything else could be very risky. I use a cell phone with the modem to make the hack – buy them across the state line for cash and give a false name, use 'em for a month and then sling 'em away. It's the least traceable way of setting up a hack. But if these Apostles people are like you say, razor sharp on surveillance, they could get on to us in ways others can't. So I'm not taking any chances.'

Muddy got up and waddled towards the kitchen, scratching at his ass unashamedly.

'What we'll have on disc at the end of this will be the workings of just a tiny part of what's clearly a vast organization. I don't know what we have yet, and I won't for some while. All this data is stored in hypertext form, it could take weeks to go through. I didn't see any reference to REGENS amongst the stuff I did get a look at, I can tell you that. Do these treatments have other names?'

Hannah sighed. 'Dozens. It's just a collective term.'

'Well, we have downloaded a whole bunch of medical files. Maybe some of what you need to know is amongst them.'

Hannah had agreed from the beginning that, if Muddy was able to come through for them, the first files they would attempt to capture to disc would be those that might give a clue as to the real fate of McKinnon's father. There was common ground here anyway. The medical data he was hoping to locate might also point to the connection between Falk, the REGENS they were developing, and the ubiquitous Fiske, all of which was central to her research.

Soon McKinnon and Hannah were going through printouts of some of the stuff Muddy had captured to disc.

'Most of the medical files seem to relate to patients

admitted to some place called the Highlands Clinic,'
McKinnon said.

Hannah turned a page. 'It's the Apostles' own clinic
in North Carolina. I seem to have stuff relating to that
too. There's another file here, in a separate section, that
doesn't seem to be a part of the rest. It only really caught
my attention because the patients aren't filed by name,
just by number. In fact no names are shown anywhere in
the file.' She passed it to McKinnon. 'Look.'

Muddy hawked some phlegm up into a tissue and
tossed it in a trashcan, then went back to surfing the
Apostles of Christ's database. 'Yeah, well, that usually
means only one thing: we're pokin' around somewhere
they really don't want us to be. When you've been
in this business as long as I have, you get to know
the signs.'

Hannah continued to scan the sheets. 'I don't pretend
to understand all the technical jargon, but it seems a lot
of the folk on this admissions list are being treated for
various forms of cancer.' She started making notes in the
margin. 'These are some of the key diseases REGENS
are designed to fight. We know Falk is owned by Fiske.
Where better to try out the new treatments than at
the Apostles' own hospital? That place is strictly for
cult members only. If the treatments are still in the
development stage, this is the one place Fiske's people
could function without interference.'

The hacker sat silently, studying the numbers written in
where the names would normally have been. For the third
time in a minute he sniffed loudly, snorting back mucus –
his personal habits were really starting to get to Hannah
now – and then he said, 'Insurance policy numbers,
that's what these are. Medical insurance policies. I've
chopped into the databases of most of the major insurance

companies in the last few years. I remember the look of those things.'

McKinnon looked up. 'Well, maybe you could hack into them again.'

'Did your father have US medical insurance?' Hannah asked.

McKinnon gave a resigned sigh. 'Nah, he was a long-time UK resident,' he said at last. 'I'm sure he wouldn't have had.'

'I'd like to know who these people are,' Hannah said. They both turned to look at her. 'I'd like to contact them or, if not them, their friends, relatives, find out what kind of treatment they've been getting up there, find out what they've been told about it.'

Muddy studied the screen again and shrugged. 'Well, it looks like there could be a dozen different companies here, so don't hold your breath.'

'How soon do you think you could have something for us?'

'Well, it's a while since I snooped around in that neck of the woods. Codes will have been changed. I may have to do some networking, get stuff from colleagues. Could take a few days.'

Jerry came through from the living room looking bleary-eyed. 'What time is Wes coming for me?' he asked.

Hannah looked at her a watch. 'In a couple of hours. You'll be hitting the road for the cabin as soon as he shows up. How are you feeling?'

His slight shoulders lifted into a shrug. 'Okay, I guess.' He eyed the pages of printout. 'If you want me to give you a hand for a while, I'd be happy to.'

'That's just what we want,' Hannah said. 'You know your way around this stuff better than anyone.'

For the next few minutes she briefed Jerry on the nature of the information she was hoping to turn up amongst the labyrinth of data. 'If you, me and McKinnon get started on this end of it, it'll leave Muddy free to make a start on the insurance company end.'

Jerry and Muddy made hacker-talk for a moment, and then Muddy said, 'You two might as well go eat or something. We're gonna need some time to get organized here.'

The deli on 48th Street was packed. Hannah and McKinnon carried their pastrami sandwiches and beers over to the only available corner and, as the effect of the food began to kick in, they began to unwind.

'Thanks for the whole Muddy thing,' Hannah said. 'You risked a lot setting it up for me, and I appreciate it. But . . .'

He sipped his beer. 'Yeah, go on.'

'Well, don't take this the wrong way, but I have this feeling that . . . well, you're gradually gonna climb aboard my project.'

'Wow! Paranoia rears its head. I've already told you, I have no intention of pissing on your fireworks.'

'How prettily put.'

'Yeah. W.B. Yeats. But I will ask you this: what was it that kicked *Chain of Command* into gear, I mean as far as sales went?'

She shrugged. 'A bunch of stuff. Mainly, a CNN feature on the Bosnian arms scandal – they had me on as an authority on the . . . Oh now wait a cotton pickin' . . . I see where this is going!'

'Climb back in your box. All I was gonna suggest is that, down the line, when you're good and ready, I'm certain I can get the network interested in this. If you

143

wanted to do a feature, with you as the primary source, to plug the book, I mean . . .'

'Well, don't hold you breath, kiddo,' she said. 'I don't expect to finish the manuscript till next year. We're talking publication next fall, the earliest.'

'Well, this'll keep.'

She looked up and forced a weary smile. 'Look, I'm not ungrateful. Most nonfiction writers would offer you their bodies, their savings, and their grandmother's tooth-fillings for a shot like that. I'm just very cautious, that's all.'

'I have no designs on your cash or your granny.'

'She'll be very pleased to hear that. Wherever she is.' She chewed on her sandwich for a moment. 'So, my bod is in serious trouble, is that it?'

'I'm just enjoying the view, right now. Is that okay?'

She fluttered her eyelids. 'Be my guest.'

McKinnon was starting to relax. 'Yeah, I vaguely remember you in that Bosnian feature now. They had you standing amongst the wreckage of that school in Srebrenica?'

'That's right. You do remember.' She sipped her beer. 'I thought that if the book was going to have any reality I needed to get down there amongst the muck and bullets, and, as the man said, get to know "what you really felt, rather than what you were supposed to feel, and had been taught to feel".'

'Hemingway, right? He also said you needed to know "what really happened in action; what the actual things were which produced the emotion that you experienced."'

'Uhuh.' Her eyes sparkled. McKinnon could see her mind at work. Then her voice took on a cultured purr: '"Could I have a chocolate bar? Or is it too close to lunch? I'm always hungry."'

She watched McKinnon struggle to place the quote for a moment, then saw his face relax. '"Go and eat one",' he drawled.

The game went on. '"I'll take one with filberts."'

'"I'll have another vermouth."'

'Good!' Hannah drained her beer glass. '*A Farewell To Arms* is my favourite.'

McKinnon tipped his head on one side and looked at her. 'Yeah, there is a kinda Cat Barkley quality about you.'

'Oh yes . . . "I'm grand now,"' she purred again. '"You say grand so sweetly. Say grand."'

'Grr-and.' It came out like an exultant growl.

They both laughed.

'You're a funny old fish, Joel,' she said, the game over. 'You know that?'

'Uhuh . . . yup.'

'I'll bet you're the toughest guy to get to know this side of Mount Rushmore. But if somebody gets inside you, really gets that ol' ticker of yours pounding, you'll go to the ends of the earth for them.'

'What makes you think that?' he asked.

'Because you and me are the same kind of people. And that's how I am.' She looked off into the distance. 'Once I decide someone's worth it . . . Well, you know how that Supremes thing went . . .'

'"There's No Mountain High Enough."'

'Yup. I'm as loopy as they get.'

'Please God, protect me from the sane! The first football game I ever went to as a kid, all I did was look at the people, thousands of them, like ants. Sane, ordinary ants. It made me scared, made me feel utterly insignificant. I remember thinking, whatever I do in life, I ain't gonna be an ant.'

145

'So what are you now?'

'I don't know . . . I just know it gets lonely out there being it, sometimes.'

She studied him. 'The business with your father, all those years ago, really tore you up, didn't it?'

'Uhuh. It messed me up for a while. Kinda cut the ground from under me. Made me want to . . . change skins, be someone else for a while. I thought I was over it, but all this Marston Moor shit . . .'

She put her hand across the table, and took his. 'Well we're survivors, you and I. It's what we do best. Next time the demons come a-knocking . . . if you need another one on your team, you know where I am.'

He smiled broadly for the first since they'd met. His eyes twinkled brightly. 'I have this funny feeling they're gonna start getting busy again around this time next week.'

'Dinner time, Thursday?'

'Uhuh.'

'Well, ask them to give us an hour or two's notice, will you? I'll need to get my hair done.'

As they strolled back to Muddy's, she slipped her arm into his again. It was a simple enough action, but it made McKinnon feel good, the best he'd felt in a long time.

Muddy made impenetrable hacker-talk with distant colleagues, and Hannah, Jerry, and McKinnon began the task of sifting through the mound of data the hacker had captured to disc from Fiske's database. After about an hour, Wes Tyrell arrived, and Hannah saw the brothers off on their trek to her cabin in the Adirondack Mountains.

Soon eyes tired, brains fogged over, and the party broke up for the night. The trio met again at nine the following morning. Muddy came through from the kitchen, dressed in pyjamas that looked like they needed soaking in salt for a week and then boiling. He handed Hannah more printouts.

'There was no way I could get into the databases of more than a handful of the insurance companies in the time.' He yawned revealing a mouthful of half-chewed toast. 'I went for the ones whose policy numbers turned up most frequently in the file.'

Hannah was hardly listening. She read through the data, ringing items with a pencil. Then she closed her eyes, and tipped back in her chair. 'Robert P. Elrington – Assistant Secretary to the Treasury,' she said, half to herself.

McKinnon came back from the kitchen carrying a mug of coffee. 'Huh?'

'Marion Fulbright, I know that name from somewhere too.'

'Junior Senator for South Georgia.'

She turned to him, her eyes bright. 'Come over here and take a look at this stuff.'

He crossed to the work station, and she passed him some of the pages she'd annotated. 'Am I going soft in the head, or are the people I've ringed who I think they are?'

He studied the sheets for a moment. 'Some of them have to be . . . Cameron S. Macfarland, there can only be one of him. He's with Food and Drug Administration, or he used to be.' He looked at her steadily. 'What the hell are all these heavy-hitters doing getting treatment at the Highlands Clinic?'

'Nothing they want known about,' Muddy said. 'Listing these folk only by their insurance policy numbers means this has to be a real sensitive file.'

Hannah shook her head slowly. 'Like I say, the Highlands is strictly for cult members only. This squillionaire textile guy I know tried to get treatment there. Couldn't get to first base.'

'Well, who's to say these people aren't members of the cult,' McKinnon said. 'Could be they're part of the thing and just shut up about it.'

Hannah looked through each of their individual medical files again. 'All being treated for cancers, tumours or melanomas . . . Or it could be that this is the only place in the country REGENS treatment is available. And the very trade-off I suspected is going on right here. "You have a potentially terminal condition; we're the only folks that can take care of it. But the catch is you have to join the Apostles of Christ to get treated."'

'Well, it seems friend Fiske has some of the key players on Capitol Hill as members of the movement, then.'

'It's like I told you, McKinnon, REGENS is power. You hold it, you hold the power of life over death. Oh, I don't mean in the sense the Hitlers and the Genghis Khans of this world did. What Fiske has is far more potent. Here, he's not the destroyer, but the deliverer. Deliverer from the oldest foe of all: terminal disease. His kind of power generates not fear and loathing, but respect, even a sense of commitment. In a sense, it's the ultimate power.'

Suddenly she got up, and began to sift through a pile of printout. 'I can't help wondering if a file I turned up last night doesn't tie in with all this somewhere.'

McKinnon watched her as she searched, with increasing impatience, through reams of paper. Finally she located the sheets she needed and handed them to him, then she bent back and tried to get the crick out of her neck.

He read quickly through what was a list of names. He recognized many amongst them. Senators, state governors, congressmen, city mayors, members of the judiciary were listed with their addresses and contact numbers. 'Cameron Macfarland is here too. So this has to tie-in to the medical file somewhere.'

'Maybe it's a list of those who've already been treated with REGENS at the clinic,' Hannah said.

'I very much doubt it! You've got a couple of hundred of the country's main movers on this list. They can't all have contracted killer diseases. And even if they had, most of these folk wouldn't be seen dead getting mixed up with something like the Apostles. There has to be some other link here.'

'Well, the admissions stuff is the best evidence I have so far that the scam I told you about is in operation. It fits with everything I know about Fiske and his thinking. He argued in *The Lost Gospel* that even the Son of God had to resort to miracles to persuade people that he was the Messiah. That Christ used his healing powers to make converts . . . "to effect cures . . . and affect the curious".'

'Well, dozens of Christian sects go that route,' McKinnon said. 'I guess they take the view that if it worked for Jesus, it's good enough for them.'

'Yeah, but that kind of faith-healing has to rely on fakery or some hit-and-miss auto-suggestive process to work. But Fiske could have the real thing, a set of cures for deadly diseases that actually work. Until another pharmaceutical company comes up with something like them, he has a unique currency he can deal in. He can play God, ignore the average Joe, keep what he has back to make powerful converts.'

'I don't see how it would work,' McKinnon said.

'Like the old dictum says: "A condemned man turns to God." It doesn't matter how rich or influential you are, if some quack tells you you've got six months to

149

live, and there isn't a thing he can do to help you, you start reassessing your life damn quick, believe me. Once you find out this is something that neither money nor all the networking in the world can fix, you start looking at any option, every option, just like anyone else in that position.'

'So he turns these poor bastards around. To do what?'

'Strengthen his influence on Capitol Hill. The stronger his lobby, the more effective the fight against those in government determined to wipe him out. And the more powerful the corporate end of the organization becomes.'

'Do you have any proof that that is what's actually happening?'

'Not yet, but that's what this exercise was all about for me. I've got names now. I'll start checking these people out, see if they've done any interesting U-turns on policy in the last year or two. See if anything they've done has directly benefited Fiske in some way.'

'Well, to have any kind of a case, you're gonna have to be able to show they're batting on Fiske's team, had the treatment and so on.'

Hannah threw up her hands. 'Well, somewhere in that database are the answers we want, I'm certain of it.'

Muddy, who'd said very little in a while, spun around in his chair. 'Dream on, lady. The Jesus freaks just got wise.' His fingers moved over the keyboard again for a moment. 'They did it. All the entry codes – all the ones we have, anyway – just got changed.'

McKinnon and Hannah were both tired when they got back to her place. It wasn't easy to recapture the mood they'd felt the day before, but the wine soon began to kick in and both sensed that something in the relationship had changed. There was a need now to be together for something other than a common pursuit.

With barely a word, Hannah took the wine glasses through to her bedroom and, after some haphazard attempts to produce atmospheric lighting – proof, if proof were needed, that this was not a regular occurrence in her life – they undressed and held each other.

Her body was more contoured than he'd imagined, her bust fuller, her waist narrower. The total assuredness she displayed as a writer vanished, and she became . . . vulnerable. Vulnerable pressed buttons inside McKinnon, always had. For the first time in a long while he lost himself in the warmth of another human being. All he knew was the softness, the scent of her skin, all he heard were the sounds that seemed to well up from the deepest part of her body . . .

CHAPTER TEN

Pieter Kleig drew deeply on his cigarette. It wasn't often he got to have one these days. But here in the Apostles' most remote outpost, in the plains of South Dakota, there were no core disciples to berate him. And who else around here had the balls to wade in against the Sentinel-in-Chief?

Here, by the window, he had a clear view of the central compound and the airfield beyond. Two young black males, dressed in the simple terracotta-coloured robes that many disciples wore, sauntered down the main pathway in front of him.

Kleig watched them warily. The skinny kafir on the right had a rap sheet with the LAPD. Two counts of theft, back in the eighties, so his file said. Kleig sniffed. Typical of the recent black intake. His kind will tell you from now until Christmas that they're men reborn, they've left the wages of sin behind, and all the rest of the horseshit they fill their heads with around here. But it was an even bet he was behind the break in on D Section a week or two back.

In the old days, in Johannesburg, I could have taken the little sonofabitch out the back, to garages behind the police station, and worked on him with a yard of rubber hose for ten minutes and got a confession out of him, and hardly left a mark on his body.

He inhaled again. But the old days were gone. Gone for ever. For Kleig they'd ended in the spring of 1993.

Kleig was a white South African, who'd served as a police officer in Johannesburg for more than fifteen years. One evening, as he was leaving his office to round up rioters who had stoned a police patrol in one of the black townships of Soweto, a call had come through from head office. 'Make a token response only . . . Hold a few troublemakers overnight.' Why the soft approach? Kleig had asked.

'Talks with the ANC are at a very delicate stage,' came the reply. 'We can't afford any disruptions.'

Kleig knew then it was time to get out. He was certain there would be no place for him in the new South Africa, and had begun to look for other opportunities.

Word of the job with the Apostles had come through an American relative. Fiske had been impressed with Kleig's administrative skills, his tenacious energy, his expertise working in sensitive areas, in 'tidying up' messy situations. He'd joined the organization the day after his interview, and had not been back to South Africa since.

This was a good job. For a man of his abilities, Kleig knew it was as good as he would ever get. Fiske, it had to be said, was a realist. He didn't need his Sentinel-in-Chief to undergo any great religious conversion. Given the nature of the work, it would have been a fairly impractical option anyway. Someone in this set-up has to keep his head out of the clouds, Kleig told himself as he stubbed out the cigarette. Someone had to knock these flakes into shape. Okay, so he'd been accused of being over zealous. But he was certain that his boss would not consider his proposals for dealing with this new crisis an overreaction.

*   *   *

154

The Lear jet turned into the wind and began its final descent. J. Richmond Fiske peered down at the vast structure rising from the dry earth beneath him. The dream he'd nurtured for more than twenty years was at last becoming a reality. He drained his brandy glass and thought: all the great religions of the world had once been little more than cults – God, how he hated that word. Their acceptance into the religious establishment had not just been a result of the universality of their message, but also their sense of permanence. Soon Christians all over the world would glimpse the sphere of influence the Apostles had now assumed, understand that they had carved a niche in society that could only broaden and deepen.

Rapid growth in Fiske's empire had begun with the realization that many of the techniques used in the induction of disciples into his church could be adapted and employed with equal success in the commercial sector. Soon middle managers of corporations in which he had an interest were being sent off to self-development courses, aimed at ridding them of their blockages and hang-ups. This, they were told, would enable them to reach their inner selves, and empower them to work better with team mates.

Fiske's natural acquisitiveness, and his need to control absolutely all that came within his sphere of influence, soon manifested itself in his gaining control of a number of the organizations where his techniques had been successfully employed. Hidden behind a smoke-screen of nominee companies, he was soon to become the majority shareholder in a wide range of high-profile corporations. Apart from the Apostles, Fiske now owned a massive merchandising business, marketing 'inspirational' products that ranged from CDs to soap. A 'Captain Christian' video game alone had grossed more than sixty million dollars in five years. In the late eighties, he had acquired Farm Fresh Frozen Foods. More than half the seventeen hundred workers now employed at the plant in Milwaukee were members of a local Apostles commune. In the early nineties, Fiske had moved into film and TV production. In the last season, five movies, all with strong fundamentalist Christian messages, had been financed by the multinational conglomerate Fiske's organization had become.

As the Lear jet turned to align itself with the runway, Fiske got a glimpse of the facade of what would soon be the Apostles' first cathedral. The cost of bringing it this far had been phenomenal. The expenditure incurred in transporting vast quantities of building material to this remote spot had already been double that budgeted for. But it will be worth every cent, Fiske told himself again.

This will be the church that REGENS built.

Initially, he'd shown little interest when the Wall Street-watchers in his pay first suggested that Falk Pharmaceuticals might be susceptible to a takeover bid. The value of their stock had plummeted when they'd announced falling profits for the third successive year, due largely, it seemed, to massive overspending by the research division. Attempts to establish the exact nature of the new products in development there proved less than illuminating. When an industrial spy established that the most costly research was related to the development of cures for currently incurable life-threatening diseases, Fiske began to change his attitude towards a takeover bid.

The more he learnt about the potential of REGENS, the more fascinated he became with the whole subject.

Although a number of other pharmaceutical companies were working on a range of similar treatments, it became evident that Falk was years ahead of them all. Furthermore, their process contained a number of elements that were patentable. It was soon clear to Fiske that if whoever bought Falk could overcome a number of obstacles related to the testing of the treatments, they might look forward to a monopoly of the REGENS market for a long time to come.

Hadn't much of Christ's initial credibility with his followers rested on his healing powers? Fiske had reasoned at the time. Christian missions throughout the world had sold health care and education in exchange for immortal souls ever since. Potential converts didn't just want to be regaled with endless tales of Christ's miracles, Fiske told core disciples. They wanted miracles of their own. How many times had the evangelical wing of the movement been confronted with, 'I need some proof of God's existence before I'll consider joining any Christian movement,' or, 'Give me some evidence that my life will be uniquely changed for the better if I join your church, and you may have a convert.'

If the Apostles of Christ could control the distribution of REGENS, could bring hope to the sick and the afflicted where no hope had existed . . . For some that might prove an irresistible enticement. Here perhaps was the greatest gift in the winning of new converts since those bestowed on the Son of God himself. As one of Fiske's marketing managers had put it, in an unguarded moment, 'It sure beats the hell out of loaves and fishes!'

The Lear rolled to a halt, and Fiske, the sole passenger, hurried down the stairway to the waiting limo. He was surprised to see Kleig waiting for him. He'd learnt long ago to interpret the contortions that frequently marked the countenance of this taciturn South African, and he sensed immediately that he had a crisis on his hands.

Kleig made no attempt at small talk. 'Something has come up I figured you'd want to know about, sir. One of the data processors at the North Carolina Commune, a kid called Tyrell, has failed to show up at the communications center this morning. No one seems to have seen him since late Friday night.'

They got into the limo and it moved off towards the perimeter of the airfield. 'His brother has gone too.' Kleig gave him a quick brief on the Tyrell brothers and their background. 'I mention the singer brother only because the boys are pretty close. The general view is that the processor brother only split because the singer did. If we find the singer, we find them both.'

'Did the processor give any indication of what he was planning?' Fiske said quietly.

'None that we know of.'

Fiske turned and fixed Kleig with an Arctic stare. 'You mean to tell me that we've had a disaffected processor, an operative privy to key entry codes, roaming the streets for nearly three days, and no one was alerted?'

'I'm afraid so.' Kleig tried to meet the old man's eyes squarely, but he turned his face away. 'But we could have a line on him any time. Sentinels assigned to the Evangelical Army Unit say the singer brother formed some kind of attachment to a woman called Hannah Rostov. She's the journalist who . . .'

'I know who she is,' Fiske snapped. 'She's doing this book on the movement, this hatchet job. And she wrote that piece in the *Times* that stirred all the debate on the child abuse issue.'

Never underestimate this man's memory for detail, Kleig told himself again. Or his capacity to bear a grudge.

'Well, we believe there's a strong chance both brothers have gone to her.'

'If they've gone to her, it's because she's made them guarantees.' Fiske continued to stare out of the limo window. 'Ask yourself, Kleig, what possible reason would she have for doing that?'

Kleig's face started to lose its natural pallor. 'In exchange for the entry codes,' he said at last.

'Precisely.' Fiske rubbed the side of his nose.

'She changed her New York address recently, has gone to some trouble to keep it to herself. We're hoping to get a look at her tax records, should have them any time. We'll be able to pick her address up from those.'

'In the meantime, I want all entry codes that this processor might have had even the briefest exposure to changed. Are you clear?'

'Yes, sir.'

'I hope so.' The stare hit hypothermic. 'I think I could be forgiven for thinking that you're losing your grip, Mr Kleig.'

Fiske was asleep in the master bedroom of the compound in Highlands when Kleig called back. The old man's fingers moved blindly around in the gloom for a moment till they locked on to the telephone receiver.

'You said to call you, no matter what time,' Kleig began.

Fiske sat up and tried to bring his mind to bear on what was being said. 'Yeah, yeah. Just get on with it.'

'We have a fix on the Rostov woman. We're working on a phone tap right now – we have no people in this district so it's taking time. There's no evidence yet that the Tyrell brothers are with her, or have contacted her. But there is another development.'

For the first time in their association, Fiske was able to detect a shake in the security chief's voice.

'We have a shot of a guy leaving her apartment. I had a man we have at the Sixth Precinct run the licence plate number of his car through the system.'

'And?'

There was a pause. Then Kleig said: 'It's . . . Joel McKinnon's car.'

'*McKinnon!*'

Here it comes, Kleig thought.

'I thought that problem had been dealt with.'

Kleig cleared his throat. 'That operation was, er . . .'

'A total screw-up. That's very evident,' Fiske snapped. He considered the implications of the liaison for a moment. 'Rostov and Joel McKinnon.' He sighed. 'If your people don't start to function as required, Mr Kleig . . .'

'I know, I know. Believe me, I'm . . .'

'Do you have a helicopter available?' Fiske asked.

'Yes, sir, I believe so.'

'Then get down here right away. We have a lot of work to do.'

CHAPTER ELEVEN

Hannah sat at the mirror in her bedroom, putting the final touches to her make-up. The bedside phone rang. It was McKinnon.

'How you doin'?'

There was a dirty laugh. 'Tired but happy. Very. You?'

'Have lunch with me and I'll tell you.'

'Can't. I'm off to see Senator Mitchelson. I want to know what he has to say about his recent treatment at a hospital that only takes Apostles' members as patients.'

'Oh, I'm sure he'll be delighted to tell you?'

'I'm not going to approach him cold, you fool. I'm gonna sneak up on him. He thinks I'm a feature writer, anxious to hear his views on law and order reform. I shall beguile him with my feminine charms.'

'Do you think he's ready for that? I mean he's been a sick boy.'

'Yeah, he's a sicko all right. My guess is he's got himself hooked up with the sickest organization in the country.'

'And if he hasn't?'

'Well, maybe someone should warn him to expect an approach from Fiske any day.'

'For Christ's sake be careful.' There was a pause. Then he said, 'Have dinner with me tonight.'

'Okay. The Hacienda at eight.'

'You got it.'

She hung up and went through to the living room. The last of her notes were pumping out of the printer.

Using data from different insurance companies, Muddy had ultimately been able to put names to seventeen of the patients they'd found on the Highlands Clinic admissions file that had previously only been identified by their medical insurance numbers.

Hannah had recognized seven of them straight away: all key players on Capitol Hill. After some detective work, she was able to upgrade five more names to that list.

If she was to show conclusively that Fiske was using REGENS to make powerful converts, who he'd then subverted to further the cult's aims, she would first have to establish a number of hard facts: that they were members of the cult, paid tithes to it like other initiates, had some kind of regular contact with it. And she'd have to be able to show that they'd consistently taken positions on key issues, under debate in Congress, that had benefited, or stood to benefit, the cult.

Proving these converts paid Fiske a percentage of their income, Hannah knew, would be immensely difficult. There was, too, the risk that he'd waived such payments in their cases, in return for the good they could do him. Without having any real idea of the difficulties involved, Hannah had broached the idea of getting Muddy to hack into their bank accounts.

'I don't do banks,' she was told. She learnt that there was a whole network of hackers, each a specialist in a different field. Bankbusters, it seemed, were a breed apart: outgoing, gregarious, good at finessing codes out of disaffected employees. Muddy had agreed to get her *bona fides* to a colleague, and set up a phone call so he could sound her out.

'You just don't make an appointment with these guys like you do when you go to your chiropodist, or something,' he told her. 'You can get seven to ten years in the joint for hacking into bank records these days, so they're real choosy about who they talk with.'

So Hannah was pushing the research for her book in the only direction she could right now. Taking the fight on to the streets, right to the doors of the closet converts themselves.

She put on a smart tight-fitting suit with mutton chop sleeves – one that had unquestionably raised the blood pressure of at least one interviewee before – locked her apartment and headed for the elevator.

Okay, hotshot, here I come.

The elevator smelt of dogs. That damn woman upstairs with her poodles, she thought as she stepped in. If she'd only wash them once in a while.

The elevator stopped again at the floor below, and two men in tracksuits got in.

A sense of danger, of being utterly vulnerable, instantly surged inside her.

Without a word, one of the men grabbed for her arms, pinning them back. The other smacked a wad of surgical lint against her mouth.

Hannah kicked out wildly, catching his shin. And then the lights above her began to spin, splitting off into a kaleidoscope of colour as she felt her legs give way beneath her.

When the elevator doors opened again, a third man appeared. The smaller of the attackers threw him Hannah's attaché case and the set of keys he'd taken from her pocket.

*   *   *

163

'For fuck's sake get off your ass, and help me with this stuff.' Wes Tyrell's voice echoed against the rough-hewn stone of the cabin Hannah owned in the Adirondack Mountains.

His brother, Jerry, curled himself into a tight ball on the sofa, and stared sullenly at the TV screen. 'You don't have to curse.'

Wes pulled the garbage bag from beneath the sink and tossed it against the kitchen door to stand with two others. 'People in the Outland curse, Jerry. We're Outlanders now, right? So if I feel like I wanna curse, that's just what I'm gonna do. Got it?'

Jerry gestured around him. 'I don't see any Outlanders. I don't see anyone, other than you, as a matter of fact. Maybe if I did, I'd feel a whole lot better.'

He unwound himself, sidled over to the garbage bags, and began to tie them up.

Wes softened his tone. 'Come to the store with me. It'll get you out of the place for a couple of hours.'

'Last night you said we shouldn't be seen together yet, and I agreed with you. And, anyway, the shopping mall in Piseco isn't really gonna do it for me, you know what I'm saying?'

'Look, you knew how it would be to begin with. We went over it a hundred times. As soon as things have settled down a bit . . .'

'I know all that. It's just that, stuck out here in this bug-hutch, I don't know, I feel . . . neither part of one world or the other. In a while, things'll start to make sense again, I guess . . .' A crack opened up in Jerry's voice. 'But right now, Wes, I miss work, I miss the kids at the commune, a whole lot of stuff.'

'You don't have an exclusive on that one. I miss Elaine, okay. As a matter of fact, I miss her like crazy. The way

164

things are, I don't suppose I'll ever get to see her again. But that's one of the sacrifices I know I have to make, to break free of the Apostles. As hard as that's gonna be, I happen to think it's worth it.'

Wes picked up the garbage bags, kicked open the back door, and began to carry them across the yard behind the cabin. Jerry watched him go. High above him the peaks of the mountains loomed, backlit now by the early evening sun.

It's all right for Wes, he thought. This is a breeze for him. As part of the rock band, he's had more of the Outland in the last year than I have in my whole life. He's adjusted. For me, the North Carolina commune was . . . everything. Gimme a PC, and a few guys to rap with now and then, and I'm firing on four.

Jerry watched his brother climb into the battered Chevvy pickup, and, without looking back, move it out on to the track that ran down to the highway.

He's pissed at me. He's really starting to wonder why he took me along, Jerry thought. I don't blame him. I'm wondering too.

For the last two years, Jerry had watched his brother's metamorphosis, watched as he systematically renounced each facet of the cult's teachings, developed something he doubted he, himself, would ever have; self-reliance. The brothers had always been close. Wes, being the elder by three years, had always made the decisions. Both knew that if he left the blood bond would prove stronger than the spiritual one, and Jerry would follow.

I can't go back to the commune, he told himself again. As much as I feel I'd like to most of the time. Not now I've passed all that data on to Hannah. I'm a traitor, a collaborator in the eyes of all those I ever knew.

Elders of the cult always depicted the Outland as a

lonely desolate place. New York had seemed so brash, and impersonal. And this place . . . Jerry looked out at the flat featureless wasteland that stretched from the mountains to the horizon.

Will the last man alive on the planet please turn off the lights.

He shook away the thought. Somehow, I must learn to adapt too, he told himself again.

He went through to his bedroom, and rummaged in the bottom of his rucksack for the book Hannah had lent him when he and Wes had left New York: *Breaking Free – Life Beyond the Cult*. He glanced at the author's name.

Okay, Dr Helen S Garrett, I'm all yours.

A metallic click . . .

Jerry's head jerked up from his book. The lock of the kitchen door. He checked his watch. Seven thirty.

'Wes?' he called.

Silence.

His heart began to hammer. He peered out of the bedroom window. The uneven expanse of dirt, bounded by a fence, that served as the cabin's front yard was deserted.

Can't be Wes. No Chevvy pickup.

Can't be Hannah. She has a key, but she's in Manhattan – we spoke to her this morning.

And no one else knows we're here . . .

'Hello?' His thin voice resonated through the building. The only sound was the whistle of the wind in the mountain peaks high above him.

Maybe I imagined it. He slid off the bed. But I have to know for sure.

He padded down the passageway, his bare feet slapping

166

against the stone flags, and went into the kitchen. Beyond, through an arch, was a small utility area. Daylight was beginning to fade now, and the freezer and washer-dryer unit that blocked light from the only window showed only as dark shapes.

The shape to the far left moved. Jerry's whole body jerked with shock. A man in a black anorak moved out into the light.

'You're a long way from home, Christian,' he said.

Jerry just stood there, blinking at him.

The man moved to the kitchen door, opened it, and let in another, a guy with red hair and a moustache.

Jerry made no attempt to run, just stood there pale and trembling. 'What happens now?' he said at last.

'We go back,' Red said. 'First, some questions: what entry codes and software did you pass to the Rostov woman?'

They must have Hannah, how else did they get the key? 'If you could find me here, you must know the answer to that.'

The other man stepped forward, and swung a fist into Jerry's stomach, instantly folding him up on the floor, choking for breath.

'Don't make me ask you again,' Red snapped.

'I'll do you a list,' Jerry said when he had breath enough to speak.

'Who has the data now?'

'Some computer hacker . . . on Central Park West. I don't remember the exact address.'

'You will. Come on, we're out of here.'

Jerry scrambled to his feet. 'I'll get my stuff.'

'Jack here will do that.' Red turned to the other man. 'Check the place out thoroughly, and follow us.'

*   *   *

167

The dark blue Merc swung right, and headed west towards Alder Creek along a road that weaved between the brooding peaks, now almost lost in the evening light.

Jerry tried to steady the small notebook he'd been given on his knee, and searched his mind for details of the data he'd stolen from the Apostles' database. Visions of Wes' panic-stricken face broke through his concentration.

'Are you done?' Red snapped.

'I'm doing my best . . . it's hard to write with the car moving. Can I ask something?'

'What?'

Jerry's miserable face turned towards the driver. 'What will happen to my brother?'

Red shrugged. 'I have no instructions about him.'

No, Jerry thought. He didn't break *omertà*.

Five minutes later, Red swung the Lincoln off the road, and eased it down a stony track, back towards the mountains. Ahead now was a copse of trees nestling in the shallow foothills.

The saliva in Jerry's mouth began to dry. Why had they made this excursion? Were they here to meet a plane . . . a helicopter?

A hundred yards into the copse, he could see a Cherokee 4x4 parked on the edge of a clearing.

'What's happening?' Jerry asked.

Red's watery blue eyes fixed him. 'Are you done?'

Jerry passed him the notebook. 'Yes. I've put down all I could remember.'

Red turned the pages of the book reading carefully. 'Okay, get out. You're changing cars.'

So that was it. But why the diversion? Why not make the change-over at the roadside?

'What about my stuff?' Jerry asked as he moved nervously across the clearing.

168

'It'll be waiting for you at the commune.'

Now Jerry could see a figure in the driver's seat of the Cherokee, dead ahead of them, could hear its engine running. He was ten feet from the front fender when the driver threw the vehicle into gear. Jerry froze in his tracks. Red stumbled into him. Then he realized that the Cherokee was actually reversing. He let out an audible sigh, and moved forward a few steps.

Then, in one moment of blinding clarity, the whole scenario became clear. A large black rectangle was suddenly revealed beneath the vehicle. *A pit*. Jerry heard the click of a handgun being cocked, felt it for a second against the back of his skull.

Then his world exploded.

CHAPTER TWELVE

McKinnon pushed away the plate of nachos he had been picking at for the last hour and peered through the knot of diners that were gathered around the bar of the Hacienda restaurant on 60th. He checked his watch again.

Where the hell was she? Up until now, Hannah had been very reliable. They both had mobile phones. If she was delayed somewhere, why didn't she call?

I'm worrying about her. It's a good long while since I worried about anyone.

She'd been on his mind most of that day as it was. Now he was starting to get a true measure of how he felt about this woman he'd known little more than a week. She was a rare creature, no doubt about that. Inquisitive, gutsy, sparky, full of raw energy. She seemed to be afraid of nothing, prepared to cut a swathe through any obstacle that stood between her and the place she wanted to go. And yet, at no apparent risk to her femininity. Now that was unusual. And, it had to be said, she was physically magnetic.

Does one fall in love with a reflection of oneself, or with the self one would like to be? Or, by the mere mention of the word 'self', does one negate real love altogether?

If I were to fall in love with Hannah . . .

How long is it since I felt I could fall in love with anybody?

Half an hour later, McKinnon decided she wasn't going to show. He paid the check, and took a cab back to his apartment.

He turned on the living room light, and checked his messages. There had been a call from some woman in NBS's accounts department with a query on his expenses, a 'howyerdoin' call from Forrest Friedman, his cameraman. And one from his secretary, Laurie.

'Someone called Wes Tyrell was trying to reach you. He left a number, said it was very urgent you call him . . .'

There was no message from Hannah.

Was the call from Tyrell linked to her? McKinnon wondered. He dialled the number the kid had left. Wes answered immediately.

'Thank God you've called, Mr McKinnon. I can't reach Hannah, I've been trying for hours. She said you were with NBS, and I just couldn't think of anyone else to telephone.'

'What's the problem?'

'It's my brother . . . He's gone. Sentinels have been here and taken him.'

'What makes you think that? Maybe he's just wandered off somewhere.'

'This is the middle of nowhere. He had about ten bucks on him. I have the only transport. There's nowhere he could have got to on his own. I'm telling you, the sentinels have taken him.' There was panic in his voice. 'And the only way they could have found this place is . . .'

'If they've already paid Hannah a visit,' McKinnon said almost to himself.

172

'Are you there, Mr McKinnon?' Wes said after a moment.

They have Jerry Tyrell. Hannah's missing. Can that be coincidence? If she doesn't show . . . Then they could have her too. That means Fiske is on to us. It was his people who were trying to shut me up in London, I'm certain of it. And I'm a lot more dangerous to him now . . .

'Look, Wes, stay where you are. I have to check some stuff out. I'll come back to you. Call me straight away if Hannah shows up there.'

He hung up, dialled Muddy's number, and got his answering machine. He tried his mobile. Muddy answered. He sounded like he was in his car.

McKinnon quickly updated him on the events of the last few hours. 'Where are you now, Mud?'

'Heading for my place on Fishers Island.'

'Well, you know the hazards of your game better than I . . .'

'Don't worry McKinnon, I know how to take care of myself. I'll stay put here. Jesus, I hope you're wrong about Hannah. I should watch your own back, if I were you.'

McKinnon hung up and took a deep breath. Right, Lesson One: Don't jump to conclusions. For the next hour he called hospitals, the police, continued to call Hannah's mobile, which appeared to be switched off, even roped in a member of the NBS newsroom staff, in an attempt to find out if there was another explanation for Hannah's disappearance. He didn't know whether to be relieved or sorry when these enquiries produced nothing.

At twelve forty-five am he decided to go to her apartment. Maybe she's there, maybe's she's unconscious or something. There might be a concierge, or a neighbour who can let me in.

There was a concierge, one who was less than thrilled at being woken up at that time. He resolutely refused to let McKinnon check her place out, and threatened to call the cops if he rang his doorbell again.

I have to begin to assume the worst, McKinnon told himself as his car bumped over the uneven road, back to his apartment. How the hell did Fiske's people get on to us? Had they been able to detect the hack into their database and somehow been able to link it to us? Or had they had a tail on the Tyrell boys from the start?

What is it we know that's so dangerous to Fiske?

Okay, we've made a connection between the Ravenscourt Group – the operation that runs Marston Moor – Falk Pharmaceuticals, and the Apostles movement, but we still have no hard evidence that supports my theory that prisoners at the jail are being used as guinea pigs to develop REGENS. We did find some evidence to show that Fiske was using these treatments to win converts in high places, who can swing things for him at government level, but nothing conclusive.

Does knowing all that we do automatically mark us out for elimination?

Maybe the question I should be asking myself is: What does Fiske *think* we know?

We got into the base using internal entry codes. His people may have no idea what we have or don't have. Maybe it's just paranoia that we might have seen something only they know they have hidden away in there. Something sensitive enough to trigger this onslaught.

Or perhaps the answer is even simpler than that. Fiske is a control freak of awesome proportions. Folk like Hannah and I who help disaffected believers in his credo to defect are, to him, the ultimate pariahs. Maybe this is retribution for aiding the Tyrell brothers' escape.

McKinnon slept little that night. The following morning, there was still no word from Hannah or Jerry Tyrell.

McKinnon was scheduled to cover a demonstration of striking grade-school teachers, taking place in Tampa that afternoon. The last call he made in an attempt to trace Hannah was to Random House – the publishers of her first book, the only associates of hers he knew. This he made from the concourse of Kennedy Airport. He was told they no longer handled her work.

By that night, back in New York, after a renewed bout of telephoning, McKinnon had come to the view that the only logical answer had to be that Fiske had ordered some kind of mass operation, had abducted Hannah and Jerry, perhaps even had them killed.

If that was right, there was only one effective way to strike back. Blow the lid off the whole thing. Take everything he had to NBS – the promise he'd made to Hannah was becoming less relevant with every hour that passed. Tell his boss, Bruce Van Stratton, that the data he'd obtained through Muddy's efforts had been sent to him anonymously through the post, and hope that, if the network bit on the story, their researchers would turn up hard evidence down the line that would make Muddy's stuff virtually irrelevant.

I'll make an informal pitch to Bruce first, he decided the following morning, as an elevator at the NBS building winched him to the eighteenth floor. If he takes the bait, I'll do him a detailed report. That's gonna take a day or two. If I still haven't heard anything on Hannah or Jerry by then, I'll give him everything I have.

*   *   *

Bruce Van Stratton stubbed out his cigarette in the glass ashtray on his desk.

'Do you have any idea what it's gonna take to stand something like this up? You're gonna have to show these people have regular contact with the sect, show up to religious gatherings, whatever, pump money into them. Most of all you're gonna have to be able to show that they took positions on key congressional issues that benefited the movement in some way. As for the Marston Moor end of it . . .'

'Yeah, yeah. I'm gonna need hard medical evidence that prisoners there are being experimented on,' McKinnon said. 'And that that work is directly linkable to Falk Pharmaceuticals and, ideally, to the manufacture of REGENS. Well, given some time, and some effective backup, that's precisely what I plan to do.'

Van Stratton took off his glasses and rubbed the bridge of his nose. 'We're talking about a massive investigation here, Joel. Something that's gonna keep three, maybe four researchers tied up for months, not to mention yourself. Don't get me wrong, you're a good guy – you've never sold me a bum steer yet. But I'd have to be very sure in my own mind that this was gonna be a runner before I started deploying that kind of manpower.'

'Like I say, I'm gonna do you a full report.' McKinnon remembered what Muddy had said about the vast volume of captured data that still needed to be checked out. 'I may even have some of the answers you need in the next day or two.'

When McKinnon had left his office, Van Stratton found a number stored on his personal organizer, and dialled out on his private line.

*　　*　　*

Three hours later, Van Stratton took the elevator to the floor below, and crossed to McKinnon's office. McKinnon was on the phone to the police, checking to see if they had any news on someone called Hannah Rostov. Material relating to the Apostles and Marston Moor investigations lay all around him.

'Okay, we have a problem in London,' Van Stratton began when McKinnon had hung up.

'We do?'

'Uhuh. I want you on the five twenty flight to Heathrow.'

McKinnon looked up. 'What the hell for?'

'To feed the pigeons in the park. What the fuck do you think for?'

'The Caulfield visit? Isn't the local office covering that?'

'Of course. But Bruckner is stuck in Budapest, and the other guy they have there . . . Well, let's just say, the last two reports he filed didn't exactly endear him to the Gnomes on the nineteenth floor.

McKinnon lay back in his chair. 'Gimme a break, Bruce. I'm really tied up here. Isn't there someone else who can go?'

'There's a couple of people. But you've just had a two-week vacation. And, anyway, London is home territory for you. You can work on your report on the plane, for Christ's sakes.'

After he'd booked his ticket, McKinnon phoned Caitlin at home.

'I just couldn't bear the thought of going another year without seeing that bright smiling face of yours again.'

'Yeah, and you want a bed for a couple of nights, huh?' Caitlin said.

'Well, that would be useful.'

177

She laughed. 'God, McKinnon, you're full of shit.'

'I'll freak if they stick me in some dingy hotel, I swear to God.'

'You can bring me some duty frees, you tight-assed bastard. Malt whisky. You know where the key will be. I'll make up the bedroom you had last time.'

As the 747 lifted on to its flight path for Heathrow, McKinnon tried to get his mind around Van Stratton's report. But his thoughts turned back to Hannah.

He'd only known her for a matter of days, but he knew the encounter had changed him. The survival instinct, or whatever it was within him that, for most of his adult life, had prevented him from getting close to anyone, had, for a brief precious time, it seemed, given way, and allowed him to feel again.

Please God, let her be out there somewhere. Alive and safe . . .

McKinnon stooped down and searched amongst the geranium pots that stood around the doorway of Caitlin's Kensington home. His fingers closed around a key, pressed into the soil in the third pot on the right.

The only thought on his mind, as he let himself into the hallway, was sleeping off his jetlag. I'm really gonna be Mr Bright and Informative feeling like this, he thought as he dialled NBS's London office.

There was silence on the other end of the line for a moment, as the production assistant searched amongst her papers.

McKinnon noticed there was an envelope, with his name typed on it, propped against a coffee pot on the kitchen table. Caitlin had obviously left early.

'Well, as far as I can see from the schedule,' the

assistant said, 'It's tomorrow you're needed, for coverage of the President's trip to Windsor Castle.'

McKinnon yawned. 'You mean to tell me I've lost a day in New York and missed out on a night's sleep for damn all?'

'I'm afraid it does rather look that way. I'm very sorry. I really can't understand where the confusion arose.'

McKinnon slept for a couple of hours, showered and dressed in fresh clothes, and went downstairs. It was then he remembered Caitlin's note.

Dear Joel, I've gone to my parents in East Grinstead in Sussex for a couple of days. I have some vital information for you, regarding your father, but I can't discuss it on the phone. Take my car – keys on the table – and come down as soon as possible. It shouldn't take you much more than an hour. Love, C.

A hastily drawn map was pinned to the note, but she'd left no telephone number.

How was it possible that she, of all people, had become the recipient of information regarding his father's death? McKinnon wondered. She was on the very periphery of his life now. They knew none of the same people. And if she did have news for him on that front, why all the secrecy?

He went around to the mews garage, started up Caitlin's car and, after carefully checking the map she'd left him, moved it out into the late morning traffic and headed south.

The Hammersmith Road was backed up solid. In the far distance, McKinnon could make out the flashing lights of a police car. Or was it an ambulance?

Above him, a helicopter crossed and re-crossed the line of traffic.

As he drew closer, he could see that the police had set up a road block. Uniformed men, some armed with automatic weapons, moved down between the lines of cars. Obviously some hood was on the run, McKinnon thought. A cop stepped back on to the pavement and carefully checked out the cars in the line ahead of him, then radioed in for instructions.

The police began to move up more quickly now. Suddenly, high above him, a voice blared through a bull horn, 'Would the driver of the blue Renault Five please move out of the vehicle with his hands on his head.'

Some guy's in trouble, McKinnon thought vacantly. Then it occurred to him that it might be him. He hadn't consciously noted the make and model of Caitlin's car. He reached across and opened the glove box. The owner's handbook told him all he needed to know.

'Sit up and move your hands to where I can see them.' A policeman stood by the window, levelling a Heckler and Koch carbine at his head. McKinnon blinked uncomprehendingly for a second. And then slowly lifted his hands upwards. More police closed around the car. The same officer shouted something again, but the hack of the helicopter, now directly above, made it hard to hear. Another man moved gingerly forward and opened McKinnon's door. 'Move out of the vehicle.'

As McKinnon stepped out on to the road, there was a metallic rattle as guns were readied to fire. 'What the hell is this all about?' he asked.

No answer. The man nearest to him motioned him to move over towards the pavement, then stepped forward and carefully searched him. A plain-clothes man pushed through the ring of police. 'Is this your car, sir?'

180

Ah, so that was it. A hell of a big operation to mount for a stolen car. 'No, it belongs to a friend of mine. I'm on my way to see her now.' As he spoke police were searching the interior. One took the key from the ignition, went around to the back of the car and tried it in the boot. Then, after a moment's discussion with a colleague, he came over to McKinnon and said. 'These have a separate boot key. Do you have it?'

McKinnon shook his head. 'No.'

The whole operation seemed to change tempo now. The Renault was hurriedly driven up on to a grass verge and the backed-up traffic directed to move past it. More police arrived with tools. A crowbar was jammed under the trunk lid and hammered into position.

'Hey, now wait a minute!' A gun barrel was pressed into McKinnon's stomach.

There was a sound of rending metal and a loud crack. The trunk lid was lifted and police gathered around. McKinnon pulled forward and strained to see. At first it looked as though the luggage space was stuffed with blankets. The plain-clothes man put on surgical gloves.

What the fuck do they think they're gonna find in there? a shaken McKinnon asked himself.

Using just the tips of his fingers, the cop carefully lifted the corner of the blanket. Beneath was a human hand, alabaster white. He pulled back more of the blanket. McKinnon's conscious mind blanked. Some animal part of it registered: blood, death. A CID man tried to lift the blankets further up, but dried blood had glued them to whatever lay beneath. The cloth was slowly peeled back. Visible under a tangle of blood-caked hair was a woman's face. One side of it was just a mass of swollen flesh. The cop pulled back the hair.

181

'*Oh, sweet Jesus!*' McKinnon's cracked voice broke through the silence. '*Caitlin!*'

His arms were jerked behind him, handcuffs snapped on to his wrists. He felt his knees begin to buckle. The plain-clothes man spun around.

'Get him out of here.'

Men's voices resonated across the exercise yard that separated the prison blocks.

'I love you Phil . . .'

'I love you Billy . . . Sleep tight.'

'I miss you, Ed, I wish you were here beside me . . .'

'See you tomorrow, sweetheart.'

McKinnon, sprawled on a bed in a cell in the Remand Centre in West London, wrapped the thin pillow around his ears in an attempt to shut out the sound. And the smell of cabbage and urine.

How in the name of hell could this have happened? he asked himself. Poor sweet Caitlin. Her only crime was to have known me. Why did Fiske have to snuff out her life, just to take me out of circulation? My God, I must represent some almighty threat to him.

The events of the last three days merged into one, long agonizing blur.

'It's like I told you, I was driving to East Grinstead . . . I was following instructions left for me in a note by Caitlin Morgan.'

A detective with pockmarked skin had taken a sheet of paper from a file and slid it across the desk to McKinnon.

'The note signed simply with the letter C?'

'That's how she always signed her letters.'

'It was typed on her PC, but there's one problem; when someone uses a computer they leave fingerprints on the keyboard. The action of typing usually means that they're overprinted too many times to be clearly identifiable, but the oils that make prints are there all right. From what we know of Miss Morgan's movements prior to her death, if she did type this note, she would have had to have done it before nine am, this morning. Then she would have had to have wiped the keyboard clean immediately afterwards. You see, there are no prints on it of any kind now, nothing.'

McKinnon began to massage his face.

'We spoke to the cleaning woman, who comes in twice a week, and she told us she always wipes over the computer screen and keyboard,' the CID man went on. 'According to her, it's the only time it ever gets done. The last time she cleaned it was yesterday. So the question I have to ask myself is: why did Miss Morgan break the habit of a lifetime, and wipe it over again, hours later, after typing a note of only six lines? I think a more likely explanation is that someone else typed the note, and wiped down the keyboard to erase all fingerprints, in case theirs were still identifiable.'

McKinnon gave a long sigh. It was a halting, uneven sound. 'Her fingerprints must be on the note.'

'Forensics say that the only prints on it are yours.' Now the detective took out a large envelope. His eyes never left McKinnon. 'And the only prints on this are yours too.'

'It looks like an envelope I left at Caitlin's place. It had press cuttings in it.'

'Well, when we found it, it contained £400,000 worth of negotiable bonds. It was under the driver's seat of the Renault. Under the floor trim. I'm told by Miss Morgan's employers . . .' He consulted his notes. 'The Badendorf Bank in Lombard Street, that they were issued and sent by courier to her home on her authority, when the bank first opened for business this morning. No one on the board there knows why she would have needed them.'

McKinnon began to get up. 'This is absolutely . . .'

Wolstenholme, the lawyer who been assigned to represent him, put his hand on his shoulder, motioning him to sit.

'I take it that you're suggesting that the bonds were my client's motive for murdering the deceased woman?'

The detective chose his words carefully. 'Right now, it would appear to have been the motive for the murder.'

McKinnon's speech was slurred from the effects of shock. 'I had no idea the bonds were in the car.' He turned to his lawyer. 'How do I make them believe that? I got off the plane from New York this morning, I went to Caitlin's house – she left a key for me – and hit the sack for about two and a half hours, to sleep off my jetlag.'

'Is there anyone who can support that?'

'I've already told you. I was on my own there. I believed Caitlin was in East Grinstead with her parents. I know it's not helpful, but it happens to be the truth.'

'The autopsy report says Miss Morgan was killed between nine and eleven this morning, so what you were doing at the time is going to be a critical issue.'

McKinnon's voice cracked. 'Look, if I'd known I was gonna to be set up for murder, I'd have made other plans.'

The CID man's eyes met McKinnon's squarely. 'I have to tell you that the reason you were stopped this morning was that we received an anonymous tip-off at eleven fifteen am, at West Kensington Police Station, to say that someone answering your description had been seen in Southgate Mews, putting a bundle that looked like it might be a body into the back of a Renault Five.'

McKinnon closed his eyes, as though his interrogator's gaze was more than his traumatized mind could handle. 'Well, if they did, they didn't see me. The whole thing is an elaborate set-up.' He sipped more water and tried to rally his thoughts. 'I'm a journalist. I've been investigating a religious cult and their connection with a major pharmaceutical company and a prison in the UK. I have evidence of their activities that's very damaging to them. They made a try to take me out of the picture here, a couple of weeks ago. One of them got messed up pretty badly in the process. I can only assume that they were able to tap into the phone calls I made to Caitlin afterwards, learnt that I was coming to London and staying with her, and put together this whole frame-up, with the intention of having the authorities take care of me.'

Silence.

'I can show you what I have on these people. Then you'll understand why they went to the trouble they did. All the papers relevant to the investigation I was carrying out are in my attaché case. It was in the car when you stopped me.'

'Nothing of that nature was found in the case you left in the car, I can promise you that,' the CID man said.

McKinnon's hands began to shake. He fought to control them. 'Well, the colleagues I was working with on this have copies.' He turned to Wolstenholme. 'Did you try those numbers I gave you again?'

He checked his watch. 'It's still very early there. Right now we're just getting their answering machines.'

McKinnon put his head in his hands. Sweet Jesus, Hannah, where are you? I need you.

McKinnon twisted in the damp bedsheets in the remand centre cell. In some distant part of his mind the station sergeant's voice droned on:

'I'm arresting you for the murder of Caitlin Morgan. You do not have to say anything, but it may harm your defence . . .'

Is my family cursed? First my father is framed for murder and shut away.

Now me.

This can be no coincidence. There is some linking element here, one I can't even begin to make sense of.

But when I do . . .

CHAPTER THIRTEEN

Hannah lay back against the wall, and tried to stop herself trembling. The knot in her stomach twisted again. She let out a low moan, and sank to her knees. In the small part of her mind that was still capable of objective analysis she tried to rationalize her fear. To do that, she knew she would have to reach back to times past. But, where there had once been clear ordered memories, there was now only a blur, disconnected images colliding one with another.

It's not the conditioning. It's the drug that's doing this, she told herself again. The stuff they got into me when I first came here.

But the great fear continued to well through her unchecked. It was as though her tormentors had tapped into some source of primordial terror that had, until now, been trapped in a time capsule deep within her.

During her first days as a prisoner of the cult – weeks ago, or was it months? – she'd waited for the induction techniques that she knew from her own researches would soon be used to soften her up. She had been ready for the low protein diet that would sap her energy, make reasoned evaluation increasingly hard, but had not expected that her first meals would be laced with some form of sedative that affected the memory – how else had they got it into her system? From then on she restricted herself to the most basic foodstuffs – to fast completely, she knew, would only worsen her condition – but it was soon clear that the damage was already done.

Neither had she been prepared for the infinite subtlety of the techniques they would used to reprogramme her.

Many in the group she was first to encounter, those billeted around her in the the same accommodation wing of the commune, had, in their Outlander existences, been in fields that in some way were allied with her own. One, a woman of around forty, had been a writer of romantic fiction, so she said. She was certainly very well read. Another, a man in his mid-thirties, had, until a few years ago, been the editor of a newspaper in Seattle. There were also a sometime playwright and an ex-TV executive amongst the group.

Was she here because she'd been classified as being suitable for inclusion in this group? Or had those around her been hand-picked for a special task – subverting and breaking her? From their behaviour, it was hard to believe. In her early months of detention in the Apostles commune – no amount of probing could elicit a straight answer about its exact location – she was treated to indifference, even mute hostility by the group.

She knew that the commune was large – the perimeter fence couldn't even be glimpsed from the area surrounding the compound. All around her, there were work shops, classes, activities of a dozen kinds, but no one made any attempt to make her take part in them. Neither was she encouraged to join the twice-daily religious gatherings. For this she was thankful. She'd felt so wiped out much of the time, she could barely get around the central compound some days.

The only activity of her day that became routine was her early evening trip to the airy leisure centre on the west side of the compound. Here she'd sit and await the return of the group from their various daytime assignments. They seemed not to mind her sitting with them, listening numbly to their chatter, although they seemed to have a mighty high opinion of themselves, and were far from welcoming. But here, at least, were like-minded souls whose conversation occasionally lifted above the prosaic.

As clear memories of her life prior to her abduction became hazier, she began to flounder. Where were the love-bombing sessions new recruits were routinely subjected to? I'm obviously considered beyond the pale, where that's concerned. A hopeless case, too deeply entrenched in my own scepticism to be worth bothering to reprogramme. If I'm not to be inducted into the cult, what do they intend to do with me? Am I to be slung on to some kind of human garbage heap? Didn't I once hear of some guy being used as a guinea pig in some ghastly medical work they were doing?

Stripped of her past, of the experiences that had given her confidence, her sense of self-worth, and denied a future, she began to reach out more and more to the group, to long for some small acknowledgement from them that she even existed.

One night, during one of the group's informal gatherings, a chance remark seemed to trigger something in the memory of the ex-journalist. He remembered seeing Hannah's name on the jacket of a hardback he'd once reviewed for his paper. '*Chain of Command* was a helluva book!' he told the others. Instantly his attitude towards her changed. He was able to summon up whole extracts from the text, to hold the others enthralled as he unravelled for them the complexities of the arms scandal that had been the *raison d'être* for the book.

This event had an uplifting effect on Hannah. Frightened, weak and disorientated, she was grateful for the small amount of approval it seemed to gain her. But a voice inside her struggled to be heard: *It's the drug doing this. Don't let their acceptance count.*

But from that point onwards the group began to open up to her, to show her warmth. They were, they often assured her, all feeling their way in their new environment, and frequently felt as lost as she did. From now on they should all lean on each other.

Many times she considered confiding in one or other of them, telling them that she was different, quite simply a prisoner here. But she knew well enough that they had all joined the sect voluntarily and, in most cases, had given up a great deal to do so, and feared that they might cut her out again if they felt she did not share their enthusiasm for the new life. The hours they spent chatting together, eating together, became the centre point of her life. She even began to do a little work, selecting second-hand clothes from the mountains of stuff gathered by open order members, pressing, making repairs to those items that she felt might find favour amongst other commune dwellers. Soon she was allowed to help make the terracotta-coloured robes core-disciples often wore.

One day, the romantic novelist came across a second-hand copy of Hannah's book amongst the latest consignment of stuff to arrive from the outside world. That night, despite Hannah's protestations, she began to read selections from it aloud to the rest of the group. In her rendering, the text sounded disjointed, the imagery devoid of realism. The voice began to trail off. Then to Hannah's astonishment, the woman suddenly slammed the book closed.

'Well,' she said, 'I don't think it takes a giant leap of imagination to know why this ended up on someone's junk heap!'

Hannah's credibility within the group evaporated as quickly as it had come. They closed ranks again and, this time, shut her out completely.

But by now Hannah was unable to reach back and find that crucial vestige of awareness that might have allowed her to rationalize her situation.

Now she lay in the darkness in the corner of her bedroom, her mind twisting in a void.

Soon the elder would come again, and they would talk. And for a few minutes she would have some tangible entity to cling to.

Soon . . .

'I've brought you some chicken soup,' the romantic novelist said. 'Jewish penicillin, that's what my ex used to call it.'

Hannah tried to focus on the woman as she set a bowl down on the bedside table.

'It'll put the roses back in your cheeks.' The woman was smiling now. 'Elder Brown said you'd been feeling under the weather, so we all thought this might do the trick.'

'All?' Hannah managed at last.

'Of course. We've all been very worried about you.'

Six months later Hannah was called to Elder Brown's office.

'You're to be transferred,' the woman told her. 'You're to join a community in the Outland. We believe you can serve the movement more effectively as an open order member. First, you'll have to prove yourself. You'll have an assignment to complete. Your preparation for that will begin tonight.'

The open order community was centred in a brownstone on 2nd Avenue. Five families, all cult members, lived there. Hannah shared a large apartment with a seasoned recruitment officer, his wife, and their two teenage children. Apart from domestic chores, she would be expected to work in the movement's office, five blocks away. Her experience as a writer would be put to good use: she would write promotional material for the sect.

But first, she knew she must contact Muddy Harbin. Mr Harbin was proving elusive, so Elder Brown had said. She'd once known him, he'd helped her research *Chain of Command*, so it was felt he might respond to her more readily than he had to those who had already tried to reach him. Seemed logical. Some Outlanders could be very hostile. She had letters to write, faxes to send, messages to leave.

On the afternoon of her first Saturday in New York, she walked the nine blocks to the supermarket with the couple's daughter, a kid called Ginny, and helped her do the family's weekly shop.

As her fingers pressed into an avocado, to check if it was ripe, she heard a familiar sound. She strained to hear the Muzak above the din of the shoppers.

I know that song . . . 'Knights in White Satin'.

Who had the hit with it, all those years ago?

It took fully two minutes for her to make the connection. That British band, the Moody Blues, that was it . . . Suddenly the hard yellow light around her began to swim. She felt her balance going, reached out to the aluminium shelving in front of her to steady herself.

Five minutes later Ginny was at the check-out with

a full trolley of produce. She looked around for her charge.

'Hannah?'

When the woman she'd been assigned to watch failed to emerge, the check-out girl said, 'Is she a tall lady with red hair?'

Ginny spun around. 'Yes,' she said, her eyes wild with concern. 'Why?'

'Well, she just went out over there, on to Second, and got into a cab.'

'Vir on seexty-sevinth, you vant?'

The cab driver's accent was so thick Hannah had difficulty understanding what he was saying.

She tried to snap her mind on to the subject at hand, get it straight in her head. She told him.

What's gonna be there when I get there? she asked herself again. Why do I need so badly to do this? Does it have something to do with Mr Harbin?

No. This is something different. Something to do with . . . the old life.

Ten minutes later the taxi pulled up at an apartment block, one of the many built in that part of Manhattan in the early thirties. Hannah peered at it. It looked pretty smart. Where someone who'd come some way in life might live.

The taxi driver tipped his head in her direction.

'Dat's seese dollas foidy, lady.'

She put her hand into her pocket. No money . . . When had she last had money? No purse . . .

'Hey, cum on, I int got ol day.'

Panic began to seize her. What do I do?

Do what you once did before. The voice within her was clear, commanding.

She got out of the cab. 'One minute.'

The cab driver slammed the heel of his hand into the dashboard in irritation.

She walked up the steps, put her weight against the glass door, and stepped into the lobby. The grey-haired concierge looked up from his newspaper. For a second his face registered nothing.

Slowly the corners of his mouth lifted, and his face broke into a warm smile.

'Miss Rostov! Good to see you! How was yer trip?'

Hannah's voice was barely audible. 'Fine, Gary, just fine. Look, I seem to have done it again.' She shook her head in the direction of the taxi.

'Come out without any money, huh?' Gary moved out from behind the reception desk. 'Still my girl!' He hurried out to the street, searching in his pocket for the cash. 'And I'll bet you've packed your key too. What would you do without your Uncle Gary?'

Hannah walked from room to room in a haze of shock.

My home . . .

Everything as I left it . . .

Plants all dead. Pity. Should have given them to the woman next door to look after while I was away. My place or . . . our place? Do I have a husband, a family? No.

Her Apple Mac stood where it always had been, on the desk by the window. Without even thinking, she entered her code and booted it up.

The software program was still in place, but, beyond that, the hard drive was blank. She took one of the backup discs out of the plastic box in the drawer beneath, and loaded it.

Blank.

She tried another. All the others: all blank.

She ran to the bedroom, took down a framed print, tapped a code into a panel, and opened her wall safe.

Empty.

What was I working on? What did I do up here all day?

'For pity's sake, who am I?' she cried aloud. 'Who was I?'

Suddenly, the deep compulsion that had driven her here seemed to overwhelm all other emotion.

'Knights in White Satin.'

I have that track somewhere. She ran to the walnut chest of drawers that stood in the corner of the living room, and opened it. CDs lay in neat rows. I have that song on a sixties compilation somewhere. She ran her finger down the titles until she found the disc she wanted. Instinctively, she turned for the CD player behind her.

Bought it in Boston . . . real cheap . . . bankrupt stock.

She put in the CD and waited . . .

Nothing.

She took it out, and looked at it. It looked like the label had been stuck on by hand . . .

By her . . . In a different life.

Of course it didn't play the fucking song! All there was on it was computer data.

She took it over to the PC, and loaded it.

Slowly she scrolled through the pages of text on the screen. Of course . . .

I'd forgotten . . .

My diary.

Hannah twisted around in her seat. How long have I been here? Ten minutes? Twenty? This'll be the first place sentinels come looking for me.

I have to get out of here.

*   *   *

Fenton Dellaplane tossed the plastic coffee cup into a trashcan, moved out of the shadows, and peered across the station concourse to the platform beyond.

Most of the passengers aboard the early evening train from New York had disembarked now, and he was getting edgy. In the last knot of people, walking towards the barrier, he saw a tall man moving at an even, stately gait. His eyes were hidden behind sunglasses, the distinctive shoulder-length hair had been swept up into a felt hat. But it was McBain all right.

Whoever has you, has the hearts and minds of the vast majority of those in the movement, Dellapane thought as he watched him come.

It was said amongst disciples that Fiske had recognized from the beginning that he lacked the personal charisma necessary to create the religious fervour needed to drive his new Christian order forward, and had begun to look for someone to front the organization for him, right from the cult's inception in the early seventies. The first man to aspire to that role had been Dr Jonathan McBain.

In 1972, McBain had left the priesthood – a calling he'd been pushed into by his mother – and tried to find work as an actor. Fiske had first seen him in a fringe theatre tryout of a play about the American Civil War cult figure John Brown, and had sensed immediately that this might be the man he was searching for. Something in his luminous gaze reminded Fiske of the picture of Christ that had hung in his grandmother's bedroom during his childhood.

For more than twenty-five years, to followers of the Apostles of Christ, the reverend doctor had been the earthly voice of the Almighty, a living icon on to which all attention was focused. Fiske, by design, remained a shadowy figure, seemingly on the perimeter of events. No more than a handful of people had any idea of the nature of his true role. By the early nineties, McBain had travelled hundreds of thousands of miles, delivering thousands of hours of lectures, and it was beginning to show. To Fiske, he was a spent force.

Whilst McBain was vacationing in Europe, the cult's creator announced that *wunderkind* Daniel Kerensky, who he'd been grooming in secret, would take over the doctor's role.

But Fiske had made a bad misjudgement, and the next year was a disastrous one for the sect. Following Kerensky's expulsion, Fiske, clearly short of a better replacement, had reinstated the old campaigner – McBain.

But the role had changed. Fiske began to hand down encyclicals of an increasingly radical nature, insisting they were relayed to the flock without alteration. Followers now wishing to have an audience with the holy one were carefully screened, answers to their questions drafted by a special team without McBain's input. Like Dellaplane and others he had met with in the year of his banishment, McBain's concerns over the future of the cult, its teachings and its practices, deepened.

Dellaplane's own disillusionment had begun less than three years after he'd joined the movement. The further he rose within its ranks – and his rise to senior elder, in charge of the Chicago Commune, had been little less than meteoric – the more his faith in the direction it was taking began to flounder.

One chill November night, a year ago, he'd reached a crisis of conscience, and had called the Outlander woman with whom he'd lived for four years: Hannah Rostov.

Given that he knew that she was deep into researching

a book aimed at exposing the very cult he was desperate to save from its own excesses, she was an odd choice of confidante. But at least she'll understand what I'm up against, he'd told himself as he dialled her number.

But Hannah had sounded cool and distant when they'd spoken. Clearly, too much in their lives had changed in the years they'd been apart for anything of the empathy they'd once known to have survived.

I allowed the Apostles to come into our lives and force us apart, Dellaplane told himself when he hung up. To Hannah, it must seem as though I chose them above her. Calling her, forcing her to confront that fact again, had ripped a scab off a healing wound. Why did I do it? Was I searching to see if there was a chance to turn the clock back in some way, a chance to begin again? Either way, it had been a mistake. If I leave the Apostles now, then I gave her up, sacrificed the best relationship I ever had, for absolutely nothing.

That realization had been a factor in his new-found resolve to stay in the sect, and fight for the changes he knew had to be made within it.

Jonathan McBain looked around furtively. Come by train, it will take longer, but it's safer, Dellaplane had urged, when they'd planned this crucial meeting a month before. Rail travel just doesn't figure in Kleig's thinking. Anything we can do to throw him off the scent has to be worth the effort.

Dellaplane moved cautiously into the light.

'Jonathan.'

The tall man turned. The mesmeric blue eyes that had transfixed cult members for more than two decades met his. Relief registered on the tense countenance.

'Fenton.'

'There's a car waiting. We've borrowed an apartment

198

for the meeting. It's about ten minutes' drive from here. Toliver is very anxious to meet you.'

Vernon Toliver was younger than McBain had expected. From the voice on the telephone, he'd gauged him to be in his late fifties, but the newest recruit to their cause looked to be little more than forty-five. He settled himself on to the sofa opposite the two men, and poured them coffee.

'We don't know each other, Jonathan, although over time I hope we may come to.'

The face that had gazed out from most of the Apostles' promotion material turned to study Toliver. 'It would seem that we have a great many objectives in common.'

'I hope so. I should tell you that it was the address you gave in San Francisco in the mid-eighties that's responsible for me being so involved with our movement today. Eleven years ago, my life was in a mess. My wife of fifteen years, whom I loved very dearly, was dead at thirty-seven. I'd sold my interest in the computer business I'd started in the seventies – the third biggest in the country at the time – and although I knew that I would never again have any financial worries, I could see the time ahead of me only as a vast dark void. The Apostles came into my life and gave me hope. There is much good in our movement – I'm sure you don't need me to tell you that. I felt that was true when I became an Apostle; I feel it now. The cruel, the degenerate, the unprincipled that is in it: that has troubled me for a long time. The more concerned I became, the more I began to take seriously the anxieties of Dellaplane, and the others who believe that there must be change.'

'If change is to come, it must come soon,' Dellaplane said. 'The government initiative is hotting up, there's no question about that. We know the Feds have taken statements from members in at least eleven states, relating to everything from our recruitment methods, initiation processes and isolation techniques to our tithing system.'

McBain threw up his hands in a gesture of frustration. 'All areas where change is desperately needed.'

'At least five hundred members have dropped out of US communes and open order groups in the last four months – that's twice the normal figure. We have to take it that many of those, too, are bad-mouthing us to authorities.'

Toliver poured them more coffee. 'We know that district attorneys in at least nine states, where we have multiple interests, are digging through public records, anything they can lay their hands on, in the hopes of finding breaches in anti-trust laws, any indictable offence they can hang on us. The Caulfied Initiative is on, Jonathan, have no doubt about that. My view, until recent weeks, was that we still had a chance of heading this thing off, of showing them that we can clean up our act, put the movement on to a new footing, one that would be acceptable to the establishment of this country. I knew that to achieve that we would need to have a clear picture of what was going on in all the hidden recesses and outposts of the organization. Without that information, we'd never know where or how deeply to cut.'

Toliver began to take files from his attaché case. 'Fiske delooped this end of the movement more than a year ago. Very little sensitive data comes this way at all now. So we decided to bring in some professional help. Not just to scope the organization itself, but also affiliated corporations in which the Apostles have a controlling interest. Given all we already knew on the development of REGENS, we decided to focus particular attention on Falk Pharmaceuticals. We put a seasoned operative in there, equipped with as many key entry codes as we could get him. He came up with the data Dellaplane has shown you.'

Dellaplane shot Toliver a look. The point was made: if you even hint at our concerns over what has become of that man, McBain will be on the next train back to New York. They can't link the spy to us; that's all that's relevant here.

McBain digested all that he'd been told for a moment. 'I was totally stunned by the report on the Falk data. I've known Fiske half my adult life. I know he can be irrational, irresponsible, cruel . . . But this! The experiments being done on the prisoners in the British jail . . .' His eyes swivelled around to Dellaplane. 'I'm not ashamed to admit it, I cried when I read what's been going on there.'

'It makes our people no better than Nazis,' Toliver said.

'As for the use being made of REGENS . . . Here is a blessing, a boon to mankind of incalculable value,' McBain went on. 'That these cures should be withheld, made available only to those who can further Fiske's political aims, is an absolute obscenity. It goes against everything I thought this church represented.' He threw up his hands, as though at a loss for words.

McBain took off the hat he was wearing and let the long greying hair fall on to his shoulders. 'If he's publicly exposed, he would totally destroy a movement that I and many others have given their lives building.'

Dellaplane got up. 'Well, the immediate problem is the Caulfield Initiative. If we're to head that off – and some of those who share our concerns believe that, in the light of what we know, we may be too late – we have to act now.'

201

There was total silence in the room for a moment, then McBain said:

'I tried to reason with Fiske for years. At first I got his standard retort: "This is not a cafeteria credo, where you just take the things you want." One night I decided to go for broke. Fiske exploded. If you've never seen him lose his temper, let me tell you, it's a very frightening sight – when you criticize the Apostles, you criticize him. At the end he turned on me, his face white with anger. I'll never forget what he said: "It's my fucking religion, McBain. I'll run it any way I see fit!" That remark confirmed my worst fears. When I drove home that night, it seemed to me that I'd wasted my whole life's work. But I came to see that the Apostles are far bigger than Fiske now, they have been for years. And little of the good that's in them is of his making.'

McBain walked over to the window and looked out at the clapboard houses that lined the street. 'Fiske used to say that the establishment church is like the Hydra: a beast with one body, but many heads, all trying to pull it in different directions.' He turned to study the two men in front of him. 'That's what I believe the Apostles has become. So maybe we should do as Herakles did – strike off a head or two.'

CHAPTER FOURTEEN

Sweltering days, cut off behind enemy lines without supplies, in remote Rwandan villages where nothing could block out the smell of the putrefying dead. Sub-zero nights spent in a bombed-out Chechnyan hotel under constant fire from Russian artillery: nothing had prepared Joel McKinnon for the months of waiting on remand.

There was a dreadful inevitability about the trial itself. He sat at the back of the court, often listening with an eerie detachment, as the prosecution case unfolded before a rapt jury.

Bruce Van Stratton, McKinnon's boss at NBS for almost five years, was one of few character witnesses to testify for the defence. He spoke well enough on the defendant's behalf, although his talk of the correspondent's coolness under fire, his initiative in difficult situations, seemed to have a mixed effect on the jury. But when he repeatedly denied that McKinnon had ever come to him with evidence of the covert activities of the Apostles of Christ – beyond that material already covered in the Kerensky story – doubts that had been gnawing at McKinnon's mind for months crystallised into hard fact.

Van Stratton was in on this! Right from the beginning. That's why he sent me to England. They'd got to him . . . Somehow Fiske got to him too.

A friend of Caitlin's, a woman he dimly remembered from the past, spoke of the burning resentment McKinnon had felt when the deceased woman broke off with him. Had it ever been that way? There were times when McKinnon began to doubt his own memory of events.

Even the police officer who'd taken McKinnon's statement following the attack on him in Southgate Mews was shipped in. The assailant, who McKinnon stated had, as a result of action he'd taken, been badly injured, if not killed, in the fight, was now made to sound like some kind of victim. McKinnon himself, in the prosecution counsel's reading of the statement, came across as little more than a self-confessed thug.

There were holes in the prosecution case to be sure: there was little forensic evidence to directly link the contents of the trunk of Caitlin's car to the man found driving it. But the evidence, circumstantial as much of it was, taken as a whole, amounted to a compelling indictment.

A thousand times a voice screamed inside the defendant's mind: Hannah, if you still live and breathe, come forward and speak for me, tell them what you know. Without you I'm lost . . .

McKinnon could only believe the worst when the efforts of two private detectives failed to find her.

In his whole life, he had never felt so alone. It came home to him now what an insular figure he must have always cut to those around him, a man who neither needed nor understood human relationships. If he saw that with such clarity, how could the jury not take account of it?

His lawyers had prepared him for the worst long before it happened. McKinnon had heard the judge speak the words many times in his dreams before they actually came: 'To be detained for the term of at least twenty years, before being considered for parole . . .'

The night of the sentencing, McKinnon sat alone at the remand centre, certain that nothing worse could befall him. He barely looked up when his lawyer entered the interview room. But there was further to fall. Much further. An abyss opened up now beneath his feet, swallowing him, drawing him down to a new hell . . .

'They're sending you to Marston Moor . . .'

The words echoed around the dank, airless space. As McKinnon's mind plummeted, his new position hit him with dreadful clarity.

So this was what it had been about all along. It was so obvious, why didn't I see it coming? he asked himself. Because even I didn't believe Fiske's sphere of influence extended that far. But he's done it. He's got me where his people can deal with me at their leisure.

The lawyer was talking now about an appeal. What was the point? I'll be a patient in the hospital wing inside three months. My medical file will show that I have some terminal disease. Only God knows what they'll put me through before they allow me to die.

Marston Moor Super Maximum Control Unit – or 'Supermax' – was built on the American model and was the most secure institution of its kind in Europe. It had been constructed on the site of a Victorian mental institution. Its architects, after submitting a number of designs that had failed to find favour with the local planning authority, and weary from fighting off conservationists – bent on preserving the old Gothic facade, claiming that it was 'part of an established skyline of exceptional beauty' – had simply incorporated the building's exterior into their design for a state-of-the-art prison.

Marston Moor was Britain's first privatised Supermax. After winning the franchise to run it, the Ravenscourt Group set in motion a carefully orchestrated strategy, aimed at softening up the all-powerful Prison Officers' Association; with the result that staffing levels were soon reduced to the point where concerns were raised amongst the new system's critics that security was being compromised. Ravenscourt's directors knew that one serious breach in that direction would bring a deluge of condemnation down on their heads, so nothing in the design of the security system itself was left to chance.

Dubbed immediately 'the Alcatraz of England' when it first opened, the jail consisted of eleven separate cell blocks subdivided by 1,700 electronic gates, operated by guards using touch-screen computers and 192 television monitors. The whole complex was ringed by eight guard towers, six gun towers faced with mirror glass and razor wire on top of two fourteen foot fences. At night, if need be, 8,000-watt floodlights could illuminate the entire area with a glare brighter than that of the noon sun. A minefield of microwave sensors above and below ground would immediately trip if so much as a rabbit attempted to cross the area between the cell blocks and the perimeter fence.

A thin layer of cloud covered the sun, still low on the horizon, as the jail came into view. McKinnon peered at it through the tiny window of the prison van. The old Victorian facade presented a forbidding sight, its stark Gothic towers, grey with age, looming above. As they drew closer, he remembered how his father's cellmate had described the place: 'The most soulless hole on the globe . . . a state-of-the-art gulag . . . a sanitized Devil's Island . . .'

The prison van swung left, pulling away from the

main drive, and up to a small gateway at the side of the complex. It was waved through, crossed a small yard and stopped under a steel canopy. McKinnon and two other prisoners were taken down steps into a brightly lit reception area and the long humiliating induction process was begun.

Through it all – the strip search, the medical, the kitting out – McKinnon uttered not a word. The governor, a small man with a bullet-shaped head and piercing hazel eyes, went through his induction blurb as though he'd been set on fast forward: 'You have been sent to this facility because you have been categorized as a prisoner who represents a real danger to the public. There is no free association here. You will be held in a single unit for an initial period of three months. If, at the end of that time, you have demonstrated positive institutional adjustment, limited interaction with one other prisoner may be allowed. Visiting hours are . . .'

McKinnon's mind was in some far distant place.

Some way, somehow, I've got to get out of here . . .

His cell was a bomb shelter of a room, twelve feet by seven feet. Almost everything in it was made of concrete to prevent the making of home-made weapons. The bed was a plain slab, with a thin fireproof mattress and pillow. Even the stool at the writing table was made of reinforced concrete, and fixed to the floor. The floor itself was smooth cement, painted green. Meals were delivered though a slot in the door, which was made of steel to minimize voice contact with other prisoners. The only window had a view of the block opposite. A ten-inch TV set, with a built-in VCR – installed as the result of a recent EU human rights directive – sat on a shelf near the bed.

At eleven am every morning, a steel door, at the other

end of the cell, opened automatically. Beyond was a small exercise area – a patch of gravel measuring about Fifteen feet by twenty feet. Two sides of it were formed by doorways that obviously gave the occupants of other cells access to the area at different times. A small tree, barely more than a sapling in a protective casing, grew in one corner. This, and the strong daylight that generally seemed to fill the area, was intended to give the impression of an open-air space. In fact, transparent roofing, eighteen feet above the prisoners' heads, encased the entire wing. Let into it, at intervals, were large sky lights which could be opened automatically each day, weather permitting.

Breakfast came at six thirty, lunch at noon, dinner at six thirty. A library provided books and videos. These could be ordered using an adapted teletext system – incorporating American home-shopping technology – available on every inmate's TV set.

The hardest part of the régime to adjust to was the isolation. At least during his months on remand McKinnon had had the sight and sound of other human beings. At first, the inactivity, the claustrophobia, was unbearable. It choked him, crushed him. He clung to the smallest live sounds: the creak of the meal trolley, the dull thump of another prisoner exercising in a cell close by. Even the rain became a welcome companion . . .

Prisoners undergoing induction were only allowed access to law books or self-help books. McKinnon had read somewhere that imprisonment rated alongside bereavement and divorce as the most traumatic of human experiences. There was a book in the library – shown on the closed circuit teletext listings – entitled *Stress And How To Fight It*.

With the remote control unit he wrote the reference number of it into the window provided on the screen, and added his prison number so that it could be delivered to his cell the following day.

He'd never before been exposed to a self-help book. Much of its rationale he found irrelevant to his position, but the little he could identify with gave him a new start point.

I must live inside my head, he told himself. Find a level where I can be free to make lucid judgements, evaluate progress. I must carry on with the investigation – it was in this place that most of the key events played out. I have a unique opportunity to find out what's really going on here.

McKinnon also began to wade through the only book he was allowed to keep in his cell. Incongruously enough, it was an early edition of Fiske's second tome, *The Road to Redemption*. Hannah had lent it to him after one of their many discussions. It had been in his attaché case when he was arrested. He guessed that he'd been allowed to keep it because the authorities thought it was something to do with his religion.

McKinnon began to learn a great deal more about the man who'd so completely altered his life. Of pivotal interest was a chapter on myths. Here, Fiske tried to explain man's enduring love of legends and the significance of recurrent themes in tales that have come down us to through Homer, the Brothers Grimm, and a dozen other sources.

The piece triggered a memory of a Greek expression McKinnon had learnt when he was covering the trouble in Macedonia, two years before: *O Ex'apotho!* He later found that had parallels in a dozen other languages. Fiske, a thorough researcher, doubtless knew of it too. Taken

209

on its own, it was of little interest, but, laid beside what Fiske had written here, it provided a crucial insight into his thinking, a key to what the piece was really about.

McKinnon's mind turned again to what he was certain was taking place only a few hundred yards away, in the prison hospital wing.

Suddenly, it was as though a door in his mind was jerked ajar.

My God! The answer to this whole thing has been staring me in the face! I was just too close to see it. I know what Fiske's up to. I know why I'm here, why I'm so dangerous to him. I was just seeing one end of the plan. The rest of it is in that database somewhere. Fiske is certain that I stumbled on to it when we made the hack. It's why he's gone to such lengths to take me out of circulation.

My God, if I ever get out of this place, I'm gonna take you down, old man. One rotten chunk at a time.

I'm one of the very few who can . . .

Precisely at eleven am, on the ninety-second day of McKinnon's incarceration, the electric door to the access area slid back as it had every morning, and he walked out into the exercise yard. Only this time there was another human being waiting for him – one of the very few he'd so much as seen in the last twelve weeks. His good behaviour had been rewarded. He was to be allowed to 'interact' with another prisoner.

The man facing him introduced himself as Ray Teal. Teal was a large man around forty. His small intense eyes peered out from a massive dome of a forehead and scrutinized McKinnon for a moment. Then he offered his hand.

The guy could be a Fiske plant, McKinnon told himself. Be careful what you tell him.

He stepped forward and shook the hand.

'How long you been in?' Teal enquired.

'Three months.'

'Huh, a beginner. Try nineteen years – five of them in here. Your first time?'

'Yes.'

'Before you ask, I'm here because I killed my ex-wife's lover.'

'I thought that counted as a crime of passion, these days,' McKinnon said for something to say.

'Not when you spend a month planning it, and two hours doing it.'

'What did you do, torture him or something?' McKinnon said before he could stop himself.

Teal laughed. 'No. He was just a hard bastard to kill that's all.'

All through this exchange, Teal locked him with his eyes, indicating with darting movements to the left and right that there were surveillance cameras watching their every move. Then he put a finger to his mouth and jerked his head in the direction of a light-fitting above them. Clearly, that contained a microphone.

'Had any visitors?' Teal asked.

'Only my lawyer so far. I don't know many people in this country.' Poor sweet Caitlin, he thought again.

Teal told him that, apart from the odd do-gooder, he, like many lifers, no longer got any visitors. Wives, having no reason to believe they'll ever live a normal married life again, divorced husbands. Children grew up, and grew away from disgraced fathers. It was the usual story.

McKinnon knew it. He'd been one of those kids.

And it's just these forgotten men that Falk targets, he thought as Teal talked. I must not be seen as one of them.

211

The only reason he'd pressed for an appeal – his lawyer had told him that without new evidence it was doubtful that any such hearing would be granted – was to keep his name in the judicial consciousness. So long as some kind of court proceedings are still ongoing, he'd told himself, I'm probably safe enough.

Teal was talking about football now. McKinnon nodded in the right places. Get to know this man, he told himself. Hardened killer he may be, but he's all you've got. If he's been here as long as he says he may know something of what's been going on. He may have heard gossip, a rumour . . .

'Do you have a cassette machine? Teal asked.

'No. I wish to God I did.'

'Well, I have a spare. You can have it till the next time we meet, if you like.'

An act of kindness. McKinnon had forgotten how it felt to have someone show him kindness.

High above them, a bell sounded and the doors to their cells slid back automatically. Teal moved into his and re-emerged carrying a cassette machine. As McKinnon took it, he noticed a piece of paper protruding from the top of the plastic carrying case. He quickly covered it with his hand. 'Thanks. We'll talk again next week.'

Back in his cell he unfolded the paper, and read it eagerly.

As you probably now realize, everything we do and say in the exercise area is monitored. If you want to communicate with me without having the guards listening in, record it on the cassette in the machine, and give it to me next week. I suspect that the induction cells may have concealed

212

cameras in them, so it's probably best to record what you have to say under the bedclothes at night.

Was this some kind of sexual overture? McKinnon wondered. There had been absolutely nothing in Teal's behaviour to indicate that it was such. More likely, it was just one tormented soul in search of another.

'If you want to communicate with me . . .'

I've been a communicator all my life. Detach yourself. Look at what you know, at what's happened to you objectively, as you would if you were still working for the network.

Write the story. Okay, right now it's for an audience of just one – but get it down. When you give it to him – if you give it to him – judge his reaction, and if it feels right, put the bite on him for information. He might even volunteer it anyway.

Over the next three days and nights McKinnon laboured on the recording, whispering the narrative into the tiny mike under the thin duvet cover. Often he ran the tape back and erased a section, and recorded it again with words chosen to convey exactly the extraordinary course of events that had brought him to the position he was now in.

The closing lines on the tape were from the heart. Simple and to the point: 'Whatever it takes, more than anyone else you know, I have to get out of here.'

Even on the morning McKinnon was due to see Teal again, he was undecided about giving him the tape, fearing that he was one of those who reported to Fiske.

At this point, what have I got to lose? McKinnon asked himself as the bell announced the beginning of the exercise period. Teal is a hardened con. He must know a few slants. Mustn't he?

A week later, Teal offered the loan of the cassette recorder again. When McKinnon got it back to the cell he found a long message recorded on to the cassette inside it.

Teal was not an articulate man. The message was fairly garbled in places, and he tended to stray off the subject. But the bottom line seemed to be that he had been much impressed with McKinnon's story.

It seemed that Teal himself had heard stories about forgotten lifers disappearing out of the system. The way he put it, it was as though they were somehow swallowed up in the labyrinth of the prison, and never heard from again. Quite how he got this intelligence, given all the restrictions on communication, he failed to explain. Whatever Teal's evidence was for believing what he did, McKinnon was surprised to find that he seemed quite ready to believe that his newfound friend was in very real danger.

All talk regarding McKinnon's situation ceased for several weeks. Then, one morning when the men met, they noticed that the surveillance camera, mounted high in the glass roof above them, had been replaced with an update. This one was motorised, designed to pan back and forth across their end of the wing.

When the camera was turned away from them, Teal whispered, 'Give me a leg up.'

For a moment, McKinnon gawped at him, uncomprehendingly.

Teal pointed to the light-fitting over them that concealed the microphone. 'Move it!'

A second later, Teal climbed on to McKinnon's

shoulders, took a lump of gum out of his mouth and stuck it over the front of what he was sure was the mike itself. Then he climbed down, and the two sat with their backs to the camera and talked freely for the first time. The conversation that followed took McKinnon completely by surprise

'Do you have money? Say forty, fifty grand in a bank somewhere, or can you get it? I have a good reason for asking, believe me.'

'I might have,' McKinnon said at last. 'Why?'

'The guy I exercised with before you was an engineer by training,' Teal began. 'He had, or he said he had, a way to get out of here. He told me some of it. Real ingenious stuff.'

'You're kidding.'

'But it's not a lot of good to him now. He had a serious run-in with some prison officers six months back, and got pretty badly messed up in the process. He's been in the punishment wing ever since he came out of hospital.'

How could Teal know all this? McKinnon wondered.

'If you're in as much danger here as you say, and you can get your hands on that kind of money, I could try and see if my friend felt like passing the information along.'

'How can you contact him?'

'There are ways, even in here.'

McKinnon thought for a moment. 'Even assuming for one minute that what he has to sell is worth that kind of money, who would I pay?'

'My friend has a retarded daughter in care in Bristol. She means a lot to him. If you could arrange to have sufficient money transferred to her relatives to enable her to be put into a private home, I know that would make him a much happier man.'

McKinnon shrugged. 'It might be possible. What would you want out of this?'

'Half the cash. I'm eligible for parole in three years. That's tomorrow in this place. The money would help me get started again.' He watched the camera begin to swing again. 'We better get that gum down before someone comes round to check the mike out.'

'My friend's name is Devereux,' Teal began when they met again a week later. 'He's ready to talk business.'

'How do I speak with him?' McKinnon asked.

Teal looked up and checked that the gum was correctly in place over the mike again. 'Order a video from the library in the usual way, from the list on your TV screen. Choose something that's seldom taken out, one they only have a single copy of. When they put it through the door of your cell, sellotape over the small indentation at the back of the cassette – that's there to stop the tape being erased accidentally – load it into your VCR, and spool on past the movie. There's usually blank tape at the end of it.' Teal held up an audio cassette mike with attached wiring. 'Then plug this gizmo into the back of the machine where you'd plug in a camcorder. You can then record your voice on to the tape, and tell Devereux what you propose.'

'How do I get it to him?' McKinnon asked.

Teal told him that he should lift the plastic flap at the front and make a pencil mark on the tape in the corner.

'Return it to the library then order it up again, only this time put in Devereux's prison number instead of your own. The despatcher will think he's ordered it, and will send it to his cell. When Devereux receives a cassette he hasn't ordered, he'll know someone is trying to reach him. He'll check to see the pencil mark is where it should be and he'll listen to the message. If he wants to respond, he'll use the same procedure to get a message to you.'

McKinnon shook his head in disbelief. 'If you say so.'

Teal fixed him with a look McKinnon had not seen before – the look the ex-wife's lover no doubt saw before he died.

'God help you if you tell a living soul about this set-up.'

CHAPTER FIFTEEN

The morning of McKinnon's 130th day of incarceration was an unusual one. He received a letter. It came with his lunch, as mail always did. The one-page note had been done on a PC. He read the signature first. He blinked at it for a second, and leapt up off his bed. Then, with trembling hands, read the letter from the beginning.

Dear Joel,
Very shaken to hear about what happened to you. Sorry this is the first time I've written, but I got caught up on a long assignment in N.C., something I got pushed into, which is why I've only just heard the news. I know you're perfectly innocent, and it's all a hideous mistake. Whatever you need, I'm there for you, you hear? It seems like only yesterday we were sitting in Srebrenica, eating filbert chocolates, and sipping vermouth – all there was left to eat or drink! – waiting for the next story to break. A few wonderful weeks together, and then torn apart. We were lovers in a war then. In a sense we are now. Don't forget what I told you, Mount Rushmore. Like the Supremes' song says . . . Yeah? I love you, Joel. Remember, there's people out here who really care for you. I'm in good shape. Your loving 'Cat'

The address at the bottom of the note was a post office box in Manhattan.

Hannah!

She was alive! She's being careful as hell. She must know exactly what's at stake, otherwise why all the coded references? 'Filbert chocolates', 'vermouth', 'Cat': all allusions to the conversation they'd had about *A Farewell To Arms*, that time in the deli on 48th. The Supremes' song: 'There's no mountain high enough . . . to keep me from you.'

'Whatever you need, I'm there for you . . .'

The long assignment in N.C. she was pushed into: N.C. has to be North Carolina, McKinnon told himself. Fiske's centre of operations. The Apostles took her. 'I'm in good shape.' But she's none the worse for it. And she's ready to help me do whatever I need to, to get out of here.

'Remember, there's people out here who really care for you.' That line isn't in there for me. It's for the censors in the governor's office, or whoever it is here who reports to Fiske's people. The message to them was simple enough: this is not a forgotten man. If you start screwing around with him, there are people out here who'll be taking notice! That's why she passed herself off as a colleague in the news media. She knows Fiske's people will be watching.

Nothing that had happened in the last year had lifted McKinnon's spirits so completely.

'Do you think your pal here, the one getting paroled, would deliver a letter on the outside?'

'For cash he might, yes,' Teal said.

McKinnon had been in regular touch with Devereux for more than a month, and had the seeds of a plan to break out of Marston Moor. But there were still some vital elements that would need to be put in place from the outside, if the plan was to work.

The bell above him sounded the end of the exercise period. McKinnon stood up slowly and stretched.

'Give me his cell number.'

That night, McKinnon recorded a brief message to the man in question and 'mailed' it to him, using the 'Cassette Express', as Teal termed it. The guy was clearly used to using the system, as the reply came through the door of McKinnon's cell promptly twenty-four hours later, in the shape of an unrequested copy of *Sense and Sensibility*. His message was short and to the point. For £300 he'd post a letter, consisting of three sheets maximum, on the outside.

McKinnon had lost count of the hours he spent working on his plan. Devereux's original idea was audacious and ingenious, but it would require considerable personal courage to execute. McKinnon felt that, provided the fates were on his side, the overall strategy had more than a chance of succeeding. But there were fundamental weaknesses in certain areas he could find no reliable way of sidestepping. But the sudden re-emergence of Hannah had put an entirely different complexion on matters.

'If something intrigues me,' she'd said, 'before I can think, is it safe, is it legal? I'm off, I'm committed, there's no holding me.'

They had been together for two weeks, but in some ways he felt he'd known her half his life. As a news correspondent he'd learnt to make character judgements quickly and accurately, and he was certain that if there was one person on the planet who could be relied on to help him, it was Hannah.

Now he set about putting into writing ideas that had

been churning around in his head for weeks. The letter, he knew, had to be brief but persuasive. Detailed but clear. And he'd have to rely on her to pay the messenger somehow.

Six hours later, McKinnon recorded a message to Teal's pal, agreeing his terms – it just fitted on to the end of the little-rented *Remains of the Day* – with instructions to pull the folded note out from its hiding place inside the cassette itself, where it was now sandwiched between the tape spools and the plastic casing.

Desperate situations call for desperate measures, McKinnon told himself as he tried to sleep. And if this is intercepted by the authorities, how much worse off can I really be?

The two interview rooms at the prison were obviously in use as McKinnon was marched down to the visiting room, a large rectangular space divided down its length by a half-inch-thick glass screen, and across its width by partitioning that created four separate booths. Prisoners spoke to their visitors by telephone.

Wolstenholme was his usual sanguine self. He sat shuffling his papers.

'Good afternoon. So, have you read the new affidavits I sent you?'

'Yeah, they seem okay.'

'Oh, before I forget, I had a call from a friend of yours.' He searched his notes. 'Cat Barkley will be arriving from the States on the seventeenth, and will make arrangements to see you the following week. Now, as regards the appeal . . .'

Hannah got the note! The seventeenth! That gives me five days.

As Wolstenholme talked, McKinnon began to take

222

decisions that he was certain would shape the rest of his life. He shot a glance in the direction the two prison officers pacing listlessly thirty feet to his left, and scanned the room, checking every detail of the layout. *Hell, now is as good a time as any. Let's get this show on the road.*

Without a word, he slipped from his seat, moved back and unhooked the fire extinguisher behind him. One of the guards let out a shout. McKinnon lifted the large red cylinder above his head and, with all his strength, hurled it at the glass screen.

The partition shook as though struck by some seismic force. A wide crack opened up across it, but it held. The alarm bell, on the wall above McKinnon's head, immediately rattled into life. Prisoners and visitors alike sat in mute astonishment as an officer closed with McKinnon, his baton raised to strike. McKinnon lunged forward and caught him with a right hook across the jaw. The man went down, his head striking the edge of the partitioning.

McKinnon turned and caught the extinguisher as it began to roll off the central table unit, and used it to fend off blows from the other man. It made a lousy weapon. He hurled it clumsily forward, but the guard pulled back.

The main doors, on the prisoners' side of the room, swung open, and men dressed in riot gear spilled in. Heckler and Koch carbines were levelled at McKinnon's head.

'Freeze!'

A man stepped forward and cuffed his hands behind him. He was dragged out of the visitors' room and down a corridor.

A powerfully built prison officer strode ahead for a moment, then stopped and spun around. McKinnon was slammed up against the wall by the men behind him.

'Getting bored, eh, McKinnon? No girls for you to slice up in here? If you need some action that badly, we'll have to see you get some.'

His right knee jerked upwards into the prisoner's scrotum. For a moment McKinnon thought he was going to pass out. A granite-hard fist hammered into his stomach. He folded forward. A second blow caught him in the kidneys.

'Don't get frisky with us. It's a bad idea.'

The mansion J. Richmond Fiske had built in the mid seventies, high in the Blue Ridge Mountains of North Carolina, had been extended and remodelled almost continually ever since. During a long and noisy period, when a museum and photo-gallery, chronicling the rise of the Apostles, was being added to the south wing, he'd moved most of his clothing and personal effects over to the original homestead that still stood in a wooded corner of the twenty-acre lot, as it had since the late nineteenth century. Fiske always referred to the place as the 'cabin', but it was, in fact, a five-bedroom ranch house of considerable charm. He never moved back.

Formal dinners and meetings were still held in the mansion that was now considered the Apostles' mecca. But, when they were done, Fiske would cross the wide, carefully tended gardens to his own private sanctuary.

Today the Council of Elders met. Conscious that the movement he'd founded would never attract thinking minds unless there was an impression of democracy at the heart of it, Fiske had set up the committee in the late seventies. Ostensibly, core disciples met once a month to discuss the agenda for the weeks ahead, and set the

224

spiritual direction for the movement. But, to the mounting annoyance of the revisionists, the meetings were in reality little more than briefing sessions, opportunities for Fiske to pontificate, and delegate in areas in which he had no interest.

This morning, there was only one topic on the agenda: the Caulfield Initiative. Fiske knew well enough that there were many in the Apostles who urgently wanted change, change that might offer Outlanders a more palatable view of the movement, and allow it to establish itself as an acceptable alternative to the mainstream churches. But, for him, the contentious issues — the recruitment, initiation and control techniques the cult employed — were the key to its existence. Without them, he knew members could not be remoulded, become of value to the spiritual family.

He'd therefore choreographed the council meeting so that it would fall at a time when three of the key advocates of change would be unavailable. He and six others, who he could count on to toe the line, would vote this morning on what action to take to counter the government offensive.

Fiske crossed the rose garden, stooping to examine roses recently brought from the hot-house. The Chicago Peace, with its yellow and peach-tinged petals, was thriving, but the spindly Elizabeth of Glamis was clearly longing for its native British soil.

He set off for the mansion, entering through French doors in the east wing, and made his way through to the morning room, a wide airy conservatory that looked out over the misty peaks of the mountains. Meetings of the council traditionally began here. Fiske greeted the six members able to attend – several of whom he knew must have been travelling since the early hours of the morning

– then seated himself at the head of the long oak table, so that breakfast could be served.

As the others began to eat, Fiske reached for the brown leather pouch that lay to the right of his place setting, and began a daily ritual that had been a part of his life for some years.

At the age of sixty, he'd been diagnosed as diabetic. Since then he injected himself three times a day with the insulin his pancreas could no longer produce. To obviate the need for him to carry a syringe, insulin, glucose, and glucometer everywhere he went, separate diabetic kits were kept at strategic places around the Highlands Estate. One was always laid up with his breakfast place setting.

Before eating, Fiske would need to take a blood test, to establish the sugar level present, so that he could then determine the corresponding level of insulin he would have to inject to balance it. He held a pen-like object above his forefinger, and pressed a button at the top, so that the sprung-loaded needle inside could draw a drop of blood. This he pressed on to a strip of litmus paper.

The table talk began to gather momentum. There was clearly a growing sense that President Caulfield was closing in. That unseen eyes followed their every move.

Fiske pressed the litmus paper into the glucometer. Dispelling paranoia is the priority this morning, he told himself. Left as things are, this spectre will gnaw away at their resolve to retain the *status quo*. I might even hint at the plans that are in hand in Washington to subvert the Caulfield Initiative. That will certainly lift their spirits.

The liquid crystal display on the glucometer, that would show the sugar level, remained blank. Fiske shook it irritably. Three letters appeared: 'BAT'. The batteries were flat. This particular machine was an oldish model, the first he'd acquired. It was kept in a drawer in the mansion dining room and only used at breakfast meetings. The batteries probably hadn't been changed since he'd bought it. His secretary, he knew, kept replacements in her office. He lifted the phone on the table to his left, and tried her extension. She was clearly not yet at her desk. He would get the batteries himself.

He left the table and crossed the hallway outside, into the administration wing.

Immediately, behind him, there was a massive explosion. A searing wall of heat lifted him off his feet and threw him into a knot of staffers, standing in the reception area. Something deep in the house fractured and gave. There was a creaking sound, and a large part of what, seconds before, had been the dining room, tipped off its mountain-top foundations, and plunged fifteen hundred feet into the valley below.

Above the ringing in his ears, Fiske could hear the crackle of flame, the snap of burning timber. Within it, he could hear the desperate screams of the trapped and injured. He fought to get a firm grip on the desk in front of him and, with considerable difficulty, struggled to his feet. He ran his hands up the back of his head. Where there should have been hair, there was now only bloody flesh. He turned slowly. His suit hung off him in shreds. Now there was shouting. Everywhere, running feet . . .

Fiske's secretary appeared in the doorway, her eyes wild with alarm. He stared back at her, clearly in deep shock, then pushed by her and staggered into the hallway.

A security man rushed to keep him from going deeper into the chaos ahead. He looked up. Conduits and pipework hung down from the ruptured ceiling. Where three of the council members had been sitting, there was now only smoke and hazy sunlight. The legs

227

of the disciple who'd been sitting opposite Fiske were visible under the charred table, but the rest of him was nowhere to be seen.

For twenty anxious hours after the bombing of the Highlands mansion Pieter Kleig assumed the leadership of the Apostles of Christ. Doctors at the Highlands Clinic, close by, were soon satisfied that the trance-like state into which the sect founder had fallen was the result of shock. They were agreed that the burns to the back of the head would probably require plastic surgery at some time in the future, but should be left to heal naturally in the meantime.

Shortly before four am, the morning after the bomb outrage, Fiske rang the bell beside his hospital bed, and asked a nurse for Evian water. After a few sips, he had her summon Kleig.

Doctors were dismissed the minute he appeared in the doorway of the private room. Fiske lay back into his pillows, his eyes defying Kleig to tell him anything other than the plain facts.

'No one in the dining room survived, Mr Fiske,' he said softly. 'I'm sorry. The explosion was caused by about thirty pounds of Semtex packed under the foundations of the house. Climbing equipment was found close to the road, west of the village, so it's probable that the assassins scaled the south face of Cherokee Ridge, and planted the bomb there, sometime Monday evening.'

Fiske closed his eyes and considered all this for a minute. 'Caulfield,' he said flatly.

'No, not in this day and age. Too provocative, even for him. Anyway, he's not about the business of giving the movement its first great martyr. Neither would it achieve any of his real objectives. This was a terrorist act, I'm certain of that, possibly the work of a rival sect, or a disaffected element within our own.'

'Within our own,' Fiske echoed. 'Watch everything they do, Kleig. They'll show themselves, they always do.'

CHAPTER SIXTEEN

The door of the cell slammed with a metallic clang. McKinnon shook himself like a cat and stared around at his new home.

The punishment cell in G Block was half the size of the one he'd been in before. Its only contents were a bed, a basin, a shower and a lavatory. There was no window of any kind and, judging by its staleness, the air was recycled.

Well, this is where you wanted to be, he told himself, as he examined the cut above his left eye and the bruises on his neck in the steel mirror above the basin. My little routine in the visiting room certainly guaranteed that. You're three cells further east than you really need to be, but at least you're on the right side of the prison now. If they have their way, you'll be in this bug hutch twenty-three hours a day for the next two months. For one hour a day, at nine pm, the door the other end of the cell will open, and you'll be allowed to stomp around in the narrow corridor beyond. You'll be totally alone, and they will watch your every move. But if Devereux has got it right, if he's levelled with me about how things work on this block, I shall be free of this place in five days.

Now he listened. Listened to the silence. It was total. The only audible sound was his own breathing. Holy God, this had better work, he thought. Hopefully, the shenanigans in the visiting room have bought me a little more time. The governor's enquiry – and there has to be one, too many people saw what went on for him to overlook it – should help keep me off the 'forgotten list' for a while longer. Five days is all I need.

You're not gonna have me, Alderbrook!

The exercise area was little more than a passageway about forty feet in length. McKinnon stepped out into it and jogged to the end. There were a number of windowless steel doors on each side of it, which he presumed gave other prisoners access to it at other times.

Well, I'll find out a lot in the next five minutes, McKinnon thought as he began a series of short sprints.

When he returned to the west end of the area for the third time, the surveillance camera above him had turned away. He moved under it, and examined the wall just above the concrete floor. As Devereux had predicted, there was a metal flap, a couple of inches square, set into it, the kind used in public buildings to cover power points. McKinnon held his breath and lifted the flap. The power point itself seemed to be loose. It was hard to get a firm grip on it, but he dug his fingernails behind it, and he gradually began to move it forward.

The camera above him was already beginning to turn back on to the corridor. With a curse, he let go, and irritably completed a few more laps of the exercise area for the benefit of the guard who was no doubt monitoring this screen, and several dozen others, in the central control block.

Devereux had developed the escape plan that McKinnon had now inherited from a cell three doors from the one he now occupied. He had intended to make his bid for freedom on a Tuesday morning at dawn. The Monday evening, the one eventuality he could never have foreseen had caused him to abort his whole scheme – the governor, needing the cell for a more deserving case, had decided to return him to his regular unit a week early.

Desperate to be left where he was – in the only block where his ploy had a chance of working – he decided to restage the one-man riot that had got him banged up in the punishment block in the first place. But the guards on duty proved to be an unappreciative audience. Devereux was badly beaten, his right knee permanently damaged in a fall, and all hopes of renewing his escape bid had had to be abandoned.

But Devereux had said the key item necessary to the success of the plan – smuggled in from the outside, via a member of the kitchen staff at considerable expense, ten months before – should still be where he'd left it.

Five minutes later, McKinnon had eased the power point out of its housing. He pulled it forward, taking care not to put too great a strain on the cables connected to it, and then began to squeeze his hand into the small square opening in the wall. He could feel nothing. He pushed his hand in harder. The ragged edge of the concrete began to cut into his flesh.

Nothing.

Soon his hand was wet with blood, his face beaded with sweat. The surveillance camera was again sweeping the area where he was supposed to be. 'Goddamn it!' He jerked his hand free and was about to turn away when something caught his eye. He stooped down to examine it. Lying across the bottom of the opening was a strand of thin green twine. Fishing line. It was still here. *If I just pull on it, I'll be here for a week!*

Now McKinnon dug into the hole with renewed vigour, this time feeling closer to the inside of the skirting board.

At last his fingers closed around something hard – a metal spool. A sense of relief welled up inside him, as he pulled free a reel of fishing line – no ordinary fishing line, as Devereux had told him. This could hold the weight of a 300 pound marlin.

McKinnon stuffed it under his jacket and began to jog down the corridor. He glared up into the lens of the camera.

I'm on my way, you dumb fuckers!

Every spare moment in the last month had been taken up with fitness training. Each night his muscles had ached from the punishing routine he'd put himself through. Now that programme was intensified. He would need to be in perfect physical shape if his bid for freedom was to succeed. As he pushed his work-out schedule to the limit, he turned over every aspect of the plan in his mind, refining it, tightening it. Each day he meticulously noted the daily routine, the movement of the guard patrols, the technical workings of the cell block itself. Under the bedclothes at night he began to prepare the handful of items necessary to the plan.

For most of the day before Day Zero, he rested, worked at keeping his pulse rate slow and even. At six thirty, a tray arrived through the slot in the door. The fare was the same as it had been at every other dinner-time that week – thin soup, cold meat, bread, water, and an orange. He ate slowly. Please God, this is my last supper in this fucking hole, he thought.

At eight fifty he began to stuff his bed with towels, clothes and balls of toilet paper. At nine pm precisely the door to the exercise area slid back, and McKinnon walked out. He moved up and down the narrow area in short sprints the way he had every other day that week.

Exactly sixty minutes later, the bell above him sounded. He walked back to the door, then ducked down, flattening himself into the dark space to the right of the doorway. The surveillance camera was almost above his head. He watched it slowly panning across the corner of the wing. He was satisfied now that this was a blind spot, and, provided he stayed in this one space, the camera could not take him in.

Devereux had said that at least six other prisoners would be exercising in other areas in the wing at this time. At ten pm, the security guard in the central control room would monitor the TV screens that covered the block, to ensure that each man was back in his cell before closing the automatic doors. The lights-out bell would sound ten minutes later. McKinnon's cell was close to the end of the block. The chances were that the guard would check on him last, by which time he would find that Prisoner 685 had already turned in for the night.

McKinnon knew well enough that this was the weakest part of the plan. *If I can just pull this off . . .*

Two minutes later there was a low droning sound. McKinnon's mouth dried. The door to his cell slowly began to close. *Ten minutes to be certain . . . If they decide to check out my cell before lights out, I'm fucked . . .*

The next ten minutes were the longest in McKinnon's life. He crouched low in the shadows and tried to keep his breathing even. Where the hell was that bell?

A discordant clanging shattered the silence and lights across the wing began to go out. As silently as he could, McKinnon stretched himself out in the corner beneath the camera, and began to wait. It would be a long night. If he slept, he risked missing his chance.

Around five forty-five am, the first glimmer of daylight began to show through the plexiglass roof. He scrambled to his feet and worked to get some blood flowing back into his leg muscles.

Soon the visibility was good enough for him to see the metal rail that ran the length of the wing, under the roof high above him. As the camera began to turn away, and the rail moved out of its field of vision, McKinnon stepped forward. In his right hand he had a heavy chunk of rubber cut from the heel of his shoe. Tied around it was one end of the precious fishing line. He swung his arm back and threw it high into the air. It fell short of the rail. He moved back into the shadows and waited for the camera to complete its cycle. He threw again. Again it fell short. The third time, it lifted clear of the rail, drawing the line up over it.

The rubber weight was hanging forty feet above him now in clear view of the camera. Please God, let the guard in central control be scratching his ass or something . . . Anything but watching the screen. With infinite care, McKinnon began to feed the line over the rail. The rubber weight began to descend, but it was already clear that it would come to rest, not in the exercise area, but somewhere to the left, on the roof of one of the other cells. He now began to manoeuvre the line towards him. As soon as the camera turned away again, he gave it a gentle yank and, to his intense relief, the rubber weight fell back into the exercise area. As soon as it was safe, he ran forward and retrieved it.

Back in his hiding place, he lifted his jacket and pulled out a three-foot length of rope made from underwear knotted and plaited together. He gave it one more powerful tug to ensure that it would hold, and then proceeded to attach one end of it to the fishing line, in place of the rubber weight. The other end of the underwear hawser was already attached to 120 feet of line, which he now pulled free of his jacket and allowed to uncoil on to the floor. Then, with his heart thudding in his chest, he settled down to wait.

At exactly six twenty am, there was a low humming sound – as there had been on every Tuesday McKinnon had been at Marston Moor. He turned around and strained to see. An automatic roof-washer appeared from an opening high in the wall that formed the end of the prison block. Large brushes on rotors, fed with water from a tank, spun on either side of a powerful motor seated on the rail. Another motor moved the entire assembly along the track as the brushes cleaned a week of grime off the inside of the plexiglass that formed the roof of the wing.

McKinnon knew he had seconds to act. As soon as the camera turned away, he began to haul the underwear rope up so that it straddled the rail directly above him. When it was in position, he hurriedly knotted one of the trailing lengths of fishing line to a makeshift harness around his waist, then taking care not to pull the rope off the rail, secured the other line to the other side. He gripped the lines that stretched out above him with all his strength and gritted his teeth.

A few seconds later, the travelling roof-washer hit the rope lying across the track. McKinnon knew that there was a risk it would just ride over it, or that it would become trapped inside the contraption and bring the washer to a halt. But his gamble paid off. The washer, heavy with the water it was carrying, began to push the rope along the rail. McKinnon was dragged slowly down the length of the exercise area. Before more than a few seconds had passed, his face was being ground into the partition wall at the end. The line was designed to hold a 300 pound game fish, he told himself, as he felt the breath slowly squeezed out of him, but how much more would it take?

The washer moved inexorably on, down the length of the prison block. The two fishing lines were now slowly drawn over the steel supports that extended from each side of the rail, bending upwards to the framework of the roof to hold the track in position. The supports turned McKinnon's rig into a basic pulley mechanism. Instead of simply pulling the lines forward after it, the movement of the window-washer now caused them to be drawn vertically upwards into the air. McKinnon felt the lines take the strain, felt the pressure on his feet gradually reduce. Above him, the motor groaned as, inch by inch, the mechanism hoisted him up towards the rail. For seven seconds he swung helpless, like some stricken trapeze artiste, in front of the security camera. For seven seconds, he closed his eyes and waited for the alarm bells to rattle into life. Then he was above the camera, only feet now from the rail itself.

The act of drawing the lines over the steel supports, he sensed, was weakening them. He felt them begin to stretch under his weight as he was slowly lifted to the roof. He made a grab for the rail and missed. There was a snap like the breaking of a bow string, as one side of the harness fell free. McKinnon made another desperate try for the rail. His right hand locked around it, the knuckles turning white as he frantically tried to get a grip with his left. The underwear rope was obviously tightly jammed under the washer now as it continued to lift him. There was another percussive twang. As the other line sheared, McKinnon threw himself upwards and locked his left hand around the rail. He felt something in his shoulder muscle give. A knife-like pain spread across his upper back. He closed his eyes and tried to centre his strength.

Then he began to swing. He took a deep breath and lifted his torso on to the rail, hooking his ribcage over it to hold himself steady. Within reach, above him, was a joist, part of the framework of the roof. He jabbed his hand out and clung to it, then pulled himself upwards again until he was standing on the rail. He balanced there in the first sunlight of the day, the interior of the prison wing stretched out beneath him. A guard, patrolling the corridors now, could look up and see him clearly, silhouetted against the light of the sunrise.

'Please God, Devereux got it right,' McKinnon intoned to himself, as he worked his way along the rail until he was directly under one of the motorized skylights. Devereux had been a mechanical engineer until he turned to crime. He had told McKinnon that, because conventional fire escapes could not be incorporated into prison design for security reasons, a number of extra safety factors had to be built in. The authorities had to be satisfied that, in an emergency, prisoners waiting to be led to safety would not die in their cells from smoke inhalation.

Well, we'll find out soon enough, McKinnon thought as he pulled out his matches and unfolded a small square of cotton cloth, part of one of his T-shirts. Steadying himself on the rail, he struck a light and held the flame under the cloth until it started to burn. Then he reached up and held it under one of the roof-mounted smoke sensors. Now the smoke was making his eyes water. And, within seconds, his fingers began to burn. He clenched his teeth and turned away his streaming eyes. Suddenly with a curse he hurled away the smouldering rag. In the same moment, the sprinkler next to the sensor, sent out a swirling gush of water. For a second, McKinnon thought the surge would sweep him off balance. Again he steadied himself, holding his singed fingers under the welcome flow.

Let it happen now! Please God, let it happen now!

McKinnon's heart pounded as his eyes searched the roof for movement.

There was a low hum. Then a grating sound. McKinnon watched a worm-drive system, inches above his head, begin to rotate. Then, just as Devereux had predicted it would, the automatically controlled skylight in front of him began to winch open, to release the smoke the sensor had told the computer system was present in the wing. At the same moment, fire alarms throughout the wing began to hammer out discordantly.

McKinnon mustered the last of his strength and, clinging to the joist above him, swung his legs up into the open frame of the skylight. He reached forward and, with a loud grunt, levered himself out on to the roof, and into the warm morning air.

He stood there for a second, breathing hard, and tried to collect his senses.

Now the hard part begins.

CHAPTER SEVENTEEN

Howard F. Bracknell's eyes snapped open. He shook his head and tried to get his mind to focus on the noise that had wrenched him from sleep. The phone. He switched on the bedroom light and lifted the receiver.

'I'm sorry to call you at this time, Governor. I thought you ought to know that we have a prisoner at large in the complex.' Chief Prison Officer Russell hastily began to update his boss on the events of the last hour.

Bracknell's wife's head emerged from beneath the bed covers. 'What is it, dear?'

The governor put his hand over the mouthpiece. 'A cock-up, by the sound of it . . . All right, Russell, I'll be right there.'

He was halfway into his trousers when the phone rang again. It seemed that the police had just called to say that a woman in a village three miles from the prison had come downstairs to find a man in prison uniform in her kitchen, trying to steal clothes from her washing machine. Apparently, when he saw her, he'd run off towards the woods at the back of her property.

Bracknell hurried out across the compound and watched as four yellow and white Land Rovers sped towards the main gate.

It had always been accepted that, in the event of a

break-out, Marston Moor Prison would be too remote to be able to rely on an immediate police response. So, like Supermaxes in other countries, it was equipped to mobilize its own armed task force. Bracknell had deployed the unit that morning for the first time since the prison's completion, five years before.

How was such a screw-up possible? he asked himself again.

Marston Moor Super Maximum Control Unit had the most sophisticated security system of any prison in Europe. And yet, apart from one fire alarm, none of the security devices had been triggered when McKinnon had broken out. Bracknell ran his fingers through his hair like a comb. How was that possible?

Bracknell had been at the helm from the beginning. The Ravenscourt Group, the corporation that owned and operated Marston Moor, anxious to maximize profits for their shareholders, had put him under pressure from the first day of his appointment to keep staffing levels to an absolute minimum. The current low levels had already attracted considerable criticism from government back-benchers and the media in general, so Bracknell knew well enough that even the smallest security breach would cause the system's detractors to fall instantly on his throat. Everything he and the board had done, over the years, therefore, had been designed to keep the Home Office on low burn, to keep them as far away from Yorkshire as possible.

And now this.

Bracknell watched the Land Rovers snake out of the complex and then turned and began to walk back to the administration building.

This man in particular has to be found.

*   *   *

Ed Sheckler wound the wheel of the Land Rover left with the heel of his hand, pulled up on to the grass verge next to the police squad car, and braked. The three other Land Rovers parked beside him. A lone police officer was stomping up and down, trying to keep warm, near the porch of a cottage in the middle of a row of agricultural dwellings.

Sheckler moved around to the back of the vehicle and collected carbines and flares. Other guards appeared with Doberman dogs, and a procession of eight moved down the pathway to the house.

'What's the story?' Sheckler asked the policeman.

'He's not come back here. There are two of our boys down in the woods.' He motioned behind the cottage. 'You'll have to go through the house.' He rang the doorbell.

'Only two men?'

'There should be about a dozen from B Section moving into the other side of the woods any time now.'

'How's the old girl?'

'Pretty shaken up.'

The door was opened gingerly. A bent women, her white hair still in curlers, stood shaking on the step.

Sheckler took off his cap. 'I'm sorry to bother you. My men and I need to come through.'

She nodded, pulled the door further open and watched the guards and their dogs move down her hallway through to the kitchen.

When she went back in, Sheckler was waiting for her. 'I know you've already spoken to the police, but could you just give me a description of the man you saw here?'

She sat down in a threadbare armchair by the fire. Sheckler saw that she had what looked like brandy in a tumbler on the table beside her. 'Tall . . . black hair

243

with a little grey in it . . . He was dressed in a blue tracksuit, I suppose you'd call it, with a yellow stripe down the leg.'

'Did he say anything to you?'

'Yes . . . he said, "I won't hurt you, I just need clothes."' She allowed herself a little laugh. 'But as I told the other man, mine are all skirts and blouses. When he saw that, he ran away.' She took a sip of the brandy. 'I don't know if this is any help, but I think he might have had a bit of an accent. An American accent.'

McKinnon. Sheckler slung the carbine over his shoulder and made for the back door. 'Thanks, you've been most helpful.'

The woman crossed to the sink, filled an electric kettle with water and plugged it in. Then she went back to the front door and opened it. The police officer outside spun around. 'Would you like some tea and toast?' she enquired.

The policeman rubbed his gloved hands together. 'Well, I wouldn't say no.'

They went through to her kitchen. 'I shall be going to my sister's in a little while,' the woman told him, as she made tea.

'That's the best place for you, love, after a shock like that.'

The woman caught sight of herself in the mirror and noticed her face was still smeared all around with night cream. 'Oh . . . I'll be a few minutes.'

The policeman didn't seem to hear. He buttered his toast and inspected the marmalade. It looked home-made.

Half an hour later, Bracknell and five members of his staff stood around the scale model of Marston Moor Prison that was a permanent fixture in his office.

'And using the fishing line, he winched himself up on to the roof of G Wing.'

'Well, that's blindingly obvious,' Bracknell snapped, walking back to his desk. 'What we need to know is where he went from there.'

'We're still working on that,' Chief Prison Officer Russell said, limply.

'A hundred and ninety-two cameras in this place and you can't tell me!' Bracknell spread his hands and leaned on his desk, and nodded slowly to himself. 'Well, there's very little point in searching the complex for him now. He's obviously got through the security net, and is out there in the woods somewhere.'

Russell shrugged. 'If that old girl is to be believed. I'm sorry to be so dogmatic in the face of the evidence.' The prison officer motioned towards the model. 'But there is no conceivable way he could have crossed to the perimeter fence without tripping something somewhere. I've checked the entire system. Everything's fully operational.'

Bracknell's mind was still chewing over Russell's first remark. *If that old girl is to be believed.* We're scouring the countryside for McKinnon, purely on the say-so of some old pensioner. For all we know, the man she saw was just a regular burglar. His heart missed a beat, and then another. *If she saw anyone at all.* Hell, she could even be in on this. When you get right down to it, anyone in on the scam could have made a phone call like that. But for that call, we would have no reason to believe that McKinnon had penetrated the outer wall. We'd have concentrated purely on searching the prison. He could have been here under our noses all the time. Christ, maybe he still is . . .

'So the only way he could have got out is through

the main gate,' Russell went on. 'Well, the main gate hasn't been opened today. Except for the task force, of course . . .'

The colour began to drain out of Bracknell's face. 'Oh my God,' he said almost to himself. He reached for the phone on his desk. 'Get me Sheckler on the radio. *Now!*'

Half an hour earlier, the old woman had dressed and hurried back down to the kitchen.

'I don't feel safe here,' she told the policeman breakfasting there. She moved over to the window and looked at the neat little garden.

'I can't say as I blame you, love.'

'I shall be leaving for my sister's in Selby as soon as I'm packed.' She could just see an armed man standing at the edge of the woods that ran along the bottom of the property.

'Well, if I'm not needed here any more, I've had another call out. I tell you what, I'll ride with you as far as Frampton. At least it'll save you being stopped at all the roadblocks.'

'Thank you. I'll call you as soon as I'm ready.' She watched as the policeman began to butter another piece of toast and hurried down the hall and out through the front door. She took keys from her pocket, unlocked the garage that adjoined the house, and moved a dark grey Audi out on to the road. Then she got out, and checked the street around her. She was alone.

She moved up to one of the task force Land Rovers and tapped three times on the rear window. After a moment, she moved on to the next and tapped again. At the third jeep, the taps were answered with a faint click from the central locking system. Very slowly the offside passenger door swung open.

The woman had noticed that the normally upright backs of the rear seats had been pushed forward into the horizontal positon, to provide maximum storage space for equipment. With some difficulty, McKinnon now began to extricate himself from the cramped foot-well beneath one of them.

The Audi had already been on the road for half an hour when Bracknell finally figured what had gone down, and called Sheckler, the leader of the task force.

Sheckler was running now, back through the woods towards the house, a line of men close behind him. He pressed the earphone of his radio a little harder into his ear.

'Don't you get it, you cretin!' Bracknell screamed. 'The security alarms never went off because McKinnon never left the place. His fucking girlfriend, or whoever, called us with some cock and bull story, and we fell for it . . . *We took him out ourselves.*' He sounded like he was choking on something. '*Delivered him right to her fucking doorstep!*'

Sheckler stood panting at the back door of the cottage. The door was locked, the lights in the building out. One of his men started to try to force open a downstairs window as the others spread out and began to scour the property. But Sheckler already knew. The birds had flown.

Police Sergeant Gregson took another swig of coffee, and strained to hear what the helicopter pilot was radioing in.

'Yeah, yeah, got it, brown panel truck. Over and out.' He screwed the top back on the flask. 'Okay, Phil, get the dogs.'

Gregson swung his vehicle off the road, and reached

behind him for the stack of orange plastic cones. What a way to start a week, he thought. Perfect. A whole week on nights. The baby howls its head off all day when I'm trying to sleep. And now this, a seven fifteen am call-out. What kind of tenth rate operation were these jerks up at the prison running anyway?

He climbed out, and began to position the cones on the road. A moment later, the constable riding with him joined him with two German Shepherd bitches, their dark faces wreathed in vapour.

The lights of a truck were already visible about three hundred yards to the south. As it approached, a Ravenscourt Group helicopter swung out over a copse of trees and hovered above the road block.

'What do they think we need down here, wet nursing?' the constable snorted.

'Who gives a fuck what they think?' Gregson threw him one of the carbines. He slung it on to his shoulder and, waving his flashlight, moved out into the centre of the road.

The panel truck slowed and came to halt a few yards in front of him. Covered by the constable, Gregson moved cautiously up to the driver's door. 'Police roadblock,' he announced as the window was wound down. He shone the flashlight around the inside of the cabin. The dark-haired woman driver appeared to be alone. 'I'm sorry, but we're going to have to take a look inside the truck.

The woman yawned. 'Help yourself. It's open.'

The constable moved around to the back, opened the two doors and released the dogs, which immediately jumped on to the tail-board. The back of the truck was empty except for some crates of bottles and small boxes. The dogs moved around inside, sniffing the stale

248

air around them, circled a few times and jumped out, even before their handler had given the order.

Gregson examined the underside of the vehicle, then walked back to the driver. 'Okay, on your way. Sorry to have bothered you.'

The woman nodded sleepily, put the truck into gear, and pulled away.

Gregson took a clipboard off the front seat of the Range Rover. 'What make of truck was that then?' he asked as he watched its tail-lights recede into the distance.

'Damned if I know.'

Three miles beyond the roadblock the truck pulled off on to a track that led up into woodland. Beyond was a shallow stream, barely ankle deep where it ran under a low stone bridge. The truck negotiated the bank with little difficulty, and moved under the bridge with inches to spare.

The driver stepped down and listened for a minute. Then she hurried around to the back and climbed in. The stale air had a sweet, slightly nauseous scent to it now. She moved the crates and rolled back the matting that covered the floor. On the left-hand side was a long rectangular lid. She unlocked it and pulled it back.

Joel McKinnon gulped for air like a drowning man. He rose up out of the coffin-shaped recess in the base of the truck like he'd been spring-loaded into it. He stood there breathing deeply for a second till the stench hit him. Then they both climbed out into the stream.

'You might have drilled the air holes a bit closer to my face,' he managed at last, as he tried to massage some feeling back into his legs.

Hannah pulled off the woollen hat that covered her head. The dark curls that framed her face came with it.

She took him in her arms. 'You're damn lucky, you have any holes at all. I'd never used a power drill in my life till then.' She peered up into the night sky. 'My God, Joel, I was never so scared in my whole life.'

He turned his face to hers. 'Listen, it worked. You were marvellous, absolutely marvellous.'

'The ouzo was the only thing I could think of that smells of aniseed. I poured almost half a bottle of it into those mats.' She screwed up her face. 'How people drink that stuff for pleasure, I don't know. Still, it certainly seems to have screwed up the dogs.' She took a map out of her coat and began to check it. 'Okay, we have forty minutes to kill. I need to know where I'm going.'

'I don't know how to thank you,' McKinnon said. 'You've taken incredible risks, and . . .'

'Well, we're not out of this yet. Nor will we be for some time. Thank me when we are.'

He sat down on the bank. 'I don't know of anyone else on the planet who could have pulled all this together in the circumstances.'

She shook her head, still amazed at the events of the last few hours. 'No, there's no one else crazy enough. If anyone had told me how I'd be living this last year of my life . . . I see sentinels in my dreams, on every street I walk down. Now I suppose I'm gonna see British policemen too.'

'Tell me about what happened to you.'

'If you'd asked me two months ago, I couldn't have told you. My head was full of a thousand images, all scrambled together, set neither in time or place . . .'

She told him a little about her time in the Apostles' commune – she still remembered nothing of the actual kidnap itself – and about how she'd ultimately been

250

transferred to an open order community, centred in the brownstone in NYC.

'One morning I went to the supermarket and they were playing this song; "Knights in White Satin" by the Moody Blues. I remembered then that I'd had it on a CD . . . in some other life. And I had this . . . this compulsion to go home – wherever that was – and play it. It was bizarre. There was this kinda battle going on inside me. One part of me was pushing me homeward, the other pulling me away.'

She told him about the taxi ride to an address that suddenly surfaced in her mind, and how the concierge had paid the fare, and let her into her apartment.

'It was the strangest experience, standing there in this place that I knew had to be mine, but remembering almost nothing of the life I'd lived there.'

She explained the significance of 'Knights in White Satin'.

'Some part of my mind was trying to snap me back into reality, using my diary to do it. Every night of my life I used to sit at my PC and write up the day's events, my feelings about them, anything of note. It was all still there, McKinnon, on the backup disc disguised as a pop CD. Fiske's people got everything else, but they missed that. I knew sentinels had to be looking for me and that the first place they'd check would be my apartment. The only other name and address I could call to mind was that of an old college friend I have in Connecticut. I got the doorman to lend me some cash and I took off there. My friend pretty much saved my sanity, Joel.

'I read for days. Sometimes it was like what I read had happened to someone else. At first, I had almost no memory of being a part of the events I'd written about, they stirred no emotions in me. But, little by little, the fog in my head began to clear. I'd glimpse a face, sense a reaction, relive part of some moment that, until then, had seemed never to have happened. There was some mail in my mailbox, and a few messages from friends and relatives on my answering machine. That's when I realized I must have been away for some time.'

'Nothing from me or my lawyers?'

'No, not a thing.'

McKinnon shook his head. 'So where did everyone think you were?'

'Those I dared to call thought I'd been in Europe.' Hannah stared into space, still trying to rationalize it all. 'It's all so crazy. Most of them had had cards from me, Joel.' She looked at him. 'I mean, actually written by me. From Byelorussia, Siberia, other places in the SIS. Somehow Fiske's people had gotten me to write them.'

'The Nazis had Jews in some of the concentration camps send cards like that to relatives. "Weather great, happy and well, wish you were here." If they could get that together fifty years ago, it certainly wouldn't be beyond Fiske's capabilities.'

'Yes, but those Jewish people were conscious of what they were doing. Very frightened, yes, but . . . Anyway, it was around then that I called NBS.'

'Thank God you did.'

'When I first mentioned your name, it was like I'd said a dirty word. Then I got through to the girl who'd been your assistant.'

'Laurie.'

'And that's when I heard about what had happened to you. When she said you'd been sent to Marston Moor, I understood how much danger you were in.'

'You must have been in a fair amount yourself.'

'I was desperate to see you, and I knew I had to get

252

you moved to another jail pronto – I couldn't just leave you there for Alderbrook's people to go to work on – but I had no clear plan until your letter arrived. God, I was relieved when that came.' She smiled at him. 'I cried, went nuts. From that point on I started putting things together. I had my married sister send me her passport – we look very similar – and took the first flight I could to England.'

'I'll make this up to you,' he said. She looked pale and tired now. He cradled her head against his chest. 'I don't know how or when, but I will.'

'When we've untangled this mess. When we've got what we need to convince the British authorities that Fiske had you set up. When we've enough to get him and his whole obscene coven closed down for good.'

'That's not gonna be too easy to do with us both looking over our shoulders all the time.'

She opened the passenger-side door, pulled out a sports bag, and tossed it to him. 'Well, we won't get anywhere hiding out in some God-forsaken corner of the globe. I know that, right know, that would be the sensible thing to do. But, as hard as it's gonna be, we're going to have to confront this thing, get as close to it as we can.'

McKinnon pulled clothes from the bag, and began to change. 'So where are we headed now?'

She looked up at him. 'Our ultimate objective is to get to Muddy.'

McKinnon looked up. 'He's okay?'

'He's fine. He's an old hand at this. He knows how to cover his ass. His cholesterol level will get him long before any sentinels do. When they came nosing around, he took off to his place on Fishers Island. I had a helluva job finding him, but that's another story. He's gonna help us, Joel. He takes the view we're all in this together now.'

Do I tell him about Jerry Tyrell? she wondered. No, not yet.

'Connecticut seems a very long way from here right now.' McKinnon thought for a moment. 'I take it you got my passport?'

She unzipped one of the pockets of the sports bag. 'I faxed the part of the letter you sent, from you to your ex-wife, to her office in Vermont, and made the follow-up call like you said to. She wasn't overly communicative, but the stuff arrived at my place about two weeks later.'

'Thank God for that.'

McKinnon had been made to surrender his US passport – records seemed to show it was the only one he'd ever applied for – when he was first arrested. The slightly faded UK passport Hannah handed him now had lain forgotten in a packing case in his ex-wife's attic.

He opened it. The photo inside showed him with black hair – in reality, it was peppered with grey – and a moustache, but gave his name as 'Mackenzie', the name he'd taken legally as his own, following his father's conviction, and discarded only when he'd become a US citizen. No reference had been made to this episode of his life during his trial, and he was fairly certain that neither the UK nor the US authorities had any knowledge that such a document existed.

McKinnon turned to the validation page and took a deep breath – the passport was valid for a further three years.

Several times in the previous year he'd promised his ex-wife that he'd arrange to have the packing case shipped from Vermont to NYC, but he was now profoundly grateful that he'd put no such plan in hand until now.

There was the distant hack of a helicopter. Hannah checked her watch.

After a moment, McKinnon said, 'I wonder if you have any idea the trouble you've got yourself into on my account.'

She strained to hear. 'I'm starting to. The agency I rented the cottage from and the guy who sold me the truck won't be able to give the police a great deal, that's one good thing.'

When the helicopter had passed over, McKinnon asked, 'So, where to right now?'

'The petrol-chemical complex at the docks in Hull. There's a low customs presence there. Most of the tankers that dock there go back empty with just skeleton crews. There's always spare cabin space.'

'How do you know that they'll have anything to do with us?'

She got to her feet. 'You're not the only one with friends in low places, Joel. When I was in Riga, in the Baltic, following Fiske's evangelical circus, I hung out with some of the riggers. A lot of them had worked as merchant seamen, mainly on tankers. They told me that Latvian ships had a good thing going all around this part of the world. It seems that the authorities here are only concerned with trying to stop people getting into the country illegally, not out. They let immigration the other end deal with that. For cash dollars, most Latvian ships will take anyone who wants to go.'

'If the riggers told you all this, maybe they told Fiske's people too,' McKinnon said.

'Unlikely. For starters, they thought the Jesus freaks were straight from the planet Whacko. Not one of them spoke a word of English, and no one I saw amongst the Apostles group spoke anything resembling the Latvian

255

dialect – I do. I'm not called Rostov for nothing. So unless they all communicated in semaphore, I think you can safely discount that one.'

'Point taken.'

'There's no evidence that UK customs are wise to the scam yet. I did some serious scouting last week, and I'm confident that the route is viable.'

'Okay. So how does that get us to the US?'

'Most of the Latvian boats make a stop-over in Rotterdam. From there, Mr Mackenzie, I suggest we take a regular flight to Montreal, hire a car and head south.'

He put up a hand. 'I'm not saying another word.'

'Come on, we'd better get going.' They went around to the back of the truck. 'We better just hope that none of the Hull security people have seen a Honda Sahara either.'

They climbed into the back. 'Well, those cops we ran into certainly hadn't,' McKinnon said.

'Well, there's only five in the country. So unless the next lot we hit did a stint in Rwanda or Somalia or somewhere, it's not likely.'

McKinnon lowered himself back into the concealed spares storage area that was a standard feature of the vehicle, designed as it was for arduous assignments in the most remote regions of the globe.

I wonder if they've found the Audi yet? Hannah wondered as she moved the truck out on to the road. There is the risk that, once they put this whole thing together, the cop who rode with me as far as Frampton will remember the licence plate number. If he does, all he'll ever know is that the last owner bought it for cash at auction using a false name. And, if he gets really busy, he'll find out that they dumped it in a derelict barn south of the village ten minutes after he got out.

CHAPTER EIGHTEEN

Senator Carl Hollingsworth looked up from his empty brandy snifter and watched his children playing on the wide expanse of lawn that ran down from a large colonial-style property. Then he turned in his seat to study his wife as she clipped sprigs of the bougainvillea from the profusion of blooms that grew around the French doors.

Until yesterday, he thought, I had everything life could offer: a beautiful family, a fine home, friends, a great career, more influence in the government of the most powerful nation on earth than I could ever have dreamt. But now, it seems, I have something else too: pancreatic cancer. The doctor says that if they'd caught it earlier, something might have been done. But as it is . . . I have six months, a year at best. Now, I'll never see my children grow up, never grow old with the woman I love.

How do I tell them? The senator fought to control the feeling of hopelessness that began to engulf him again.

Right now, I would give anything to make this dreadful thing go away.

His mobile phone rang. The call was from an old friend, one of the two people he'd told. 'Look Carl, this may sound like a long shot, but I wouldn't be calling if I didn't think this was worth looking into. Remember Steve Wallis at the State department? He was diagnosed as having the same thing as you, two years ago. Same prognosis too. Apparently, a pal of his put him on to some private clinic in South Georgia. They've made some kind of breakthrough in that area. There has to be something in it. Hell, look at Wallis now! He beat the crap out of me at squash less then a week ago. I think you should talk to him. I mean, what harm can it do?'

Elaine Brody walked out into the warm afternoon air, crossed the concourse of the Sanderville Business Center, and silently thanked God. The long battle with her estranged parents, to get access to the money her aunt had left her, was nearly over, so her attorney said.

How dare they interfere, she thought again. If I want to pay it all over to my church, it's nobody's business but mine!

She took the elevator to the underground parking lot. Now she could relax a little. She might even enjoy the drive home. This expedition into the Outland had been her first in ten months. She had been a member of the Apostles of Christ for almost seven years and had built a new life in the closed order commune in North Carolina. The trauma of her exit from her family's home in Walnut Creek, California, was just a memory. Now the worries of the last few months could be forgotten too.

She crossed the lot and made her way over to a Cherokee jeep. As she turned the key in the lock, she heard a voice behind her.

'Don't turn around, 'Laine, It's me . . . Wes.'

She froze.

'Just carry on with what you're doing. Wind down the window and make like you're checking a map or something.'

For a moment, Elaine was too shaken to do anything. Then she let herself in to the jeep, lowered the window, and made a fairly unconvincing play of checking the money in her purse. Now, in her peripheral vision, she could see part of Wes Tyrell's face in the shadows by the wall.

'I've been worried sick about you . . . Where have you been?' she said.

'On the move.'

'Do you think we're being watched?'

'It's possible. Look, I need to speak with you.'

'Where?' she asked, risking a glance at him.

'Take the freeway out to the airport. There's a shopping mall about seven miles past it.'

'Yeah, I know it. The Oakbridge Center.'

'Park there, and window-shop for about twenty minutes. Then go to the second floor of Nieman Marcus . . .' For the next minute he gave her explicit instructions. As soon as he was sure that she'd understood, he jumped the low wall behind him and disappeared into the maze of parked cars.

Elaine moved the jeep out on to the exit ramp, her mind racing. She'd met Wes three years before, when he'd come to the North Carolina commune to visit his brother who worked with her at the central database there. She'd dined with the boys that evening in the refectory, and had taken them back to her apartment for coffee. Wes had played the guitar late into the night, sung everything from Tina Turner to Billy Joel. She'd often thought since that, had they both been living in the Outland, they might have slept together that first night. But in Apostles communes, there were strict rules regarding such matters, and it had been six months until she had visited him at the commune in Georgia, where he was based, and stayed the weekend.

Any hopes Elaine might have had of them settling

into some regular routine had been dashed when it was announced that the 300-strong Evangelical Army, of which Wes's band was a key part, would be taking to the road for a year. They had stayed in touch as best they could by phone and letter, and had enjoyed one last weekend together before the brothers' defection. Elaine had known for a long time her lover did not share her unquestioning devotion to the movement, but she'd not realized until his return from the world tour what an effect his exposure to the Outland had had on the little belief he had left. She'd been very shocked when he'd told her, that final weekend, of his intention to leave with his brother. She'd lain awake for nights, torn between her loyalty to her lover and her allegiance to her religious family – she'd thought many times of calling her divisional councillor and tipping him off – and had castigated herself repeatedly for her lack of faith when she finally elected to keep silent until the brothers had gone.

When Sentinel-in-Chief Pieter Kleig began to question all those who'd known the brothers, Elaine began to worry that her past relationship with Wes might affect her position as a data processor at the base. But, when she was interviewed, it had turned out that the sentinels knew nothing of that last weekend the lovers had spent together, and appeared to assume that the relationship had petered out the year before. It seemed too that Jerry was the main focus of their enquiries, and she had been able to convince her interviewer that she had known him only as a fellow member of staff.

In the months that followed, she began to accept that she would never see Wes again. But now her heart and mind raced, as they had that first time, more that a year before. If God had not wanted me to love this man, she thought, as she changed lanes on the freeway, then he would not have given me this great a passion. Wes returning to my life is a sign. This is my opportunity to bring him back to the Apostles' abiding love. But even as that idea crystallized, she knew that, in truth, it was not a mission in the name of the Almighty that was driving her to this assignation, but a warm ache in her loins.

She turned into the parking lot of the shopping mall, parked and crossed slowly to the Saks franchise. She found it hard to believe the sentinels might still be watching her, if they had ever watched her at all. Still, Wes had thought it was a real enough danger, and he was the one out there living on the edge. Best do as he said.

Certainly no one followed her across the lot. She pretended to busy herself at the perfume counters, even tried some new fragrance that had just hit the market. If she was to sin today – to make love with a man who was now deemed beyond the pale by her religious family – what was a little vanity along the way? And if Wes had been around women on the outside all these months, might he not expect her to smell as they did?

Twenty minutes later, she crossed to Nieman Marcus, took the elevator to the second floor, and then made for the ladies' room. Instead of going in, she moved beyond it, climbed over a barrier marked 'staff only', and took the stairs beyond, to the staff parking lot below.

She pushed through the hedge that marked the boundary of the mall. In front of her was the rear entrance of a Holiday Inn Hotel.

'It's me. Elaine. I'm sorry I'm late,' she said. The apology was the agreed code to signify that she was alone.

The door of 526 opened a few inches and Wes peered cautiously out.

'Before you ask, no, I wasn't followed.'

261

He looked at her directly for the first time. 'You wouldn't know if you were being followed, believe me. I just hope we've managed to throw them off your scent for a while.'

She moved forward, and he took her in his arms. Her breath was heavy on his neck. He took her chin and kissed her.

'How's Jerry?' she asked.

'I thought you might know. The sentinels took him, months ago . . . I've been out of my mind with worry. Obviously, you haven't seen or heard from him either.'

'No, nothing. Poor Jerry . . . So you're on your own out there.'

'You make it sound like the Gobi Desert. I have some friends. They've been very good to me, as a matter of fact.' A mirthless smile played at the edge of his mouth. 'I take it Fiske has had me excommunicated from the church,' he said sarcastically.

She nodded. She looked as though she was going to say something, then decided against it. She crossed to the minibar in the corner of the room and took out some Cokes.

The supreme arrogance of the man! Wes felt a consuming anger rising in him again. How could I have spent the better part of my life actually believing that he was empowered by the Almighty to decide who should get to speak to him and who shouldn't? If he's harmed Jerry, I'll kill him. If it takes the rest of my life . . .

Elaine passed him a Coke. 'But I'm sure if he thought you'd . . .'

'I don't give a damn what he thinks any more, Elaine. I know your feelings, but just try to respect the decision I've taken, and understand that what I've done is the right thing for me.'

262

'But *The Lost Gospel* says . . .'

He put his finger gently on her lips.

Her eyes brimmed with tears. 'If you don't come back to God, then how are we to have any future?'

'We'll find a way.'

She embraced him. Then, without a word, they undressed.

Wes's body seemed leaner to her, tauter. Was it possible that life in the Outland was agreeing with him? She wondered, as his hands began to move over her breasts and down her stomach. She fought hard to relax. There was an air of unreality about the whole moment. For many months she'd struggled to resolve the unresolvable: Wes was out of her life now, a pariah in the eyes of everyone but her. She must forget him, she had no other choice . . .

And yet here they were, making love as if nothing had changed.

Let him love you. She felt his stubbled jaw against her inner thigh. Let him love you, there may never be another time.

Max Marshak held the sensor at arm's length and, for the tenth time in the last hour, made a slow 360 degree turn. The illuminated arrow on the circular display panel floated around in a detached kind of way, like the needle of a compass at the North Pole.

'Sonofabitch!'

He turned around and surveyed the row of shops behind him. It was like she'd evaporated into the air. The micro-transmitter couldn't be on the blink already. It was an updated model, injected during her last medical. Maybe someone had tipped her off about it, maybe she'd even had it removed.

Marshak tried to calm down. More likely she'd found

a double somewhere and had moved out of range of the sensor, too fast for it to be able to track her. Marshak switched channels. The needle on the sensor swung immediately to the south east. Well, the Cherokee's still where she left it, outside Saks. And the bug is still in place under the driver's side front wing. Maybe Tyrell has finally come out of the woodwork. Could be he's picked her up from here and they've taken off together.

He wiped the sweat out of his eyes. There'd been three defections from the North Carolina commune already this month. If we lose another one . . . Correction: if I lose another one . . . another data processor . . .

Following the defection of the Tyrell brothers, Kleig had issued a directive that sentinels should, until further notice, monitor every move made off-commune by the data-processing staff. To make this practical, they and other cult members working in classified areas had, as their annual medicals came up, been implanted with micro-transmitters, developed from those used by zoologists to tag wildlife. The commune doctor had developed a technique that ensured the bug, no larger than a pin-head, could be secretly put in place during a standard blood test.

Until an hour ago, Marshak had treated this latest assignment as one more mind-numbingly dull exercise born of Kleig's paranoia. Jerry Tyrell was dead, for fuck's sake! And Wes was a smart kid, his file had made that clear enough. He wouldn't go within ten miles of the Brody girl. Now, as Marshak searched the mall yet again, he revised that view: he wouldn't go near the Brody girl, unless he had all the angles covered.

Check out the Cherokee. If that produces nothing, best radio in for back-up, he told himself as he crossed the parking lot. Okay, so if she is with Tyrell, where's the first place they're gonna make for . . .

He stopped, and turned around slowly. What the fuck is happening to my brain? he asked himself. All this sitting around is making me daffy. He stared up at the Holiday Inn on the next lot.

Wes Tyrell lay with his eyes closed, listening. Elaine was in the shower. She was singing a ballad by Mariah Carey.

He moved silently from the bed, and checked the bathroom door: it was pulled to. Her purse lay on the minibar. He lifted it carefully, and searched for her address book. In the back, scrawled at different angles, were telephone numbers: ones that had been his when he was on tour with the Evangelical Army. He'd seen them there months before. On the facing page there had always been a list of eight-digit numbers. Most had now been crossed out in pen. Beside them, new numbers had been written in. Wes took paper from the desk drawer, checked for the sound of running water again, and then quickly copied the new numbers down.

There was no good way to say goodbye, he had always known that. When she asked about meeting again, he knew he would have to lie. He knew, too, that she'd see through that. Was this the cowardly way or the brave way? he asked himself as he struggled into his clothes.

He opened the door of the room with infinite care, turned down the corridor and was gone.

Two minutes later, Elaine called from the bathroom, 'Can you call up for some iced tea, babe?' She gave her hair one last rub with the towel. 'And maybe a sandwich too . . . Wes?' She opened the bathroom door.

'Wes, where are you?' She ran to the door of the room and opened it.

A fist slammed into her face, sending her reeling.

'I believe you spoke to the senior consultant at the Highlands Clinic this morning,' the attorney said.

Senator Hollingsworth shifted uneasily in his chair. 'Yes, this morning. He told me he'd been though my medical records, and – there are no guarantees of course – but he felt that, provided no time was lost, there was an eighty per cent chance of inducing a lasting remission.'

'Well that's absolutely wonderful!'

Hollingsworth's eyes were large with barely concealed fear. 'I can't tell you how I felt when I heard. I've been through . . . hell. I was dreading telling my family. Now at least I can give them a little hope. Anyway, the clinic said I'd have to talk things over with you first.'

The lawyer walked over to a table in the corner of his office and poured them coffee. 'Yes, well, there are a few matters we need to discuss.'

'Money.'

'The treatments aren't cheap. Your medical insurance should cover the fees but, if it doesn't, I don't imagine they'll present too much of a problem to a man of your means. No, there are concerns of another kind. These treatments are fully developed, but not yet available to the general public. And won't be for another year or two. The only hospital carrying them out is the clinic in South Carolina.'

'I can be down there tomorrow,' Hollingsworth said.

'I don't think you quite understand. The Highlands is a private clinic. It's owned by a religious sect. Beds are only available to their members.'

'I'm sure they'll make an exception in my case.'

266

'They make no exceptions,' the attorney said.

Hollingsworth's brow furrowed. 'What are you saying? I'd have to join the sect to get treated?'

The attorney sipped his coffee. 'Well, not to put too fine a point on it, yes, that's exactly what I'm saying.'

'Good God man, I'm a practising Methodist. My whole family is . . .'

'I'm just telling you the position as I understand it.'

'What is this sect?'

The attorney paused. 'It's called the Apostles of Christ.'

'The Apostles . . .' Hollingsworth stood up, swaying slightly. 'They're an appalling bunch! My God. If you think . . .'

'I can't comment on what you've heard.' The attorney's voice was matter-of-fact. 'All I know is that they've spent tens of millions of dollars developing treatments that are years ahead of anything else currently available.' He lifted the phone to his secretary. 'Still, if you feel that strongly about it, I'm sure you have other courses of action open to you, so I suggest you . . .'

'I don't.' Hollingsworth reached for the chair to steady himself. 'You know very well I don't.' He sat down slowly. His voice began to shake. 'I'm a senator, for Christ's sakes. Can you imagine for one minute what would happen if . . .?'

'No one is suggesting that this would be something you'd need to go shouting about. If you wanted it that way, no one who is important to you need have any idea that you're involved with the sect.'

Now his eyes were beseeching the lawyer. 'Look . . . Maybe there's a way I could arrange for some kind of . . . donation to be made, some kind of . . .'

'This isn't about money. It's about trust, understanding.

An understanding they'll need to have with you before they take you as one of their own, share with you what they have to share.'

Hollingsworth's eyes narrowed slightly. 'Are you a member of these . . . Apostles?'

'What I'm a member of, Senator Hollingsworth, is entirely a matter for me.' Now there was a coldness in his voice. 'Whether you join this outfit is entirely a matter for you. It's of no importance to me whether you do or not. Nor should it be to anyone else.'

'Are you saying that if I don't join, they'll just let me die?'

'I'm saying that if you don't join, they don't believe you can be cured. I'm not suggesting there's any medical basis for that, but they take the view that recovery is only ultimately possible if God wills it to be so.'

The corner of the senator's mouth lifted into a mirthless smile. 'And he only looks favourably upon those who accept the true faith, is that it?'

The attorney shrugged. 'It may sound hokey to you and me, but it's not a lot different to what Catholic missions have been selling around the world for centuries.'

There was a long silence in the room. The only sound was the ticking of the clock on the mantelpiece. Then Hollingsworth said wearily, 'What would I have to do?'

'Speak to them yourself. Go through some kind of initiation process, I should imagine. Nothing too strenuous. It could be done over time. They might even agree to let you do it back to back with the treatment.' The lawyer's eyes met with the senator's. 'To be frank with you, at this point, what have you got to lose?'

'My integrity,' Hollingsworth said softly.

'Is your integrity going to provide for your wife, put your kids through college when you're dead?'

Hollingsworth put his head in his hands and sighed. There were months of pain in that sigh.

'Who is it I have to call?'

The Apostles commune in North Carolina was now the movement's largest: 9,500 people were housed in an area of prime farmland, covering an area of close to fifteen thousand acres.

A fifty-acre lot acquired on the western boundary in the mid eighties had been designated the sentinels' headquarters and training facility. The timber-framed building that had once stood at its centre had been replaced with offices and accommodation blocks. The only indication that the property had once been a flourishing dairy farm was the low-built brick milking shed that stood on a stretch of wasteland behind them. It was to here that most errant cult members were brought for 're-education'. Few who had reason to be on the lot had any illusions as to what that involved, and most kept clear of the place, closing their eyes and their ears to the late night arrivals and departures that indicated that it was again in use.

Fifty yards beyond, at the eastern boundary of the lot, stood three unpretentious clapboard houses, the largest of which was home to Pieter Kleig.

Before Kleig's appointment, sentinel commanders had been recruited from within the ranks of the cult itself. But by the late eighties, Fiske knew that future security chiefs would be called upon to implement directives of a more radical nature than any demanded of their predecessors, and that what he needed was an objective professional, one who would discharge, without misgivings, assignments of a kind which ran directly counter to the sect's teaching. Pieter Kleig had proved to be just such a man.

The South African had been given authority to build

up a small élite unit of field operatives within the sentinel force itself. This was made up of those drawn from the more extreme element within the sect – men and women who could be counted on to be efficient enough in the field but who, for the most part, lacked leadership qualities – and a few specialist outsiders. The rationale for recruiting them was straightforward enough: many assignments required that the sentinels involved have an extensive understanding of Outlanders and their environment, a qualification which ruled out most second-generation cult members, who Fiske considered the most reliable of the youth constituent.

Kleig sat at the desk in his office and studied the most recent developments in the investigation into the bombing at the South Carolina mansion. He chain-smoked as he read the Outlander unit's report that had come with the post that morning.

Not surprisingly, Fiske had held him personally responsible for the security breaches that had made the outrage possible, and made it very clear that the South African's whole future with the movement rested on his exposing those behind it.

Over the last months, Kleig had spread a broad net, deployed all the facilities at his disposal, but had, so far, failed to establish a single solid lead.

The report on the investigation into the previous year's incident at the Falk Pharmaceutical Research Center in Pittsburgh made little better reading. It seemed an early breakthrough had now stalled completely.

Kleig had seen to it that all traces of the incident had been erased and the security guards who'd been involved had been carefully briefed.

Staff employed in the division of the facility where Corrigan had worked were told, in a confidential memo sent to each, that he'd stolen valuable data, relating to products under development there, and had disappeared with it. The police had so far failed to locate him or the material. The memo stated there was evidence to suggest that Corrigan intended to sell the data on the open market, and that once word of this began to get out, there was a possibility that they, as employees of Falk, might be approached for information regarding his whereabouts. Should that happen, they were urged to inform a member of the management immediately.

Kleig had set this initiative in motion, as much as anything, for the benefit of the local police, and, to a lesser degree, to test the validity of his own cover-up exercise. He was, consequently, more than a little surprised when a senior manager at the research facility called him some months later to report on an interview he'd just had with a laboratory assistant employed there.

The girl was concerned about some questions she'd been asked by the man she was dating. It seemed that he'd picked her up at a local singles bar, a few nights before. She'd had no reason to doubt he was anything other than what he claimed to be – a Coors Beer representative – until he started asking her about Corrigan. Plainly anxious to further herself with the company, she'd gone through his wallet when he'd been in the shower after a love-making session, and had made notes on what she'd found.

Sentinels soon established that most of the documentation was phoney. But a ticket from a dry-cleaner in nearby Altoona, soon provided them with the lead they needed. When lover boy returned to get his clean clothes, they traced him to his real place of work – the branch of the Cordell Detective Agency in the town.

State-of-the-art Korean surveillance equipment was

eventually able to penetrate the office's security screen, but failed to reveal the identity of the agent's client. It seemed that he'd either already reported in to them, and was awaiting further development on the case before opening up lines of communication again, or was contacting them by some undiscovered means.

Plans to break into the agency's premises had been dropped the previous week for the simple reason that their office was located almost opposite the local police precinct.

Kleig closed the report. Well, if the private eye needs a new development on the case to prod him into calling his client, then we shall give him one, he thought.

He began to put together a plan aimed at breathing some life back into the enquiry.

An hour later, the phone on his desk rang. The call was from the re-education unit. It seemed the Brody girl had finally confessed to seeing Wes Tyrell at the Holiday Inn near the commune, and she had, in all probability, allowed computer access codes to fall into his hands.

Kleig put down the phone for a moment. Of one thing he was certain: Fiske must never know. The Sentinel-in-Chief was already in little doubt that, were it not for the fact that his special talents were so essential to the upcoming promotional campaign, he would have been kicked off the lot weeks ago. If Fiske was to learn there'd been yet another crucial leak . . . The girl would disappear. The disappearance would be put to good use. There would be rumours, nothing more. Rumours that would ensure that other data processors on the lot would act a little more prudently than she had done.

'Bring her here,' the operative at the re-education unit was told. Kleig hung up. Tonight I shall have a little company, he thought.

He lived alone in the house. He'd realized long ago that he was incapable of cohabiting peaceably with anyone. Back in Johannesburg a string of incidents, involving attacks on female partners and other women, had been successfully buried by the South African Police. His records made no mention of any impropriety. But in America, he'd known from the beginning that he would have to learn to curb the bouts of pathological violence that periodically engulfed him, or end his days choking up his lungs in a gas chamber, or some such.

These days he targeted only those the cult considered beyond the pale, those who would be little missed inside or outside its boundaries. Alone in the cellar of the house with them, he'd act out the savage sexual fantasies that haunted his dreams. A handful of the girls returned to the commune. The vast majority ended up interred in the humus and sedimentation tanks of the sewage treatment works that served the sect.

Kleig watched, now, from the window of his office, as a panel truck pulled up outside the property, saw the driver hurry around to the rear doors and unlock them.

Elaine Brody stepped down and eyed Kleig's house dully for a moment, then a hand touched her shoulder. Her pale face and sleep-starved eyes registered nothing. She trudged wearily forward.

Kleig walked to the front door to meet her, and felt his penis begin to stiffen in his pants.

CHAPTER NINETEEN

McKinnon scratched at the half inch of stubble covering his chin and studied the island, visible now across half a mile of flat water. He sniffed the Chardonnay air.

'After Marston Moor, that motel in Montreal seemed like a real good place to be. But this . . . Sweet Jesus, Hannah, no one will ever know how good it is to be out of there.'

She put an arm in his and studied his face. 'Yer know, I think I'm gonna like you with a beard.'

'It's just as well.' They watched as the jetty came into view, and a guy of about twenty, his long blond hair tied back in a ponytail, jumped over the side of the ferry and secured the bow.

Hannah put on her rucksack and reached for a totebag. 'We could have holed up somewhere more remote, where we're less likely to be recognized, but Muddy's here and I thought . . .'

'Fishers Island is fine. How the hell did you find Muddy? You never did tell me. I mean, if the sentinels couldn't get a fix on him . . .'

'It took some doing, believe me. I knew that was the reason Fiske's people let me go, to lead them to him, so I had to tread very carefully. I was pretty sure that no normal means of communication was likely to make him break cover, so I finally convinced Laurie that I was on your side, and wanted to help – good kid that – and she admitted that she had some e-mail addresses hidden away, for some of your "shady contacts" she called them. When she said e-mail it stirred something in my memory . . .'

'About how hackers communicate in Klingon.'

'Right. Muddy said his codename in English was: "May your Blood Scream".' She laughed. 'I went out and bought a book called, *How to Speak Klingon*, and translated a letter I'd written to him using his code name – don't ask me to pronounce it.'

'And he responded.'

'Uhuh. But he was very nervous. He was certain at first that I was working for Fiske, or the cops, or the FBI. I think when he realized that I just wanted to see you out of jail and the Apostles brought to account for what they'd done, to all of us, he started to soften.'

'Well, I guess he has as much interest as we do in seeing that happen now,' McKinnon said.

'I think he takes the view that the sooner we have something on Fiske's set-up that can be handed to the authorities and made public, the sooner the focus will be turned away from him, and he can go home.'

McKinnon picked up the backpack, which was packed with clothes Hannah had spent the day before buying for him, and they went ashore.

'I wasn't too struck with your hacker friend, when I first met him,' Hannah said.

'I wouldn't go so far as to call him a friend.'

'Well, some of his personal habits grossed me out, but I guess he's grown on me. Hell, Joel, we turned his whole life upside down. He's been incredible about it, about everything.'

Muddy Harbin was waddling down the boardwalk towards them. His pudgy face, smeared all around with the ice cream he was eating, lit up into a smile. At least McKinnon took it as a smile. With Muddy, you could never be certain.

'Christ, the beard, the backpack . . . All you need is the guitar.'

McKinnon took his hand. 'Great to see you, Mud. Hannah says you've been great, very supportive.'

Muddy shook his head. 'I had a fair idea of the risks I was taking. We've all got ourselves in a mess – you worst of all – so we gotta help each other now, right? Get these bastards off our backs now, and nail them once and for all.' He turned to Hannah. 'A lot has been happening since we last spoke. First off, the Tyrell kid came through.'

Hannah's face brightened. 'He got the new codes?'

'Uhuh. Enough to get us started again. Getting back into the holy of holies, though, was a piece of brilliance of my own making.'

The clapboard house Muddy owned on the south side of Fishers Island, off the coast of Connecticut, was much like a dozen others they passed on their walk there, except that his badly needed a paint job, and the window frames replacing. He produced a small black box about the size of a TV remote control unit from his jeans pocket, and proceeded to wave it around the open-plan living room.

'All but one of the codes Wes Tyrell turned up were useless. Our religious friends have changed their encryption system. They're now using a thing called PGP: Pretty Good Privacy. If you hack into their database without the key, all you get on the screen is a load of gobbledegook.'

'So how did you get in?' McKinnon asked

'By sheer genius . . . Oh, and by having a brother-in-law with the Software Surgery. Ever hear of that outfit?'

277

They hadn't.

Satisfied that the area that was now home to much of the equipment McKinnon had last seen in the hacker's New York apartment was still free from bugs and surveillance devices, Muddy got down on his hands and knees, and began to rummage around inside the fireplace.

'The one file I could get into can't be of any great importance to Fiske, because it wasn't encrypted. Neither is it to us, except that it allowed me to plague the bastards.'

'You planted a virus in the system,' McKinnon said. 'Jesus.'

'Yeah, a real virulent sonofabitch. That took the smile off their faces, I can tell you. They had data evaporating, literally falling off the screens, before their eyes. They shut down the base, to the extent they could, and they did just what I wanted them to. In fact, the only thing they could do.'

'They called the Software Surgery,' Hannah said. 'Uhuh.'

Hannah and McKinnon watched Muddy's elephantine rear twitch around for a minute, and then waited while he coughed soot out of his lungs. In his left hand now was a plastic bag from which he produced a computer disc.

'They're based in Raleigh, North Carolina. They're the only outfit in the country who run an emergency antidote service that could handle something on that scale. They got busy – you can't hang around with something like that – and whadda you know, it just so happened that my brother-in-law was the one who could save the day.'

Muddy loaded the disc into the Apple Mac set up on the dining-room table. 'See, this voice spoke to him from heaven – well, from here actually – and told him exactly the kind of virus he was dealing with. And while he was

278

cleaning up the mess, and while the encryption system was down, he put me on-line to the whole fucking works.'

McKinnon chuckled. 'Muddy, you're a winner.'

'Naturally, I went for the personal files, the medical and pharmaceutical stuff. It's not all stored together and, given the time available, I just had to get what I could get.' Muddy's fingers rattled over the keyboard for a moment. 'This is some of the personnel file, detailing the membership of the cult. I put the hypertext to work, and it came up with these.'

Hannah and McKinnon studied the list displayed on the screen.

'As you can see, all these guys are heavy hitters, of one kind or another, on Capitol Hill. I also have lists identifying members of the judiciary, industrialists, and the media. Like I say, at this point they only tell part of the story. But each has a full medical history on file – I've only had a chance to look at a few. They show a range of conditions, many of which have been treated at the Highlands Clinic.'

Muddy began to move through the lists.

'Jesus, Mr Fiske has been a busy boy over the last year or so,' McKinnon said.

'You wanted hard evidence of Fiske's infiltration into the corridors of power,' Muddy said. 'Well, there it is.'

McKinnon sighed. 'It's great going, Mud. But I'm afraid we're gonna need a helluva lot more than this.' He repeated Bruce Van Stratton's view, expressed more than a year before, 'To stand this up, we're gonna have to show these people have regular contact with the sect, show up to religious gatherings, pump money into them. Most of all, that they've influenced decisions that have benefited the cult in some way.'

279

Hannah got up and stretched. 'Well, that process begins first thing tomorrow.'

McKinnon wrapped a towel around his midriff, went to the window of Muddy's guest room and looked south across a mile of shimmering water.

'I still can't believe we made it here.'

Hannah hung the last of her clothes in the only closet. 'Well, this is about as free as we're gonna be for a while.'

He drew her to his side and kissed her gently. 'I don't know how things would have worked out between us if all this craziness hadn't taken over our lives. And I don't think it matters. All I know is how I feel now. You were the only light on the horizon while I was in that place. Not just because of the testimony I knew you could give, but because of who you were. Because I knew we mattered to each other, and that, if the opportunity arose, you'd do everything in your power to help me.' The blue eyes ringed with black held hers. 'You're the first person who's come through for me in a long time, Hannah. I suppose part of what I'm feeling is gratitude, but there's also a deep sense of wanting to be around you now. If we ever get us out of this mess . . .'

She put her finger to his lips. 'You're a great guy, Joel, except for one thing: you talk too much.' He caught her around the waist, and swung her gently off her feet on to the bed.

When Hannah woke at first light, McKinnon was gone. She put on her robe and went downstairs to find him in front of the computer in the living room.

Muddy was up too, scrambling eggs in the kitchen

and trying to pick his way through the second verse of 'Daydream Believer'.

McKinnon took a sip of his coffee and looked up. 'Did you sleep?' he asked.

She came over and put an arm around him. 'Well, you obviously didn't.'

'I had too much on my mind.'

Muddy came through from the kitchen, and set two unappetising plates of scrambled egg in front of his guests.

'Mud, are you still in touch with that bank specialist colleague of yours?' Hannah asked.

'I can be.'

'Could we still use him to get into the bank accounts of some of these high profile people?'

Muddy waddled back into the kitchen. 'Want to see if they're paying tithes to the cult?'

'Uhuh.'

'It'd take time and, knowing him, money. Lots of it. But if you want, I'll give him a call. I might be able to talk him down. He owes me one. First we'd have to find out where these people bank.'

'Maybe you could work with Muddy on that,' Hannah said, turning to McKinnon.

He took a mouthful of egg. 'Why? What are you gonna be doing?'

'As soon as I feel it's safe, I'm gonna take off for Washington for a day or two. Start getting myself up-to-date with what's been happening down there. I want to find out how our heavy hitters have been voting in Congress recently, and whether Fiske has been a beneficiary.'

'Good idea,' McKinnon said distractedly. 'Look at this, Hannah.' He rolled the data on the screen back to the beginning. 'This is a file Muddy found in the personnel section. These people don't seem to have been dragged into the cult yet. Fiske has their medical records as well, so they must be folk he has his eye on for the future. If I'm right, he seems to have his sights set pretty high.'

Hannah picked her way through the file. 'I can't believe this is a future targets list. Christ, it would put about seventeen senators and close to fifty congressmen in Fiske's pocket.'

'Drawn from both sides of the house, that's the interesting thing,' McKinnon said. 'With that big a slice of the action, you could pretty much force through any legislation you wanted. You'd effectively have a third political party hidden in the ranks of the other two, a floating majority that could put its weight behind whatever decision Fiske wanted to carry the day, irrespective of either official party line.'

'The Vatican has been doing that in Italy for years.' Then Hannah spotted a name towards the end of the file, and caught her breath. 'Good God! Is that who I think it is?'

'Well, how many of them do you think are walking around?'

'Well, unless there are two guys with the name Arlen J. Gallagher, Fiske would seem to have his eye on the US Vice-President. Can we take a look at his medical file?' Hannah said.

A few moments later McKinnon had it up on the screen. Hannah moved a chair up beside his, and began to scroll through it.

'There must be an error here,' she said at last. 'It shows he's suffering from stomach cancer – okay. If they say so. But the date of diagnosis . . . That's ridiculous, that's in four months' time. Unless Fiske's people now have an astrologist on the team, how on earth can they know that?'

McKinnon suggested they check out the medical files of others on the future targets list. In each case, they were shown as suffering from some critical condition, with the date of diagnosis given as being at some future time.

For a minute the only sound was Muddy's discordant humming in the kitchen.

'What the hell does Fiske know that they don't?' Hannah said at last.

CHAPTER TWENTY

Fiske's eyes scanned the faces of those seated in front of the podium. He fought back the pain and weariness and began.

'When the idea of REGENS was first presented to me as a practical reality, I found myself asking the inevitable question: just because we can, should we? I mean, the scientists tell us that by the year 2020 the world's population will have doubled. What service do we really do mankind, in the long term, by making such treatments generally available?'

Fiske took a breath, and sipped some more water. The gathering of core disciples watched him in silence. The founder's appearance at such a meeting was rare enough, but the fact that he'd insisted on making the address today, in all the circumstances, only added weight to what he had to say. No one present had any illusions as to the impact the bombing of the Highlands mansion had had on the movement. Six members of the Council of Elders had died, the founder himself had narrowly escaped death. It was a marvel to many who listened now that he was able to stand before them as he did. His voice was steady, his stance solid and assured. How was it possible, after all that he'd been through? The Good Lord himself clearly watched over this man.

'And if we make REGENS available only to a select

few, who should be the ones to benefit? Then, as has happened throughout my life, I found myself coming to one clear conclusion: those within our movement! It is they who should benefit!' Fiske listened to his voice resonate through the hall, to the burst of applause that followed it.

'I say this quite unashamedly: those who will carry forward our message will be chosen. REGENS will bring us new friends, new allies. They are a gift from Almighty God to us, his new . . . chosen people.'

When the audience reaction had died down, he added, 'Even then, we must not use these gifts unthinkingly. The feeble-minded, the deformed, the disabled; God has told us what value he puts upon them by making them as he has. What real good can come from interfering with that?'

Kleig moved through the small knot of people gathered around the great man. Fiske sat wearily in an armchair studying a video-tape of his performance.

The coaching had been beneficial, there was no doubting that, he thought. The general delivery was better. The traces of that damned St Louis accent were barely perceptible now. But the voice . . . It was mellower, more rounded. The cadences were more measured. But it was not an orator's voice. It never would be.

He listened to his disciples' rapturous applause for a moment, and thought: perhaps that no longer matters . . .

Kleig moved into his line of vision. Fiske looked up, then beckoned the South African forward.

'I was going to get through that address if it killed me. If there are heretics out there, who would have me dead, I wanted them to be certain that they had failed utterly.'

'I had some plants amongst the delegates,' Fiske said.

'Whatever is to be gained from them will be added to what we already have on the conspiracy.'

'What do we have, Kleig?'

The South African searched for words. 'This matter is still our number one priority,' he said lamely. He fingered the lapels of his jacket. 'There's another matter that needs your attention.' He took a breath. 'McKinnon has broken out of Marston Moor Prison.'

Fiske's eyes swivelled upwards to meet his. 'When?'

'Some days ago . . . I, er . . .'

Fiske struggled to stand up. 'Why wasn't I told?' Some of those around him turned at the tone of his voice.

'I was hopeful that he would be recaptured . . . I didn't want to bother you with this unless . . .'

'And where is he now?'

'He's on the run. The authorities there believe he's already left the country.' The Sentinel-in-Chief hesitated. 'And I'm afraid that's not all. There is some evidence to suggest that Hannah Rostov is with him.'

For the first time in their association, Kleig saw Fiske's composure crack. The flesh on his face sagged, pulling down the side of his mouth. For a fragment of time, the South African saw him look as he would in ten or fifteen years, when he would be a very old and decrepit man.

'You should never have allowed Rostov to leave the commune,' Fiske said at last.

'Well, we thought she'd lead us to the hacker.'

Fiske's eyes blazed. 'What you've done is turn a minor annoyance into a massive headache.' He closed his eyes, and rocked slightly in his chair. His voice was barely audible. 'If they do have evidence of the Blue Ridge Project . . .'

'If they had it, why didn't they go to the authorities

right at the beginning? Why didn't it come up at the trial?'

'That was then. Who knows what they may have now?'

An eerie calm seemed to take Fiske over. 'I'm starting to have a feeling about Mr McKinnon,' he said, almost to himself. 'This is by nature a curious, intuitive beast. If we're patient, Kleig, he'll come to us.' The eyes opened and bored into the South African's. 'We just have to be certain that we're ready for him when he does.'

Kleig's moves to breathe some life back into the Corrigan investigation were to reap benefits that even he could never have foreseen.

The one solid lead in the case had come from the young lab assistant who'd alerted her boss to the fact that a man she'd been dating had asked about Corrigan.

Kleig's thinking had been clear-headed enough: we're gonna have to give him something worth communicating.

The detective had ceased his attentions to the lab girl some months before. And she, feeling she was just being used, had made no attempt to restart the relationship. But she was now to be the bait in a trap.

On Kleig's instructions, she was given a day off work and sent to a beauty salon in the city. Then she and a plain female friend, acting as camouflage, were despatched to a bar, which the Cordell agent was known to frequent most Friday nights. A 'chance' re-encounter was then carefully engineered. Before long, the agent – ever the professional – began to pump her about Corrigan again. Although the alcohol she drank, to give her Dutch courage, rendered her, at times, almost incomprehensible, she was able to pass on the key information in the form she had been briefed to. She let slip that the former lab technician had been in touch.

'He seemed scared . . . wouldn't say where he was calling from . . . wanted to come to see me, but I didn't want to get involved. He said he'd call again in a week . . .'

Predictably, the agent reported straight back to his client, in a call from his car phone, the following morning. The call was monitored and the number traced by an Apostles surveillance team set up in the centre of the city.

Kleig was astonished to learn the paymaster was Apostles Elder in Charge of North-Eastern Communes and Open Order Groups, Fenton Dellaplane. Quite what Dellaplane's motives were for initiating these enquiries could not be firmly established from the transcript of the one call. Kleig knew he had to consider the possibility that the Apostles elder had somehow gotten wind of Corrigan's infiltration of Falk, and was merely trying to establish, for his own peace of mind, whether or not this was a government-inspired operation that might, down the line, have repercussions on the whole movement. Hardly a capital offence. Before he said anything to Fiske, he would have to be certain.

Sentinels shifted the focus of their enquiries to Dellaplane's office at the Chicago commune. For the next months, every communication that went through it was monitored, every activity made by the elder and his staff logged.

It was soon clear that Dellaplane was making a number of late-night excursions from the commune, and going to some lengths to ensure that their purpose remained secret. He was repeatedly able to give the surveillance team the slip. Then a chance remark, picked up in the transcript of a phone call, implied that he had some kind of apartment in the city that he kept especially for clandestine meetings.

The following week, the catering manager at the Chicago commune was informed that a member of the refectory staff, at the cult's Kansas operation, would be transferring to Chicago and should be taken on as part of his staff there.

It was this new employee that would soon serve Fenton Dellaplane many of his meals.

Within weeks, Dellaplane began to complain of headaches, giddiness and nausea, and soon made an appointment to visit the commune's medical center. The locum who saw him – he'd apparently just moved down from North Dakota to help out – decided to take extensive tests.

Although Dellaplane would never know it, the procedure he would use for the blood test was unique. As the syringe pierced the flesh of his arm, the plunger inside was depressed a further few millimetres, and an electronic tagging device, no larger than a grain of salt, was forced through the large-gauge hypodermic needle.

Some days later, Dellaplane was told that he was merely suffering from some kind of minor viral infection. But, by that time, sentinels were tracking his every move. Within days, they were able to follow him to what was clearly some kind of safe house. They bugged the place and taped the conversations of those meeting there.

Not even Kleig, who, by nature, saw intrigue and deceit in every ill-lit corner, could have foreseen what that would produce. After reading through the transcripts, he was certain that he had not only unmasked those behind the industrial espionage at Falk, but also the conspirators responsible for the bomb outrage.

*   *   *

Fiske sat slumped in the corner of the balcony that ran the length of the first floor of the Highlands ranch house. His mint tea and breakfast lay on a tray before him, untouched. He looked up from the report Kleig had given him, his battered face – lacking the make-up he'd worn during his appearance in front of the core disciples – a sickly blue-grey.

At last, he said, 'I might have expected this from McBain. This is just the kind of betrayal he's expert in.' There'll be no more front men. This is the end of them. The Apostles need to hear no other voice than mine now. 'But Dellaplane,' he went on, 'I knew his revisionist views well enough. But I never dreamed he could be a part of something like this.'

Kleig took a third helping of scrambled egg and bacon from the serving dish on the trolley at his elbow. 'Well, at least we know Corrigan wasn't reporting to the Feds.'

'Yes, but McBain and the others in this now have details of the Blue Ridge Project. And the research programme at the prison in Britain.'

Fiske rarely bothered to wear his coloured contact lenses since the bombing. His insipid blue eyes looked unfamiliar in the early morning light, almost colourless, like those of some desert reptile.

'If they should fall into the hands of the authorities, I needn't tell you what the consequences would be . . .'

'We have to move fast, Mr Fiske. Move fast and cut deep.'

CHAPTER TWENTY-ONE

'I don't know if this is relevant but, given our conversation last night, I thought you should see it.'

Muddy's fingers moved over the keyboard of his computer with the assurance of a concert pianist.

'This file is normally stored off-line,' he went on. 'That almost certainly means it's considered highly classified.' He turned to McKinnon. 'I just keep wondering if it's somehow tied up with your theory on the future targets file we found.' A technical drawing of some kind flickered on to the screen. 'This was amongst Fiske's copies of what have to be Falk files.'

'What theory is this?' Hannah asked. But McKinnon's attention was on the elliptical image displayed on the screen.

'At first I thought it was some new kind of pill,' Muddy went on. 'Then I noticed the scale that it was drawn to, and realized it had to be almost invisible to the human eye.' He sidled off into the kitchen. 'I've done work for a number of pharmaceutical outfits over the years, and I reckoned I was owed a few favours, so I sent it over to a contact I have at a research facility in Houston. He told me he thought it was some kind of germ warfare – he called it a "bacteria time-bomb".'

He came back carrying a pot of coffee, and sat down in front of the computer again.

'It consists of a capsule, barely visible to the human eye, that's designed to hold some kind of virulent bacteria.' Muddy pointed to one end of the drawing with the spout of the pot. 'A thin membrane would be stretched over the open end of the capsule to keep the contents in. If the capsule was taken orally, the design of the outer casing would ensure that it would cling to the wall of the stomach or the small intestine.'

'To stop it being passed out of the system?' McKinnon asked.

'That's right.'

As he poured them coffee he explained that, from the accompanying data, it seemed that the synthetic material covering the end would be like a hypersensitive version of the membrane that forms the human stomach lining. The intention clearly was that the hydrochloric acid present in the stomach should gradually eat away at the membrane until it perforated, thereby releasing the bacteria into the victim's system. The thickness of the membrane would determine the time-lapse before the 'bomb' detonated.

Muddy turned to McKinnon. 'Is this ringing the same bells for you as it is for me?'

'Jesus, Mud, you've cracked it. This has to be the key to the whole scam.'

'What scam?' Hannah said impatiently. 'What is this theory of yours?'

McKinnon got up and started to pace. 'Well . . . When I was in jail, I went over what we had on Fiske a hundred times. A few insights and pointers, that's all it added up to. Christ, if we'd had more, I'd have used it at the trial, gone to the media with it. But we didn't.' He took a sip of his coffee. 'Fiske didn't go to all the lengths he did to shut us up for knowing what we knew. He did it for knowing what he *thought* we knew. We were only able to capture to disc a few scraps of inconclusive data in the first hack. But how could he be sure of that?'

He turned to Hannah. 'When I was arrested I had your copy of Fiske's second book, *The Road to Redemption*, on me. The prison authorities thought it was something to do with my religion, so I was allowed to keep it. If you remember, in one of the early chapters, Fiske gets into this whole thing about man's obsession with pagan legend and ritual, and the effect that had on the development of Christianity. He looks at all the early European folk tales, and older stuff that turns up in Greeks myths. Central to it all is sorcery, necromancy, the casting and lifting of spells. Reading about it at Marston Moor, thinking about what was going on in the hospital wing, just across the compound from me, made me think of something I picked up on when I was in Macedonia, covering the trouble there. Do you know the Greek term often used to mean "spell"? *"O Ex'apotho!"'*

Hannah looked up. 'I'm sorry, I just don't see where any of this is going.'

'The thing is, Hannah, in a certain context, it's also the term they use for cancer. That dual usage exists in half a dozen other European languages.'

She closed her eyes and tried to piece all the information together in her mind. '"The casting and lifting of . . ." Wait a minute. Are you saying that Fiske doesn't just cure people to make converts, that he actually gives them the disease in the first place?'

'In certain cases, yes. That kind of thinking would fit with his whole philosophy. I think he targets specific individuals, vital to him, and uses something like the device Muddy turned up to transmit the disease.'

'You can't give people cancer in a pill, Joel. Even I

know that. The hydrochloric acid in the stomach would neutralize it on contact.'

'No, that's not right,' Muddy said. 'My pal at the research facility said the most likely bacteria the capsule would carry would be a thing called a heliocobacter – it gives you stomach cancer. It's unusual in that it's one of the few bacteria that gives off CO_2. If ingested in a cooked meal, it's capable of neutralizing the stomach acid and surviving in the stomach.'

'And that's what the Vice-President is diagnosed as having,' Hannah said almost to herself.

McKinnon poured himself more coffee. 'No, that's the whole point. It's what he's *going to be* diagnosed as having. That's how they know, Hannah. They gave him the fucking disease in the first place, using this little gizmo Muddy's turned up! Tell me, how else could they possibly be able to foresee the future?'

Hannah said nothing for a while. She was clearly chewing over all he'd said.

'Look, I didn't say anything about this to you before,' McKinnon went on, 'because I just couldn't figure out how in the normal course of life you could give a perfect stranger one of these diseases.' He rapped the computer screen with his knuckle. 'But we seem to have a pretty convincing answer to that one now.'

She crossed her arms. 'I'll buy that Fiske is doing this to a bunch of deadbeat cons who no one gives a damn about. But senators and congressmen?'

'You said to me that you couldn't imagine that Fiske was waiting around for public figures, who might be useful to him in the future, to catch terminal diseases on the off-chance that he might get a shot at curing and converting them. It was all way too hit and miss, too dependent on chance. But this takes the chance out of it.'

'It does makes sense of the diagnosis dates,' Muddy said.

'How could Fiske possibly get to a US Vice-President with one of these bacteria things?' Hannah asked.

McKinnon shrugged. 'If he can turn congressmen and senators, why not a valet or a cook, someone who could plant one of those things in a meal or a drink.'

'But surely most of his food is checked before he eats it. If it didn't show up then, it'd show up in the regular medical examinations these people have.'

'Well, the great advantage of something like this device is that, unlike poison, it wouldn't disperse evenly into food or liquid. So one could check out a dozen samples, and still turn up nothing. The thing would just exist as a microscopic little blip on the stomach wall until it detonated. If that was timed to happen straight after a yearly medical, it might have months to do its damage before being detected.'

Muddy nodded. 'And the amount of damage it did would be crucial, too: too little, and the patient would be able to turn to regular medical technology for treatment, too much, and they'd be beyond the help of even REGENS. Fiske would need to wait for the targeted individual to realize they were in trouble and seek help, of course. To go through all the emotional changes, to become vulnerable.'

'"The condemned man turns to God,"' McKinnon intoned. 'When that point comes, Fiske knows there's a whole host of folk up on Capitol Hill ready to steer him towards the Highlands Clinic.'

'But even if you're right, what real use is the Vice-President to Fiske?' Hannah said. 'Gallagher is a fucking joke. The biggest ditz to hold the office since Dan Quayle.'

297

'That's no doubt why Fiske thinks he can turn him,' Muddy said.

'The President gives him no authority,' Hannah said. 'And I don't think anyone in Washington seriously believes he'd be a credible runner in a future election.'

McKinnon thought for a moment. 'Well, you know what they said about Quayle: "He's just a heartbeat away from the Presidency."' Hannah turned around in her seat and looked hard at him. 'Caulfield is committed to wiping out everything Fiske has created,' McKinnon said. 'And we've seen how efficient the Apostles' killing machine can be. When Fiske is certain Gallagher's in his pocket, he has a bullet put in Caulfield's head . . .'

'And Gallagher becomes President,' Hannah said.

'What other possible attraction could turning him have? And it doesn't take a massive leap of imagination to figure out who calls the shots from then on. Fiske would have the Presidential veto and the concealed floating majority to do pretty much what he liked with. As long as the turned congressmen and senators hold on to their seats, it doesn't matter which party takes control – Fiske has it covered all ways.' McKinnon shook his head. 'Christ . . . It doesn't bear thinking about.'

'Well, this has to be what Fiske is so sensitive about us getting on to,' Muddy said.

McKinnon laughed. 'Are you surprised?'

'I still don't see how these capsule things could be made to work accurately,' Hannah said. 'Everyone's resistance to disease is different. In the stuff I've read about REGENS development it says that lifestyle, racial mix, blood type, a hundred factors have to be taken into account. How could Fiske's people possibly allow for all that? Christ, it would require enormous pre-planning and research.'

'Well,' said Muddy, 'perhaps that's what the experiments at Marston Moor are all about. Not about REGENS at all, but about bacteria time capsules. Maybe they use those guys to check out all the stuff they need to know.'

Hannah looked at McKinnon. He seemed now to be in some far-off place again. He put his hands to his head and began to rock back and forth in his chair.

'Jocl, are you okay?'

A photograph in a magazine a couple of years back . . . Gallagher arriving somewhere . . . His bodyguards carried containers of blood. They went everywhere with him. His blood group was so rare, he had to have some on hand in case someone took a shot at him.

'Muddy, let me see Gallagher's medical file again.'

As soon as it came up on the screen, McKinnon read through it carefully. Then he looked up.

'Gallagher is fifty-seven. My father would have been around the same age if he was alive today. Gallagher is of Irish stock.'

'Scottish,' Muddy put in.

'Scottish. My father is of Protestant Irish stock: close enough. The Caulfield administration was returned to office last November, my father died in January . . .'

Hannah got up and spun around. 'Where on earth is all this going, Joel?'

'Gallagher has a rare blood group.' He pointed a pen to a line on the screen. 'Group A FIN.' His voice was calm and level. 'Only a handful of people would have remembered the fact. But I have more reason than most. You see, I have the same blood group. Which means my father had it too.' His face was pale. 'Muddy has to be right. If everything you say about the profile needed on a subject is correct, then who better to test the process out on than the forgotten men at Marston Moor? But if Gallagher has been targeted, Fiske's people would have needed to find themselves a very special guinea pig to act as a model for him. Someone whose own profile not only matched the target's closely, but one who had a blood type that less than one in five hundred people have – A FIN.

'The details would have been in my father's prison records, for Alderbrook to see. Once Fiske had developed his plans for Gallagher, and Alderbrook had established the kind of guinea pig he'd need for the thing to work, who would he find better than my father?'

McKinnon began to pace the room, and began to arrange the facts he had in as logical an order as he could. 'My father's ex-cellmate said he saw my dad alive, but in a helluva state, only days before the story broke that would have resulted in his conviction being quashed. In the normal way they'd have just let him die, like the other forgotten men I found on Alderbrook's list. But if the doctors there were doing some crucial stuff on him, they must have crapped themselves when all that broke. He was meant to be a forgotten man! How were they gonna explain away the state he was in when the authorities came knocking? They hastily gave him a deadly shot of something, and solved that one, but it would have raised too many suspicions, perhaps jeopardized everything that was going on up there, if they'd announced he had died that very week. So they backdated his death certificate a month or two to make it look less coincidental. And they didn't put the cause down as being some kind of cancer . . .'

'Because cancer takes months to kill,' Hannah said. 'And they'd have to explain why they hadn't made a damn good effort to notify the next of kin of the condition he was in.'

'That's right. So they changed the cause of death to cardiac arrest, because everyone accepts that you can drop dead from that without giving any warning. Everything was going just fine until the son, an NBS journalist, started asking awkward questions. The cellmate tips him off to the date discrepancy, and suddenly there's a real problem. Next thing you know, the cellmate is dead, and two thugs have made a damn good try to take the son out too.' McKinnon turned to face Hannah. 'That's one helluva lot of trouble to go to, if there's nothing to hide.'

'The troublesome son survives,' Hannah said. 'Joins forces with a known opponent of the Apostles, me, and together we hack into the files in Fiske's database, where the truth regarding all this lies.'

'Meltdown!' McKinnon said. 'Alarm bells must have gone off all over Fiske's operation. Why else would they go to such lengths to shut us down?'

Muddy got up and scratched his ass, a clear sign that he was concentrating. 'I'm sitting on the outside here, listening to all this, and the question I need an answer to is this: why go to the bother of getting you all the way to England and banging you up in Marston Moor Prison? Why not just whack you with a truck on some back street in New York?'

'Because they weren't finished with my father when they were forced to kill him. In view of all we know, why keep someone that sick alive otherwise? My DNA and blood group are as close to my father's as they're ever gonna get . . .'

'And if things didn't pan out with the hit on Gallagher as they were supposed to,' Hannah said, 'they could go back to the drawing board with you.'

'Correct.'

Hannah got up. 'Well, the logic is impressive, I'll give you that. But logic is not evidence. And if we're ever gonna get out of this mess, that's what we're gonna need.'

Muddy began to clear the breakfast table. 'Well, if the evidence we need isn't amongst the new stuff I've captured to disc, we're screwed. And my guess is it isn't. There are references to other units in this file, which I'm certain would tell us a lot more, but they're all stored off-line. So . . .'

'Where? How?' McKinnon asked.

'According to the procedure index, they're stored on disc in a silo in some place in South Dakota.'

'Probably in the commune there,' Hannah said. 'You think that's where all the really hypersensitive stuff is?'

'That's what my gut tells me.' Muddy looked up. 'Why, thinking of paying them a visit?' Muddy laughed, and went through to the kitchen 'Good idea. Why don't we give Fiske a call? Maybe he'll arrange a tour.'

McKinnon got up and stretched. 'Well, as we sit here, I'm a wanted man, a convicted killer on the run. I'm not suggesting we're losing sight of this, but there's a lot of very ugly people out there looking for me, for all of us. To fight back, to lift the lid off the whole thing, we need sight of key correspondence, contracts, confidential memos, banking data. Most of all, I need to be able to show that someone at the Home Office in the UK is in on all of this, and being paid by Fiske's people to send interfering SOBs like me to places like Marston Moor. And it seems to me there's only one way we'll ever get to that position. Sooner or later, we're gonna have to get inside that commune in South Dakota, and take a look at the stuff stored there for ourselves.'

'You're out of your mind, Joel,' Hannah said. 'You'd be on the loose about three minutes in there.'

'What do you think I did all the time I was a foreign correspondent, sit around hotel lobbies? This is my field of operations, Hannah. It's what I do. Okay, I walked right into the Caitlin mess, but that won't happen again. I know what I'm dealing with now.'

Muddy came through from the kitchen. 'Well, if you're serious, the process you're talking about is called "nesting".' He patted his ample gut. 'It's hard to believe it now, but in my youth. I was one of the best nesters in the game. In industrial espionage-speak, that's an operative who specializes in breaking into silos where off-line data is stored, sifting through it, and moving it out, via an on-line laptop and cell phone. I used to do all my own entry work too.' He surveyed himself in the mirror that hung over the fireplace and sighed. 'But I guess those days are gone.'

'How much do you need to know to be an entry man?' McKinnon asked.

'A great deal,' Muddy said. He looked him up and down for a moment. Then he said, 'Nothing I couldn't teach you, I suppose.'

CHAPTER TWENTY-TWO

Fenton Dellaplane slammed down the phone, and began to pace the living room of the small rented apartment in the Lincolnshire suburb of Chicago.

McBain's PA says she took him to Kennedy herself; the limo driver this end says he never came through. Maybe McBain has just chickened out. Please God, if he has, he doesn't lose his head. He's been a basket case since the fiasco at the Highlands mansion. Getting him to meet at all was a major undertaking.

If Fiske is on to us . . . How? Dellaplane had long ago come to the view that Corrigan, the industrial spy he'd put in place at the Falk research facility, had somehow been uncovered, and had come to a bad end at Kleig's hand. At the beginning, he'd agonized over the consequences the man's exposure might have for him, and the rest of the conspirators. But he had gone to considerable lengths to ensure that Corrigan had no knowledge of who his real paymasters were and, when months passed without any sign of a comeback, he had decided that Fiske had done as it was intended he should, if things went amiss, and seized on the obvious aggressor as the mastermind of this act of espionage: President Caulfield. And nothing that had happened in recent weeks had given Dellaplane reason to believe that Fiske had come to any other view about the incident.

When the idea of assassinating Fiske and key members of the Council of Elders had first been mooted, Dellaplane had voiced bitter objections: 'We are meant to be men of God, for pity's sake. Not some blood-hungry terrorist organization! There must be some other way to make him listen, to make him understand that change is vital if we're to survive as a spiritual force.'

But the more he and the other revisionists talked, the more it became clear that negotiation would be fruitless. No decision that Dellaplane had taken in his life had caused him to search his conscience more deeply. Certainly, Fiske was now totally out of control. The data that Corrigan had unearthed had shown that unless immediate action of some kind was taken, he would plunge the country into a crisis it might take decades to recover from. The issues concerning the public image of the sect could not be addressed until this potentially disastrous course of action was reversed.

The night he made his decision had been the last time he and his partner of four years had spoken. What had he expected to hear in Hannah's voice – forgiveness? Forgiveness for choosing the Apostles of Christ movement over her? Had he wanted her to say; 'It's all right, darling, come home. You have no decision to make'? Perhaps. Now he would never know.

He'd finally resolved that there was simply no other way. Fiske, and the staunch reactionaries that surrounded him, would have to be purged from the movement.

Plans had been laid with infinite care. A tiny dissident element amongst the sentinels, posted at the Chicago commune where Dellaplane was senior elder, had agreed to carry out the operation.

Media speculation over the bombing of the Highlands mansion laid the blame for the outrage on everyone from white supremacist groups to Islamic fundamentalists. The only fact upon which all were agreed was that Fiske's diabetes had, in the bizarrest of ways, saved his life.

Was this God's will? Dellaplane agonized in the aftermath of the mission's failure. Had he decreed that this sick, perverse man should be saved? If so, then what is destined for us?

McBain is not coming. Perhaps he's already dead.

Dellaplane was suddenly gripped with a terrible dread. In that instant, something deep in him sensed that he was utterly alone and exposed.

He caught his breath, and tipped forward as something hard-edged twisted in his stomach. He took his coat from the chair in the hallway, and hurried for the front door.

A man in a dark shirt and jeans stood blocking his way. The eyes that bore into Dellaplane's were totally without humanity – windows into a damned soul. Without a word, he pointed the barrel of a Mauser 9mm at Dellaplane's head and fired.

At almost the same moment, there was the sound of elevator doors opening down the corridor, and the babble of children's voices. The killer froze for a moment, then took off down the stairs.

Paramedics, arriving at the scene twenty minutes later, were astonished to find that the victim of the attack still had a pulse.

The black Merc swung off the country road and began to roll down an uneven dirt track. The driver switched on his lights and negotiated the potholes carefully. A mile down, he pulled into a clearing and braked. The headlights of a grey stretch limo, until now hidden in the trees, cut through the darkness. Men got out of both cars and moved to the bright space created at the point where the headlights crossed.

The sentinels on each side of Jonathan McBain pushed him forward, then stepped back a few paces. He stumbled but did not fall. His face was pale, his eyes sunken and dull. He searched the gloom for a moment.

Is this how it ends? he thought. Here? like this? Ahead, he could hear the crunch of footfalls in the dry earth. Walking slowly towards him was a small grey-haired man, dressed in a blue tracksuit. McBain didn't need to see his face to know who he was.

'I got it right the first time, when I kicked you off the council.'

McBain eyed Fiske wearily. You look as beat up as I do, old man.

'Sure I screwed up with Kerensky, but the bigger mistake was letting you have your old job back.'

Silence.

'*Judas.*' Fiske spat the word at him.

McBain shook his head as if to say, And that's the best you can come up with?

'I don't think so, Jeffrey. For me to be Judas, you'd need to be Jesus Christ.' McBain sighed. 'The older I get, the less I think I know. But on that particular one, I'm pretty solid.'

Fiske turned away and began to walk back to the car. 'Get him outta here.'

'I told Marcie, I said to her, if we go back to living as open order disciples, it'll be the same old shit.' Regis Lamont leaned out of the window at the rear of the grey panel truck and checked the street. The nearest sign of life was in the Italian restaurant a hundred yards away. 'Sure we could have our own place again, but it would be bills, mortgage repayments, and more bills, just like before. No built-in baby-sitters, no friends around us when we wanted them.'

Warren Kaplin checked the wiring between the microwave oven and the car batteries, arranged on the floor of the truck, one last time. 'Did you pay in all your savings when you became closed order members?' He switched on the cooker and a light went on inside. There was a low hum as the heat-proof glass plate began to rotate.

'Yeah, of course we did. She knows that, she knows the terms we agreed.' Lamont swivelled around in the van's cramped interior and levered the lid off a plastic icebox. 'But if I get into that, she just gets mad. So I concentrate on the day-to-day stuff, try to talk her out of it that way.' He took out a small parcel, wrapped in cooking foil, and began to undo it. 'I tell her about the awareness sessions, the enlightenment classes we'd have to attend.' He took out the white half-frozen human hand inside and laid it on a paper plate Kaplin provided.

'At least three nights a week,' Kaplin intoned as he laid it in the microwave.

Lamont took a clinical thermometer from its plastic case and began to shake it. 'That's what I told her. I said, be happy, be content with the life we have in the commune. It isn't as though we just stumbled into it. We gave the whole thing a great deal of thought.' He shone a small flashlight on to the thermometer and checked that the mercury level was at its lowest position, then he passed it to Kaplin, who carefully placed it between the stiffened fingers of the severed hand. Kaplin then set the cooker to a little above defrost. There was a low humming again, and the two men settled down to wait.

'I've been through all that a dozen times with my wife,' Kaplin said. 'I'll tell you the truth – and this is not something I'd say to many people – she misses a drink.'

'And that's a reason to change your whole life around? Of course not.'

They watched a young couple move down the street, deep in conversation.

'I mean, I ask you, what's so fucking wonderful about their lives? Probably spend two hours a day commuting to work. Half their lives sucking round some toe-rag of a boss. I've done it, pal. You can keep it and shove it.'

They sat and listened to the drone of the traffic for a while, then Kaplin checked the hand again. It was now a gentle shade of pink. He pulled the thermometer free and struggled to read it again. 'How the hell nurses read these things, I'll never know.'

Lamont curled up his nostrils. 'Smells like a side of fucking ribs.' He gave a hoarse laugh.

'You're sick, you know that, Christian? Okay: ninety-eight point six, or close enough. Come on, we got work to do.'

The smiles faded. The two men got on to their knees and bowed their heads.

'Oh, Lord, we ask you to bless this endeavour . . .'

Lamont rewrapped the hand, and they got out of the truck, locked it, crossed the street, and began to walk down to the apartment block on the right. An illuminated sign above the wide entrance read 'Trump Tower'. Kaplin went ahead, put his weight against one of the heavy glass doors and approached the secur-ity desk.

'I have to collect a package from 1203.'

The security guard put down his paperback and glanced up. 'I'll try them for you.' He pressed a button under his desk, and they waited for a moment.

Kaplin drummed his fingers. 'He said something about leaving it in the manager's office.'

There was clearly no one home in apartment 1203. The guard scratched the side of his nose. 'No one said nothin' to me.'

'Well, I've driven in from Connecticut, so maybe you could check.'

The guard scrambled irritably to his feet. 'Okay, stay there.'

The minute he was out of sight, Lamont crossed the lobby, and the two men made for the elevator. At the twelfth floor they got out and hurried to apartment 1203. To the left of the door was a small alcove. Set into it, tilting upwards from the horizontal, was a glass panel with the shape of a human hand recessed into it. Kaplin checked to see that they were alone, then lifted the foil package from under his jacket. He unwrapped the severed hand again, and laid it on to the imprint, prising the stiff fingers apart until they fitted exactly into the indents provided. There was a faint buzz as the computer scanned the palm print, and checked it against the one in its memory. Meanwhile, sensors noted that the blood temperature was that of a living human.

There was a faint clicking sound and the door of the apartment swung ajar. The two men moved quickly inside, and began to search, putting papers and software discs they found into a bag.

Fiske had been in no doubt that the Reverend McBain had chosen the Trump Tower apartment as his main base because it was acknowledged as having the most sophisticated security system of any block in the city. He was equally sure that secreted within it were documents that would cast further light on the activities of the conspirators in the Apostles' midst.

The cult's creator was, above all things, a practical man. McBain had been confronted with evidence of his complicity in the assassination bid, but had remained obdurately silent. When all Kleig's expertise failed to break him, Fiske was forced to fall back on his powers of ingenuity in order to get to the data he needed.

By the time the solution – how to overcome the apartment's security system – had presented itself, McBain's need for a right hand was no longer an issue.

CHAPTER TWENTY-THREE

Wes Tyrell sat in the corner of Muddy's kitchen, his head in his hands.

Muddy stood behind him, his hands in his pockets. 'I know how it looks on the file, kid. But there could be another explanation.'

'*There's no other explanation!*' The sound was almost a shriek. 'The personal file you accessed says all I need to know.'

Hannah passed him a herbal tea. 'It just says Jerry left the commune when you did.'

His voice was barely audible now. 'It's a dead file. It means he's dead, Hannah. If he's not with the Apostles, where is he?'

All those present – Muddy, Hannah, and McKinnon – considered different theories they might offer as consolation, but thought better of it.

'I knew Jerry was dead . . . I knew it inside. But Elaine . . . I can't believe they got to Elaine too.' Wes began to sob again. 'And it's all my fault.'

'Maybe she did leave the cult, like her file says,' Hannah said softly.

'She would never leave. She was in it up to her neck.'

Wes got up and wiped his face with the back of his hand. 'That Fiske . . . So help me God, I'll see him in hell.'

He walked to the door, then, after a moment, turned back. 'I hope the map is useful.'

'It's invaluable,' McKinnon said. 'Thanks for doing it.'

Wes shrugged. 'I only used to go up to the South Dakota commune when Jerry was there, so I don't know it well. But it should give you some idea of the layout.' He paused. 'If I were you, I'd figure on making your play on a festival day. Everyone is at worship for long stretches then. The administration sector – that's where you're gonna be heading for – is usually deserted.'

'Good idea,' Hannah said.

Wes opened the door, checked outside, and walked on to the boardwalk that ran alongside the house. 'The next big deal on the calendar is Thanksgiving. Apostles get in a real froth at Thanksgiving. It's the best shot you'll ever get.'

'That's in ten days,' Muddy said.

'Can we be ready by then?' McKinnon asked.

'If we're not ready by then, we never will be.'

McKinnon pulled his coat over his head to keep off the rain, and peered out from a doorway opposite the north-eastern entrance of the Apostles of Christ's commune in South Dakota. He checked his watch: seven forty-five am.

To his left, he could see an articulated truck lumbering down the road toward the perimeter fence. He could see the trailer rocking this way and that. It was the second to come this way in an hour.

He pulled back into his hiding place amongst some outbuildings and surveyed his bedraggled companion. 'Are you really up for this, Mud?'

Muddy shook the rain out of his face. Hunched against

the wall, he looked small and rather vulnerable, but there was a resolute expression on his face. 'The rain's good. It helps. You do your bit, I'll do mine. Okay?' he said.

McKinnon whispered into the tiny mike pinned to the inside lapel of his jacket. 'Okay, Hannah, we're gonna take a shot at it.'

Hannah sat amongst a selection of Muddy's computer equipment in a motel bedroom, about five miles away.

'Okay. Good luck. And, for Christ's sake, be careful.'

McKinnon watched the truck come. Everything we need to know is in that dump somewhere, he told himself. I just hope that all the toys work like they're supposed to.

The truck ground to a halt at the main gate, shooting up spray. When the security guard moved forward to check the driver's papers, McKinnon and Muddy broke cover and climbed between the two sections of the truck, flattening themselves against the bodywork of the trailer. The guard waved the truck through, and hurried to get out of the rain.

The truck moved down a narrow roadway and turned off left. They clung on, checking each block that passed. When the rig slowed to turn again, McKinnon jumped free. Muddy hung back for a second, then swung the shoulder bag that contained his precious equipment behind him, and jumped too. He fell forward on his knees, grazing them slightly, quickly recovered himself, and the two ran for cover amongst some huts.

McKinnon checked his wrist compass and signalled Muddy to move off to the left.

'Inside, heading for target area,' he radioed to Hannah.

The place seemed deserted. They threaded their way through a complex of low buildings until they came to a five-storey brick structure, on the south-eastern corner of the commune. That was where Wes Tyrell had said the communications centre was housed. They took up a position amongst some trash cans opposite, and, when McKinnon felt it was safe, he moved off to inspect the only door.

It was wood with a metal frame. No window – that was good. It was locked, but didn't appear to be bolted on the inside. He circled the building quickly, and decided this was the only feasible way in. He took a metal box, around the size of a cigarette packet, from the totebag that was slung across his back, pressed it hard against the door lock, and hurried back to his hiding place.

The directional smart-charge, detonated from a small remote control unit, split the lock with a crack no louder than a handclap.

He tried the door again. It budged a little, and finally gave after some judicious kicking. While Muddy stood watch, he hastily removed the only visible sign of damage, a small burn mark, with some wire wool. Then he and Muddy hurried inside, and made their way to the computer room on the third floor.

Muddy spent the better part of two minutes reconnoitring the room from a transom window, and decided to bypass it – and the security system that doubtless protected it. Relying on instincts developed over many years of field work, he began, with McKinnon's help, to cut through the partition of the adjacent room. The small battery-driven power tool – a Taiwanese import designed for marine salvage work – sliced through metal, wood and plastic with little effort. McKinnon guided it, while Muddy poured water from a thermos over the moving blade, in an attempt to simulate the cooling effect of the sea-water that would normally surround it.

When a section of partition, large enough for Muddy

to climb through, had been removed, he turned to McKinnon.

'Okay, I'll handle this on my own from here. You know what you have to do. Go!'

McKinnon watched his elephantine rear disappear through the opening, gathered up tools and hurried back to the entrance.

'Muddy on "nest",' McKinnon radioed in from his hiding place outside. 'He'll contact you when he needs you.'

'I'm as ready as I'll ever be,' Hannah replied. She knew Muddy was unlikely to actually steal any software – if subsequently caught, this would radically reduce any criminal charges that might be brought against him – but would put all data he felt might be useful to their investigations on-line to her, via the laptop, modem and mobile phone he had with him.

Fifteen minutes later, McKinnon heard voices in the distance. He peered out and, after a moment, a uniformed security guard came into view.

Jesus! Stay cool, he told himself. There's plenty of time.

The security guard came on, moved up to the door of a building three away from the one Muddy was working in, and tried the door. Satisfied it was locked, he moved on.

Okay. Serious problem.

McKinnon whispered into his lapel mike. 'Mud?'

'Uhuh. What's happening?'

'We've got a patrolman.'

'Can't quit now. If you have to, draw him off, and get out. I can take care of myself?'

'Sure?'

'*Do it!*'

McKinnon eyed the man. Well, there's little doubt what's gonna happen if I just sit here on my ass. What had Muddy said about the 'shit end of being the entry man'? Well, this was it.

McKinnon showed himself just long enough to be certain that the guard had seen him, and then took off at a sprint, down between the buildings ahead of him.

The guy will radio in for backup. Has to. Any minute the alarms will go off . . .

But, for the next few minutes, the only sound was his own footfall, and that of his pursuer. As he ran, McKinnon sensed the same adrenaline rush, the same feeling of elation mixed with fear, he had during the escape from Marston Moor. Soon his throat burned. He fought for breath and ran on.

A truck, laden with crates of bottles, pulled out of a side turning. As it slowed and turned, McKinnon threw himself forward. His fingers found a hold on a metal ring at the back. For a second, it seemed as if his arm would be wrenched from its socket. With an almighty effort, he levered himself up on to the tailboard and clung on. *If the guy driving this is in radio contact, I'm fucked.*

He looked back and saw a jeep, occupied by a security guard with a dog, pull up to the panting security guard, and then roar off in pursuit. He watched with eerie detachment, as they began to gain on him.

The truck rumbled on into the centre of the vast commune, towards what looked like a new town centre. McKinnon tried to reach Hannah again. Her mobile was busy. A good sign: Muddy was probably downloading stuff to her. Lights at an intersection changed behind the truck, but the jeep sped on. A woman in a blue Chevvy, set to side-swipe it, braked and swerved. There was a hollow metallic crunch, and the jeep was thrown violently right, all but demolishing a small newspaper concession on the corner.

This is my chance, McKinnon told himself. He was dimly aware of the jeep backing up, trying to disentangle itself from the debris, as he judged his moment and jumped free, landing hard on the corner of the sidewalk. The truck made a turn and was gone.

He scrambled to his feet, and ran down the narrow street to the right. Long before he reached the end, he could see that cordons had been drawn across the road. Beyond, a wide square was thronged with people. As he drew closer, he could see that the women wore elegant hats, the men were all dressed in what looked like morning suits. The rain had given way to patchy sunshine now, but many carried umbrellas.

What the hell . . .?

Barking. McKinnon spun around. Way in the distance two uniformed men with dogs were running towards him. Every impulse screamed; *Lose yourself in the crowd!* McKinnon swung himself over the railings, and began to run towards a knot of people in front of him. On the roof of the buildings around him, motorized surveillance cameras scanned the square. A beautifully groomed woman of about thirty and her lady friend eyed McKinnon's approach with obvious distaste. McKinnon, still soaking from the rain, ran on in his sopping anorak and jeans and thought, how long can I last, dressed like this?

The security men had now passed the cordon, and were heading his way. He moved gently between the top-hatted men and their elegant spouses, and made for the densest part of the crowd. Here, liveried ushers shepherded them towards a cobbled roadway that rose on a slight incline. Between their shoulders McKinnon could see the vast entrance of a church building, its twin spires silhouetted against an angry sky.

Security men, some in plain clothes, stood on a grassy bank to his right, and surveyed the crowd with binoculars. A helicopter hovered overhead. Is all this for my benefit? McKinnon asked himself. Surely not. So some society long dong is getting himself hitched. What's the big deal?

Somewhere high in the heavens there was a low rumble, and again rain began to fall in sheets around him. The colours in the clothes of those ahead of him were suddenly eclipsed by a hundred small circles of black and grey, as umbrellas were raised to shield the coiffures of the rich and the righteous. McKinnon moved up to a woman of about twenty-five, who was dressed in a pink satin suit, and shot her a toothy smile.

'Damn shame this, isn't it?' he offered in his best New England accent. He craned to see over the heads of those in front of them. 'My wife's here somewhere with my clothes . . .'

The young woman moved her open umbrella in his direction. 'You'd better get under here.'

In his peripheral vision, he could see the security men on the bank, pacing nervously back and forth now, their binoculars hanging at their waists. McKinnon pulled closer to the girl. She lowered the umbrella in the direction of the downpour. Let's see you jerks find me in this shell game.

The two Asian women ahead were dressed in sarees, and several oriental couples were decked out in kimonos. The profile of the patrician-looking man to McKinnon's right immediately struck a chord. Cosgrave . . . Wasn't he with Food and Drug Administration?

McKinnon pulled away from the girl a little, and, as

unobtrusively as he could, tipped his mouth towards his lapel mike. 'Hannah, are you there?'

'Yup. What's happening?' came the reply.

'I've stumbled into some kind of shindig. Muddy okay?'

'Working well.'

'Edward Cosgrave. Do we have anything on him?'

McKinnon moved slowly forward as Hannah checked through data, some of which had been downloaded from the South Dakota silo only minutes before. After what seemed an eternity, she said, 'We don't have a file on him as such. But there's a list with his name on it amongst stuff Muddy's just sent me.' She rolled hastily through the pages. 'There must be five hundred names here.'

McKinnon pressed the earphone in a little tighter to hear.

'Is this something new?'

'I haven't seen it before.'

McKinnon walked on, and looked back. The woman ten yards behind him was familiar too. Could that be Marion Fulbright? Wasn't she still with the Treasury? If she was, she was shorter in the flesh, a good bit older too . . . She ignored his gaze, and looked away.

McKinnon had Hannah run a search on her.

'Same story . . . Same list.'

'List of what, though?'

'Search me.'

What on earth could be important enough to drag these heavyweights out to this God-forsaken corner of the map on Thanksgiving? McKinnon wondered.

He glanced at the programme the girl was carrying. 'Do you want to see?' she asked demurely. He turned the pages slowly. As his mind made sense of the words, elegantly embossed on the thick glossy card, he knew

321

why security here was pitched at the level of some kind of superpower summit: 'The Consecration of the First Cathedral, Dedicated to Jesus and the Apostles of Christ.' Fiske's Apostles of Christ. On an inside page there was a picture of the bishop, who was soon to be enthroned.

McKinnon looked around him, taking in the elegant buildings that flanked the square. What the hell was this place? Fiske Town? How could people with such high public profiles possibly risk being seen at such an event? There could only be one answer. They were all converts, so they had nothing to fear from one another – they've been assured that the town is secure. If one non-believer got word to the outside world about this gathering, about those who have stood up to be counted here, it could lift the lid off a lifetime's work, and Fiske knows it. That's why this place is where it is. Hannah had said that part of the reason the cult had flourished unchecked for so long, was that its churches were largely anonymous buildings, tucked away in back streets. But a new cathedral wasn't the kind of thing that went unnoticed. So where better to have it than here, deep in the plains of somewhere like South Dakota? McKinnon scanned the buildings stretched out around him. This cathedral was to be Fiske's Temple of Solomon at the centre of his Jerusalem.

That's why security was so tight. No outsider was to know the true scale of the Apostles of Christ movement, the international influence it commanded, the depth of infiltration into the inner sanctums of government that had already been achieved. And I'm no ordinary outsider. I have to be *the* prime target. Fiske has spent a mint trying to have me iced already. Sentinels have been scouring the planet for me for a month. If they take me here . . .

Pieter Kleig eased his neck around in the starched wing

collar and swallowed. Then he turned his attention to the man in front of him.

'We've got a good full face shot of the intruder on one of the security cameras. I thought you should take a look at it.'

Kleig undid the top button of his shirt and loosened the grey silk necktie as he followed the sentinel through to the control room at the centre of the bunker, set fifty feet below the cathedral building.

'Where is he now?' the Sentinel-in-Chief asked.

'Somewhere down in the square.'

'What do you mean "somewhere"? There are a hundred and sixty operatives down there. You're telling me that's the most precise fix they've got?'

'Well, with all the umbrellas up, it's hard to be certain.'

Kleig was no longer listening. He stood swaying uncertainly in his black patent evening shoes, staring trance-like at the image on the high definition monitor in front of him. His hand shot out, gripping the edge of the control panel till the knuckles went white.

The rain shower began to ease. As Fiske's guests gradually lowered their umbrellas, McKinnon saw sentinels moving through the crowd in his direction. With a muttered 'thank you', he left the girl, and pushed off to where the throng was thickest – at the cathedral entrance. Here, sentinels flanking both sides of the Romanesque-style doorway were scanning every face in the crowd. Something in their vigilance told him they'd been given a specific objective.

He began to hang back, letting the bulk of the guests move ahead of him. He could make a dash across an expanse of the square that had opened up to his right, maybe lose himself in the buildings beyond. But then what? Fiske has chosen this place because it is totally isolated. I need to buy myself some time. If I can get past those monkeys on the door, I may have a chance. They'll hardly risk a scene inside the cathedral itself. Not on Fiske's big day. When the service is over, I could have a problem or three. But I'll have the whole ceremony to figure that one out.

Now there was only a handful of guests left to go in. A tall man, in front of McKinnon, stripped off his raincoat and laid it on the overnight bag he was carrying. McKinnon stepped forward and, as unobtrusively as he could, trapped the trailing collar of it under his foot. A second later, he buttoned himself into it, and lifted the collar around his neck.

McKinnon recognized the man in front of him immediately as Senator James Mitchelson. That profile of his was unmistakable.

Hannah was directed to go through the same process as she had for the others.

'Same list, same story, but something more . . . Mitchelson's name has turned up at the end of one of the future targets files – those shown with future diagnosis dates. There's a date under his name too – February last. Looks like he's a contact or something.'

A contact. Was the main list a list of covert contacts that could link a prospective member, who would soon be desperate for specialist medical help, to the cult that could provide it?

McKinnon covered his mouth with his hand. 'Marion Fulbright married, Hannah – I read something about it a year or two back. She uses her husband's name too now. The list may not have been updated. Run a search again, tell the program to look for all possible matches.'

324

A moment later Hannah said, 'Bingo! You're right. She's now Doctor Marion Fulbright-Collins. She's turned up at the bottom of a target file too – some guy with a diagnosis date shown as being in four months.'

A doctor. A contact like Mitchelson . . .

'There's some stuff under her name, too . . . June twenty-seventh, this year, "The Hilton Hotel, NYC; Amnesty International Fundraiser". Then there's what looks like some medical stuff: Gamma viru. Density 1/250.'

McKinnon weighed up all the information. A time, a place? Maybe that was when she last met him. But what was the significance of the medical data? Viru: was that virulency? Bacteria were measured by their virulency. What tied all three together?

The only possible answer hit him. The woman wasn't *a* contact! She was *the* contact! She'd hit the guy with a bacteria capsule of that specification on that date, at that function. She'd given the poor bastard on file some God-awful disease, that would be in the right state of development to be treated with REGENS in four months.

She and Mitchelson, and Cosgrave, and . . .

McKinnon looked around him

About five hundred others . . .

Was this the targeting group? The hit group? Covert core disciples who carry more than a message?

Who carry disease. Human vermin.

This isn't just a family get-together. No one comes this far, risks this much for that. This has to be some kind of convention, or mass briefing session, with the ceremony thrown in as light relief.

McKinnon looked at Mitchelson. He searched his memory. I did a piece on him a year or two back.

325

What was he peddling then? A campaign to save some old colleges . . .

McKinnon moved up to his side. 'Jimmy! Good to see you.'

The senator shot him a wary glance.

'It's me, Mike. Mike Austin. We were at Wallbrook together.'

Mitchelson's face softened a fraction, but he still looked very ill at ease as he searched his memory. 'Is that right?'

'Do you still see any of the crowd?'

There was a pause.

McKinnon saw two sentinels to his left begin to close in.

The senator gave a nervous smile. 'It's a funny thing you should say that . . .'

The senator and McKinnon, conscious of a dozen sets of eyes following his every move, followed the last of the guests into the cathedral. In his peripheral vision, McKinnon could see several sentinels radioing in for fresh orders. As he and Mitchelson passed, one took a step forward towards him, then seemed to think better of it and moved back to join his anxious-looking colleagues grouped around the vast bronze doors.

Fiske, dressed in an immaculate grey morning suit, paced nervously, his cellphone an inch from his face. *'He's where?'*

Kleig's voice was breathless, he was clearly running. 'In the nave of the cathedral. There was nothing they could do . . .'

Fiske took a deep breath, and considered the matter for a moment. An aide moved up to where he and the bishop stood in the vestry. 'Three minutes, sir.'

A strange calmness seemed to possess Fiske now, one that had gripped him at such times before. He walked to the door that stood ajar in front of him, and stole a look at the congregation gathered in the body of the cathedral that was the culmination of a life's work. He picked out a face here, noted another there. To allow McKinnon's presence to intrude upon this moment was unthinkable. He was an irrelevance, an irritation that would soon be scratched.

For more than twenty years, I've had to endure McBain and Kerensky, sit by and watch as they received the acclaim I should have had. For more than twenty years, I've hidden myself away, so that no one should say, 'Who is this runt of a man that dares to set himself up as a godhead?'

Today that era ends. This building and all it stands for shows that I have that right. Today, before me, stand those who will change everything. A hand-picked army. Men and women who will change this country into the theocracy it should always have been: church and state as one body, capturing the hearts and the minds of the people.

My church . . . my state . . . my body . . .

'Are you there, sir?' Kleig sounded distinctly uneasy. To his astonishment, Fiske said, 'Perhaps we should look on this as a blessing. McKinnon's come to us, I told you he would. He's saved us a great deal of trouble. Tell central control to lock all exits. His only way out will be the way he came in.'

327

CHAPTER TWENTY-FOUR

Once inside the cathedral, it was immediately clear to McKinnon that to get a seat in the nave, one had to have an invitation with a number on it, or give one's name to a woman seated at a table inside the door who then consulted a list. Now the crowd around him thinned as guests peeled off to find the seats they'd been allocated. Suddenly McKinnon felt very exposed. All around the nave, the eyes of sentinels locked on to him as orders were radioed in. Heavyset men dressed in ill-fitting morning suits began to move down the aisles towards him.

To his immediate right was a narrow doorway. Beyond it, a spiral staircase. The usher standing in front of it shifted to the right to help untangle a couple of half-open umbrellas, and McKinnon made his move.

He was up the staircase before the first sentinel had reached the passage. The spiral reached high into the roof to a long gallery. Work here was still far from complete. McKinnon picked his way between ladders, clambered over tools and building materials that littered the way ahead. He could hear the bare boards beneath him creak as sentinels ran to close with him.

Powerful resonant chords rose from an organ beneath him and the voice of a choir, hundreds strong, filled the vast nave. Now the congregation rose to their feet and lent their voices to the chorus.

Ten yards behind him, McKinnon could hear the tramp of feet. He ran on, swinging a wheelbarrow into the path of his pursuers, pulling down timber that had been stacked against a wall, anything that came to hand that might be used to slow them up another few seconds. There .was bright daylight at the end of the gallery now. Maybe there would be a second staircase and a way out. A feeling in his gut told him he would never reach it without taking more drastic action.

The open door, in the architrave ahead, looked good and solid, the lock on it clearly designed to keep out the most single-minded of intruders. Men burst into the space behind him. He dashed through the doorway and turned to ram it shut, but the sentinels were too close behind. A spade lay against a wall. He lifted it, swung it around his head and caught the first man through the door a sturdy crack across the forehead. If he made a noise, McKinnon never heard it. The swell of the organ and choir directly below drowned all other sound now. As the wounded sentinel went down, McKinnon could see that the man immediately behind was levelling a Glock 9mm automatic at his neck. He dipped low and swung again. The edge of the shovel sliced into the man's right temple, throwing him back into the path of those behind him. McKinnon dropped his weapon, stepped over the first man, and threw his weight against the door, slamming it. The key snapped the deadlock home with a satisfying click. He pulled it free, tossed it down the gallery, and took a gulp of air.

As he tried to run forward, a hand locked around his right ankle, throwing him forward on to his knees. He twisted and yanked, trying to get to the spade, then heard the click of a gun behind his left ear. The man he'd first hit struggled to his feet. The right side of his face was a sheet of blood. Pieter Kleig stood there swaying, trying to keep the gun steady, mopping at the gash in the side of his head with the collar of his morning coat.

As the sentinel commander struggled to figure out his next move, the music beneath them wound to a finish. For a moment there was total silence. Then there was the sound of a man's voice as the first lesson was read.

McKinnon turned his back and began to move off. Kleig shook himself. Blood sprayed across the dusty loft. A puzzled look spread across his broken face.

What's the fucker doing? I've got a gun on him.

Then the reality of the situation struck him. If I use the gun, I disrupt the service. I ruin the Apostles' greatest moment.

Clearly McKinnon had already figured that out. He shot Kleig a wan smile and reached down for the spade again, daring him to come on.

Fiske's voice, way below, reading from *The Lost Gospel* filled the silence.

'Take this gift, the greatest gift I have to offer, my love and the abiding love of my father who is in heaven . . .'

Another spade lay in a wheelbarrow to the right. Kleig made a dash for it. McKinnon swung at him as he went, trying to cut him off. His next blow was deftly parried. Kleig seemed to find new strength.

'Through him, and through him alone, will you find peace and understanding.'

He swung his weapon upwards, trying to catch the interloper in the crotch. McKinnon jerked his hips back and landed a blow on Kleig's shoulder, dropping him to his knees.

Below them, a congressman's eyes left his prayer book and scanned the ornate roof above. Two rows behind him, the wife of a State Department official

331

found herself suddenly distracted by a faint banging above her.

McKinnon dived to the left, but a second too late. Kleig's spade smacked into the right side of his ribcage, crushing the air out of him. Kleig stopped to wipe his eyes, and McKinnon made another move towards the pool of light at the end of the gallery. Suddenly the sound of the organ was deafening. He clamped his hands to his ears and pressed on. Might Kleig risk a shot now?

Thousands of glistening pipes rose all around him. Some part of McKinnon's mind registered that he was now in the organ loft. Kleig limped on behind him, cursing. His fingers raked through his pockets. Where was that fucking silencer? He looked up, his eyes blinking at the shaft of daylight ahead. McKinnon mustn't get to the cupola. Whatever happens he mustn't get that far . . .

With the last of his strength, he threw himself forward, bringing McKinnon down heavily amongst the organ pipes. He twisted the man over on to his back, clamping his shoulders against the floor with his knees, and closed his hands around his throat. McKinnon was all in now. Somewhere, beyond the pain, he could feel his consciousness beginning to slip away. Suddenly his arms were the heaviest things in the world. Cling on to the sound . . . don't let go . . .

Till now, the piece the organist below had been playing had called only for low notes, produced by the highest of the pipes surrounding the men.

In some distant place McKinnon could hear a wheezing rattling sound. He knew it came from within him.

The organist changed register. One hundred and twenty decibels of pealing, piercing, treble notes broke from the shoulder-high pipes, an inch from Kleig's face. His whole body shook, like someone had wired him up to

332

the national grid. Something gave inside his head. He clapped his hands to his ears. There was only silence and agonizing pain.

McKinnon's head was below the shortest pipe. The volume even there was close to deafening, but the three feet or so made the difference. To him the noise became a lifeline, pulling him, choking and coughing, back into some semblance of consciousness. He tried to sit up. Kleig, astride his chest, was still writhing in agony. McKinnon reached out to take what he knew might be his last chance at life. He gritted his teeth, wrenched at an organ pipe above him, breaking it free. With a gasp of exertion, he struck his assailant a single bone-splintering whack across the side of the head. Kleig tipped over backwards, his head dropping out of sight into the part of the framework that supported the organ pipes. There was a hollow snap beneath him.

Immediately, the sound of the organ faltered and faded a little.

As Kleig struggled to right himself, McKinnon saw that a narrow blast of air was now blowing his sodden hair around.

Sunday school. A lifetime ago. The organ in the church in Finchley . . .

Kleig, his head a ball of red, was thrashing wildly, desperate to get a foothold. One open eye fixed McKinnon with a dreadful determination.

You'll ruin everything, Kleig's mind screamed. Tear everything down . . . Somehow I must stop you.

McKinnon reached down into the open flooring in front of him.

The air to make the organ work was produced by a massive pump.

He could feel air being forced out of a split in the side

333

of a thick rubber tube. Kleig had pulled himself upright now. With his last particle of strength, McKinnon tore at the broken edge of the tubing. The sound of the organ below became erratic. As the line broke free, it cut out with a rasping wheeze. The blast of air was so forceful that he had the greatest difficulty in holding the pipe steady. Dust began to blow in every direction. He braced his back against a beam and locked the tube under his left arm. Then he reached for Kleig's head, dragged it back by the hair till the mouth was stretched open. He gripped the pipe tightly. It vibrated in his hand like some headless serpent, and then, with all the force he could muster, he rammed it deep into Kleig's throat.

Air, pumped at a pressure sufficient to fill five miles of pipework in a fraction of a second, instantly burst his lungs. Kleig staggered back, his chest heaving, his eyes bulging from his head, and lurched out into the pool of daylight – the open gallery that ran around the dome of the cathedral. He paused for a second against the stone balustrade, and then, without a sound, tipped forward, dropping a hundred and twenty feet to the altar steps below.

Fiske's hands were spread out across the altar in an act of supplication. They jerked free as Kleig's body connected. A spray of dark blood drenched the altar cloth.

For a second, there was total silence in the cathedral. Then a great cry went up, a deep unearthly sound that echoed through the beams and masonry like the wail of banshees. Faces gawped in horror, eyes blinked in shock.

Fiske turned towards the nave. His mouth moved but no sound came out. His eyes flickered to those in the congregation who'd resisted attending the service till the last day, who'd openly feared that to be caught publicly aligning themselves with the most controversial sect in the country could prove to be an act of the greatest folly. He had given them his personal reassurance: 'Security will be of the highest level. Only chosen disciples will be allowed entrance. You'll be amongst fellow believers. You'll be safe . . .'

Now he saw only panic in their eyes. Something had clearly gone terribly wrong. Now there would be police, publicity.

Senators, congressmen, state governors, and others in high office, who'd taken what Fiske alone could offer, and done his bidding since, surged forward first, in a desperate attempt to get to the emergency exits. But those seated close by, who were already there, found them locked by some kind of remote-controlled device. They screamed at those behind them to hold back, but before many could make a sound, the air was crushed out of them, as they were slammed back against the doors. Others were trampled underfoot as the mob surged forward.

Fiske, desperate to avert a second disaster, screamed into his short wave, *'Open the doors down there! Open the doors!'*

One man, with less to lose than some, reached for his mobile phone and called 911. Before he was done, a sentinel ripped the phone from his hand.

A traditional turkey dinner and a chilled bottle of Labatts; little else had invaded Vern McCreight's thoughts in the last half hour. But now the voice of the flight controller at Police HQ in Sioux Falls, still a sibilant rattle in his headset, was turning that into a distant possibility. His partner, Shaun Rafferty, checked the navigation screen in front of him and gave Vern a bearing, and he swung the Bell helicopter into the wind and headed south west.

The Apostles of Christ's arrival in the area had attracted some media attention, seven years back, when it was announced that it was they who had bought the five-thousand-acre lot to the south of Wessington Springs. Most folk in the county took the view they were isolated enough there to be of little threat to anyone. Rafferty and McCreight had flown over the new complex a hundred times in the last year, watched as the cathedral had begun to dominate the skyline, but never once had they had reason to make a landing there till now.

McCreight checked his watch. 'What time does your family eat on Thanksgiving?'

'Usually around five. Hey, so some Jesus freak calls in a 670. Doesn't mean it has to be the Alamo down there. More likely he just shot up some bad stuff. We could still make it.'

The Wessington Springs commune was clearly visible a couple of miles ahead when the voice of the controller at the airfield there came on the line, asking them to identify themselves.

'SFPD. Answering a 911 call from an Edward S. Hart. He's reported an incident involving a fatality.'

'Is this some kinda joke? No fatalities here, I assure you. It must be a mistake.'

'Well, we have to check it out anyway.'

There was a pause, like the controller was doing some checking of his own. 'Look, you're not needed here, fellas. The sheriff knows the score. We handle our own law enforcement. If there was a problem, believe me . . .'

Rafferty tightened the focus on his binoculars. Way below him, he could make out people running, bursting from the cathedral building. Some rushed for cars, others collapsed or ran to the aid of those who were clearly injured.

336

'Jesus, Vern, it's like a war zone down there.'

'Clear down!' McCreight bellowed into his mouthpiece. 'I need to call in for back-up.'

He swung the chopper into a tight turn, levelled off, and made a landing in a parking lot next to the cathedral. Two sentinels pushed through the crowd and began to run towards them, clearly with the intention of heading them off.

'Don't even think it,' Rafferty said. The two men skidded to a halt and stood eyeing the cops nervously. Rafferty and McCreight elbowed their way through, into the chaos that seemed to spread out in every direction. All across the compound there were shaken, distraught people. A woman's face, her eyes wild with fear, loomed up an inch from Rafferty's.

'*My husband got caught in the crush . . . You have to do something.*'

McCreight spun around as they pushed on. The unconscious man being carried away on a makeshift stretcher behind him had a familiar face. He'd seen it on CBS only the day before. Senator . . . what was it?

'*Don't just stand there! Get some paramedics in here!*' one of the men with the stretcher party screamed as they hurried by.

'They're on their way,' Rafferty called. The two cops ran towards the cathedral building now.

A party of three, seemingly unhurt, veered sharply to the right as they approached, immediately attracting their attention. McCreight changed tack, and tried to head them off. The three broke into a run. A chauffeur-driven limo braked hard ahead of them, and they clambered in. Rafferty noted the licence plate as the car sped towards the entrance of the complex, then was forced to dive left as a large Merc skidded and swerved after it.

*   *   *

McKinnon moved slowly up to the coping that ran around the walkway on the cathedral roof, and looked down. Beneath him, to the right, was a fire escape. It looked as though it could be reached from the doorway he could see across the roof. The pain in his right shoulder was a dull stomach-churning ache now. Arm movement was limited, but his grip seemed positive enough. He struggled across to the door, put his weight against it, and began to work his way down the steel ladder to the ground.

In the distance, at the edge of the complex, he could see a line of cars snaking out on to the highway. He was certain that they carried senators, congressmen, and others who had no wish to be found there when the police arrived in force.

His head swam as he tried to get Hannah on the cell phone.

'Drop everything!' he told her. 'Get out on the road! Take the licence plate numbers of every car that comes by – they have to come by you, there's no other route.'

'Why? What's happened, Joel?'

Now he could see two sentinels heading towards the foot of the ladder.

'Just do it, Hannah.'

He stopped. What the fuck do I do now? Go all the way back, and face the likelihood of the same thing the other end?

He moved down and, as one of the sentinels reached out to grab him, kicked out wildly. The man caught his leg and, with a powerful yank, pulled him off the ladder. He dropped about six feet, his head striking the cobbles of the path beneath with a dull crack. The flickering lights around him cut out like someone pulled a switch.

One of the sentinels took a knife from his pocket and

moved forward. He turned McKinnon over on to his back. There was a click as the blade locked into place.

Behind him, the howl of a siren broke through the din of the crowd, and a police car rolled over the grass at speed towards them.

CHAPTER TWENTY-FIVE

The Lear jet hit turbulence. The cabin lights flickered uncertainly for a moment, and the dozen or so members of Fiske's coterie, most of whom stood in groups in the centre aisle, frantically trying to reach different divisions of the organization on cell phones, were thrown off balance.

Fiske, standing at the rear of the plane, made a grab for the seat back to the right of him. For a second, the scrambling people around him merged with images of the mayhem he'd seen play out in the cathedral less than an hour before.

An aide struggled down the aisle towards him. 'Excuse me, sir.'

Fiske fought to bring his mind back from the edge of the abyss that had opened up in some distant part of his consciousness. His eyes, filmy and bloodshot, met the aide's.

'You'd better come, sir.'

With some difficulty, Fiske eased himself out of the seat and moved down the plane to the open area, amidships. The CNN report playing out on the TV set in the corner showed the bodies of the wounded being carried on stretchers from the nave of the cathedral.

'It now seems certain that at least two men died, and as many as twenty-seven others were injured tonight, when panic broke out during a religious meeting at an

Apostles of Christ commune, near Sioux Falls in South Dakota. Cult members had been attending a ceremony at a new cathedral there, and the casualties occurred during a dash for the emergency exits, after a security man, employed by the sect, fell to his death from a gallery inside the building. The Apostles of Christ, one of the fastest-growing religious sects in the country, have been linked to controversy many times before . . .'

Fiske turned away. He appeared to stumble. An aide ran to help him. He pushed him aside and moved uncertainly back down the aisle.

Another aide hurried up from the rear of the aircraft, and whispered into Fiske's ear, 'There's no doubt, sir. The man in the organ loft was McKinnon.'

'Where is he now?' The voice was calm, so quiet the aide had to struggle to hear the words above the drone of the engines.

'Two of our operatives had him, but had to give him up to the police. We believe he was amongst those taken to hospital in Sioux Falls.'

'Thank you.' Fiske sat down and sipped at a large cognac.

So he's free. He was a witness to everything. More than a witness: an integral part. He and his father. Their destinies and my own are intertwined, so it seems . . . Hopelessly entangled . . .

Someone will listen to McKinnon now. It's just a matter of time.

Pain. Blinding head pain . . . cushioned in something. The last effects of a powerful pain-killer.

McKinnon lay still, his eyes tightly closed. The most primitive of animal instincts kicked in automatically. Play dead. Listen . . .

342

All around him, the hum of low voices, the clack of heels hurrying on a hard floor. A woman sobbing somewhere. The voice of a man calling out. He sounded delirious.

McKinnon opened his eyes a little. Hard white light . . . Beds . . . Men and women in white coats. A hospital ward. There were women patients in here too. This was an emergency ward somewhere. To his far right, he could see a uniformed policeman sitting at a bedside taking notes.

McKinnon's eyes snapped open. What do they know? Do they know who I am?

Sometime later – McKinnon had no way of knowing how long – a scrubbed female face loomed into his vision. 'Ah, so you're awake. How are you feeling?'

Give nothing away. Not yet. McKinnon reached upwards to find a bandage around his head. 'My head's killing me.'

She took his pulse. 'Do you know what happened to you?'

McKinnon thought for a second. 'Yeah, pretty much.'

A long forefinger was thrust up in front of his face. 'How many fingers do you see?'

'I'm seeing double, if that's what you're asking.'

The nurse consulted the clipboard above his head. 'Yes, well, you may for a while. You have a skull fracture – a relatively minor one. You also have two cracked ribs, some ligament damage, and a number of superficial injuries: contusions of the neck, and back.'

'At the risk of sounding corny, where am I?'

'The St Teresa Hospital in Sioux Falls.' The nurse took out a pen. 'We couldn't find any identification on you when you came in . . .'

You bet your sweet life you couldn't.

343

'So we couldn't notify anyone you were in here. Could I have a name?'

In his peripheral vision, McKinnon could see that the cop had moved down the ward to question the occupant of a bed closer to him. A name? Sure. 'Wheeler. Mark Wheeler, twelve Mayfield Avenue, Finchley, England.'

She wrote that down, and put the clipboard back on the wall. 'You're a long way from home, Mr Wheeler.'

McKinnon's nose took in the smell of disinfectant. 'Yeah.'

'There's a phone beside your bed if you need to call someone.'

'Thanks.'

'I'll get you some more pain-killers and some water.' She gestured behind her. 'You can see how things are here right now, so it may be a while before I can do any more for you. Press the bell to your left, if you really need to.'

'The light is hurting my eyes. Could you pull the curtains around?'

She did as he asked, then hurried off. McKinnon searched his mind for Hannah's number, lifted the phone and dialled.

Hannah let out a shriek of relief.

'Dear God, Joel, I thought you were dead. Why didn't you . . .?'

'I couldn't. You heard what happened?'

'Are you kidding! It's all been on TV, radio, you name it. Are you okay?'

'A little bashed about that's all. A security man bought it, I know that. Who else?'

'A senator got crushed. There's a lot of injured.'

'Look, I can't say a lot now, there're cops all over the place. Just tell me, did Muddy get out all right?'

344

'Yes, he's fine. He did great. He really got the goods on them this time.'

'Good. I'll call you back the minute it's safe.'

'Police in South Dakota have confirmed that the Republican senator for West Virginia, Lawrence S. Pendleton, was killed last night during a religious ceremony at an Apostles of Christ commune, near Sioux Falls.'

The CNN report carried much of the same footage – the wreckage inside the cathedral, caused by the fleeing congregation, the injured being carried from the scene – as it had the night before. 'The FBI are anxious to establish why it was that a Republican senator came to be attending a meeting of one of the country's most controversial sects. They're also keen to speak with the cult's reclusive founder, J. Richmond Fiske, who is understood to have been one of the first to have left the scene after an incident in which two people died, and more than twenty-seven were injured . . .'

Hannah studied the report for a moment longer then turned to the tall raven-haired woman sitting to her left. 'It seems that you have no more idea than any of the other networks on what really went on down there.'

ABC TV's head of current affairs, Lauren Silverman, turned off the set and ground her cigarette into the ashtray on her glass-topped desk. 'The word we have is that there were at least a dozen other heavy hitters in the congregation. I must have heard thirty different names bandied about in the last eight hours.'

'And?'

'Our people on the ground down there haven't found a scrap of hard evidence to back that up.'

'And my guess is they won't. No one will. The Apostles impose a code of silence on their members as strict as the Mafia's code of *omertà*. Only theirs is backed up by mind-massaging techniques that come straight out of *The Manchurian Candidate*. Believe me, I know. Even those on the periphery of the cult know better than to rat on them. Joel McKinnon is a professional journalist. He was at the centre of the whole thing. He identified at least seven key movers at the ceremony. I got the licence plate numbers of eighteen others who had good reason to want to be out of there before the authorities arrived.'

She then told her of the data she now had in her possession, showing conclusively that they, and hundreds of other highly placed government figures, were closet members of the sect and were being used to bend Congress to Fiske's will. She told her how Fiske used REGENS to turn them.

'I can show that many of those present at the ceremony are part of an elite force, charged with the task of planting bacteria capsules, designed to infect their targets with life-threatening diseases, ones that only REGENS can cure. I have evidence to show that the capsules themselves were developed using prisoners as human guinea pigs.'

Lauren blinked slowly. She was clearly having difficulty taking all this in.

Hannah fixed her steadily. 'I believe I can show a conspiracy to subvert and take over the government of this country that reaches into the White House itself.'

Lauren walked over to the window, and looked down at the street, twenty storeys below. She threw up her hands in a gesture of frustration. 'I'd kill for the lowdown on this. Who wouldn't? If what you're telling me is on the level, we're looking at the greatest political crisis this country has faced since the fifties. But, Hannah, you're asking for guarantees I alone can't give.'

Hannah folded her arms. 'Well, this doesn't move

346

one step forward till I know we have a deal with the authorities.'

Lauren was clearly choosing her words with care. 'We don't know each other, Hannah. But I've been in current affairs a long time . . .'

'Joel says you run the tightest ship in the business.'

'If we can't stand this up, no one will, I can promise you that. What I can't promise you is exactly how the FBI will react. In the normal way, we'd go with this, and worry about them down the line. But, as you'll appreciate, this is a very sensitive situation. In the circumstances, we'd have to play it straight with them right from the beginning. We've certainly managed to – how shall I put it? – come to an understanding with them on certain issues in the past, but Mr McKinnon is a convicted killer, on the run from a maximum security prison. Presented with the evidence, and a full and accurate account of what really happened in the UK last year, I can't see how they can avoid intervening on his behalf. But, as I'm sure you realize, these things take time. The British authorities are sure to begin extradition proceedings against him the minute he surfaces. Exactly what the Feds will choose to do in response to that, I can't tell you.'

'Well, before anyone starts screaming that I'm with-holding information, they need to know that I have no better idea where Joel is right now than they do.'

'Good.'

'He discharged himself from the hospital in Sioux Falls yesterday. He'll call me from wherever he is, when he's ready to. If I can't give him the assurances he needs, I can promise you he won't come in. If he doesn't come in, you don't get what you need to proceed with this.'

Lauren lifted a phone. 'I'm gonna get legal affairs on to

this right now. In the end, it's gonna depend on how much we have to bargain with. My understanding is that the FBI are mounting a massive investigation into everything to do with the Apostles as we speak.'

Hannah got up and began to gather her papers together.

'Well, I've got a three-year start on them. Joel and I can point them to stuff happening on Capitol Hill right now. Very few others in this country can. And you believe that, or I wouldn't still be here in your office.' She moved over to the door. 'Fiske knows he's in big trouble now, and every minute we stand around playing "Getting to Know You", crucial records, that could rivet him and everyone connected with him to the wall, will be going into the shredder. I have a lot at stake here too. Just about everything, as a matter of fact. I don't know how you're gonna pull it off, and to be honest, I don't care. I just know that if I don't have a clear understanding with you by midnight tomorrow, including an assurance that Joel will get bail while this plays out, then I go straight to NBC and begin again.'

Lauren Silverman sat down to a meeting with ABC's legal team, certain in her mind that she held the keys to what could prove to be the most important story of her career. The attorneys present emphasized what she already knew: the FBI's principal concern would be that Joel McKinnon was an escaped killer, wanted in Britain, a country with which the US had had an extradition treaty for over a century. Anything he or Hannah Rostov might have to tell them, concerning the Apostles of Christ – regardless of its current notoriety – would doubtless be overshadowed by that fact.

It was agreed that she should approach Warren K. Morgenson, the recently appointed assistant director of the FBI, who had once been a journalist himself and would, it was felt, have a better appreciation than most of the value McKinnon and Hannah's information might have to the rapidly widening investigation the agency was mounting into the affairs of the cult.

Morgenson listened patiently for an hour to what ABC's head of current affairs had come to say to him.

The timing could not have been more propitious. Only that morning he'd attended a meeting with the Attorney-General, who, as a result of the controversy surrounding the incident at the Wessington Springs commune, had ordered that the investigation into the affairs of the Apostles be stepped up, and a report filed regarding the relationship that it was believed might exist between high-ranking members of the government and the cult. Such was the media frenzy, the Secretary of State had considered ordering the FBI to raid the sect's premises there and then, but was prevailed upon to wait until more hard evidence, showing conspiracy to corrupt, could be gathered.

Morgenson thanked Silverman for setting up the meeting, and promised to call her back that evening. He then began to turn over in his mind everything she'd told him.

Her informants had provided her with tantalizing samples of the evidence they had. One schedule, showing the link between Marston Moor Prison, Falk Pharmaceutical and the cult, immediately filled gaps in the Agency's own information regarding the reach of Fiske's corporate interests.

Morgenson was then forced to confront one fact: if McKinnon was lying, and his story that he'd been set up for the murder of the woman in the UK by Fiske's people

349

was one massive invention, how was it that he'd ended up in the one maximum security prison in England Fiske controlled? A fax to a contact in the British Home Office soon established that there were at least seven other jails in the UK to which he could have reasonably been sent, and that Marston Moor had been overcrowded at the time. Lauren Silverman had promised that data, obtained from the Apostles' own files, would show that there had been collusion between those acting for the cult and a Home Office official, to ensure that McKinnon would be sent there nevertheless. Once there, she said, the intention was to make sure that he never left alive.

If the ABC woman was to be believed, McKinnon and Rostov had information regarding areas of Fiske's activities of which the FBI currently knew nothing, including some which might bear crucially on the security of the President himself.

All in all, it seemed like it was going to be important to have these two on hand for some time to come.

If the data they provided revealed corruption inside the Home Office, and showed that a private prison franchise had been awarded to an organization owned by one of the most dangerous religious sects in the world, and that hideous medical experiments had been carried out on prisoners there, the British government would soon have a great deal to occupy it. If Silverman's submissions held water, the Crown's case against McKinnon would become unsupportable. This would be an ill-judged moment, then, for the UK authorities to start jumping up and down, waving urgent extradition applications.

Early that evening, Morgenson called Lauren Silverman at home, and told her that if McKinnon came in, he would be put into one of the more salubrious safe houses the agency had in the city, with the promise of relative free-dom of movement, in the care of one of their operatives, until some kind of deal could be hammered out with the British. He agreed that he, Hannah and a third party, Muddy Harbin, would be granted immunity from federal prosecution regarding the hacks they'd made into Fiske's database – a condition that ABC's lawyers had stressed was important to have established – and confirmed that Silverman, or a member of her staff, could be present at all key interviews conducted with McKinnon and Hannah, and that all press statements issued prior to the network's exclusive coverage of the story on an agreed date would be subject to her approval.

As soon as Morgenson hung up, Lauren Silverman called Hannah on the mobile phone number she'd been given.

At six fifteen am, the following morning, an FBI jet touched down on a private landing field in Sioux Falls. At six thirty am, it was joined by a helicopter, carrying an ABC camera crew. A little before seven am, a battered taxi rolled on to the tarmac, and Joel McKinnon, his bandaged head hidden under an improbable-looking hat, stepped uncertainly out. Hannah hurried over to him. She put her arms around him, and kissed him gently.

'How're you feeling, babe?'

'Pretty spaced. You?'

'Beat. It's been a helluva few days.'

'I'll bet.' He warily studied the two agents standing a few yards off. 'These guys better be on the level.'

CHAPTER TWENTY-SIX

A Hughes 500 T-tail helicopter moved out of the clouds, and hovered over Fiske's compound in Highlands, North Carolina. The pilot could clearly see FBI vehicles moving up the steep road to the entrances, on the west and north-eastern perimeter fences.

The chopper's nose dropped, and it made its descent, landing in a parking lot to the left of the mansion, which was still partly hidden under a forest of scaffolding.

Armed agents, in helmets and flak jackets, poured into the buildings, as trucks and jeeps rolled on to the gravel drive.

Twenty minutes later, the agent-in-charge crossed Fiske's office, passed empty bookshelves and display cases, and moved out on to the balcony. The Blue Ridge Mountains were now clearly visible in the early morning sun.

He looked down. There was no escape route this way. He held the mouthpiece of his mobile phone a little closer, to cut down the sound of the safe door being drilled out on the floor above him, and called Morgenson.

'Well, if Fiske was here, sir, he's long gone. The only staff here now are a couple of Mexicans. They say they haven't seen him in months.'

The view from Morgenson's office on the fifth floor

of the FBI building in downtown Washington DC was of a rubble-strewn building site. Apart from the nights they would spend in the agency's safe house, it was all McKinnon and Hannah would see of the outside world for almost a week. Although McKinnon's concussion had eased somewhat, he still found it difficult to concentrate for long, and the early interviews had often ground to a halt. When he needed to rest, the focus had turned to Hannah. Morgenson had soon realized that he was in the company of the greatest authority on the Apostles of Christ he was ever likely to debrief.

When the data she and McKinnon had provided on the movement was put together with the FBI's own material, gathered as a part of the Caulfield Initiative, a sufficiently complete picture of the cult's activities emerged for Morgenson to feel justified in authorizing raids on Fiske's compound in North Carolina, the Highlands Clinic, the cult's commune in South Dakota, and the head offices of Falk Pharmaceutical Inc. Delays, he pointed out to the Attorney-General, could result in valuable evidence being destroyed.

As more records covering the cult's activities became available, and further layers of Fiske's operation were peeled back and the discoveries made public, media interest ballooned. By the third day, most TV networks had cancelled a proportion of their night-time scheduling to make way for news and comment on the revelations. In the corridors of Capitol Hill there was talk of very little else.

Aubrey Stamford-Smith stood holding the phone, swaying slightly. The only sound in the room was the drone of traffic along Queen Anne's Gate.

354

'That's a preposterous suggestion!' he said at last. 'I . . . I give you my word that no such policy . . .'

As the Prison Director continued with his tirade, Stamford-Smith reached for the remote control unit on his desk and switched on the TV that sat in the corner of his office. BBC2 had coverage of Prime Minister's question time, live from the House of Commons. He watched, with an eerie detachment, as the Shadow Home Secretary got to his feet, and asked permission of the Speaker to put an unlisted question.

The Director's voice hammered in Stamford-Smith's ear. 'If there is a particle of truth in this . . .'

But Stamford-Smith's attention was on the TV now. The shadow minister's voice broke through the wall of shock that was rapidly encasing him.

'Would the Prime Minister like to comment on American media reports that claim that inmates of Her Majesty's Super Maximum Security Prison at Marston Moor, in Yorkshire, have, for a period of more than three years, been subjected to cruel and inhuman medical experiments . . .?'

Stamford-Smith hung up the phone, and switched off the TV. He locked the main door of his office, and stood staring into the flames of the fake coal fire.

Almost immediately the black phone on his desk rang again. Then the grey one next to it. Before long, there was knocking at the door and the sound of agitated voices in the corridor.

The knocking, and the calls for him to answer, became more urgent. By the time he let himself out of the private entrance that led out to a back street, pressmen and TV crews were beginning to move into the street.

He stopped in the doorway of a men's tailoring business for a moment, and pretended to window-shop.

If I go home, what will that solve? he asked himself.

How long he stood there he did not know, but a crash of glass behind him made him turn. A small gathering of people across the street from his office were pelting the windows of the building with bottles. One shattered the central pane of the room he had been in only minutes before. A squad car skidded to a halt on the corner, and the mob ran for cover.

Stamford-Smith pulled the collar of his coat up around his ears, and pushed off into the crowds of homeward-bound shoppers and tourists. He turned the corner and made his way down to St James's Underground Station.

The paper-seller, seeing him coming, reached for the *Evening Standard* as he had a thousand times before. But Stamford-Smith hurried by him, oblivious to all around him.

The platform for westbound trains was packed with commuters. Those with connections to make at the main line station of Victoria, jostled for position at the platform's edge. Stamford-Smith forced his way through and watched for moving lights in the tunnel to his right.

McKinnon was always going to be a problem, he'd known that from the first day the file had been passed to him. Committing him to the facility at Marston Moor was never going to be the end of the matter. From the day news that he'd broken out had filtered through to his office, he'd waited. For what, he was uncertain.

The lights at the end of the tunnel-opening to his left were those of a train.

For today. He'd waited for today.

The District Line train began to thunder down the platform. Stamford-Smith closed his eyes, gritted his teeth and threw himself forward.

*   *   *

'Using all the data gathered,' Morgenson said, 'we've put together a list of more than a hundred and fifty people whose membership of the cult, and activities on its behalf, are, as the Secretary of State put it this morning, a cause for the gravest concern.'

It was early evening on the fourth day after the Wessington Springs incident. There was complete silence in the office as Hannah and McKinnon scanned the schedule in front of them.

'A really useful mix,' Hannah said at last. 'The high, the mighty. Key movers from a dozen fields.'

McKinnon began to ring names on the list in pencil. 'It's interesting that Fiske seldom targets the top man in a government department; he usually goes for the next man down, some nice faceless fella, with a low public profile.'

'Agents have started taking testimony from as many of these folks as we've been able to pin down,' Morgenson said. 'As you might expect, none has so far admitted to being a member of the Apostles of Christ movement. A few have said they received treatment at the Highlands Clinic – needless to say they deny any knowledge of it being tied to the cult.'

'The Apostles' records speak for themselves,' Hannah said. 'All these people have been making regular payments to the cult.'

'The consistent line we've been getting is that they believed they were simply making donations to support a hospital that they feel saved their lives.'

McKinnon laughed. 'Sure!'

Morgenson went over to a fridge in the corner of his office, and began to pass out cans of beer. 'It wouldn't be a bad angle, except that they all come out with it, like it's some well-honed alibi. However, as you can

357

see from their statements, we have made some progress with the relatives of the senator who was killed, and the congressman who was amongst the injured – I understand he's just come out of a coma. They're obviously scared shitless, but they seem to want to get a lot off their chests. They, too, admit to being treated at the Highlands Clinic, but they go a lot further. It seems that the cult started leaning on them within weeks of the treatment beginning.'

'It was a safe enough card to play, given that no other facility in the world could offer the men the same hope of recovery,' McKinnon said.

'If their testimony is to be believed, Apostles' lobbyists in DC have hustled them into voting their way on a half-dozen key bills this year already.'

Hannah crossed to the window to get some air. 'Well, I'll take a small bet that it turns out to be the pattern with all the other closet converts who have a foot in government. I'll think you'll find Mr Fiske has been softening up the system with chilling efficiency for a long time.'

Morgenson changed files. 'Well, he and his people are already gonna be charged with first degree homicide, attempted homicide, corruption, coercion, acts in violation of the First Amendment, international agreements on germ warfare, civil rights and probably a few others the legal profession has yet to find a name for. Our initial focus will be on those who attended the Wessington Springs ceremony – the bunch you call the targeting group. Your list, checked against those identified, or traced through their car licence plates as being there, gave us this.' He began to pass papers around. 'Four hundred and sixty-nine names in all. Investigating that lot is gonna take one hell of an operation. All the evidence suggests that these people are the hard core. They're not going to break easily. In many cases we're gonna have to set up phone taps, run surveillance . . .'

'And all that time they're gonna be sending out panic signals, destroying evidence,' McKinnon said.

'Right. Nevertheless, raids carried out on the homes of some thirty-seven individuals already indicate that they were involved in what I can only describe as some mass infection programme.'

'And the future targets?' Hannah asked. 'What's the story with them?'

'Well, obviously they're a matter of prime concern,' Morgenson said. 'Trying to get the cooperation of local medical authorities has been a nightmare, but we hope to be able to contact and test everyone on that list within the next few weeks.'

'You're gonna have to tread very carefully there, aren't you?' Hannah said. 'Many of these people may not have been hit with the bacteria yet, or if they have, they may not yet be aware that they're suffering from some potentially life-threatening disease. If you handled this wrong, you could cause absolute panic.'

'All our people have been carefully briefed, I promise you. And I can tell you this: from the reports I've had back already, it seems that we were absolutely justified in making the moves we have. The individuals tested have all shown signs of having been targeted.'

McKinnon looked up from his papers. 'And what's the update position regarding the Vice-President?'

'Well, the only evidence we have to support the suggestion that he, too, has been targeted is in the stuff you found on him in the files. That's proved to be grimly accurate as regards the others, so we're taking the threat seriously. But, as you can appreciate, it's a sensitive business. I

359

hope to speak to Mr Gallagher myself when he gets back from Europe at the weekend.'

Morgenson took another file from the pile on his desk.

'It's too early to know what kind of charges will be brought against Falk – we're going to need data from the Home Office enquiry into what's been going on at Marston Moor to get a full picture of their activities – but the board of the corporation are under pressure to make some kind of a humanitarian gesture, and provide REGENS to help these folk out.'

'Thank God for that,' McKinnon said.

Hannah turned to him. 'These aren't the only people that are gonna need professional help. If the cult falls apart now – and I don't see how it can survive – a good many of the initiates are going to need some kind of exit counselling before they can be returned to the community.'

McKinnon shook his head slowly. 'I wonder how many thousands of lives Fiske will have ruined by the time this is over.'

The staff nurse flicked through the TV channels until the familiar face of the ABC lunchtime anchorman stared back at her. She turned up the sound, and checked the patient in room 119 one more time.

The man with the heavily bandaged head gave a barely perceptible nod. She took his pulse and thought, you're a first, kiddo. In fifteen years, I never saw a man survive a bullet in that part of the brain.

Doctors still had to fully ascertain how much was left of that brain. The patient – apparently one Fenton Dellaplane – had remained wholly detached during the various tests that had been taken, and had uttered not a single word since he regained consciousness a week ago.

When the nurse had gone, Dellaplane studied the news report on the US authorities' investigation of the Apostles of Christ. He was dimly aware that the story had dominated the news for the last few days, but this morning, for the first time since he'd been shot, he was able to bring his full attention to bear on it.

He lay back on his pillow and watched a film report of the storming of Fiske's compound by the FBI.

So, the hand of God, a God that knows us only as sinners, has intervened, he thought. The movement, as Fiske shaped it, is finished. Perhaps that's for the best. It'll make way for something new, better. Something I might have a hand in creating. After all, there's going to be a lot of lost souls out there now, needing to find something to believe in again.

Maybe, then, Hannah would see me in a different light, perhaps even stand beside me.

But first there must be a cleansing process. A purging of the past . . .

McKinnon put down the fax, and stared vacantly out at the building site opposite Morgenson's office.

It seemed that records recovered in raids on the hospital wing of Marston Moor Prison, the Harley Street offices of Dr Alderbrook, and the south London home of Aubrey Stamford-Smith had finally laid bare the truth regarding the fate of the 'forgotten men'.

'I knew my father died a hideous death in that hellhole,' McKinnon told Hannah. 'Inside, I've known it for a long time. Now I can be certain, I can start to face it, face the fact that I let him down.'

Hannah got up and put a hand on his shoulder. 'I didn't know him, but I don't think he'd feel you let him down, if he knew what you'd been through on his behalf.'

He looked at her. 'To get any solace from that, one would have to believe in a hereafter, in God.' He surveyed Morgenson's office. Every surface was covered in crisp new files. 'I think I've rather lost sight of God . . . And he of me.'

Morgenson came in and sat down at his desk.

'It's too early to be certain yet, but it looks as though all the stuff relating to the targeting of the Vice-President has been destroyed, and erased from the database.'

Hannah slumped into a chair. 'Here we go.'

'So where does that leave us with the Gallagher enquiry?' McKinnon asked.

Morgenson made a space between the files, and began to go through a long fax. 'One of our people met with the Vice-President's representative last night. They had his lawyer come back to us this morning, which would be interesting in itself, except that they're saying he's fine. According to them, he's not suffering from any disease and he certainly hasn't been approached by any of Fiske's people.'

McKinnon shrugged. 'What the fuck do you expect them to say?'

'Well, on that basis, we don't have the remotest justification for claiming that he, too, has been turned. And before you ask, we can't get to Gallagher's current medical records direct because they're classified.'

'I never imagined we would get to them through him,' McKinnon snapped. 'The clinic's own records should . . .'

Morgenson turned to one of the new files. 'Well, it looks like a lot of them have been junked too.'

Hannah threw up her hands in dismay. 'Jesus, I knew it. I just knew it!'

'Our people have been going through the records we

got from the clinic all night. It seems like very little of the material you got from the database is still on file there.'

There was total silence in the room for a minute. Then McKinnon said, 'So all we have to support this end of the case is our copy of Fiske's future targets list and Gallagher's medical records.'

'And we may have major difficulties in validating them,' Morgenson said.

McKinnon looked up. 'How so?'

'Just because this office is prepared to overlook the fact that much of the evidence you have regarding Fiske's activities was obtained illegally, doesn't mean everyone else will.'

Hannah turned around in her chair. 'I thought that evidence was evidence, whether it was begged, borrowed or stolen.'

'Essentially, that's true. The problem is that, well, to put it into the broadest terms, nothing you have is on company paper or signed by anyone in Fiske's organization. What I'm getting to is that the only link between the key data and them, is the word of . . .'

'A hack, a hacker and a killer on the run.'

'Well . . . Yup, that about says it. So, as far as the Gallagher aspect of the investigation is concerned, we're floundering.'

Hannah massaged her forehead. 'And if the Vice-President's involvement with Fiske can't be substantiated, then the security implications for the President himself . . .'

'There aren't any security implications for the President, Hannah,' McKinnon said. 'It's as simple as that.'

Morgenson's secretary came in and handed him a stack of faxes. As soon as she'd gone he said, 'We're gonna tell the Vice-President's people that there's a distant risk that he may have been exposed to some bacterial infection and see which way he jumps. Given what we have, it's really all we can do.'

Hannah stared at Morgenson. 'So you mean to say that Fiske could have the Vice-President in his pocket as we speak, could have plans in hand to hit the President and put Gallagher in his place, and there's nothing we can do about it?'

Morgenson sniffed. 'Right now, not a whole helluva lot, no.'

Hannah stirred the simmering spaghetti sauce again, then tasted it.

'Well, this isn't the best I've ever done – you need better olive oil and fresher herbs – but it sure beats the hell out of junk food.'

McKinnon sat slumped in an armchair across the living room of the safe house in Washington DC.

'So what happens with you when all this is over?' he asked.

She sensed the question had been coming for the last hour. 'Gonna finish the book, of course. We're gonna be beating publishers off with baseball bats.'

'Sure.' He looked up. 'Whadda you mean "we"?'

She put her hands on her hips. 'Don't get cute with me, Joel. You know damn well I wouldn't dream of doing this book without you now.'

His mouth lifted into a smile. It was the first she'd seen on his face in days. 'Okay!' He came over, and put a finger into the sauce.

'Hey!' She caught him around the waist, and kissed his neck.

'Pretty good.'

'Told yer. So, is this love?'

'Anyone who can make spaghetti sauce like that gets my fawning adulation.'

'Sounds like a deal to me. Just don't get sloppy with the fawning bit, that's all.'

He saluted. 'I should warn you, I'm hell to collaborate with.'

'Tell me something I don't know.'

Hannah's mobile phone rang. She took it from her purse. For a moment, she didn't recognize the caller's voice.

'It's me, Hannah. Fenton . . . Are you there?'

'Yes, I'm here. So . . . How're yer doin'?' she said awkwardly. 'Or is that a pretty dumb question right now?'

Does she know what happened to me? Dellaplane wondered. From her tone, she doesn't. Tell her no more than she needs to know. 'Yeah, it's a pretty dumb question. So the Apostles are the big news story, huh?'

'So it seems.'

'They must be busting down the door for that book of yours now, yeah?'

'I've had a few interesting calls, seeing as you ask.'

'Yeah, and one or two from the Feds, I should imagine, you being the great oracle on all things Fiske.'

His speech was slurred. He sounded like he was on something. How much does he know? Hannah thought. And what does it matter now anyway?

'Yeah, yeah. I'm the Cultbuster Kid. What are you calling for, Fenton?'

'*Are* you in touch with the Feds?'

Ah, so that was it. He wants me to put in a good word for him. How touching. 'I may be,' she said coldly.

'I know the Apostles are finished, Hannah . . . I have some files over at my bank. I want you to have

them. When you've read them, you'll know what to
do.'

She wandered through to the living room, leaving
McKinnon to finish fixing dinner.

When she came back, she looked as though she'd been
crying. She told him about the files.

'So what upset you?' he asked.

'He seemed to have some idea that, now the Apostles
were finished, I might go back to him.'

'And?'

'He wouldn't know me. I'm a different me.'

'Maybe he's a different him.'

'I think he is.' She sighed. 'But he's just five years too
late, that's all.'

The following morning, agents at the North Carolina
commune finished digging out the sedimentation tanks
in the sewage treatment works that served the Apostles
community. The identities of many of the young women
whose bodies were found there would never be known.

Wes Tyrell was one of the few to enter the little local
mortuary. Elaine Brody's crumpled body would haunt
him for the rest of his life.

Many records relating to the sentinels' operation had
been destroyed by the time FBI agents broke into their
headquarters on the North Carolina lot. But files hidden
under the floor of Pieter Kleig's residence, and those
given up by Fenton Dellaplane, finally lifted the veil on
the activities of Fiske's private Gestapo.

A dawn raid on a basement flat in Earl's Court, London,
resulted in the arrest of James Scrivens for the murder of
the man McKinnon had known only as Jessop.

Scrivens, under duress, agreed to turn Queen's evidence, and testify against other sentinels, many of whom

had yet to be tracked down, and, in a long statement outlining his activities for the cult, admitted to the killing of Caitlin Morgan.

This eventuality convinced McKinnon that, rather than wait in the US for the outcome of extradition proceedings pending there, he should return to England voluntarily, in the hope of finally untangling the mess that had resulted in his conviction for murder.

The day he and Hannah were due to leave, they received a call from Morgenson asking for them to stop by his office for coffee.

Morgenson passed them a report. 'I thought you might be interested in seeing this. I haven't been authorized to show it to you, but I figured, well . . . we owed it to you.'

McKinnon took the two sheets of typescript from the envelope. Hannah moved up to his side and read over his shoulder.

The document was a medical report. Vice-President Gallagher, it seemed, had recently undergone tests to establish if he was the carrier of what, they gathered from the technical jargon, was, effectively, a bacteria time-bomb.

It seemed that the papers Hannah had received from Fenton Dellaplane had finally convinced his advisers that there was a very real possibility that he'd been targeted with the device, and there was an urgent need to take action.

Oncologists at the Naval Hospital at Bethesda had scanned his stomach and intestine using specially modified equipment capable of identifying a microscopic foreign body. After five hours, they'd located a capsule, less than 1/100th of an inch in diameter, attached to his stomach wall. Its general specification matched that shown in the data McKinnon and Hannah had handed to the FBI. Analysis of the capsule confirmed that it contained a particularly virulent strain of heliocobacter – the only cancer bacteria that can survive the hydrochloric acid present in the stomach. Tests on the synthetic material, which covered an opening in the outer casing, however, showed that that was highly susceptible to this acid. Despite the fact that there was evidence to indicate that the capsule had been in the patient's stomach for many months, the team were, at first, at a loss to understand why the sensitive material hadn't perforated weeks before, releasing the deadly contents of the capsule.

After a discussion with Gallagher's personal doctor, the reason became apparent: the Vice-President had suffered from stress for many years. His doctor had prescribed a medication usually associated with the treatment of stomach ulcers – its principal property was that it drastically reduced stomach acid. The medical team were in little doubt that this had saved his life.

It was hard to tell from the report if the irony was intentional or not, but it closed, adding that the medication, one of the most successful generic drugs ever manufactured, was a product of Falk Pharmaceutical.

Morgenson turned to Hannah. 'Needless to say, you won't be able to put any of this in your book.'

'*Our* book. We're gonna blow a hefty chunk of the publisher's advance before we give a second's thought to that.'

'If what I read about the deal in the *Post* yesterday is right, it sounds like you could be busy for some time.'

'Just watch us.'

'So where can I find you if I need you?'

Hannah took McKinnon's arm. 'It depends on how

things go in England.' She shrugged. 'As soon as we can, we're gonna head for Guanajuato in Mexico.'

'Ah yeah. Don't they call that "The City of Eternal Spring"?'

'Uhuh. When this is done, we'll need all the spring they can sling at us.'

McKinnon put his weight against the heavy doors of the main entrance of London's Old Bailey, and he and Hannah began to pick their way through the posse of journalists on the pavement outside.

He stopped at the kerb, and took a long, deep breath. The air, soured by exhaust fumes, was far from good. But to him, at that moment, it tasted better than any he'd breathed in a long time.

They crossed the road, hurrying to shake off the media. Hannah took McKinnon's hand in hers.

'So, what do you feel, now it's all over?' she asked.

There was a long silence. A chill wind was blowing up from the Thames now. McKinnon lifted the collar of his coat.

'What do I feel? I feel like a beer, Hannah. I want to walk down that street knowing no one's gonna be watching me, and have a long, cool beer. Come on.'

She studied his face, trying to figure out what he was thinking. 'We did good, you know.'

McKinnon scanned the street, looking for a bar. 'Yup.'

'We did everything but get Fiske.'

He picked out an illuminated sign, and began to guide her towards it. 'It's not over yet.'

EPILOGUE

Ice-cream wrappers, bags that had held McDonald's hamburgers, blew around in the weeds, flew this way and that across the dry earth. A day earlier, the arena at Cedarwood County Fairground in New Mexico had rung to the sound of a rodeo audience, to the hooves of quarter horses, and the lowing of steers. But now it was host to a different crowd. Quiet thoughtful groups of people, few older than thirty, sat in the tiers of wooden seats, listening intently to the man speaking from the podium at the south end of the stadium.

He was tall with dark wavy hair and luminous green eyes. Much of what he had to say about his vision of the Almighty had a familiar ring, but his voice had a haunting, almost mesmeric quality that held his listeners enthralled.

In the back row of the seats, close to the podium, two men in straw hats and sunglasses studied the speaker intently. The elder of the two took off his shades.

'I've seen all I need to see,' Fiske said.

Two years had passed since the disintegration of the Apostles of Christ movement. There was little sign that the traumatic events of that time had marked him. Quite the reverse; he was twenty pounds leaner, and the flesh around his face was taut and lightly tanned. The small, almost colourless, eyes sparkled.

'I told yer you wouldn't be wasting yer time if you came out here,' the younger man at his side said.

'We'll make the approach after the show.'

Fiske began to move down the aisle towards the arena. The younger man hurried to keep up. 'The important thing is to keep it simple and to the point,' Fiske said almost to himself. 'Make him feel that the Church of the Redeemer is only a step away from his own vision of the future.'

High in the seating, a short distance to their left, a thin figure, his face hidden behind dark glasses, watched them. As they walked towards the backstage area, he slipped from his seat and, staying low, started to close the distance between them. Whenever Fiske's head made even the slightest turn, the thin man craned to catch a glimpse of his face.

The sermon came to an end. The audience rose to their feet in an ovation. The evangelist stepped down from the podium, and was joined by two men in suits.

Fiske stopped, took off his glasses and stood on tiptoe to get a clearer view of them. The thin man, trailing him, took off his glasses too.

Wes Tyrell had aged more than his years. His lean face was etched with deep lines. His dull eyes studied Fiske. Now he could see his face clearly.

There's no doubt. I've got you at last. It's taken two years of my life, but it's been worth it.

He no longer heard the roar of the crowd. Those who moved around him seemed to float. He screamed Fiske's name above the din.

You destroyed Jerry . . . Elaine . . . All that I've ever valued in life.

Fiske turned. Tyrell pulled a Magnum from his anorak, steadied it with his left hand, and fired.

The shot resonated through the stadium like the sound

372

of a string snapping inside a piano. It tore off Fiske's left ear, creasing his skull badly. He went down, a look of complete bewilderment on his face.

Tyrell closed with him, as those nearby peeled away and fled.

Fiske lifted his head, and ran a trembling hand around to where his ear should have been. He squinted at the figure silhouetted against the dying rays of the sun.

Who is that man? Why has he done this?

He struggled to bring his mind back from the edge of panic. It can't end now! There must be a way. Talk with him, reason with him.

Fiske wiped the blood from his eyes. 'Who are you?' he asked.

Tyrell stepped forward and pressed the Magnum against his forehead.

'Only God knows that now,' he said, absently.

And then he fired.

Raising Cain

Gallatin Warfield

There is trouble in the mountain valley in Maryland where attorney Gardner Lawson practises. A mysterious religious cult has arrived, settling in an abandoned granite quarry deep in the hills.

Known as CAIN (for Church of the Ark, Incorporated), this fanatical group attracts media attention after an elderly black man dies in unusual circumstances.

The dead man's son is police detective Joseph Brown, who's convinced that CAIN was responsible and begins secret investigations. When the CAIN leader is also found dead, 'Brownie' becomes the prime suspect for murder. Gardner Lawson now decides to resign as State's Attorney in order to conduct his close friend's defence.

Lawson's subsequent inquiries and a high-tension trial compel many to confront their innate prejudices – and force hidden secrets out of the shadows.

0 7472 4507 X

The Weatherman

Steve Thayer

A major serial killer thriller . . . a tour de force

Chief among all the complex and original characters in this astonishing novel is the shifting weather and landscape of Minnesota – demonic, majestic, bizarre, magical. And on Minneapolis-St Paul's 'Sky High News' it is TV weatherman Dixon Bell, a hulking eccentric uncannily precognitive of the elements, who pulls the highest ratings. His alter ego, busy breaking the story of a killer who snaps the necks of local young women, is hard news producer Rick Beanblossom, a Vietnam veteran like Dixon, a Pulitzer Prize winner who hides his napalmed face with a mask. Rivals for beautiful, ambitious anchor queen Andrea Labore, they develop an ambivalent friendship when Dixon becomes a suspect in the killings and Rick sets out to prove him innocent.

Electrifying, from the opening rollercoaster of a flash tornado to a cataclysmic and controversial death chair scene, *The Weatherman* grips like a vice and has more twists and turns than the Corniche.

'I read *The Weatherman* with mounting excitement and a sense of involvement which few novels can elicit in me these days . . . This is a wonderful story, one that will stay in my memory for a long time' Stephen King

0 7472 5083 9

HEADLINE FEATURE

A selection of bestsellers from Headline

BODY OF A CRIME	Michael C. Eberhardt	£5.99	☐
TESTIMONY	Craig A. Lewis	£5.99	☐
LIFE PENALTY	Joy Fielding	£5.99	☐
SLAYGROUND	Philip Caveney	£5.99	☐
BURN OUT	Alan Scholefield	£5.99	☐
SPECIAL VICTIMS	Nick Gaitano	£5.99	☐
DESPERATE MEASURES	David Morrell	£5.99	☐
A CERTAIN JUSTICE	John Lescroart	£5.99	☐
GRIEVOUS SIN	Faye Kellerman	£5.99	☐
THE CHIMNEY SWEEPER	John Peyton Cooke	£5.99	☐
TRAP DOOR	Deanie Francis Mills	£5.99	☐
VANISHING ACT	Thomas Perry	£5.99	☐

All Headline books are available at your local bookshop or newsagent, or can be ordered direct from the publisher. Just tick the titles you want and fill in the form below. Prices and availability subject to change without notice.

Headline Book Publishing, Cash Sales Department, Bookpoint, 39 Milton Park, Abingdon, OXON, OX14 4TD, UK. If you have a credit card you may order by telephone – 01235 400400.

Please enclose a cheque or postal order made payable to Bookpoint Ltd to the value of the cover price and allow the following for postage and packing:

UK & BFPO: £1.00 for the first book, 50p for the second book and 30p for each additional book ordered up to a maximum charge of £3.00.
OVERSEAS & EIRE: £2.00 for the first book, £1.00 for the second book and 50p for each additional book.

Name ....

Address ....

....

....

If you would prefer to pay by credit card, please complete:
Please debit my Visa/Access/Diner's Card/American Express (delete as applicable) card no:

Signature .... Expiry Date..............